PRAISE FOR DEV

'Another triumph from Max Brooks! . . . I can't wait until he turns every monster from childhood into an intelligent, entertaining page-turner.'
STEPHEN CHBOSKY, No. 1 *New York Times* bestselling author of *Imaginary Friend* and *The Perks of Being a Wallflower*

'Max Brooks has written the next great epistolary novel. *Devolution* is phenomenal.'
JOSH MALERMAN, *New York Times* bestselling author of *Bird Box*

'One of the greatest novels I've ever read. The characters soar, the ideas sing, and it's all going to scare the living daylights out of you.'
BLAKE CROUCH, *New York Times* bestselling author of *Dark Matter*

'*Devolution* is spellbinding. It is a horror story about how anyone, especially those who think they are above it, can slowly devolve into primal, instinctual behaviour. I was gripped from the first page to the last!'
LEE STROUD, creator of *Survivorman*, filmmaker, and author

'A masterful blend of laugh-out-loud social satire and stuff-your-fist-in-your-mouth horror. One elevates the other, making the book, and its message, all the more relevant.'
DAVID SEDARIS, *New York Times* bestselling author of *Calypso*

'A bloody good read.'
ANDREW HUNTER MURRAY, bestselling author of *The Last Day*

'Unputdownable.'
JOHN MARRS, bestselling author of *The One*

'Thrilling and terrifyingly prescient. I love Max Brooks!'
JENNY COLGAN, bestselling novelist and journalist

'For any fan of Bigfoot or cryptozoology, it's a referential treat.'
GUARDIAN

'Dark, gripping and visceral, *Devolution* is a unique journey into terror.'
WATERSTONES

'Delightful . . . A tale of supernatural mayhem that fans of King and Crichton will enjoy.'
***KIRKUS REVIEWS* (starred review)**

'Drawing you in with likeable characters in a real-world situation, then smashing your trust to pieces like a giant ape crushing a skull with his bare hands. *Devolution* will make you think twice about booking that remote weekend getaway in the woods.'
***SCI-FI NOW*, 5★ review**

'Grisly page-turner . . . Brooks' eye for rich characterisation, pointed social commentary and nail-chomping suspense is as sharp as ever.'
TOTAL FILM

'Timely, terrifying, and utterly terrific.'
SFX MAGAZINE, *****

'Part survival narrative, part bloody horror tale, part scientific journey into the boundaries between truth and fiction, this is a Bigfoot story as only Max Brooks could chronicle it – and like none you've ever read before.'
LIVE FOR FILM

'This survival-horror from bestselling *World War Z* author (. . .) is a scary and unnerving epistolary novel that explores the boundaries between truth and fiction.'
CULTUREFLY

'Tense and exciting (. . .) You'll enjoy believing.'
EVENING STANDARD

BY MAX BROOKS

NOVELS

The Zombie Survival Guide: Complete Protection from the Living Dead

World War Z: An Oral History of the Zombie War

GRAPHIC NOVELS

The Zombie Survival Guide: Recorded Attacks

G.I. Joe: Hearts & Minds

The Extinction Parade

The Harlem Hellfighters

A More Perfect Union

FOR YOUNG READERS

Minecraft: The Island

Minecraft: The Mountain

DEVOLUTION

MAX BROOKS

DEVOLUTION

1 3 5 7 9 10 8 6 4 2

Del Rey
20 Vauxhall Bridge Road
London SW1V 2SA

Del Rey is part of the Penguin Random House group of companies
whose addresses can be found at global.penguinrandomhouse.com.

Copyright © Max Brooks 2020

Max Brooks has asserted his right to be identified as the author of
this Work in accordance with the Copyright, Designs and Patents Act 1988.

First published in the United States by Penguin Random House in 2020
First published in the UK by Del Rey in 2020
This edition published by Del Rey in 2021

www.penguin.co.uk

A CIP catalogue record for this book is available from the British Library.

ISBN 9781529101423

Printed and bound in Great Britain by Clays Ltd, Elcograf S.p.A.

The authorised representative in the EEA is Penguin Random House Ireland,
Morrison Chambers, 32 Nassau Street, Dublin D02 YH68

Penguin Random House is committed to a sustainable future
for our business, our readers and our planet. This book is made from
Forest Stewardship Council® certified paper.

To Henry Michael Brooks: May you conquer all your fears.

What an ugly beast the ape, and how like us.

—Marcus Tullius Cicero

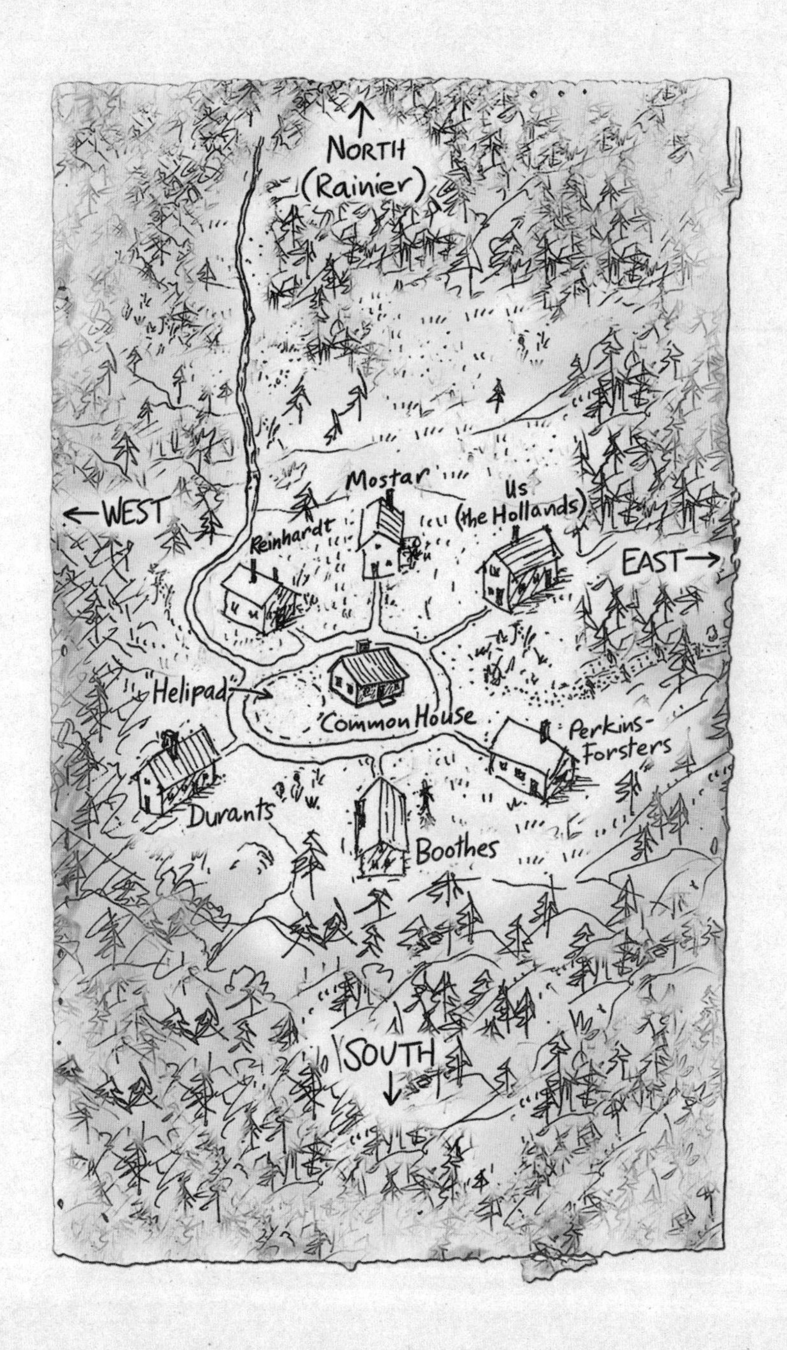
NORTH
(Rainier)
WEST
EAST
Mostar
Us
(the Hollands)
Reinhardt
"Helipad"
Common House
Perkins-Forsters
Durants
Boothes
SOUTH

DEVOLUTION

Introduction

BIGFOOT DESTROYS TOWN. That was the title of an article I received not long after the Mount Rainier eruption. I thought it was spam, the inevitable result of so much online research. At the time I was just finishing up what seemed like my hundredth op-ed on Rainier, analyzing every facet of what should have been a predictable, and preventable, calamity. Like the rest of the country, I needed facts, not sensationalism. Staying grounded had been the focus of so many op-eds, because of all Rainier's human failures—political, economic, logistical—it was the psychological aspect, the hyperbole-fueled hysteria, that had ended up killing the most people. And here it was again, right on my laptop screen: BIGFOOT DESTROYS TOWN.

Just forget it, I told myself, *the world's not going to change overnight. Just breathe, delete, and move on.*

And I almost did. Except for that one word.

"Bigfoot."

The article, posted on an obscure, cryptozoological website, claimed that while the rest of the country was focused on Rainier's wrath, a smaller but no less bloody disaster was occurring a few miles away in the isolated, high-end, high-tech eco-community of Greenloop. The article's author, Frank McCray, described how the eruption not only cut Greenloop off from rescue, but also left it vulnerable to a troop of hungry, apelike creatures that were themselves fleeing the same catastrophe.

The details of the siege were recorded in the journal of Greenloop resident Kate Holland, the sister of Frank McCray.

"They never found her body," McCray wrote to me in a follow-up email, "but if you can get her journal published, maybe someone will read it who might have seen her."

When I asked why me, he responded, "Because I've been following your op-eds on Rainier. You don't write anything you haven't thoroughly researched first." When I asked why he thought I'd have any interest in Bigfoot, he answered, "I read your *Fangoria* article."

Clearly I wasn't the only one who knew how to research a subject. Somehow, McCray had tracked down a decades-old list of my "Top Five Classic Bigfoot Movies" for the iconic horror magazine. In that piece, I'd talked about growing up "at the height of the Bigfoot frenzy," challenging readers to watch these old movies "with the eyes of a six-year-old child, eyes that flick constantly from the terror on the screen to the dark, rustling trees outside the window."

Reading that piece must have convinced McCray that some part of me wasn't quite ready to leave my childhood obsession in the past. He must have also known that my adult skepticism would force me to thoroughly vet his story. Which I did. Before contacting McCray again, I discovered that there had been a highly publicized community known as Greenloop. There was an ample amount of press regarding its founding—and its founder, Tony Durant. Tony's wife, Yvette, had also hosted several online yoga and meditation classes from the town's Common House right up to the day of the eruption. But on that day, everything stopped.

That was not unusual for towns that lay in the path of Rainier's boiling mudslides, but a quick check of the official FEMA map showed Greenloop had never been touched. And while devastated areas such as Orting and Puyallup had eventually reconnected their digital footprints, Greenloop remained a black hole. There were no press reports, no amateur recordings. Nothing. Even Google Earth, which has been so diligent in updating its satellite imagery of the area, still posts the original, pre-eruption photo of Greenloop and the surrounding area. As peculiar as all these red flags might be, what finally drove me back to McCray was the fact that the only mention of Greenloop *after* the disaster that I could find was in a local police report that said the official investigation was still "ongoing."

"What do you know?" I asked him after several days of radio silence. That was when he sent me the link to an AirDrop link of a photo album taken by Senior Ranger Josephine Schell. Schell, who I would later interview for this project, had led the first search and rescue team into the charred wreckage of what had once been Greenloop. Amid the corpses and debris, she had discovered the journal of Kate Holland (née McCray) and had photographed each page before the original copy was removed.

At first, I still suspected a hoax. I'm old enough to remember the notorious "Hitler Diaries." However, as I finished the last page, I couldn't help but believe her story. I still do. Perhaps it's the simplicity of her writing, the frustratingly credible ignorance of all things Sasquatch. Or perhaps it's just my own irrational desire to exonerate the scared little boy I used to be. That's why I've published Kate's story, along with several news items and background interviews that I hope will provide some context for readers not familiar with Sasquatch lore. In the process of compiling that research, I struggled greatly with how much to include. There are literally dozens of scholars, hundreds of hunters, and thousands of recorded encounters. To wade through them all might have taken years, if not decades, and this story simply does not have that kind of time. That is why I have chosen to limit my interviews to the two people with direct, personal involvement in the case, and my literary references to Steve Morgan's *The Sasquatch Companion*. Fellow Bigfoot enthusiasts will no doubt recognize Morgan's *Companion* as the most comprehensive, up-to-date guidebook on the subject, combining historical accounts, recent eyewitness sightings, and scientific analysis from experts like Dr. Jeff Meldrum, Ian Redmond, Robert Morgan (no relation), and the late Dr. Grover Krantz.

Some readers may also question my decision to omit certain geographical details regarding the exact location of Greenloop. This was done to discourage tourists and looters from contaminating what is still an active crime scene. With the exception of these details, and the necessary spelling and grammatical corrections, the journal of Kate Holland remains intact. My only regret is not being able to interview Kate's psychotherapist (who encouraged her to begin writing this diary) on the grounds of patient confidentiality. And yet this psychotherapist's silence seems, at least to me, like an admission of hope. After all, why would a doctor worry about the confidentiality of her patient if she didn't believe that patient was still alive?

At the time of this writing, Kate has been missing for thirteen months. If nothing changes, this book's publication date may see her disappearance lasting several years.

At present, I have no physical evidence to validate the story you are about to read. Maybe I've been duped by Frank McCray, or maybe we've both been duped by Josephine Schell. I will let you, the reader, judge for yourself if the following pages seem reasonably plausible, and like me, if they reawaken a terror long buried under the bed of youth.

Chapter 1

Go into the woods to lose sight and memory of the crimes of your contemporaries.

—Jean-Jacques Rousseau

JOURNAL ENTRY #1

SEPTEMBER 22

We're here! Two days of driving, with one night in Medford, and we're finally here. And it's perfect. The houses really are arranged in a circle. Okay, duh, but you told me to not stop, not edit, not erase and go back. Which is why you encouraged paper and pen. No backspace key. "Just keep writing." Okay. Whatever. We're here.

I wish Frank could have been here. I can't wait to call him tonight. I'm sure he'll apologize again for being stuck at that conference in Guangzhou and I'll tell him, again, that it doesn't matter. He's done so much for us already! Getting the house ready, all the FaceTime video tours. He's right about them not doing this place justice. Especially the hiking trail. I wish he could have been there for that first walk I took today. It was magical.

Dan wouldn't go. No surprise. He said he'd stay behind to help with the unpacking. He always says he'll help. I told him I wanted, needed, to stretch my legs. Two days in the car! Worst drive ever! I shouldn't have listened to the news the whole time. I know, "ration my current events, learn the facts but don't obsess." You're right. I shouldn't have. Venezuela again, the troop surge. Refugees. Another boat overturned in the Caribbean. So many boats. Hurricane season. At least it was the radio. If I hadn't been driving, I'd have probably tried to watch on my phone.

I know. I know.

We should have at least taken the coastal road, like when Dan and I first got married. I should have pushed for that. But Dan thought the 5 was faster.

Ugh.

All that horrible industrial farming. All those poor cows crammed up against each other in the hot sun. The smell. You know I'm sensitive to odors. I felt like it was still in my clothes, my hair, up in my nostrils by the time we got here. I had to walk, feel the fresh air, work out the muscles in my neck.

I left Dan to do whatever and headed up the marked hiking trail behind our house. It's really easy, a gradual incline with terraced, woodblock steps every hundred yards or so. It passes next to our neighbor's house, and I saw her. The old lady. Sorry, older. Her hair was clearly gray. Short, I guess. I couldn't tell from the kitchen window. She was doing something in front of the sink. She looked up and saw me. She smiled and waved. I smiled and waved back, but didn't stop. Is that rude? I just figured, like unpacking, there'd be time to meet people. Okay, so maybe I didn't actually think that. I didn't really think. I just wanted to keep going. I felt a little guilty, but not for too long.

What I saw . . .

Okay, so remember how you thought sketching the layout of this place might help channel my need to organize my surroundings? I think that's a good idea and if it's halfway decent, I might text you the scanned picture. But there's no way any drawing, or even photograph, can capture what I saw on that first hike.

The colors. Everything in L.A. is gray and brown. That gray, hazy bright sky that always hurt my eyes. The brown hills of dead grass that made me sneeze and made my head ache. It's really green here, like back east. No. Better. So many shades. Frank told me there'd been a drought here and I thought I saw a little blond grass along the freeway, but way out here it's like a rainbow of green—bright gold to dark blue. The bushes, the trees.

The trees.

I remember the first time I went hiking in Temescal Canyon back in L.A. Those short, gray twisted oaks with their small spiky leaves and thin, bullet-shaped acorns. They looked so hostile. It sounds super dramatic, but that's how I felt. Like they were angry at having to live in that hot, hard, dusty dead clay.

These trees are happy. Yes, I said it. Why wouldn't they be, in this rich, soft, rain-washed soil. A few with light, speckled bark and golden, falling leaves. They mix in among the tall, powerful pines. Some with their silver-bottom needles or the flatter, softer kind that brushed gently against me as I walked by. Comforting columns that hold up the sky, taller than anything in L.A., including those skinny wavy palms that hurt my neck to look up at.

How many times have we talked about the knot just under my right ear that runs down under my arm? It was gone. No matter how I craned my neck. No pain. And I hadn't even taken anything. I'd planned to. I even left two Aleve waiting on the kitchen counter for when I got back. No need. Everything worked. My neck, my arm. Relaxed.

I stood there for maybe ten minutes or so, watching the sun shine through the leaves, noticing the bright, misty rays. Sparkling. I put my hand out to catch one, a little quarter-sized disc of warmth, pulling away my tension. Grounding me.

What did you say about OCD personalities? That we have such a hard time living in the present? Not here, not now. I could feel every second. Eyes closed. Deep cleansing breaths. The scented, moist, cool air. Alive. Natural.

So different from transplanted L.A. with lawns and palms and people living on someone else's stolen water. It's supposed to be a desert, not a sprawling vanity garden. Maybe that's why everyone there is so miserable. They know they're all living in a sham.

Not me. Not anymore.

I remember thinking, *This can't get any better.* But it did. I opened my eyes and saw a large, emerald-tinted bush a few steps away. I'd missed it before. A berry bush! They looked like blackberries but I went online just to be sure. (Great Wi-Fi reception by the way, even so far from the house!) They were the real thing, and a crazy lucky find! Frank had said something about this summer's drought killing the wild berry harvest. And yet here was this bush, right in front of me. Waiting for me. Remember how you told me to be more open to opportunities, to look for signs?

It didn't matter that they were the tiniest bit tart. In fact, it made them even better. The taste took me back to the blueberry bush behind our house in Columbia.* How I could never wait till August when they'd ripen, how I'd just have to sneak half-purple beads in July. All those memories came rushing back, all those summers, Dad reading *Blueberries for Sal* and me laughing at when she runs into the bear. That was when my nose began to sting and the corners of my eyes started watering. I probably would have lost it right there, but, literally, a little bird saved me.

Actually two. I noticed a pair of hummingbirds flittering around these tall purple wildflowers sprouting in a Disneyesque patch of sun. I saw one stop at a flower and then the other buzzed right next to it, and then the most darling thing happened. The second one started giving the first little kisses, moving back and forth with its coppery orange feathers and pinkish red throat.

Okay, so I know you're probably sick of comparisons by now. Sorry. But I can't help thinking of those parrots. Remember them? The ones we talked about? The wild flock? Remember how we spent an entire session talking about how their squawk-

* Kate McCray grew up in Columbia, Maryland.

ing drove me crazy? I'm sorry if I didn't see the connection you were trying to make.

Those poor things. They sounded so scared and angry. And why wouldn't they? What else should they feel when some horrible person released them into an environment they weren't born for? And their kids? Hatched with this gnawing discomfort in their genes. Every cell craving an environment they couldn't find. They didn't belong there! Nothing did! Hard to see what's wrong until you hold it up to what's right. This place, with its tall, healthy trees and happy little birds trading love kisses. Everything that's here belongs here.

I belong here.

From the American Public Media radio show *Marketplace*. Transcript of host Kai Ryssdal's interview with Greenloop founder Tony Durant.

RYSSDAL: But why would someone, particularly someone used to urban or even suburban life, choose to isolate themselves so far out in the wilderness?

TONY: We're not isolated at all. During the week, I'm talking to people all around the world, and on the weekends, my wife and I are usually in Seattle.

RYSSDAL: But the time you have to spend driving to Seattle—

TONY: Is nothing compared to how many hours people waste in their cars every day. Think about how much time you spend driving back and forth to work, either ignoring or actively resenting the city around you. Living out in the country, we get to appreciate our city time because it's voluntary instead of mandatory, a treat instead of a chore. Greenloop's revolutionary living style allows us to have the best parts of both an urban and rural lifestyle.

RYSSDAL: Talk for a minute about this "revolutionary living." In the past you've described Greenloop as the next Levittown.

TONY: It is. Levittown was the prototype for prosperity. You had all these young GIs coming home from World War II, newly married, anxious to start a family, hungry for a home of their own, but without the means to afford one. At the same time, you had this revolution in manufacturing; streamlined production, improved logistics, prefabricated parts . . . all from the war, but with tremendous peacetime potential. The Levitts were the first to recognize that potential and harnessed it into America's first "planned community." And they built it so fast and cheap that it became the model for modern suburbia.

RYSSDAL: And you're saying that model's run its course.

TONY: I'm not the one saying it, the whole country's acknowledged it as far back as the 1960s when we realized that our standard of living was killing us. What good is all this progress if you can't eat the food or breathe the air or even live on the land when the ocean rises up over it? We've known for half a century that we need a sustainable solution. But what? Turn back the clock? Live in caves? That was what the early environmentalists wanted, or, at least, how they came off. Remember that iconic scene in *An Inconvenient Truth* where Al Gore shows us a scale with gold bars on one side and Mother Earth on the other? What kind of a choice is that?

You can't ask people to give up personal, tangible comforts for some ethereal ideal. That's why communism failed. That's why all those primitive, hippie, "back to the land" communes failed. Selfless suffering feels good for short crusades, but as a way of life, it's unsustainable.

RYSSDAL: Until you invented Greenloop.

TONY: Again, I didn't invent anything. All I did was look at the question through the lens of past failures.

RYSSDAL: You've been very critical of previous attempts . . .

TONY: I wouldn't call it critical. I wouldn't be here if it wasn't for those who came before me. But you look at those huge, government funded eco-cities like Masdar* or Dongtan.† Too big. Too expensive. And definitely too ambitious for a post Sequestration‡ America. Likewise the smaller, Euro models like BedZED§ or Sieben Linden¶ are nonstarters because they depend on punishing austerity. I liked the Dunedin** project in Florida. It's comfortable and manageable, but it just doesn't have any wow, and this . . .

RYSSDAL: We should note that Tony is gesturing to the houses and land around us.

TONY: Tell me this isn't the definition of "wow"?

RYSSDAL: Is the story true about you hijacking a Cygnus corporate retreat and pitching the project only after you'd hiked them up here?

TONY: [*Laughs.*] I wish. They knew a sales pitch was coming, and they knew it had something to do with a plot of land that the federal government was planning to auction off to the private sector, but they didn't hear my proposal until we were standing . . . actually . . . on the very spot we're standing now.

* Masdar City: A sustainable city project built in Abu Dhabi, UAE.

† Dongtan: A planned eco-city on Chongming Island, in Shanghai, China.

‡ Sequestration: An act of budget austerity controls set in place by the Congress of the United States in 2013.

§ BedZED: A sustainable community of one hundred homes completed in 2002 in Hackbridge, London, UK.

¶ Sieben Linden: An off-grid settlement in Germany.

** Dunedin: An Eco Home Village in Dunedin, Florida, USA.

RYSSDAL: And nature did the talking.

TONY: And me. [*Both laugh.*] Seriously, like Steve Jobs playing the orchestra,* my orchestra is this land. When you're here, surrounded by it, connecting to it on a visceral level, you realize that that connection is the only way to save our planet. That's been the problem all along, destroying the natural world because we've created so much distance from it.

I asked my friends at Cygnus to imagine two different endgames for this soon to be privatized land. Clear-cutting by a Chinese timber company or . . . or . . . the minimal footprint of a micro-eco-community that personified the new Green Revolution. Six homes, no more, ringing a common house in the top-down shape of a turtle, which, according to some Native American beliefs, is the foundation on which the world is built.

I described how the Tlingit-style houses would look like they literally grew right out of the forest.

RYSSDAL: Which you can see now.

TONY: Exactly, but what you can't see is that these homes are all built from 100 percent recycled materials. Wood, metal, insulation are recycled blue jeans. The only new material is the bamboo for the floors. Bamboo's really important to the planet. That's why you see it growing all around the neighborhood. Not only is it one of the most versatile and renewable building materials ever, it also helps to sequester carbon. There are also what you'd call "passive elements," like the giant floor-to-ceiling windows in the living room that allow you to warm or cool the whole house by raising or lowering the curtains.

But passive elements only go so far. When it comes to

* While "I play the orchestra" was spoken by Michael Fassbender and written by Aaron Sorkin for the 2015 movie *Steve Jobs,* it cannot be confirmed that Jobs himself ever uttered this phrase.

active, green technology, we've got it all. See how the roofs have this bluish-purple tint? Those are solar panels. Peel and stick, like old-fashioned wallpaper, and "triple junction" so they can harvest every photon on a cloudy day. And those converted amps are stored in Cygnus's patented battery that not only fits invisibly into a wall, but is 13.5 percent more efficient than the competition's.

RYSSDAL: Suck on that, Elon Musk.

TONY: No, no, I love Elon, he's a good guy, but he does have some catching up to do.

RYSSDAL: Like the solar profit program?

TONY: Exactly. If you harvest more energy than you need, why not be able to sell it back to the grid? And I don't mean a rebate like in some states, I mean sell, for cash, just like the Germans have been doing for almost two decades. That's not technology, that's just good business, making money while you sit on your ass.

RYSSDAL: And speaking of sitting on your . . .

TONY: I was getting to that. The houses don't just harvest sunlight, they also collect methane gas from, wait for it, your own poop. Again, nothing new. Biogas has been used in developing countries for years. Even some American cities are tapping into the deposits from their own landfills. Greenloop's taken all that hard-won experience and kicked it up to American suburban standards. Each house is built on a biogas generator that breaks down what you flush. But you don't see it, or smell it, or even have to think about it. Everything is regulated by the Cygnus "smart home" system.

RYSSDAL: Can you talk a little bit about that system?

TONY: Again, nothing new. A lot of homes are getting smarter. Greenloop's just gotten there faster. The central home program is either voice or remote activated, and with a constant eye toward energy efficiency. It's always thinking, always calculating, always making sure you don't waste one amp or Btu. Every room is riddled with both thermal and motion sensors. On the highest efficiency setting, they'll automatically shut down all light and heat to every unoccupied space. And you don't have to do anything more than just live the way you've always lived. You don't have to sacrifice an ounce of comfort or time.

RYSSDAL: And that goes back to the same political will that allowed Washington State to change its solar energy policy.

TONY: And put up half the money for its construction, and built the private road up from the main highway, and laid all those miles of fiber-optic cable.

RYSSDAL: Green jobs.

TONY: Green jobs. Who keeps all those fancy electronics running? Who cleans off the solar panels? Who mucks out the used-up waste in those biogas generators, carting it away along with the garbage and recycling and kitchen scraps, only to bring that organic waste back as compost to be spread around the fruit trees?

You know that every citizen of Greenloop generates between two and four service jobs for their fellow Americans? All bused in on electric vans that charge up at the Common House. And that's just the service sector. What about actually building those solar panels and biogas generators and wall batteries? Manufacturing. Made in America. This is the Green Revolution, the Green New Deal, and what they're now calling the Green Green Society. Greenloop shows what's possible, just like Levittown did before it.

RYSSDAL: Although, we can't ignore that Levittown had a racial segregation policy.

TONY: No, we shouldn't ignore it. In fact, that's exactly my point. Levittown was exclusive; Greenloop is inclusive. Levittown wanted to divide people. Greenloop wants to unite them. Levittown wanted to separate humans from the natural world. Greenloop wants to reintroduce them.

RYSSDAL: But most people can't afford to live in this type of community.

TONY: No, but they can afford a piece of it. That's what Levittown was all about, not just showcasing the homes, but every new convenience that was in it: automatic dishwashers, clothes washers, television. A whole way of life. That's what we're trying to do with Greentech, and as far as solar power and smart homes, it's already happening. But if we can put all these planet-saving ideas under one roof, literally, and plant just enough Greenloops around the country for those ideas to trickle down to the general public, then we'd finally have our Green Revolution. No more sacrifice, no more guilt. No more conflict between profit and planet. Americans could have it all, and what's more American than having it all?

Chapter 2

Happiness: a good bank account, a good cook, and a good digestion.

—Jean-Jacques Rousseau

JOURNAL ENTRY #2

SEPTEMBER 23

Last night we were invited to a "welcome potluck" in the Common House.

I realize I haven't explained that building at all. Sorry. It's like any planned community's homeowners association shared space and laid out like a traditional Pacific Northwest longhouse. I googled "longhouse" last night. The images almost match this structure. It's got a large, multi-use space with a bathroom and kitchenette on one side and a cozy cobblestone fireplace on the other. That fire gave off such a beautiful glow, mixed with the pine candles and the natural light of dusk. The Common House runs east–west, so all we had to do was leave the large, double front doors open for that spectacular view of the setting sun. I'm surprised how warm it was, certainly no colder than the nights in L.A.

It was such an idyllic setting, and the *food*! Black buttery edamame salad, quinoa with grilled vegetables, and salmon right from the nearby rivers! We started with this amazing soup course: vegetable soba made by the Boothes. They live two houses to the left of us. Vegan foodies. They actually *made* the soup, not just mixed and cooked it. The soba noodles were from scratch. Raw ingredients delivered fresh that day. I've had a lot of soba since moving to L.A. I've even had it at Nobu, where Dan and his one-time partners wanted to celebrate their company launch, and I'm pretty sure it didn't compare to this.

"From our own hand." That's what Vincent says. I like him, and his wife, Bobbi. They're in their sixties, both short and happy and look like your stereotypical aunt and uncle.

They also weren't judgy about those of us who aren't vegan. Does that sound judgy from me? You know what I'm talking about: all the vegans in Venice, especially the new ones. The way they'd look at Dan's leather shoes or my silk blouse or how one of them called a fish tank a prison. Seriously, we were at someone's house for a party and this guy totally went off on them about their koi pond. "How'd you like it if you were imprisoned in a tiny air bubble at the bottom of the ocean!" The Boothes weren't like that. They were so nice. And Dan *loved* their housewarming gift.

Think of an all steel, upside-down *T* that you grip in the palm of your hand. The neck of the *T* extends through your fingers, a long, narrow, sharpened spoon tapering to a pointed edge. Bobbi explained that it's a coconut opener, specifically for digging into the "pores." That's what those little black covered holes are called. Never knew that. I also never knew that coconut water is the best natural hydrator in the world. Vincent explained that it comes the closest to the liquid inside our own blood cells. Bobbi joked "not that we need homemade transfusions" but turned earnest when she explained the benefits of coconut water on a hike. They go hiking every morning and go through piles of coconuts in the summer.

"And I guess you can also poke someone's eye out," Bobbi added, watching Dan. He had the opener in his hand and was stabbing the air. He looked about twelve years old, and sounded like it too. "Dude, this is so sick! Thank you!"

I guess I should have been embarrassed at that point, but the Boothes just smiled at him like proud parents.

There were some actual parents there too. The Perkins-Forster family. They've only been here a few months and are the second to last residents before us.

Carmen Perkins is . . . I'm not sure she's a germaphobe, I mean, I just met her. But the hand sanitizer. Using it right after she shook our hands, making sure her daughter used it, offering it around to everyone. She's totally nice though. She kept saying how wonderful it was that we, Dan and I, "complete the circle." She's a child psychologist. She wrote a book on homeschooling in the digital age with her wife, Effie. Carmen kept calling her "Euphemia."

Effie's also a child psychologist, I guess. That's how Carmen introduced her, at least. "Well, I'm not technically licensed—" Effie started to say but Carmen cut her off with a hand on her arm. "She's working on her degree, and already a lot smarter than me," she said, which made Effie blush a little.

I don't know if Effie's physically smaller than Carmen but her posture makes it look that way. Shoulders shrugged. Soft voice. Not a lot of eye contact. A couple times before answering one of our questions, she glanced quickly at Carmen. Permission? A couple times after. Approval?

Effie also spent a lot of time and attention on Palomino, their daughter. The name, according to Carmen, is a "place holder," which they gave her during the adoption. I sensed a little bit of defensiveness, especially when Effie elaborated that a "place holder" name was something Palomino could change if she ever found one she loved more. Carmen explained that when they first met her in the orphanage in Bangladesh, she was clutching a worn and torn picture book on horses. I tried to ask her about horses, and Dan about how she liked living here. Neither of us got an answer.

You know that famous *National Geographic* picture of the Afghan girl with the green eyes? Palomino's eyes are brown but have the same haunted expression. She just stared at us with those eyes and didn't say anything for a second, then went back to her "fidgeter," a little homemade beanbag. Effie gave her a hug and began to apologize. "She's a little shy."

Carmen cut her off with, "And it's not her job to please us with conversation." And went on to tell us about how the book was one of her only possessions, that and a loaf of bread in a plastic bag. When they met her, she didn't know when she was going to eat again. Effie shook her head, hugging the girl again, and said she'd been so malnourished, all these vitamin deficiencies, mouth sores, rickets. She started to talk about what her people had gone through, the "Rohingya" minority (which I'll have to google later) at the hands of the Myanmar government. Carmen shot her another silencing look and said, "But we don't need to trigger her with those memories. What matters is she's safe now, healthy and loved."

That prompted Alex Reinhardt to comment on the deplorable state of many ethnic minorities in South Asia. Have you ever heard of Dr. Reinhardt? He looks like the *Game of Thrones* author, without the Greek fisherman's hat. He does, though, wear a beret, which, I guess, he's entitled to. I'd heard his name a couple times in school, seen his books advertised on Amazon. I think I might have caught the end of his TED Talk someone next to me on a plane was watching.

I guess he's kind of a big deal. His book *Rousseau's Children* was apparently "groundbreaking." That's the word Tony Durant used. Reinhardt gave a slight, almost embarrassed shrug at that, but went on to describe why it essentially launched him into the academic spotlight.

I hope I get this right. I'll try to relate what he explained to me. Jean-Jacques Rousseau—not be confused with Henry David Thoreau as Dan did that night—was an eighteenth-century French philosopher. He believed that early humans were essentially good, but when humanity began to urbanize, separating themselves from nature, they separated from their own nature as well. In Reinhardt's words, the "ills of today can all be traced to the corruption of civilization." In *Rousseau's Children,* Reinhardt proved him right by studying the Kung San hunter-gatherers of Africa's Kalahari Desert. "They have none of the problems," he said, "that plague our so-called advanced societies. No crime, addiction, war. They are the embodiment of Rousseau's thesis."

"And unlike Rousseau's ideal, the women aren't reduced to being virtuous sex slaves in a male-dominated society." That was Carmen. She said it nicely, smiling, but with a sarcastic roll of the eyes. Effie giggled at that and Reinhardt, reaching for another helping of quinoa, looked like he might have been working up to a less than friendly comeback.

"Rousseau was human," said Tony, "but he did influence countless generations in countless fields, including Maria Montessori." That diffused the situation, that and his unbelievable smile. His eyes. They turned to me and I actually felt my forearms prickle.

"Alex here," Tony said, and clinked Reinhardt's glass with his own, "was the spiritual inspiration for Greenloop. When I read *Rousseau's Children,* it codified my vision for sustainable housing. Mother Nature keeps us honest, reminds us who we're supposed to be." At that, Yvette, his wife, slipped a hand around his arm and gave this gentle, proud sigh.

The Durants.

Oh my God . . . or Gods!

It's ridiculous how beautiful they are. And intimidating! Yvette—she looks like an Yvette—is angelic. Ageless. Thirty? Fifty? She's tall and slender, and could have walked right out of *Harper's Bazaar.* The honey blond hair, the flawless skin, the bright, sparkling hazel eyes. I shouldn't have googled her beforehand. It just made it worse. Turns out she actually was a model for a while. A couple of older magazines called *Cargo* and *Lucky.* Figures. All these insane fairy-tale pictures of her on Aruba and the Amalfi coast. Nobody deserves to look that good in a bikini. And no one who looked, looks, that good should also be so nice.

She was the one who'd invited us to dinner in the first place. Right after I got back from my hike, all sweaty and gross with

Dan sleeping on the couch and boxes of crap everywhere, the doorbell rang and there was this glamorous, glowing nymph. I think I said something eloquent like "um-uh" before she gave me a big welcoming hug (which she had to stoop down for) and told us how happy she was that we'd chosen Greenloop.

And if her light, upper-class English accent doesn't already make her sound like a genius, she's also getting her PhD in psychosomatic illness therapy. I don't know who Dr. Andrew Weil is (one more thing I'll have to look up), but she used to be his protégé and invited me to take her daily "integrative health yoga" class, which, of course, gets armies of online subscriber views a day.

Gorgeous, brilliant, and generous. She presented us with a housewarming present called a "happy light," which is used to simulate the exact spectrum of the sun to dispel seasonal affective disorder. I bet she doesn't need it, either for depression or for keeping her flawless overall tan.

Tony joked that he didn't need one because Yvette was his happy light.

Tony.

Okay, I'm supposed to be honest. Right? That's what you told me. No one but the two of us will read this. No barriers. No lies. Nothing but what I think and feel in the moment.

Tony.

He's definitely older. Fifties maybe, but in that rugged, older movie star kind of way. Dan once told me about this old comic book—*G.I. Joe*?—where the bad guys took DNA from all the dictators in history to create one perfect supervillain. That's kinda the opposite of what I feel like they did with Tony, only Clooney's skin, Pitt's lips. Okay, maybe Sean Connery's hairline but that never bothered me; I mean, I tolerate Dan's man-bun. And those arms, they kind of remind me of that guy Frank used to have a poster of in his room. Henry Rollins? Not as big and buff, but ripped and inked. When he reached out to shake Dan's hand, I could see the muscles rippling underneath his tattoos. It was like they were alive, those tribal lines and Asian characters. Everything about Tony is alive.

Okay. Honest. It reminded me of Dan. How he used to be. Energized, engaged. How he used to effortlessly command a room, every room. That speech he made to our graduating class. "We don't have to be ready for the world. The world better get ready for us!" Eight years? That long ago?

I tried not to compare, sitting there next to who he'd become, across the table from who he thought he'd be.

Dan.

Writing this now, I feel guilty about how little attention I paid to him during dinner, and how I didn't even as a reflex reach out for him when the ground began to shake.

It was just the tiniest of jolts. The glasses rattled, my chair wobbled.

Apparently, that's been happening on and off for the last year. Just a slight tremor they said came from Mount Rainier. Nothing to worry about. Volcanos do that. It reminded me of our first month in Venice Beach, when the bed started rolling, not shaking, rolling like a ship on rough seas. I'd heard of the San Andreas Fault but didn't know about all the mini fault lines crisscrossing under L.A. I can see why so many easterners don't survive their first earthquake. If Dan wasn't so set on "Silicon Beach," I would have totally packed it in. I'm glad I stayed, glad I realized the huge difference between a few shakes and the supposed Big One. That little tremor in Greenloop, less than a truck rumbling by, reminded me of what you said about the difference between denial and phobia.

Denial is an irrational dismissal of danger.

Phobia is an irrational fear of one.

I'm glad I was rational then, especially when everyone else didn't seem to mind. Yvette even got this sympathetic smile on her face and said, "How unfair is it to leave California earthquakes for this."

We all laughed, until the next tremor happened—the human one!

That was when Mostar showed up.

The old lady I saw in the window earlier. Not Ms. Or Mrs. or Mostar Something. Just "Muh-star." She came in late, apologizing that she'd been distracted in "the workshop" and needed the extra time to let the tulumba cool. That's what her dessert was called. Tulumba. A big plate of what looked like cut up churros under a syrup glaze. We already had desserts. The Durants brought them along with their salmon: some honey-dribbled apple slices right from their tree and gluten-free artisanal ice cream with local berries. I was looking forward to comparing it with my nightly fix of Halo, especially when everyone else had warned me how good it was. Mostar must not have gotten the message. Or didn't care? Dan didn't care that there was more dessert. He tore into the tulumbas. He must have had, what, five? Six? Chomping and moaning with each one. So gross.

I politely took one. I could already smell the fried dough. I don't even want to think about how many calories. Maybe that's why almost no one else took any. The Boothes said something about animal butter. The Perkins-Forsters mentioned Palomino's gluten allergy. That was kind of inconsiderate of Mostar to do that. She must have known about all these dietary restrictions. Maybe that's why Reinhardt only had one as well. I would not have expected that, given how he looked. Sorry. Body shaming. But seriously, given how he plowed through everything else, I figured he'd join Dan in a total snarf-off. Instead, he just nibbled at the edge of one. Polite and chilly. You could feel the room temperature drop.

"Eat." Mostar plopped down at the end of the table. "Go on, put some meat on those bones." She's like this old-timey stereotype nana, right down to the foreign accent. What is that? Russian? Israeli? A lot of rolling *r*'s.

She's really short, shorter than Mrs. Boothe, who I think only comes up to my forehead. Maybe five feet or less? And built like a barrel, like if someone threw a dress on a keg. Her olive skin is wrinkled, especially around the eyes. Wrinkled and dark. Raccoon-ish, like she hasn't slept in a year. Is that mean? I don't want to be mean. Just an observation. Her eyes were pretty though. Light blue accented by the dark circles. Her hair was silver, not gray or white, and tied back in a bun.

Her whole energy was really different from everyone else's. Like if the vibe of most people in the room was slow, wavy lines, she'd have this hard, sharp bounce. God, I lived in SoCal too long.

But really, everything about her was hard, the way she moved, the way she talked. She kept staring at me, watching me peck at her dessert. Everyone else was looking at me. It felt kind of weird, like how I reacted to her tulumba somehow had this deeper meaning. I know I'm reading way too much into this. You told me to trust my instincts, but really, I started feeling so uncomfortable that I lost my appetite.

Tony must have sensed it, God bless him, because he rode to the rescue with a full intro of Mostar. "We're so lucky," he said, "to have a world-famous artist in residence." Glass is her medium and she's been sculpting in it for years. That was where he'd met her, at an exhibition at the Chihuly Garden and Glass in Seattle. Yvette added that she had been on her way to lead a "crystal yoga" session when they just happened to see her exhibition. Seamlessly, Tony wrapped up the story by explaining that he'd proposed an "epic collaboration" between the two of them: a full-scale model of her hometown, wherever that is, that would be completely 3-D printed.

That's a big thing for Cygnus, perfecting a 3-D glass technology that is "leaps ahead of Karlsruhe."* I thought I'd be bored by this conversation. Dan's college phase taught me more than

* The Karlsruhe Institute of Technology, which has pioneered the process of 3-D glass printing by embedding a silicon base with polymer nanoparticles.

enough about 3-D printing. But Tony's enthusiasm was hard to resist, the way he talked about Mostar's project being a "game-changing win for everybody." Cygnus displays their new breakthrough, Mostar gets to live in paradise rent free, and the world will eventually get to see a resurrected piece of history.

"Which is the subject of my new book," Reinhardt cut in, "resource conflicts of the 1990s."

Resource conflicts?

I wasn't sure how that subject fit into what we were discussing, and why Mostar's hometown needed to be "resurrected." I also wasn't sure if probing too deep was appropriate for the dinner table. I didn't want to trigger Palomino. While I was wrestling with the choice, Mostar took it away by waving her hand at Reinhardt. "Oh, these nice young people don't want to hear about all that."

Then she turned to me and asked, "So how did you get here?"

I got a little nervous at that, my jaw muscles stiffened slightly. I thought maybe if I could distract her with just my story, she wouldn't ask about Dan. I tried to talk about my job but it was just so boring. No, I'm not putting myself down again. I like what I do and I know I'm good at it, but who wants to hear about a CPA at a wealth management firm in Century City? I tried to focus more on my connection to this place. Everyone knew and loved Frank, and Mr. Boothe (who used to work with him) told me that he'd been the one to encourage Frank and Gary to move up here when the place was being built. Bobbi shook her head sadly when she said, "I'm sorry it didn't work out with them." But then Yvette added happily, "But we got you in the conscious uncoupling."

That lightened the mood again, until Mostar ruined it. I guess I can't blame her. I mean, why wouldn't you ask? She didn't know. No one did. It's just small talk, getting-to-know-you stuff. It's the standard question. "And what do you do?"

My gut tightened when she turned to Dan. The words seemed to roll out in slow motion.

"And-what-do-*you*-do?"

Dan just looked up from his plate, got that squinty, lemon lick look. He talked about how he's an "entrepreneur in the digital space." That usually saved us in L.A., probably because nobody really cared about anyone else but themselves. Even here, everyone just nodded and seemed ready to move on. But Mostar . . .

"So, you don't have a job."

The whole room got silent. I could feel the skin of my face. What do you say? How do you reply?

Bless you, Tony Durant.

"Dan's an artist, Mosty, just like you and me." He smiled, tapping his temple. "How much of our process takes place up here, unseen, untimed, and definitely unpaid!"

Carmen jumped in with, "Did you get paid for all your sculptures before they were done?" which garnered a nod and meek "yeah" from her wife.

"There's paycheck work and there's project work." Vincent shrugged, which prompted Reinhardt to talk about how Europeans have a much more balanced sense of identity than Americans. "Across the pond, who you are isn't just what you do." It was a little confusing given that he was actually saying this to a European (I think) but I really didn't care. I was so grateful to everyone for coming in and saving the moment. Maybe a little too much, because Tony now swerved back to a more neutral stance. "Mosty's just trying to understand Dan's journey, albeit in her own unique way."

And when he added, "And she is quite unique," the room's chuckles became laughter. Even Mostar seemed in it now, smiling with raised hands in this "you got me" gesture. It didn't appear to bother her at all. Not an ally in the room and she looked totally okay with that. I would've died.

Not that I feel bad for her, though, especially when we said good night, and she gave Dan a sidelong glance. More like a smirk, like "I'm totally onto you." I'm sure that's why I couldn't sleep last night. I tried to convince myself to read instead of re-watching *The Princess Bride*. I've loved that movie my whole life. It's worth the melatonin-reducing light from the screen. I needed the familiarity, the comfort.

I feel . . .

I wish . . .

I can't wait for our Skype session next week. Maybe I'll call you and see if we can move it up. I really need it. Especially after today.

Dan and I didn't talk about what happened at dinner. Why would we? When was the last time we really talked about anything? I could tell he was upset. You can always tell by the couch time. If he comes to bed an hour or so after me, he's miffed. If it's the middle of the night, something's really under his skin. If I find him asleep in the morning, iPad on his stomach . . .

He's there now. Awake, but not helping me. I think he can hear me unpacking upstairs. I've just been reassembling the shelves. Three of them, two large and one waist high, with long steel support poles. They're heavy, and loud. He must have heard me banging them together. Maybe not with his music. Did I mention that you can sync different rooms for different devices? I guess it's supposed to give everyone their own personal space, but since Dan's claimed the living room and those are the biggest speakers . . .

I can hear it through the door. His early '90s loop.

Goddamn "Black Hole Sun."

Wow, I am really angry. I'm not used to feeling this way. I don't like it. Maybe a walk later, hike the trail, clear my head.

I need it. The knot is back.

From my interview with Frank McCray, Jr.

Kate Holland's brother has aged considerably from the social media photos taken barely a year before. His cherubic features have narrowed, his hair thinned and grayed. The former Cygnus attorney is intense, impatient, with an undertone of muted anger behind each word. As he reaches his right hand out to shake, I notice the other resting on a holstered Smith & Wesson 500 revolver.

We meet at his "temporary base camp," a motor home parked at the end of a paved road at the foot of the Cascade Range. Before meeting in person, he warned me that there wouldn't be too much time to talk. He reminds me of that fact again as he invites me inside. While neat, clean, and meticulously organized, the vehicle's cabin is crammed to the roof with equipment. I see camping gear, freeze-dried food, the hard, black plastic case for a very expensive weapon scope, and several boxes of various firearm ammunition.

McCray ushers me to a narrow bench at the dinette, then sits across from me, next to a bulging backpack and sheathed hunting rifle. Between us sits a small, well used BioLite camp stove, the kind that uses thermodynamics to charge personal devices. McCray removes a stained bandana from his checkered flannel shirt pocket and resumes cleaning the stove. A cold north wind rocks the camper, a warning of the winter months ahead.

Before I get a chance to ask my first question, he launches in with:

It's my fault what happened to them. Not the volcano, obviously, or how it drove those creatures right toward them. I didn't set up the situation. I just put them right in the middle of it. "Oh no, you're doing me a real favor, please. I can't sell the house till the market recovers. Please come take care of it for a while. Too many memories for me to live there. I promise you'll love it."

That was me, always pushing, always thinking I knew better. I was so goddamn proud that I'd gotten her into therapy, and how she was just starting to make progress. Her need to nurture, her fear of abandonment. I think, with a little more time, she might have been ready to admit that she blamed Mom for Dad leaving us, and how that blame kept her enabling Dan. Just a little more time. But then Gary and I split, and the house needed a sitter, and I thought . . . I *thought* . . . if I could just nudge her a little closer to the truth, build up just a little more pressure . . .

He spits into the bandana, then attacks a particularly stubborn stain.

I mean . . . even if she blamed me at the time, she'd totally thank me later, after it all worked out one way or another . . .

The camper rocks in the wind.

I thought I had all the answers.

Chapter 3

Monkey, you want to reign over all the animals, but look what a fool you are!

—Aesop

From the American Geosciences Institute (published online one year prior to the Rainier Eruption).

Citing "priority realignment," the president has requested a 15 percent cut from the budget of the U.S. Geological Survey for the coming fiscal year. The budget proposal would eliminate implementation of an earthquake early warning system for the West Coast, the Geomagnetism Program that would aid in the forecasting of geomagnetic storms, and an immediate suspension of the National Volcano Early Warning System. This last aspect is particularly worrisome, as Washington's Mount Rainier has shown recent signs of renewed activity.

JOURNAL ENTRY #3

OCTOBER 1

I'm sorry I wasn't more open during our session. I shouldn't have used up all our time talking about how beautiful it is up here. Avoidance? You're probably right.

And I'm sorry I haven't written more this whole week. Too busy settling in. No, that's not all. I'm still getting used to the idea of writing stuff down. Even in this letter format you recommended. Yes, it's easier to write once I get going, but the idea of sitting down every day, talking about what I've done. Not even on paper, not even to myself. It's just hard. Looking in.

And, to be fair, there's a lot to get used to.

I know telecommuting isn't new. But it is for me. I never realized how much I craved the structure of going into an office; dedicated work space, work people, work time.

At least the house is comfortable. So much nicer than our rental back in Venice. Clean, high-tech, effortless. Frank even told us that he'd left a "housewarming present." Literally. All that methane in the biodigester. Every time I think about sleeping, eating, living above a giant tank of my brother's poo, I just try to remember that it's also one less bill to pay.

Unpacking's been slow, breaking down all those boxes, organizing all our stuff. It's all gotta be just right, you know me. A place for everything, and everything in its place.

I have been settling into a nice routine though. I need that. Structure. I wake up every morning with this majestic view right outside my window. The tall, green trees rising up to the top of the ridge behind the house. The way the leaves sparkle in the sun. The birdsong alarm clock. Not that I've ever needed one. Always up, always ready. But it's so nice, for a change, to rise with excitement instead of nerves. I can't remember the last time I did that. Middle school? When was the last time I didn't open my eyes with a mental checklist ticking in my brain? Stuff to do. Problems to solve.

I still have them, of course, but knowing that my day will start with a hike in the woods helps. I've been doing that every morning. Up and dressed, quietly as I can so as not to wake up Dan, and out the door. Easier to be quiet when you don't have to worry about turning off a burglar alarm. Nobody sets theirs, no need! Then out and up the trail behind the house.

Dawn is so peaceful here. Just me and the sun, and Yvette! She's up way before anyone, in the Common House, teaching online classes around the globe. I haven't brought myself to take one yet. Even though she won't charge me. "Just perch yourself behind the webcam and it'll feel like a private lesson." I keep meaning to do it. Too intimidating, and, let's be honest, it does get in the way of my hike!

I can't believe I get to do this whenever I want! Will it ever get old? How can it? I love that crisp, cool air in my lungs, on my cheeks, down my back when I warm up enough to take off my fleece. Frank warned me about when the weather turns, in a month or so, when it supposedly nosedives into real cold. I won't mind. It'll be nice to have real winters again, like we did back east.

So far, I've been doing the same hike every day, the trail that loops around the neighborhood up to the ridge that overlooks everything. And I do mean *everything*!

Mount Rainier is out of a storybook. The white peak rising in the distance. The morning light turning its snow an orange pink. You'd expect a princess to live in a castle on the summit, or an angry dragon to sleep under its base. Sounds crazy, but I feel strangely safe every morning when I see Rainier, like it's watching over us. I know the tremors we've been feeling (we've had one or two since that first time at dinner) are coming from the mountain, but I can't reconcile them with this protective giant ruling all he surveys.

The Boothes don't think I'm crazy. I mentioned it to them yesterday morning. They also do a pre-breakfast dawn hike. They're so nice, so inclusive. I ran into them yesterday morning on my way up the ridge. I felt really uncomfortable at first, like I'd intruded in some way. Yes, we should probably talk about this, why on a public path I felt like their rights trumped mine. But they just waved me over.

We chatted all the way up the trail. Bobbi asked how well I knew Seattle, and I confessed that I'd never really spent any time there. Vincent couldn't stop talking about how wonderful it was, "cultured" was the word he used. The fish market, the theater scene, MoPOP.* Bobbi offered the use of their pied-à-terre, a condo they have in Madison Park and visit a couple times a month. "Otherwise we'd go crazy." That was Vincent. "Just knowing that Seattle is only ninety minutes or so makes all the difference." Bobbi added, "Depending on traffic." And they laughed together.

They're so cute, the two of them, with their matching Patagonia outfits and double walking poles. When we reached the top of the ridge, watching the morning light color Rainier, it was nice, and, yes, sad to see them holding hands. When they'd been telling me how easy it was to get to Seattle "if you time it right," Vincent started going on about the national highway system.

"Practically erased distances," he said, "especially when you think it used to take months, years, to cross this continent! And do you know the Eisenhower administration only managed to get the project built by selling it as emergency runways in a nuclear war?"

Bobbi grinned and shook her head. "Yes, dear, and I'm sure she's very excited to hear about national security infrastructure."

I suddenly stiffened, thinking that Vincent would be hurt, defensive, surly. Like Dan. But he gave me this over-the-top, "What, you're not!" and the two shared a laughing hug. Their comfort, their ease.

I've tried to invite Dan. Not in the moment, of course. I would never think of trying to shake him awake. A few days ago, when I'd gotten back from my hike and he asked, "How'd it go?" Instead of answering, "Great," and going upstairs to shower, I actually sat down next to him on the couch to talk about it. I told him about the smell of the trees, the sound of the birds. I even described Rainier's inspiring peak.

And he pretended to listen. Pursed lips, exaggerated nod, eyes not meaning to but flicking down at his iPad every couple seconds. *Okay, wrap it up. I didn't really care, I was just being polite.* I

* MoPOP: Museum of Popular Culture.

knew what he wanted, but somehow, I found it in me to say, "You should totally come with tomorrow morning."

See, I did take something from our last session. I tried putting myself out there, giving him the chance. I did my part. But he just nodded again, even raising his eyebrows to prove that he'd heard what I'd said. "Maybe, sure." Then went back to his screen.

Message received. No argument but no commitment.

Dan.

That's something else I have to get used to, being together 24/7. I don't want to say it was *okay* before, but at least back then, our old routine gave us space. He'd be sleeping when I went to work and still up when I went to bed. In between we had, what, a couple hours together if extra work or phone calls didn't keep me occupied. Yes, weekends were tougher, when he wouldn't want to go out with my friends or would disappear down to Intelligentsia* for a half-day coffee. I never realized how much it upset me, or, maybe I did, but the tension, the resentment, it always diffused first thing Monday morning.

It's not diffusing anymore. We're trapped together all the time.

Did I just say "trapped"? It's starting to feel that way. Is that why Frank wanted us to move up here, to trap me here with Dan all the time, force me to watch him sit on the couch with his tablet while I unpack the house, organize everything, do everything?

And the part that really gets me, now that I think about it, isn't just the sitting around all day, it's doing it with the curtains open so everyone can see him. Here I thought keeping them open would make me feel exposed. Now I feel . . .

Embarrassed. Yes. I do. Embarrassed for him. On display. Doesn't he care?

He did when Mostar saw him! So did I. Gasoline on the fire. That's the only way to describe what happened.

* Intelligentsia: A popular coffee establishment on Abbot Kinney Blvd.

It was delivery day, the one day every week when all our online orders come in. The HOA has organized this special to minimize the "environmental impact." That's how Tony puts it. "What's the point of clean air if we're just going to pollute it with drones?"

The drones were insane. I was sitting in my home office, wrapping up a conference call, when I heard this crazy buzzing sound. Like an angry swarm of giant bees. I'd heard regular drones before, the high-pitched whir from the annoying little ones that fly around over the Venice canals. But these were deeper, louder, and a lot more numerous.

I came outside to see Tony standing on the grass behind the Common House, one tan, muscled arm shielding his eyes as the other waved down the first laptop. That's what they looked like: large, flat, and black. A robotic insect—no, arachnid, because of the eight legs. Each straight leg ending in a rotor spinning too fast for me to see. It still amazes me that those rotors could lift the grocery basket under its belly.

"New from Cygnus," Tony called over his shoulder as I approached. "Y-Q* Mark 1. Twice the payload and thrice the range of the HorseFly models UPS and Amazon use." The drone hovered for a second, descended slowly, then gently settled on the large grassy patch big enough for a real helicopter. Did I ever mention the helipad?

No, I just looked back over my first description of this place. Sorry. We've got one. Part of our HOA dues includes a medical insurance package that pays for an emergency medical evac. According to Tony, if anyone gets sick or hurt for any reason, they can zip us to a downtown Seattle hospital. "Faster than driving from right there in the city."

He really has thought about everything.

Anyway, as the drone's rotors stopped, Tony opened the basket, checked the contents of the bags, removed them, and tapped

* "Y-Q" stands for Yi qi, a late Jurassic, bat-winged dinosaur found in China.

an app on his phone. The blades *zeeeezzz*ed back to life and then it was gone. "I'm sure yours is coming," he said, turning to me with those sapphire eyes that made my fingertips tingle.

I just nodded and pretended to look past him for what should have been my incoming drone. I hadn't ordered my food by air. I'm still not ready for that. But Tony didn't know that, and I wanted any excuse to spend just a few extra seconds with him.

"Pretty amazing"—he nodded at the next approaching automaton—"civilization coming to us." And with a wink that tickled my vertebrae, he said, "Now if only they'd legalize 'certain products' nationally so we could order those online as well."

Even walking away, the feeling I got from his confident stride, the muscles in his back showing through his thin T-shirt . . . And there was Yvette, waving to me, opening the door for her husband in a twenty-first century version of—what was that '50s show all my professors used to rail against? *Ozzy and the Beaver*? Whatever. Their life looked pretty damned good to me.

As I watched them disappear inside, the second Y-Q landed a few feet away. "Here it is!" That was Carmen, calling back to her house as Effie, in the doorway, fumbled to get her Crocs on. We hadn't talked much since we'd moved in. Carmen had been gone for a few days at a conference in Portland and Effie always seemed busy homeschooling Palomino. She was there too, trailing behind Effie as the three of them gathered around the now-silent drone. She wouldn't say anything to me, even as I tried to include her in my morning greetings. "Hey, ladies. Hi, Palomino." Nothing, just a blank, silent stare. Creepy kid.

Our awkward moment was compounded as Carmen riffled through both bags before sending the drone on its way. "No broccolini?" A glare at Effie, who tried to come up with an answer, but ended with an embarrassed sigh. Carmen must have suddenly remembered I was there because she recovered with, "Well, I guess we'll just have to survive somehow!" They both chuckled. Effie's seemed a little forced.

I was almost happy when Mostar came along. Almost.

"What, no van yet?" Loud, terse, barreling in from behind us. Carmen and Effie traded a quick, almost imperceptible look, then both smiled at me and started back for their house. "We've got to get together for dinner soon," said Carmen, then, Effie, looking embarrassed like she didn't think of it first, said, "Yes, yes, yes, soon, next week."

That was when the van rolled up. I almost didn't hear it. So quiet! All electric. And that wasn't the crazy part. No driver! A cab with a steering wheel, but nobody behind it. Okay, it's not like I haven't seen driverless cars before. Tons of videos on Dan's iPad and a few, I think, in L.A., but those always had people behind the wheel. Something about a city ordinance, that they can only be used in "assist" mode, like an autopilot in an airplane. Not in this van though. Just a giant, empty land drone.

"Finally!" Mostar stomped over to the building's charging station, connected its cable to the van, then typed her password into its side access panel. With a chirp and flashing green light, the back doors slid open. And there were the groceries: Mostar's, Reinhardt's, the Boothes', and mine. I'm not much for ordering food online. I've done it a few times, Postmates, FreshDirect. But I like physically going to the store, smelling the produce, picking out just the right branzino. I used to spend hours roaming the aisles, which, now that I think about it, might have also been an excuse to get away from Dan. Maybe I was lingering on that thought too long, and maybe Mostar thought I was weirded out by the idea of a driverless car. "The only thing I miss is a delivery boy to help me."

I saw she was struggling a little bit with her grocery bags. "You need some help?"

She smiled with, "Oh, that would be lovely, thank you," and gestured to three large paper sacks. I set down my grocery bags and hefted one of the sacks. The label said something about a "silicon-polymer blend."

"Careful, it's heavy. Raw materials for my work."

I must have been wobbling, because Mostar asked, "You all

right?" and when I said I was fine, she just clucked over at our house.

"Why isn't your man helping?"

My man. Who uses that kind of language? So possessive.

But there he was, on the couch, on display for all the world. She grimaced at the sight, then at me. "C'mon, let's get him."

I felt like a character in an action movie, or a cartoon making fun of that movie, the iconic scene where someone screams "Noooooo" in slow motion. I didn't do it, but it's exactly how I felt as she trundled right up to our living room window, knocking hard on the glass, shouting, "Hey, c'mon, Danny, get up!"

It definitely looked like a cartoon, Dan flopping off the couch, flustered, terrified.

"Danny! Give us a hand!"

I'd just reached Mostar as Dan came blundering out the front door. If he was the deer in the headlights, then I was in the car's passenger seat.

Mostar didn't notice our silent exchange, or didn't care.

"Danny, I got two big sacks in the van. Just like the one your wife's carrying." He hesitated, slack-jawed, "Uh . . ."

"Go on, your highness!" And then she hit him! Not hard, just a slight slap on the arm. "Go!" I caught my breath, so did Dan, but he took off for the van just as Mostar turned back for her house.

It was the first time I'd been in her home. I'm not sure what I was expecting.

Those sculptures!

They line her walls. All glass! So beautiful, delicate. A lot of natural settings like birds and flowers. And flames! A lot of flames. Some blue and simple, like a stove's gaslight. Others red and crazy, like wood fire. One particular piece, an explosion? Bright yellow expanding to orange, red, and fringed with cloudy brown.

My favorite were the golden lilies. They're exquisite little flowers about a foot high; three thin green stems topped with orange lightening to yellow petals. And all growing out of what looked like a maelstrom of burning detonations. I can't imagine the kind of skill, patience, and talent it took to make.

I was entranced, lost in their colors and shapes. The way the light would pass through them, all of them, as I walked by.

"You like them?" She gestured to the flowers and said, "My early work. Paddle and parchoffi, before I got into this 3-D printing racket."

We were standing in the entrance hall, not far from the open door to her workshop. I could see the printer humming, next to what she described as a "space age kiln."

"It's really quite simple," she said, waving her hand over the machinery. I hadn't asked for a lecture, but got one anyway. She prattled on about making a 3-D CAD file, converting and importing it to the printer, loading it with the raw silicon-polymer blend, then waiting for it to extrude a nearly finished piece before popping that piece into the kiln to melt away the polymer. I do have to admit, this new process seemed interesting, and the finished objects were undeniably cool.

There were at least a couple dozen of them, all lined up on shelves above the workbench. Rows of little houses, none more than an inch or two high. And one larger, arching structure. A bridge, maybe. All cute, and I guess amazing when you factor in how they were made, but nothing compared to the handblown works of art right in front of me.

I wish I'd said something profound, insightful, anything except what I did say, which was, "They're wonderful."

Mostar smiled warmly and put a hand on my arm. "Thank you." Her eyes shifted to the flowers rising from the flames. "I like to think that beauty can come from fire."

Okay, this is going to sound weird, I know, but as she said this, for just a split second, she was someone else. Nothing you could put your finger on. Something with her voice, her face, the muscles around her eyes. Just for a second, and then one of those small rumbles hit and my heart practically jumped right out of my mouth. I must have made a move toward her sculptures, because her hand shot in front of my face.

"It's all right, don't worry. I put that, what do you call it? That pasty material, like you use for earthquakes in California. I've stuck it to all their bottoms." Her eyes scanned the shelves. "Can't be too careful, eh?"

"Got it!" Dan lumbered in with the other two bags, one under each arm. He hesitated in the doorway, expecting, I guess, a big expansive thank-you.

"What, you want a medal?" Mostar motioned to the workshop. "Over there next to the printer." Dan hopped to, placing the sacks where he'd been told, then came out to receive, yet again, another slap on the arm.

"Look how helpful your man can be."

I wanted to melt through the floor.

But I looked at Dan's face. He wasn't upset. And he didn't have that "Oh God, what's happening?" face anymore. This look, I didn't recognize it.

"Now go help your wife and get your groceries." Mostar gestured to the van. "Go on now, she'll come help you put them away in a minute."

He didn't say anything, rushing out the front door. Neither did I, stepping into her workshop to lay down my burden. I thought I was done, just a few more seconds to escape. But she waited for me at the front door. That knowing expression from the first night we met.

"What was it?" she asked, watching Dan carry our groceries home. "Couldn't get the job he wanted? First business failed? Couldn't get back up because his parents never let him get knocked down?"

How did she know!

"Trust me, Katie, fragile princes aren't new."

I don't know how I got out of there. A mix of nods and thank-yous and slipping out of her grasp like an eel. I don't know if she watched me leave. I don't care. I'm never speaking to her again. Crazy bitch.

But what she said.

I wasn't mad. Not then. Shocked, I guess. Even now. X-rayed like that. Violated. Too oversensitive? I don't care. It's how I feel. All I wanted to do was get away, get past it, find some way to feel better.

I couldn't go home. Dan was there. If he was angry, or hurt . . . I couldn't deal with him right then. I couldn't go back. I haven't really talked to you about that time. When things didn't work out, those silent, sullen days, weeks, waiting for the phone to ring. Waiting for the universe to recognize his genius. I had to recognize it. The endless compliments, reassurance, validation. The endless need. And when I needed him?

I thought about calling you, right there, scheduling an emergency session. I'm not sure why I didn't, or why I decided to turn and head for the Durants' house.

I rang the bell before deciding to. "Kate, what's wrong?" Yvette answered, clearly pained to see what I was trying to hide.

I babbled something about having "a day" and if it's not too inconvenient, if it's not the right time, but since she asked if I'd like . . .

I'm not a crier. You know that by now. In control. Put together. But when she reached out to hug me, I came really close to losing it.

"It doesn't matter," she said over my shoulder, rubbing my back. "Whatever it is, I know how to fix it." She released me just long enough to grab a couple of yoga mats and air pillows next to the door. "I was hoping you'd finally take me up on my offer." She led me over to the Common House. "I've got the perfect meditation session for this."

When Yvette instructed me to lie down, drew the shades, lit the fireplace, and hit the soft, soothing music app on her phone, I knew my unconscious choice had been right.

Her words, her guided imagery. She took me through these woods, just like I'd done on a physical hike. "Allow the forest to heal you," she said. "Release your pain. This land gives you permission to unburden yourself with each step."

She guided me up that familiar hiking trail, "dropping my anguish like stones."

Unwinding my back, my jaw. I could feel my breathing slow as I mentally climbed the trail.

"And there she is," said Yvette, "waiting with open arms."

And then she said a word I'd never heard before. The name of who, what, was waiting for me.

Oma.

Guardian of the wilderness.

Yvette explained that Oma was a spirit of the First Peoples, a gentle giant that arrogant Eurocentric white men have perverted into the name "Bigfoot."

I've obviously heard that word before, along with "UFO" and "Loch Ness Monster." I don't know much about it though, just what I've seen in those stupid beef jerky commercials. Screwing with Sasquatch? Is that the phrase? Is Sasquatch the same as Bigfoot? The creature in the commercials was a dumb brute. A grouchy neighbor just begging to be punked. I tried to get past those ridiculous images. Those "mutilations of truth," as Yvette described it, "like everything else our society has done to what came before it."

Oma wasn't anything like that. She was tenderness. She was strength. "Feel her energy, her protection. Feel her soft, warm arms around you. Her sweet, cleansing breath surround you."

And I could, imagining those giant arms embracing me, holding me. "Safe. Serene. Home."

Again, the tears nearly came. I felt a sob make it halfway up my throat. Maybe the next guided imagery session, the next time Yvette takes me to meet Oma. And there will be a next time.

I've actually never done meditation. I think we talked about this. I can't let go. That one class I took, I spent the whole time trying not to laugh. And all those times at home. When Dan was out, alone on the floor with the ear buds and the scented candle. My mind couldn't stop checking boxes. Laundry, errands, work calls. I just couldn't seem to focus.

But I didn't have Yvette back then. Or Oma. Yes, my practical side still thinks it's silly. Like that first thought I had about Mount Rainier watching over us. But is it so wrong to want to be watched over? When you're feeling small and scared—which, let's be honest, is pretty much how I feel all the time—isn't it okay, just for a moment, to want someone, something bigger than you to have all the answers, to have everything under control?

Chapter 4

Vancouver! Vancouver! This is it!

—Final radio report by USGS volcanologist
David Alexander Johnston before being killed by
Mount St. Helens's eruption on May 18, 1980

JOURNAL ENTRY #4

OCTOBER 2

I thought it was an earthquake. I woke up to this loud *bang*. It felt like a giant foot had kicked the house. I thought it was the kind of quick, bomb-type earthquakes we've gotten back in Venice that are over before you're fully awake. I switched on the light and saw that the front bedroom windows were cracked. I could see lights going on in the other houses.

"Look at this!" That was Dan, behind me, standing at the back window.

"Look!" Again, motioning urgently for me. I could see a red glow on the horizon. I guess I was still groggy, still waking up. I wondered why he was so excited about distant city lights. But then I realized that wasn't a city. It was Rainier.

I squinted through the cracks but couldn't really believe what I was seeing. Dan must've mistrusted his vision too because he darted out onto the back balcony. No mistaking the artificial dawn.

Another rumble hit, and this time we grabbed each other. It wasn't as bad, this one. I heard a few things clatter downstairs and the windows rattled a little bit. At the same time, the glow behind Rainier brightened.

"Is that an eruption?" I know Dan wasn't asking me specifically, but I went inside and turned on the TV. The cable was out, so I grabbed my phone and saw we still had full Wi-Fi. But when I tried to go online, I couldn't seem to connect.

I tried dialing 911. The call failed. I tried calling Dan's phone. Same. I switched off my phone and tried it again. Dan did the same with his devices—iPads, TVs, laptops. They all showed a perfect signal, but weren't working.

That was when Dan noticed the blinking app that monitors all house functions. It showed we were now on backup battery. Power from the grid was cut.

From my interview with Frank McCray, Jr.

Why would they have a satellite phone, or a two-way radio? Those are technologies that imply you're cut off from civilization, which they certainly were not. The whole point of Greenloop was to ensure that its residents were as wired in as anyone on the Upper West Side of Manhattan. Better even. As a telecommuter community, they had to have the fastest, most reliable connection possible. That means cable, not air. Satellite dishes aren't as reliable, especially in the kind of weather we get up in the Pacific Northwest. Everyone's data stream flowed through solid fiber-optic cable. And why would, how could, that cable ever fail?

JOURNAL ENTRY #4 [CONTINUED]

The doorbell rang and we both jumped. It was Carmen. She asked if we were getting any cell reception. We told her our situation, including the power problem. You could see she hadn't thought to check that. She looked back at her house, where Effie was standing in the doorway with a blanket-wrapped Palomino.

Dr. Reinhardt shuffled over in a kimono, which made me stifle a nervous giggle. He asked what was going on, what that loud crash was. His breath was so bad, even from six feet away. I just pointed up the ridge behind our houses. You could still see a faint crimson flicker. He looked, paused, then turned back with this hesitant yet arrogant "Oh yes, of course that, I've seen that, I just mean . . ." As he was struggling for the words (any words, I'm guessing, to save face) Carmen asked about his Wi-Fi connection. He responded, kind of self-importantly, that he didn't own a "pocket phone." Dan started to ask him about the power supply to his house, but was cut off by someone shouting, "Meeting!"

We all looked over to Bobbi Boothe waving her phone flashlight at us while Vincent shone his on the ground. They were halfway to the Common House, where I could see Tony and Yvette waiting. Yvette was already at the kitchenette, filling up the kettle while Tony took teacups from the cupboard.

Tony waved everyone to take a seat and asked if anyone was hungry, if they wanted him to run back to his house for some snacks. When we shook our heads, he joked that the only hunger was for information. I saw that both he and Yvette still wore their calm, reassuring smiles. Maybe a little bit stiffer? Forced? But that could have totally been me projecting my own anxiety.

Tony began by stating that obviously something was happening up on Rainier. Some kind of "activity." And while we couldn't be sure of anything yet, by now, we all knew that "our cable is out."

The way he talked, that casual confidence. "Our cable is out." He assured us that it'd probably come back soon, maybe a few minutes, an hour, and then we could all see what was really happening up on Rainier.

"What about the car radio?" That was Vincent Boothe. "We've all got Sirius satellite, right?" He rose suddenly. "I'll go listen to the news!" As he ran out to the little BMW i3 parked in his driveway, Tony held up his hand in an over-the-top salute. "Uh . . . yeah, Vincent . . . why don't you go listen to the news."

I laughed with the rest of the room.

"If there is an eruption," that was Reinhardt, "there must be at least a few fatalities, given the proximity to population centers." He talked about how, during Mount St. Helens, there were scientists, like someone named David Johnston, and people who refused to evacuate, this guy named Harry Truman. (Really? Harry Truman? Like the president?*) Waving his hand to the window, he said, "And St. Helens was in the middle of nowhere. With Rainier . . ."

Yvette cut him off with a playfully scolding "Alex" and an exaggerated nod to Palomino, who was wrapped tightly in Effie's arms. Reinhardt glanced over his shoulder at the girl, gave her a thumbs-up (Seriously? A thumbs-up?), then melted back into his chair.

Tony reclaimed the room by saying, "Until we do find out what's happening, the worst thing we can do right now is drive ourselves crazy with speculation. Stress, anxiety"—a warm, friendly glance at Palomino—"does that ever help?"

"Should we leave?" That was Bobbi. "I mean, can't we just get in our cars and drive in the other direction?"

"We could"—Tony nodded with eyebrows raised—"and that's a valid impulse, but until we know more, we might be making things a whole lot worse for ourselves." He must have expected the quizzical looks. "We're safe up here. Rainier's too far away to hurt us, right?"

Was it? Tony seemed to think so.

"But if we panic and head down into the valley . . . there's only one road out, and it's sure to be jammed with panicked people

* Harry R. (Randall) Truman, a casualty of the Mount St. Helens eruption, not to be confused with Harry S. Truman, thirty-third president of the United States.

right now. Remember the Malibu wildfires? All those cars stuck on the Pacific Coast Highway? Not moving. No bathrooms. Remember that?"

I did. Watching the endless coverage. That thin snake of cars wedged in between the hills and the ocean. I remember hearing constantly that they'd barely moved inches in hours. I remember feeling guilty that I was safe and comfortable at home, able to see the pulsing orange line creep right over the distant hills.

Tony asked, "Do we really want to do that to ourselves? Wade into that chaos? Maybe even hinder emergency vehicles trying to get to people who really need help? And if they don't? If it all turns out to be a false alarm?"

He gestured to the wall, in the direction of Mr. Boothe's car. "Again, we don't know anything right now. And if Vincent comes in here telling us he's heard about an evacuation order, trust me, I'll be the first—no . . . the *last* one to leave, after I've made sure all of you get out of here safely. But until that order comes, until we know more, the worst thing we can do right now is panic."

"So, what *do* we do?" That was Carmen, and Tony seemed to brighten. Yvette even shot him a knowing look, like she was prompting him to say what they'd been waiting for. "Perfect question," he said, and spread his hands in a jazzed "check this out" gesture.

"This situation, the one we find ourselves in now, is *exactly* what Greenloop is designed for!" He paused for a moment, letting his enthusiasm wash over us. "Think about it. We're not in physical danger, just temporarily out of touch. We have power from our solar panels, water from our wells, heating from our own biogas. Is anyone going to starve if we don't get a FreshDirect grocery fix in the next few days . . . Sorry, Alex." Reinhardt laughed, his big belly shaking like Santa Claus's. Everyone else chuckled too. You could feel the tension drain out of the room.

I felt it too, my back and jaw relaxing. Is that how he does it?

Calming fears, stoking excitement? Is that the secret to his success? Making you want to believe? I did. His energy, his passion. It's infectious. I was right on board by the time he said, "So we'll have to unplug for a little while. And isn't that what we all should be doing anyway? Limit our screen time to enjoy the world?" He gestured out the door behind us. "Isn't that why we moved here?" Nods and affirmative *mmms* followed. "And yes"—he put his hands up with a slightly mischievous smile—"I know how some of you will have to wait a little longer for the sequel series of *Downton Abbey* to drop." His eyes flicked to me. I felt myself blush; was he guessing or did I mention it to him at dinner?

Tony added, "I feel your pain." We all laughed, except one.

"And what if it's not 'a little while'?" When Mostar spoke up, my jaw re-clenched. "What if it's weeks? Months?" I felt Dan stiffen next to me. "I agree with you, Tony, about staying put, but not because it's a false alarm. What if the roads aren't just jammed? What if they're gone? We might not just get caught in traffic, we might get killed out there."

For a second, Tony thought she'd finished agreeing with him, and opened his mouth to speak.

"But," Mostar continued, "staying put and staying safe isn't enough. We could be cut off, physically unable to get out, and if Alex is right about the eruption affecting all those other towns, we could also be forgotten."

I suddenly felt dizzy.

Forgotten?

"And winter's on its way, remember? When the weather turns, when the snow starts piling up . . ." Mostar gestured to Tony. "We might have electricity, water, heat, but what about food?"

Carmen looked ready to say something, and Mostar, reading her mind, continued, "This week's groceries won't last till spring!" Out of the corner of my eye, I saw Bobbi check her phone. Was she trying the FreshDirect app? "What else do we have?" Mostar asked. "A few fruit trees? Your herb garden?" That was to Bobbi, who hid her phone like a busted teenager.

"We need to pool our resources." Mostar went back to scanning the room. "Compile a central list of everyone's supplies, and work out how to make those supplies last as long as they can."

Reinhardt huffed. "Well, that's a bit of an invasion of privacy."

Mostar turned on him. "You want to try going for help, Alex?" She gestured toward the volcano. "One road. That's it. And if anyone is thinking about walking . . ." She threw her arms out dramatically in opposite directions. "A volcano on one side and mountains on the other." She turned to the Cascades. "Anyone know how far it is to the next town, the next cabin? We don't know our neighbors, or even if we have any. We don't know anything about this land past the end of the hiking trail. Do you want to try stumbling around out there without a working GPS?"

"But can't our phones . . ." That was Carmen, her eyes bouncing between Mostar and her phone. "I had these friends who hiked the Pacific Crest Trail and they'd downloaded this map or app . . ."

"Do you have it already?" Mostar swung her eyes around the room. "Do any of you? Because it's too late to get them now." I noticed nobody checking their phones. "Do any of you have a paper map, or a compass, or any emergency supplies?" No one answered. "If you don't like my idea, then come up with a better one."

Tony tried to say, "Look, Mostar—" but she interrupted with, "You must have one, Tony. Supplies? A plan? You built this place. You talked us into coming here."

"You're scaring her." Effie's voice was so soft, I barely heard it. I peeked over to her holding Palomino, who honestly didn't look that scared. I was. At that point, I was the most terrified I'd been all night, and not just because of what Mostar said. Her tone, it was softer with Tony than with Reinhardt. Less challenge. More question.

"You must have at least thought about what might go wrong."

I watched her face change when he didn't answer, those saggy eyelids raising, the full lips rounding. "Didn't you? Right now, all I'm hearing is 'don't worry, it's not as bad as you think.' But what if it is? What if it's worse?"

"You're scaring her!" That was Carmen, sitting straight up with a clear, commanding voice. Mostar paused at that, and it gave Tony the moment to jump in.

"Mosty, we . . . we all hear what you're saying, and we respect your legitimate concerns." Mostar opened her mouth to say something but Tony held out a hand. "And, yes, I've thought about it, but more important"—a nod to the window—"they've thought about it."

"They?" Mostar cut in. "Who's they?"

"They," Tony repeated with just the barest hesitance, "the experts, the . . . emergency services. Those in charge. They've thought about Rainier, and planned and trained for this exact moment."

"They better for the taxes we pay," said Reinhardt, and it got a laugh from the room. Tony joined in with, "Exactly, they get paid to think about these situations so we don't have to." He was starting to relax, we all were, but dammit, she just wouldn't shut up.

"But what if 'they' can't handle this? What if it's too big and they don't find us before—"

"Mostar, enough!" Carmen again, followed by an "I know, please!" from Bobbi and a groaning "Mosty . . ." from Reinhardt.

"No, it's okay." Tony raised his arms gently. "Mosty's got a right to feel what she feels, and she's right about us all needing to take care of each other. That's the"—he paused, licked his lips—"that's the unspoken social contract," he emphasized the last three words, "that every community agrees to. People helping people when times are tough because it's the right thing to do. Right?"

If he was expecting support or maybe gratitude from Mostar,

he didn't get it. Mostar just glared at him before examining the rest of us. Her face was placid, her head nodded almost imperceptibly. Don't take this the wrong way, but it kind of reminded me of our first session, when you just listened with this expression like you were getting the lay of the land. That's how I felt with Mostar, like she was thinking, *So this is how it's going to be, this is what I'm dealing with.*

She was still silently sizing us up when Yvette spoke. Standing next to her husband and taking his hand, she said, "Tony just made such a good point about being free to feel the way we feel." She smiled at him lovingly. "I don't want to speak for anyone else, but, right now, I can feel the stress hormones flooding my body because I'm just so worried about all the people I know will worry about me."

Nods from Bobbi, Effie, Carmen. Reinhardt gave a long contemplative "Mmmm . . ."

"Family, friends, people out of state and even in other countries who are going to wake up tomorrow to this terrible news. Maybe some are already awake and trying to reach us." Her voice, the concern, the empathy. "And some are probably calling the authorities right now, making sure we're not forgotten."

From my interview with Frank McCray, Jr.

"Please stay on the line, your call will be answered as soon as possible." And I did. With FEMA, the USGS, the federal and state park services, the governor's office, state and county cops. I don't even want to think about how many hours I spent in that goddamn Chinese hotel room, forgetting to shower, or eat, or sleep as I texted and Skyped and email blasted anyone I could think of who might know anything about what might be happening to Greenloop, all with CNN in the background, the newsfeed on my laptop constantly updating, and my phone remaining "on the line" for a human voice that never came.

JOURNAL ENTRY #4 [CONT.]

Yvette made sure to address the room as a whole, but I could see her eyes linger on Mostar for just an extra beat. "I know it's hard to wait, feeling helpless, thinking about our loved ones, and"—she turned to the window—"those poor people out there who might really need help." She sniffed hard, dropped her head slightly as Tony slid a muscular arm around her shoulders.

"We can't be there for them, so we need to be here for each other." Yvette rested her head on his shoulder. "We can't let ourselves be destroyed by survivor's guilt, or what we hear on the news, or what we think our loved ones might be thinking about us." Another glance at Mostar. "We've got a lot to process, and we need to pool our emotional resources." The two smiled down at her, and Yvette said, "We need to keep our minds occupied, so tomorrow morning I'll be doing a meditation class here for anyone who needs it."

Tony hugged her again and said, "And my door's always open, if anyone needs to vent or share news or partake of some emergency single-malt scotch." Amid the chuckles, he finished with, "We're gonna keep calm and care for everyone's heart and soul. *That*"—he gave a confident glance to Mostar—"is our social contract."

Applause.

The Boothes, Reinhardt, the Perkins-Forster family. And me.

I couldn't believe how lucky we were to have them as our leaders. Silly term, simplistic, but what else can I call them? I felt so relieved, so secure, walking a few steps behind them as we all filed out. I did see something weird though, or maybe just thought I saw it. As they stepped out the door, Yvette glanced up at Tony with a look I'd never seen on her. Just a slight widening of the eyes, a subtle narrowing of the lips. They didn't say anything, sauntering home arm in arm. Just before they got to their door, I saw Yvette's head whip back over her shoulder. What was she looking for? To see if we were looking at them? Why?

I didn't get much chance to wonder. Soon as we closed the

door, Dan turned and asked me, "What do you think?" It's been a while since he's asked my opinion, about anything. At first, I was going to answer honestly, telling him how happy I was that Tony had put everything in perspective. What stopped me was the look on his face. Lost, searching. Genuinely open. It was the same look he'd shown at the meeting, specifically when Mostar spoke. Did he disagree with Tony? Did he really think, or at least wonder, if she might be right?

"Maybe . . ." Dan hesitated. "Maybe we should just drive down to the bridge . . . or maybe a little farther to the main road, just, you know . . . just to see what's going on?"

Before I could answer, loud sharp knocks sounded from our back door. We headed for the kitchen just as Mostar came tramping in. No apologizing, or even waiting for a response. Did I mention nobody here locks their doors at night?

Then she turned to Dan. "Do you know how to fix anything? Do you know how this house works?"

Dan, blank-faced, shook his head.

"Learn."

The word felt like a thousand pounds.

"There's probably a manual," Mostar continued in her flat, curt tone, "but it's probably"—her hands waved to the sky—"in the 'clouds.' So, you're going to have to use your head. Plumbing, electricity, all the crazy computer stuff that you kids should probably already know."

Dan was about to say something, but Mostar bulldozed in with, "And if you don't already know, learn."

Dan's lips moved. Her finger shot up. "But not now! First things first." And that finger lowered in the direction of our garage. "We can't use my workshop. Too much to move. I'm guessing yours is practically empty, so it'll be easy to build a garden."

Garden? Wait, what!

"Go on then," and she gave him a gentle shove toward the garage. "Whatever's in there, get it out, clear the floor. And get out a shovel, if you have one."

Before I could say anything, before I could even think, that pointing, smacking hand had wrapped around my wrist.

"Let's go, Katie."

And we were off to her house.

"Keep the curtains drawn," she said as soon as her kitchen door slid shut. "Don't let anybody see you. We can't let anyone know that we're in this together." I finally did manage to speak, something forceful and brilliant like "Uh . . ."

"We can't have them turning against you, not yet." She continued, this crazy little tank rolling over me, "You're a peacemaker, and we're going to need those skills first thing tomorrow." She let go of my wrist long enough to hand me a pen and yellow legal pad. "But first things first." And with a sweeping gesture to the pantry, cabinets, and fridge, she declared, "Go through it all. Catalog everything edible, right down to the last calorie. You must know how to do that, you're an American girl. I bet you've been dieting all your life." With a gentle shove toward the fridge, she headed for the back door. "Go home as soon as you're done and do the same with your own food!" As she turned to leave, I blurted something like, "But . . . wha . . ."

And she stopped, looking at my face and seeing all the confusion and, yes, anxiety leaking out from every pore. She sighed deeply, put a hand on my shoulder, and said, "You're right. I'm sorry."

Of course, I was expecting her next words to be something like, "I'm sorry I'm acting crazy. You're right. I'll stop. Go back home. Forget my meltdown. I'm sorry I scared you."

If only.

"I'm sorry I'm not more prepared." She scowled, clearly annoyed with herself. "I trusted Tony and Tony trusts 'they.'" She shrugged. "And maybe he's right. Maybe 'they' are cleaning up things right now. Maybe 'they' will be here tomorrow to fix the Internet and apologize for the inconvenience." She smiled sarcastically. "And then you can thank me for keeping your mind occupied with this engaging little project. And you'll even have a funny little story to tell your friends about the crazy old woman next door who thought the world was coming to an end." She looked ready to laugh, but sobered quickly. "But if I'm right . . ." Another shrug, a pat on my cheek, and then she tramped back to my house while I stood flustered and alone in hers.

That was two hours ago. I cataloged everything: eggs, cheeses, salami, bread. She has a lot of bread. And a lot of pickled stuff: cucumbers, peppers, and something that looks like sauerkraut. I even went through her juices and soda (no diet versions there) and logged every condiment and spice I could find. From jams to oils to something called "Vegeta." I'm not sure what the calorie count on that one is, but I've dieted enough to guestimate everything else. It's all so heavy, especially compared to our, my, calorie-negative stuff like celery and LaCroix.*

There's not a lot though, I should make that clear now. I'd say under normal conditions, three meals a day and snacks, she has enough for maybe two weeks at most. It's a little surprising, but Frank already warned me about that. He said that Greenloop's drone deliveries and smaller pantries were specifically designed to combat food waste. What was the number he cited? Thirty to forty percent of American food is thrown out each year? Thirty million tons?† I don't see how Mostar could contribute to that. It reminded me of East Coast city living, where people run to the local bodega for one tomato or a handful of string beans.

Still, her food stocks looked positively decadent next to ours. We'd thrown out so much before leaving, so many sacks and cans of stuff we'd never eaten (more waste). Now all we have at home is this week's delivery and the leftovers from the welcome dinner. It shouldn't take too long to catalog that. Which I'm about to do.

I'm in our own kitchen now, as Mostar and Dan work around me.

* LaCroix carbonated drink is considered to be calorie neutral not calorie negative, while opinions are divided on the legitimate calorie-negative qualities of celery.

† According to a 2014 EPA study, Americans waste 38.4 million tons of food per year.

They've cleaned out the garage. And now they're filling it with dirt.

Yes. Dirt.

They're outside right now, scraping up soil with stainless steel mixing bowls (neither of us has a shovel) and filling the plastic cleaning supply buckets we both have under our sinks. They're working at it like crazy, going back and forth across a bridge of Mostar's bath towels that she's laid from the kitchen door to the garage.

I offer to help but she waves me away. "No, no, specialization. You do your job, we'll do ours." She must think I'm still writing down a list of food. Not that she bothers to check. She's like a machine. So is Dan. A little slower, a little dazed. Once or twice we exchange wide-eyed looks. She catches one of those looks and probably thinks we were still questioning her decision to keep me from helping. "Division of labor!" She barks that over her shoulder. "That's how it works."

How *what* works?

I'm hiding my journal now under the yellow legal pad.

Does this wackadoo actually think we're going to be stuck here all winter? And why are we letting her do this? Why doesn't Dan just stand up to her and say, "Enough!"

Why don't I?

Okay, yes, I know what you'd say. Two betas, shared passivity, the whole reason our marriage got to where it got to in the first place. Nobody wants to take the lead and, as you say, take "responsibility" for leadership. I get all that, but . . .

But . . .

What if she's right?

I shouldn't even be thinking that now. I don't know what to think. Tony has to be right. I know he is. This is crazy. So why don't I say anything? I'm so tired. It's almost dawn.

I've got to get back to work. I need time to shower and dress and head over to Yvette's meditation class like everything's okay. Mostar's making me go.

Silver Skis Chalet, Crystal Mountain Resort, Washington State

The resort is abuzz with activity, the staff rushing to prepare for reopening. Their vim and vigor could not contrast more with the hollow-eyed, shuffling exhaustion of the departing government personnel. Most of the men and women here have been deployed since the early days of the eruption. No one seems to question my presence. No one asks for my I.D. Likewise, I try not to get in their way, searching the sea of army, National Guard, state police, and FEMA uniforms for the gray and olive colors of the United States National Park Service. Fortunately, the first one I spot is Senior Ranger Josephine Schell.

Her "field office," a converted room on the second floor, smells like cigarette smoke, coffee, and feet. Josephine plops behind her cluttered desk, rubbing her eyes, yawning.

To me, Greenloop was the *Titanic,* right down to the design flaws and the lack of lifeboats. They were extremely isolated, miles from the one public road which was miles from the nearest town. And, of course, that was the idea. With modern logistics and telecommunications, the world must have still felt very small. But then Rainier cut those connections, and the world suddenly got very big.

Most people don't realize how truly vast this country is. If you live on the East Coast, or in the Heartland, or just in and around a big western city, it's hard to grasp how much uninhabited land is out there. And the nature of that land, the type of terrain we're talking about . . .

Ever seen that satellite map of the United States at night? Those big, dark patches between the prairie and the Pacific Coast? A lot of that darkness is hostile, unforgiving ground. Beautiful from a car window or the edge of a designated path, but see how long you last straying too far from that path. Greenloop was in one of those dark patches, a mountainous, primeval rain forest as treacherous as anywhere in North America. Steep, nearly vertical slopes. Sudden cliffs lined with slippery moss. Whole fields of loose sharp stones. Throw in hypothermia, fog, foliage so thick it's like hitting a brick wall. That's what would have been waiting for anyone trying to go for help.

She gestures behind us to the emergency equipment and personnel.

And as far as help coming to them? Sure, Mrs. Durant had a point about their loved ones calling in. The problem was, so did everyone else's. We're talking millions of people from all around the world, jamming the phone lines, night and day, trying to check up on someone they knew. Even if they did manage to get through, their queries would have been logged along with every other grain of sand on the beach.

It was a total clusterfuck and Ms. Mostar knew it. I can imagine how her personal history predicted everything going to hell. But even if it hadn't, if the USGS had been properly staffed, funded, and heard, if the local services hadn't been gutted by the last recession, if FEMA hadn't been folded into the Department of Homeland Security, if the Defense Logistics Agency hadn't had to buy most of their supplies from the private sector, if the ash hadn't closed the airports and that damn drone hadn't hit the Guard helo, if most of the Guard and the army hadn't been deployed to Venezuela, if the president was competent and the media was responsible, if the I-90 sniper had been on his meds . . . if everything hadn't conspired to combine the greatest national unrest since Rodney King with the greatest natural calamity since Katrina, if everything had gone exactly according to plan, we still wouldn't have found Greenloop for one simple reason. We weren't looking for them.

Josephine gestures to the wall-sized map behind her, specifically to the three grease-pencil perimeter lines around Rainier.

This one here.

She refers to a yellow line stretching from Rainier to Puget Sound.

That's the limit of the natural disaster effect. And this big one . . .

She moves her hand across the wavy red line that extends all the way up past Seattle.

That's the extent of the civil disturbance. I know, right? And here . . .

The last, perfect blue circle surrounds the volcano.

That's our search sector. Hikers, mountain bikers, campers, those schoolkids—oh my God, those kids, the parents screaming at the governor, the governor screaming at us. Those thirty-six hours, especially after we found the abandoned school bus. Thank God they were okay, but some of the others, the folks who got caught in traffic and just abandoned their cars. That was what fucked us, really, combing the woods trying to find all those lemmings who tried to walk away. That's why the search spread out so far. But as far as it got . . .

She stabs her finger at a point on the map well outside all three perimeters.

Look where Greenloop is . . . was. They were officially safe, and they weren't alone. I can't tell you how many backwoods cabins and communities are out there, mostly because they don't want to be found. And most of them survived being cut off all winter, because they knew exactly what they were getting into. They either had the skills and supplies to hole up or the ability and gear to walk out. And a lot of them loved it. No. Seriously. They welcomed the challenge. They accepted the trade-offs. They weren't anything like the folks at Greenloop.

Those poor bastards didn't want a rural life. They expected an urban life in a rural setting. They tried to adapt their environment instead of adapting *to* it. And I really can sympathize. Who doesn't want to break from the herd? I get why you'd want to keep the comforts of city life while leaving the city behind. Crowds, crime, filth, noise. Even in the burbs. So many rules, neighbors all up in your business. It's kind of a catch-22, especially in the United States, a society that values freedom, when society, by nature, forces you to compromise that freedom. I get how the hyper-connectivity of Greenloop gave the illusion of zero compromise.

But that's all it was, an illusion.

Her eyes wander to the vast expanse of empty map behind the volcano.

It's great to live free of the other sheep until you hear the wolves howl.

Chapter 5

All animals are competitive by nature and cooperate only under specific circumstances and for specific reasons, not because of a desire to be nice to one another.

—Frans de Waal, *Bonobo: The Forgotten Ape*

From my interview with Frank McCray, Jr.

As far as emergency supplies, or lack thereof . . . Look, I don't blame Tony, even back then, when they first discovered what was left of Greenloop.

You can't blame Tony, not as an individual. That's just how the tech industry thinks. They don't plan for what can go wrong. They "move fast and break things." It didn't occur to Facebook that the Russians might hijack their platform to hijack our elections, even though they'd been doing it to other countries for years. It doesn't occur to Google, still, that while they're racing, balls out, to corner the market on driverless cars, terrorists could hack those cars and drive them into crowds.

Hell, I was at a Menlo Park conference once where a guy showed us how he'd hacked his hand, literally. Attached electrodes to the skin above the muscles in his forearm to play the piano. He didn't know how to play. Just typed in the commands, clicked "execute," and *shazam*! "Mary Had a Little Lamb." And that was just the beginning. What about a full exo-suit that could stimulate the entire body?

"Think of the possibilities." That was what the guy kept saying. Disabled individuals. The elderly. "Think of the possibilities."

I could think of a few. I raised my hand and asked, "Isn't it possible for someone to hack that suit once you put it on, force you to pick up your perfectly legal assault rifle, and walk down the street to the local preschool?" He looked like I'd just kicked over his sandcastle. He hadn't wasted one neuron on that thought, because, in his mind, it was just that. A waste. All positivity all the time. Learn to fly, even if it's in the *Hindenburg*.

Move fast and break things.

JOURNAL ENTRY #5

OCTOBER 3

Potatoes. That's why Mostar sent me to Yvette's meditation class. "We need them," she said. Again with "need" and "we." She's convinced that potatoes are the "perfect" survival food, that you can actually live on them alone. I was charged with trying to get a few seed potatoes for the garden.

Which I'm not supposed to mention, along with any defense of Mostar. "If they say anything, go along with it." She was very clear about that. "Agree, contribute, laugh with them, even at my expense. Be diplomatic."

Nobody needs to tell me how to do that. I'm a diplomat by nature, and still not really on board with Mostar's crazy plans. But I will say my mental needle's moved a little bit in her favor since I heard the news. And there's been a *lot* of news. Vincent listened to the car radio for an hour after the meeting, until Tony offered to relieve him. According to both of them, the reports from Rainier are pretty bad.

There's something called a "lahar," a boiling mudslide. According to the radio, it's what killed thousands of people at a place called Armero* in the '80s and it's exactly what's happening to Rainier now. The reports seem to focus on the far side of Rainier, the side facing all those towns: Orting? Puyallup? (Did I spell them right?) I've heard of Tacoma, which is supposed to be in danger right now. We seem to be safe, just like Tony predicted, but it looks like we're also cut off. The valley below us, the main road, Vincent thinks he heard something about it being covered by a lahar.

"Some people might have been killed." That was Bobbi. "They tried to drive away and got stuck in their cars when the mudflow came."

Yvette sighed. "That could have been us," and she reached out for a group hug. "Imagine what could have happened if we'd all just driven down into the valley last night, if Tony hadn't predicted the road being gone . . ."

Wait, wasn't that Mostar?

Hadn't she been the one to talk about the road being gone? What happened to Tony's argument about false alarms and traffic jams? No one seemed to remember that. Or maybe they did, and figured the result was the same. Both Tony and Mostar had pushed for staying, but now, Yvette said with moistening eyes, "Tony saved our lives."

I kept my mouth shut, nodded with all the others. I didn't even react when Yvette said, "I wish Mostar was here." This was after we broke our embrace, when we were just taking our places on the floor. "We all need each other now more than ever."

It was a test, the kind I've been passing since preschool. Sometimes obvious. Sometimes snarky. This one came wrapped in concern. "I hope she's okay." That was Carmen. Sympathy all around. "After what she's been through."

What has she been through? I might have asked but got cut off by Yvette. "Has anyone talked to her?"

* On November 13, 1985, the eruption of Nevado del Ruiz in Colombia caused the deaths of approximately 23,000 of the 29,000 people living in the nearby town of Armero.

There it was. The line in the sand.

Shaking heads, myself included. A pained sigh from Yvette. "Maybe she'll show up tomorrow. I think she needs healing more than anyone."

That gave me a little churn of stomach acid. I can pass the test but it always comes at a price. I hate lying, hate conflict, hate having to choose sides. At that moment I hated Mostar for putting me in this position as much as I hated myself for allowing her to.

I tried to play along. Tried to focus, relax, feel the "physical manifestations of this traumatic event" and give myself "permission to release my pain and guilt with deep cleansing breaths."

I tried to picture "Oma," that guardian of the woods spirit Yvette had mentioned in our last session. The embrace. Warm, soft arms holding me. It worked the last time. Not now. I wasn't in the mood for guided imagery.

I tried to act like my "burden had been lifted" when the session ended, and tried to appear as nonchalant as possible when asking for potatoes.

"I was thinking of making hash browns this morning." More lies. More acid.

And all for nothing.

Again with the concern, and this time it seemed sincere. Carmen and Effie looked truly sorry that they didn't have any, and Yvette told me to stop by for anything else.

Bobbi, though. I won't say she acted weird. I mean, how would I know what's weird when I don't know her well enough to know normal. But I know what it feels like to be uncomfortable, so well that I'm pretty good at reading it in others. Bobbi seemed genuinely uncomfortable when she answered. I could be wrong. It could be the news.

I watched everyone head home, Bobbi with this, yes, weird look over her shoulder, Yvette over to Tony, who, I just realized, was still sitting in his Tesla listening to the radio, Carmen and Effie waving up to Palomino, who stared down at them from her upstairs window like in a ghost story.

I'm sorry. That's not fair. But it is how I felt. Spooky little horror-film girl maniacally squeezing her beanbag fidgeter.

I had to go for a walk. Clear my head. Dan was asleep when I got home, and I assumed Mostar was mercifully out as well. "We'll work at night," she'd said before I left, "so no one will see us."

Craziness. I had to get out, calm down. I can't sleep when I'm overtired. I figured if I could just recapture the comfort of that first mystical day.

Bad idea. I should have gone right to bed.

Remember what you told me about empathy, about how I've got too much of a good thing? Picturing other people, visualizing others' lives as clearly as I live mine.

That's what I ended up doing on my hike, trying and failing to stop imagining those people in the path of the lahars. I pictured this tsunami of steaming mud, bulging with boulders, torn-up trees, pieces of broken homes. I pictured people in their cars, listening to the radio, distractedly looking down at their phones, complaining about the traffic while they yell at their kids in the back seat to get off their tablets and look at the world.

Maybe they see something in the rearview mirror, or wonder why people are suddenly running past their cars. I thought about what would have happened to me if I was there. My car getting bumped from behind. I'd turn back angrily, but never angry enough to raise my middle finger. I'd probably reach for my insurance first, have it in my hand, ready to talk about damages like a civilized adult as I turn to open the door. Maybe the door couldn't open because another car was jammed too close. That's when I'd see it, twisted halfway around to look behind me, hearing the rumble as this cliff, not a wave, a cliff, like I'd once seen in that YouTube video of the Japan tsunami.

Knowing me, I wouldn't think to open the window and slide out to run. I'd probably close the door, close my eyes, convince myself it wasn't happening as the metal and glass squeezed around me. Smashed, drowned, boiled alive.

But then I realized that nightmare fantasy couldn't have happened because the eruption had been at night. Most people wouldn't be on the roads. That's what our neighbors told us about the Northridge quake. When we first moved to L.A. Who was it? That old couple across the street who had to sell their house. What were their names? Hadn't the wife said something about how lucky the city was that the quake hit at night when everyone was safe at home? The idea gave me a moment of relief, a very brief moment because then I pictured those homes in the path of the lahars.

Would they have been asleep, like us? Dreaming? I pictured myself, snug in bed, translating the rumble into whatever subconscious story I was living. Would I have woken in time to see the roof collapsing down on me? The sharp edge of a snapped beam or splintered stick of furniture lancing through my chest?

Hopefully, I wouldn't have woken up. Hopefully, a lot of them didn't either. But the ones who did. The ones who might still be alive, pinned under rubble? How many were hurt? Trying to call for help? Gasping with one lung? Coughing up blood? Broken bones. Pain. Fear.

Why do I go there? Where's my, what do you call it, "ego-defense mechanism"?

Maybe I was trying to build one on that hike, surround myself with a wall of pleasant senses, positive memories. I should have realized it would only make things worse. Rainier was smoking now, angry. Standing on the top of the ridge, I could see little black columns rising in the distance behind it. Forest fires? Burning homes? The mountain's smoke was darkening the sky, a gray blanket blotting out the sun.

As I turned from the sight, heading farther down the trail, I tried to find the blackberry bush from before. It was there, but all the berries were gone. Even the hard, little green ones. I tried pulling one of the branches aside, pricked my finger on a thorn. Reflexively I drew my hand to my mouth. The wound wasn't deep, but enough to taste my own blood. The flavor made my stomach rumble. I realized then how hungry I was, and that sensation sent my mind swirling back to last night's calorie list.

After cataloging all our food, Mostar'd told me to come up with a "ration plan." I figured that was simple enough. No different, I thought, than any of the thousand diets I'd been on my whole life. I calculated our ages, heights, levels of physical activity, and approximate fat reserves, which I can't believe I'd actually written down! I even used the two calorie calculators on my phone (yes, I have two), which allotted 1,200 for me, 2,100 for Dan, and another 1,200 for Mostar although I'm not really sure about her exact age.

I thought I was being harsh, but when I showed it to Mostar, she just shook her head and laughed. "So American."

I felt myself flush. I'm proud that I managed to push back. I explained the dangers of crash diets, the risks of long-term health damage.

Again, she clucked. "This isn't dieting, Katie, this is rationing. Dieting is choosing to eat less. Rationing is eating less because you don't have a choice. It can drive you crazy, that lack of control. Especially for Americans. You've never known starvation, not like the rest of the world. Not even in the darkest days of your Civil War, when you still grew enough wheat to sell for profit."

How does she know that? *Why* does she know that?

"Here"—she swiped the pad from me and started scribbling—"I'll show you what I mean."

Eight hundred calories for Dan.

Five hundred for Mostar.

And one thousand for me.

"Not right away," she explained, "not while we're still setting up. But in a week or so there'll be nothing to do but sit back and digest ourselves, which is why I've given you the most, bye the by, since you've got the least," and she reached over to tap my butt. I gave a surprised squeak, turned to say something about violating personal space, but she was back outside for another pot full of dirt.

I should say that I actually had no intention of following her crazy punishment plan then. Just another diet to cheat on. But now, after hearing the news and realizing that this crazy old lady might not be so crazy after all, I started to rethink everything she'd said last night. I even started to feel guilty about expending so many calories on this hike!

And as I looked for other bushes that could have been missed before, I realized, angrily, that I might very well be standing in the middle of a natural buffet. The leaves, the bark, the mushrooms. So many mushrooms! White, black, brown, pink, purple. Purple! Are any of them safe to eat? How would I know? So much for my so-called smartphone, this useless little rectangle I still carry out of habit.

All right, not entirely useless. But even though it still functions as a clock, calendar, flashlight, step counter, Dictaphone, notepad, camera, video recorder, video studio, videogame arcade, and God knows how many other applications that would have been mind-blowing just twenty years ago, the one thing I need it for, the one thing it was originally designed for was communication.

"Siri, what can I eat here?"

I don't know what made me feel worse, that I suddenly didn't have the world's knowledge in my pocket or that up until that moment, I'd always assumed I was entitled to it. I couldn't have been more grateful for the hummingbirds that flew across my vision. They were darting around those same flowers, giving each other those little loving kisses. I was so happy at first, hands to lips. Thank God! That's what I was thinking. Thank God there's at least one beautiful thing left. But then I looked closer and saw that they weren't kissing. One was trying to kill the other, stabbing rapidly with its needlelike beak. That was what they'd been doing that first day, when I'd only seen what I'd wanted to see.

And then they flew away, startled by the same sound that made me jump. I saw the ferns ahead and to the right of me whipping back and forth. They were moving in a line, too fast for me to react. Something burst out of the bushes right in front of me. It was small and brown and I'm pretty sure it was a rabbit, although it was gone in a split second. Two quick leaps shot it across the trail and into the opposite underbrush. It didn't stop, or even slow. I watched the motion line recede, and started to wonder if maybe something might be chasing it.

Then I smelled it. Just a quick whiff in the breeze. Rotten, like eggs and old garbage. It brought back a memory from last night's meeting, when the group was breaking up. Carmen had complained about a horrible smell, a trace of sulfur when they'd opened the window. Reinhardt explained it away as gas emissions from the volcano. He's probably right. That's what I thought as the smell wafted away.

Then the howl, faint, distant. Not a wolf, or, at least, not like the wolves I've heard in movies. I know what coyotes sound like and I'm pretty sure that wasn't one of them. I'm still not sure it was an animal. It could have been the wind shifting through these tall trees, or some trick echo across the mountains. What do I know about what sound does up here? The howl faded into a trio of short, deep grunts, the last one sounding just a little bit louder, or closer, than the others. I didn't move, holding my breath, listening for another sound. Any sound. The whole forest seemed to go still.

Then I felt eyes on me.

I know you'd say it was all in my head, and I can't think of any reason to argue. Standing there, all alone, under that eerie, smoky sky with a guilty head full of apocalyptic musings. But I've had that feeling before, on the playground or when Mom judged my outfits from across the room. That intuition is how I met Dan, freshman year, through the crowd and the music. I just knew. I felt. I looked up and there he was.

I didn't see anyone this time. Even when I turned back to the house. I didn't run. I'm proud of that. I just walked slowly, purposefully, and the feeling was gone halfway home. And now all I feel is embarrassed. I can't believe I freaked out for no reason, that

I let imaginary monsters pollute my happy place. I feel ridiculous, sitting at the kitchen table, looking out the back door, hearing Dan snore blissfully upstairs. The wind's kicked up, the sound of the trees is so soothing. Maybe I should go back out there, finish my walk on a high note.

Nope. Just tried. Legs like oatmeal. *Mmmm,* oatmeal. I just finished an instant pack. Half, actually. Enough to quiet my stomach.

I can feel the irritation coming on. Dieting angst. I'm still not 100 percent sure that I should be torturing myself with Mostar's batshit "rationing." Even if she's right about being cut off. How long can we possibly expect it to last?

I really need to sleep. Crawl in bed next to Dan. With earplugs. And maybe half an Ativan. A good night's, day's, rest. Give the world a chance to get itself together. And if it hasn't, at least I can get myself together with a nice evening stroll in the woods.

From my interview with Senior Ranger Josephine Schell.

I call it a "Massoud Moment," connecting the dots only after it's too late. I got the name from Ahmad Shah Massoud. He was this Afghan guerrilla leader who fought the Russians and then the Taliban. I don't expect you've ever heard of him. I didn't until the day he died. I'd just gotten into New York. It was a late flight, like one or two in the morning? The cabdriver at JFK was listening to the BBC World Service. They were talking about how Massoud had just been assassinated by terrorists pretending to be journalists. I wasn't paying much attention and I think I might have even asked the driver to switch stations. I mean, c'mon, I was just starting my vacation. I'd never been to New York, my friends were waiting. We had *Producers* tickets.

That was September 9, 2001, and I only learned later that killing Massoud was the opening act of the World Trade Center attack. I couldn't have known that at the time. Nobody would've expected me to connect the dots. Still, I think about that moment a lot, about connecting the dots. I've thought a lot about it since. . . .

She glances up at the map.

We found these bones. Pieces of them. Smashed fragments, like someone'd gone crazy with a hammer. You could tell they were deer, hooves, a few teeth, patches of fur. There wasn't much left. No meat. Licked clean. Same with the leaves. Just enough residue to tell they'd been splashed with blood. I remember seeing this rock, big . . .

She holds out her hands in the size and shape of a soccer ball.

. . . with blood, marrow, bits of brain on one side. And it was reasonably fresh, a few hours maybe? But I didn't stop to check. We didn't have time. Remember this was Day Three after the eruption. None of us had slept, all those missing people . . . that's why, looking back, I didn't think much of the tracks. I probably wrote them off as ours, everybody just tramping sloppily through, nobody paying attention to anything except getting where we needed to be.

It wasn't until *after* we'd discovered Greenloop—shit, it wasn't until after I'd read her journal . . . that entry about discovering the remains? That was when I started asking around. And some of the other rangers, guardsmen, a few civilian volunteers, they had this "oh yeah, right" moment. And when I began to map and time-stamp everyone's recollections . . .

She stretches an arm to the map, touching a collection of small, black pins I hadn't noticed before.

That's the first discovery, Day One.

She touches the next pin.

Day Two.

Again.

Day Three. My team.

She continues to move her fingers down the pins, drawing a clear, straight path toward Greenloop.

The "Massoud Moment," connecting the dots.

Chapter 6

A lie will gallop halfway round the world before the truth has time to pull its breeches on.

—Cordell Hull, secretary of state to President Franklin Delano Roosevelt

JOURNAL ENTRY #6

OCTOBER 4

Ash. Falling from the sky. Big, lazy flakes. On the houses, the driveway, the windshield of my car. That's where I am now, writing all this down, listening to the radio.

I should be sleeping. That's what Mostar's doing. The garden's done. Dirt and compost from Mostar's bin, all mixed together. Dan even came up with an irrigation system. He's connected both our garden hoses to the garage sink, snaked it in curly waves across the entire garden, poked holes every few inches, and tied off the end with packing tape. He calls it a "drip line." All on his own, no prompting.

And he's moved on, again, to his new job of figuring out how the house works. "One thing at a time." He's asleep now, I think, but after finishing the garden he got right to work syncing his iPad to every system of the house's CPU, learning how everything operates, losing himself in kilowatts and British thermal units. No prodding from us, no rest. More work in a few hours than I've seen him do in years. Who is this man?

Mostar's moved on too. She plans to pick, slice, and dry all the fruit from our trees. Plums, pears, apples. Even the sour little crabapples on her tree that I never would have touched before this. "Every calorie counts." She would have started this morning but it has to be, in her words, "after dark, so no one sees me."

And my new job. I'm the gardener. I'm supposed to care for and keep an eye on all the seeds we planted. Not that we planted that many.

I picked through every item in both our houses and all I could come up with were some Chinese peas and a couple of sweet potatoes. I'm not sure if those have the same nutritional value as "the real thing"—Mostar-speak for conventional potatoes. "Better than nothing." So sure, despite her utter lack of knowledge on how to plant any of it. Cut up the yams to plant the eyes, which Dan seems to remember from a sci-fi book he read recently, or plant them whole? Which we did. And what about the peas? Soak them first? Wrap them in a wet paper towel, which I vaguely remember from kindergarten, or just stick them in well-watered ground, which we did.

Mostar had no idea. She even said so. "No idea." She confessed that she's a "lifelong city girl" and that the only plant she'd ever taken care of was a tomato vine on her windowsill, which she managed to kill, by the way. And none of that seemed to bother her. Confidence, clarity. "We need to try." She said this as I poked the last pea in mud. So satisfied, chubby hands on her broad hips. "We need to try."

And now I'm with her. The needle's moved again. I've been listening to the radio. A lot.

I just wanted to learn more about what's going on, get a better picture. Especially when I saw that Tony's car was missing today. Maybe he pulled it into their garage but I'm pretty sure that's their gym. He couldn't have been gone long. When I came out of our garage/garden this morning, his Tesla was still there. He must have driven off when I was showering. He must have tried to go for help. But if a lahar really has covered the valley, how far can he get?

But what if the road's clear? Vincent only *thought* he heard that story. Maybe Tony just wants to see it with his own eyes. Go Tony!

And yes, I admit, I feel kind of adrift, vulnerable now that he's gone. I was hoping to ask him about the news before going to Yvette's class. I could really use his grounding voice. Yvette must be so worried about him. I could hear the edge in her voice today, the slight rush in her timing. I guess that's also a kind of courage, staying here to keep us all happy while Tony risks his life out there. That's another reason I started listening to the radio, to maybe hear some good news I could tell Yvette to make her feel better.

Okay, that's not true. I started listening just for me.

And wow, do I regret it.

It's been about an hour and I'm more frazzled than ever.

If our valley isn't covered, a lot of others are. They act like funnels, channeling the mudslides. My nightmare scenario, picturing people trapped in their cars. That's exactly what happened. They don't know how many people were buried. And not just in their cars. I was also right about people being killed at home, either in their beds, or else up and awake without ever being warned. That's a huge problem now, getting the word out in time. They did this whole story on how most people get emergency messages from their cellphones instead of landlines the way they used to. A lot of people turn off their phones when they go to bed, or forget to charge them, or else ignore unknown callers because they think they're telemarketers.

And what's this about being cut off from the south? One of the slides reaching all the way to Tacoma, cutting the 5, the way we drove in? Something about rerouting to the I-90, and trying to organize evacuees north to Vancouver. What's "contraflow"?*

* Contraflow lane reversal: A term commonly used in natural disasters by which all lanes of a road are used to channel vehicles in one direction.

They keep mentioning that, and how people trying to drive out are getting really frustrated and angry.

Tacoma must be an important port. A lot of ships are jamming Puget Sound. A lot of accidents, especially with the little private boats. Ferries can't get out. Something called the USNS *Mercy* can't get in. I'm only catching snippets about why nothing's flying. Something with the ash in plane engines and covering the airports, but also something about a crash, a drone hitting a helicopter. Everyone was killed, including some rescued hikers. I've heard two different stories about where the drone came from: an army type looking for people or a private one trying to get pictures to post on social media. Both stories talk about "suspending UAV supply drops." Is that why I haven't seen a plane or helicopter, or even a drone, since all this started?

We might be cut off from Seattle, but it sounds like Seattle might be cut off from the world!

I don't get how this could have happened. There's too much coming at me. One report on budgets and politics. Budget sequestration? Shutdowns affecting "long-term talent retention"? What does it mean to "destroy the administrative state"? And what is the USGS? Someone from there complaining about local businesses not wanting to hear the warnings, accusing them of "another Mammoth Lakes."*

The USGS guy is also trying to dispel what I guess are rumors going around. Lots of rumors. He sounded really frustrated the way he talked about Rainier not exploding sideways toward Seattle or triggering a tsunami or setting off a chain reaction where all the other volcanos erupt as well. He must be hearing these rumors a lot. And the reporter wasn't helping. She kept bringing up these horrible eruptions in history, Krakatoa, Fuji, Vesuvius. She asked about how many people "could die" and "hypotheti-

* Mammoth Lakes, California: On May 27, 1982, a false-eruption warning damaged both the town's economy and confidence in the United States Geological Survey.

cally, what's the worst-case scenario," and when she tried to get him to imagine what the "Yellowstone super volcano" would look like, he said, "Jesus, why are we even talking about this!"

Anger. And violence.

A local station, 710am, talking about a shooting at a Whole Foods on Denny Way. Where is that? More about long lines at other stores, fistfights, a hit-and-run at a gas station. A truck driver was pulled out of his cab and beaten almost to death. It was a bread truck. It was looted and burned.

I'm listening to a press conference now. The signal's going in and out. This woman, I think she's the governor, trying to answer all these questions coming at her. So many of them, the reporters, the things they're asking. It can't be true that rescuers are focusing on "corporate assets" like Boeing and Microsoft. They can't be choosing rich neighborhoods like Queen Anne over middle-class ones like Enumclaw. That's what one reporter asked, along with another one who shouted, "Isn't it true that the USGS intentionally withheld warnings so the eruption would clear these towns for high-end development?"

A question about martial law. Oh my God! I've heard that question! Earlier today! When I got in the car, I flipped past some rant, not a news station, I think, maybe talk radio. Some guy, gravelly, frantic voice, railing against the "deep state," and how this was all a conspiracy of withheld warnings to cause this catastrophe "as a pretext for using federal troops to disarm the public." Those are the *exact* words I'm hearing now. Is the reporter just repeating the same rant we both heard?

The governor's talking now. She sounds mad. Writing as I hear it:

"Settle down! Please, all of you! We need you to listen carefully to what we're saying now. We cannot afford rumors. We cannot afford speculation. A lot of people are in real danger. They need accurate, honest reporting. They need the facts. You need to be responsible for what you're putting out there! You don't want to cause a panic! Please, think before you speak. Think about the consequences of your—"

Tony!

In my rearview mirror! His headlights, pulling back up to his house!

From my interview with Frank McCray, Jr.

Again, you can't just blame Tony, or even the whole tech industry, for not being prepared. They all should have had emergency supplies on hand, but, really, who does? How many people in L.A. have earthquake kits? How many midwesterners are ready for tornadoes or northeasterners for blizzards? How many Gulf Coast residents stock up for hurricane season? I remember partying in New Orleans before Katrina and people talking about "when" the levees fail. Not "if," "when!"

And that's just the dramatic stuff. How many have a fire extinguisher in their kitchen or emergency flares in their car? How many of us have opened the medicine cabinet in the middle of the night to find that one pill bottle we so desperately need has a long-expired label?

And when it comes to supplying everyday life, being caught unprepared wasn't unique to Greenloop. Neither was the one-click, online delivery system they depended on. The whole country depends on that now. No one remembers that Christmas in the late '90s, before the dot-com bubble burst, when everyone thought they could click their way through Santa's list. They didn't understand that the gifts they were ordering still had to be transported, in most cases, from overseas, on very big, very slow ships. The result was that a lot of my friends didn't get their e-toys on Christmas morning, while their parents spent the night before rushing from one sold-out Toys "R" Us to the next. And that was when we still had Toys "R" Us.

And what did we all learn from that giant kerfuffle? Speed up the distribution network— instead of preparing for what happens when the network fails. Go into a grocery store, any big chain, what kind of food do you see? Canned? Pickled? Dried? Not anymore. Not like it used to be. When I was a kid, most grocery stores had a very small fresh meat/fish/produce section. Now that's all front and center. The business model of America's food industry is same-day delivery of farm fresh ingredients.

But what happens when the delivery trucks don't come? What if they can't? That's what happened in Seattle during Rainier, that plus the power cuts. How much farm to table food spoiled in the first forty-eight hours?

And when it came to emergency supplies? FEMA doesn't stockpile. Not anymore. Too inefficient. They contract out to the private sector, the big box stores, who don't stockpile either because it's too inefficient. All stock has to be turned over within twenty-four hours, and if a crisis just happens to hit at the exact moment you're waiting for a shipment . . .

You can't blame the people in Greenloop for having their cupboards bare. The whole country rests on a system that sacrifices resilience for comfort.

JOURNAL ENTRY #6 [CONT.]

Tony was filthy, covered in ash and what looked like mud from the waist down. His knees and elbows were scraped and he was missing a hiking boot. As I got out of the car to meet him, I saw a few others coming out of their houses. Carmen, Vincent, Yvette (in workout clothes with a towel around her steaming neck). He saw us all coming and waved up with a smile. He saw us just half a second after we saw him, long enough for me to notice the look on his face. Dazed, slack-jawed, staring straight ahead. Even when he saw us, the smile seemed definitely forced.

Yvette asked what had happened when she got close enough,

then, as an afterthought, she remembered to hug him. Tony nodded to her, then to all of us, with that confident demeanor of his.

"Well, now I know what a 'lahar' looks like." He took a sip from the water bottle on his hip and said, "I wanted to see . . . you know . . . for myself . . ." (I was right!) ". . . and yeah, I never got to the valley because the bridge . . . well, it's gone . . . the river, mud, a lot of . . . stuff . . . debris . . . yeah, it's gone . . ." His words kind of trailed off, like he was going to say something else. But his eyes unfocused as he took another swig.

In that pause, I noticed Yvette's eyes sweeping across us. I'm not sure what she was looking for, what she took from our faces, and, what, our body language? But she must have seen something because even before Tony finished his drink, she kissed his cheek, rubbed his chest, and said, "But they're still coming for us. They're coming." The first time was to us, the second, to Tony.

"Oh yeah," Tony agreed, and sort of snapped back into himself, "totally. They're on their way."

Really? Didn't he hear the same news reports I did? The growing chaos, the grounded aircraft. Why would he still believe that "they" were on their way? Did he believe it or was he just saying it? And why would he just say it? To convince us, or himself? And why didn't anyone contradict him? Vincent had obviously been listening to his car radio as well, and I think I saw a look pass between him and Bobbi.

At last Carmen said something. "Did you see anyone on the other side of the bridge? A rescue team or other refugees?"

Tony responded with, "No. No." The first "no" was to Carmen, the second was to the ground.

Did anyone else notice Yvette squeezing his arm?

I did. I clocked everything. His eyes, his words, how he kept licking his lips before and after drinking water.

I don't think Yvette saw me, but she must have worried about his response, because she quickly jumped in. "We're not refugees, Carmen. The term is 'evacuee,' which we aren't either, remember?" That last "remember" must have come out too hard, because suddenly she gave this very noticeable sigh. "But now that you bring it up"—hand up to chest, a sudden wet blink—"we should really get ourselves ready to take care of any evacuees that happen to find us." Her gaze went up to the woods above the house. "If someone tried to get away on foot. There might be people near us right now, wandering out there, lost and scared."

I noticed the others nodding. I did too. Playing along, just like Mostar would have wanted. That's why I didn't bring up the drone crash. That's why I stayed silent while Yvette nudged Tony into saying, "Yeah, yeah, we . . . uh . . . we need to be ready . . . you know, to take care of those people. Until we're all rescued. We need to be ready. Ready . . ."

As they walked back to the house, he broke away from her grasp. I couldn't hear what they were saying. I'd gotten back into my car by then. But through the rearview mirror, I watched him motion slightly for Yvette to go back in the house. She must have tried to argue because his pushing gesture quickened, along with the nods. She looked at him for a moment, then around at the neighborhood, then went back inside. I watched Tony wait till the front door closed before going to his trunk and retrieving a big, bulging hiker's backpack. He got it halfway out, and looked like he was going to swing it up onto his back. Then he stopped. That was what really got my attention. I hesitate doing things all the time, second-guessing if I'm going to pick this up before that, realizing I should do *X* before *Y*. I do it more than most people, so I'm always hyperconscious of it. I've never seen Tony do that. He stopped, mid-swing, looked over at the door again, then looked all around the neighborhood, then quickly dropped the pack back in the trunk.

I could be reading this completely wrong. I know I am. You and I talked a lot about projecting and I'm sure I was projecting my own guilt of spying on Tony. He didn't have anything to feel guilty about. He was going for help. He was doing that for us! And the way he acted in front of us. He was tired, that's all. Poor guy's probably been up all night. I'm sure once he gets a good night's rest, he'll be back to the old Tony, the real Tony.

Did I just write "real"? What does that even mean? I shouldn't be doubting him like that. I feel guilty now just writing this part down, just like I felt guilty watching him disappear back into his house.

That was when Mostar tapped my windshield.

"Katie!"

I practically jumped out of the seat.

"Katie!" She was whispering loudly. "Quick before it leaks through!"

She was holding a Whole Foods bag, something bulging at the bottom with a spreading red stain.

I reached for my door, realized I'd put on my seatbelt (habit?), then followed her into my house.

Opening the door, she rushed past with a whispered, "Quick, shut your blinds!" She ran over to the counter. "I would have done this at home, but I need you to see it." She reached into the bag.

My back teeth locked at the first hint of bloody fur, then a protrusion, long and thin. An ear. She told me to get out a bowl and a wide pan or a cookie sheet, and the sharpest, smallest, thinnest knife we had. As I turned, she added, "Oh yes, and some rubber gloves. We don't know if it has fleas or ticks."

I didn't want to look, didn't want to acknowledge what I knew had to be coming. And it did. I turned back, gave a pair of gloves to Mostar, and tried to keep my eyes averted. But she wouldn't let me. "You have to watch." She snapped on the gloves, slid the dead rabbit out into the saucepan. "You have to learn every step."

I can't see death. You know that. I've told you about that time in New York when I couldn't walk through Chinatown with all the ducks hanging in the windows. I told you about how I can't even eat at any of those restaurants with the lobsters in the tank because it feels like death row. I told you about when Dan and I went out to Catalina for Valentine's Day and I got seasick down below because our spot on deck had this dead fly crusted to the railing with one of its wings flapping in the wind.

I know it's hypocritical. I eat fish and chicken. I wear leather and silk. I enjoy all the benefits of killing without ever having to do it myself. I know all this but I just can't. I can't see death.

"Look!" Mostar demanded as she held up the bloody rabbit. "You can't miss this." I was so light-headed, so sick to my stomach, I didn't even think to ask why. Why can't *you* be the animal killer and I'll take care of the garden?

It was similar to the rabbit I'd seen running before. Grayish brown fur, long ears, white feet. Big brown eyes. Open eyes. Looking right at me.

As she held it up, I could see the wound marks on its belly and back. Mostar smiled, without looking at me as she reached for the knife. "The trap worked! I dug a hole right by the apple tree, lined the bottom with sharpened sticks, leftover chopsticks just sitting in a drawer. I made a roof of twigs and leaves and baited it with apple chips and the last of the maple syrup."

She held the rabbit up by its head, over the sink, then massaged her hand down its body.

"We have to squeeze out all the pee from its bladder."

She then laid it out in the pan, on its back with the knife at an angle to the chest.

"Just pray that the sticks didn't puncture any of the organs. If they leak out onto the meat, it'll taste terrible."

I grabbed the end of the table, steadying myself, as Mostar sliced into the fur.

"From the neck down to the anus," she said. Then setting the knife down, she stuck her fingers right into the incision, and started to peel the skin away.

"So far, so good. I don't smell anything."

I felt the bile rise.

"We're also lucky that I heard it thrashing around in there. If I hadn't gotten there in time to snap its neck, it might be too stiff to work on."

I burped a metallic sting.

"You need special care with this step." The blade cut into the bloody wound. "Not straight down and not too deep so you don't accidentally pierce an . . . oh . . . here we go. Through the heart and . . . yes, the intestines. You smell that? At least we got to it early enough before the contents could saturate the flesh. We can still wash it, and with a little extra spice, maybe some paprika or cumin . . . or Vegeta. You can pretty much save anything with Vegeta."

Some organs were pink, others gray. They came out easy, one slow, gentle pull.

"Here, this one is for the parts we nicked . . ."

WE!

". . . oh, looks like we got the stomach too."

Both bowls filled with the slippery little bits while she went to wash her hands in the sink.

"Can't waste anything. Can't afford to now."

Back to the fur, peeling it away.

"See how you can pull the legs right out? Just like removing your trousers. Grab the foot . . . look . . . just like so . . . with one hand and pull the leg out slowly with the other."

Both hands on the counter now, my mouth filling with hot saliva.

"Just breathe." Her voice never changed its steady, instructional tone. "Deep. Steady. Pretend I'm Yvette." And she giggled a little at that.

My vision tunneled. I must have swayed because Mostar caught me.

"Sorry, Katie, I shouldn't joke." That sounded genuinely contrite. "Go get a washcloth, run it under cold water, put it on the back of your neck."

I obeyed. She waited. I felt a little better, but not much. I tried to focus on my breathing, the coolness on my neck.

"There we go, both back legs, now the front . . . over the elbows . . . and grab and pull the fur just up to the neck, like you're pulling off a jumper."

Up and over the head, still attached, exposing the neck.

"You don't have a cleaver, do you? No, of course not. Neither do I. Just bring me the big knife over there, would you?"

She placed the long chef's blade across the animal's neck, holding the handle with one hand and resting her other palm on the other.

"These counters were made for taller people, eh?"

Crack.

"There, we'll set the head aside for later, give us a chance to figure the best way to get the brains."

Thank God the eyes faced away.

"At least we won't have to tan its hide. We need it for food a lot more than we need fur for clothing."

A head, a skinned carcass, two bowls of organs. A quick hand wash from Mostar, then the same, damp hand on my arm.

"You don't have to do the rest. I'll wash and fix it all for stew."

Relief melted my shoulders. My eyes suddenly teared.

"You did very well, Katie." Her smile, was it pride? Sadness? "Better than me my first time." She began washing the organs in the sink. "And at least you'll never have to do this to cats."

CATS?

"Oh, don't worry." She gave me a mischievous smile. "I never did that. One of my Italian colleagues would tell these stories about what her mother did to survive during the other war."

Other war?

I could see her consciously pausing, leaving me an opening to ask. I didn't.

"It made me grateful, Katie." She started up again. "I never complained once about ICAR beef or 'cheese spread,' fermented powdered milk with a little salt and yeast. Even worse than béchamel and that horrid bread crumb carrot paste." She looked back proudly at the mutilated animal parts in front of us. "Still, it was food, more than a lot of people had in similar circumstances. Have you ever read about Leningrad, Katie? Those poor souls scraping paste off the back of wallpaper, boiling leather for soup, making sure their children never went out alone . . . well . . . we did too, but not for that reason."

That did it. Not the blood, the organs, the meat, the death right in front of my face.

The stories.

The hints.

"Mostar, do you . . . is it okay if I just take a quick . . ."

"Of course, Katie." She waved over her shoulder from the sink. "Go get some air, come back when you're ready."

I slid open the back door, taking long, deep gulps.

I'm not sure why I headed back down the driveway, retracing Tony's steps toward the bridge. The hiking trail was closer. A need to escape? A subconscious bolt? I'm sure you'd have a ball with this.

You'd probably also take pride in my need to psychoanalyze Yvette. For some reason I'm not as guilty doubting her as I am with Tony. Why had she been so quick to prompt him about a rescue? Was it a power thing? Admitting Mostar was right? Is that why, during our morning meditation, she'd spun the truth about who'd predicted the lahars? And why she'd given us that not-so-subtle loyalty test? Would agreeing with Mostar mean giving up some control of the group? Is control that important to her?

I spun on these thoughts for about half an hour. I'm not sure how far down the road I got. Nowhere near the bridge. You really do forget the difference between walking and driving. I probably could have gone a little farther though. I almost did, distracted with my psycho-musings, but when I rounded this little bend, I noticed a big boulder sitting right in the middle of the road.

I should say now that my eyes were already dry from lack of sleep, and the little particles of ash didn't help. That was why I couldn't be sure how big the boulder was, or how far away. I remember thinking that it must have rolled down there within the last few hours. How else could Tony have gotten around it to see that the bridge was actually gone? I could even see the tire marks, four of them to mark the two directions. I remember feeling a sense of finality, that bridge or no bridge, we couldn't drive out now with that giant rock in the way.

Then I saw the rock move.

It shifted in place, grew, then disappeared behind the trees. I also thought I saw it change shape, lengthen, narrow, even spread out limbs like a tree. Arms? I rubbed my eyes, blinked hard.

When I looked again, the road was clear. The boulder was definitely gone. Then, as the wind shifted in my direction, I smelled it. Eggs and garbage.

I didn't consciously consider what to do next. No internal debate. This was reflex. I turned and started walking back. My eyes kept scanning back and forth in a shallow arc, like they teach you on the first day of driver's school. I tried to keep my pace steady, my breathing constant. I tried not to dwell on what I'd seen. An animal, a deer. Maybe that "boulder" was just a speck in my eye.

But the smell was getting stronger, and I couldn't keep from speeding up. I thought I saw something move off to my right, a sudden space opening between two trees.

I quickened again.

Silly. Irrational. Tired. Information overload from the news mixed with memory flashes of the bloody, butchered rabbit.

A light trot, at first, long controlled breaths. That feeling. The back of my neck. Being watched. My trot became a jog, my breath thundering in my ears.

I could not have imagined the howl. I definitely heard it, just like the other day. Deep, rising pitch, echoing off the trees. Lightning kicked up from my stomach.

I ran.

Sprinting, gasping, the world shaking in front of me.

And fell. Just like in one of those stupid, cheesy horror flicks when the dumb blonde eats it just before the knife-wielding psycho gets her. At least I had the presence of mind to close my eyes, hold my breath, but after face-planting in the ash, I couldn't help but inhale.

Coughing, choking, eyes blurry and stinging, I tore forward.

Don't turn! I remember that clearly. Shouting in my brain. *Don't turn! Don't think! GOGOGO!*

Thighs burning, lungs.

I ran until I saw the roofs poking just above the driveway rise. The endorphins hit. Made it. Home. Safe!

Dan!

He was coming toward me, Mostar behind him.

Shocked expressions, both of them, utter surprise.

I must have looked ridiculous, covered in sweat and ash, rasping and wheezing. I still *feel* ridiculous. Falling into Dan's arms and then dry heaving on his chest.

It was a few minutes before I got enough wind back to explain where I'd been. I even admitted that I thought an animal might have been chasing me. I didn't say what it was. No details. It couldn't have been that large, given how big the trees were. It probably didn't exist at all. But the smell, could I have imagined that?

Mostar's face was this mix of bewilderment and . . . concern? I'm sorry, I'm so fried. Dan keeps telling me to go to bed. But I want to get all this down first. Sorry if my words are getting fuzzy.

That look on Mostar's face. I don't pretend to know what it was, or why, when Dan was helping me home, she kept her eyes on the woods.

Chapter 7

Contact, contact, contact. Ten o'clock, in the trees. Sniper! Sniper! Rattler Six is hit! Rattler Six is hit!

—Transcript of radio call from the 369th Sustainment Brigade, United States Army National Guard on Interstate 90 southeast of Tanner, Washington

JOURNAL ENTRY #7
OCTOBER 6

Animals! They're everywhere. Squirrels, chipmunks, rabbits. I get little guilt shivers whenever I see rabbits look over at me, like they know I helped chop up their sister. There are deer too. I've seen half a dozen. I can see their ribs. They look thin, hungry. And nervous. All the animals seem skittish. Three times I watched them freeze. Every single one. Like someone hit pause on a movie. And they all stared back in the same direction, toward Rainier. At first, I thought it might be something with the volcano. Animals are more sensitive to that stuff, right? Aren't house pets supposed to know when an earthquake is coming?

It didn't. Have anything to do with Rainier, I mean. Nothing else happened each time they froze.

Are they afraid of something besides the volcano? They're all moving in the same direction, migrating, it looks like, away from the eruption. But the freezing. Are they being—okay, I just had to stop before writing that word. It sounds melodramatic, but . . .

Pursued?

Are they being chased like that rabbit that time? I keep thinking about what chased me. If it wasn't in my head. A bear? I'm kind of two minds about that. Being pursued by a real bear would mean I'm not totally losing it or . . . or I'm just totally wimpy to run from a dust speck in my eye. But the first option would also mean there's a real bear out there. Do bears attack people? What was that movie where Leo gets mauled by one for, like, twenty minutes? Was it based on a true story? If there is a bear out there, I can't blame the animals for being scared of it.

They're not scared of us though, not the way they're chomping through all the fruit trees. Well, all except ours. Good call, Mostar. But the Perkins-Forsters, the Boothes, the Durants. No one's tried to shoo the animals away. And Palomino's even feeding the deer! I'm not sure if the girl actually liked it. She wasn't smiling. Effie was enjoying herself, crouching behind Palomino, holding her arm up to the deer's snout, constantly whispering into her daughter's ear while Carmen stood approvingly at the kitchen door.

And Bambi sure liked it. He ate three apple slices in as many seconds, slices that Pal and her moms might really miss later. Look, I get it. I love animals too. And I do feel for them. The drought, the bad berry harvest. And now they're being driven out of their homes. Of course they're hungry. But so are we! Spinning on this makes me wonder if these cute little critters aren't actually more dangerous than a bear. After all, if they're eating our food supply, aren't they threatening us with starvation? Death by competition. I can't believe I'd ever think this way, but after hearing about the riots in Seattle . . .

That's where I am now. Not in Seattle, in the car, listening to news about Seattle. The violence has "tipped over." That's how they're putting it. "Food riots." Mobs are looting grocery stores, beating people up. Killing some. Stabbings, shootings. And not just in the city. Something about a sniper on the I-90. That's the main east–west highway across the mountains, the one they're depending on for supplies.

This guy, it sounded like just one guy, the "I-90 Sniper," he hid in the trees and started shooting at these army trucks. The road's closed now. They don't know if there are more snipers out there.

From everything I'm hearing, the army and the cops are being "redeployed" to Seattle to "restore order." And they're recalling some of our troops home from Venezuela, but it sounds like that's going to take a long time. Some reporters are speculating about how long it's going to delay relief efforts in the actual disaster zone, and how many more people are going to die while they wait to be rescued.

I feel so bad for all these people, and guilty that my first thought wasn't for them. We're really gonna be stuck all winter. No doubt about that anymore. That mental needle I've talked about, it's pointing 100 percent toward Mostar. We're stranded. That's it. Everything we do, everything we think about, has to be devoted to surviving.

At least we don't have to worry about injury or exposure. That's what the radio said will be the number one and number two causes of death out there. But for us it's food.

Food.

Last night, over a dinner of rabbit stew, I showed Mostar my "calorie calendar." Applying her ration plan to how much edible material we had, I figured we'd run out somewhere around Christmas Eve.

"Okay." Mostar just nodded at what I thought was a devastating fact. "Good to know."

"Good!" I couldn't believe what I was hearing. "How is that good?"

Mostar chewed a mouthful of stew, winced at something, then spat a shard of bone into her napkin. "Good to know if we're getting to that point with no relief, we can half our rations, then half them again. People have lived on a lot less for a lot longer. Trust me."

She raised her stew mug, downing the last gulp, then ran her tongue around the inside border. "Bowls next time. Easier to lick."

"But what about when our food does run out?" I pressed. "When there's nothing."

"Then we eat nothing." Mostar poured the remaining water from her glass into her mug, covered the mug with her palm, then sloshed it around for a few seconds. "We can live for a month or so like that."

She drank the cloudy contents, licked her palm, then added, "But it'll probably never come to that, Katie, because by that time the garden should be ready for harvest."

"Will it?" was all I could manage. "And how much can we expect to get from two sweet potatoes and half a handful of peas?"

"No idea." Mostar shrugged, completely unfazed that the whole endeavor might have been a giant waste of calories. "But I'm sure some of our neighbors will have come around by then and even if they don't have too much extra food to share, some of that food might have seeds for the garden. And"—she raised her well-washed mug to the window—"there're always more opportunities out there."

I saw the target of her toast was a skinny squirrel poking through our now-empty apple tree.

"I might be able to make more of those traps," she mused, "but we've got to be careful that none of our neighbors step in one. We can't afford to alienate anyone. Cooperation's more important than a quick meal."

I'm not so sure. There are a lot more rabbit stews out there. And how long could we live off just one deer? I know Mostar's at least considered it. The way she looked at the doe sniffing around our yard.

That's exactly how I looked at the buck Palomino was feeding. As I watched the girl giving away more precious apple slices to that walking feast, my eye caught a couple squirrels just chowing down on the Boothes' herb garden. Bobbi was at her kitchen window, doing dishes, I guess. She was watching the rodents with this pained expression. Was she afraid to chase them away while her neighbor was being so "kind and generous" to these poor defenseless creatures? Or was she genuinely conflicted, caught between ingrained ideology and the cold hard truth?

I don't know, and right now I really don't care. I know what I was thinking, and what I saw, and smelled! I thought maybe I'd go over there to save the herbs. I wasn't going to be aggressive, just walk loudly enough to scare the squirrels, then claim ignorance and maybe later accept a belated thank-you. I was trying to do something nice. That's all. But as I got closer to her house . . .

I know she saw me. Her head didn't move but I saw her eyes flick in my direction. I know that's why she closed her window, and the curtains. And as she did, the faintest breath of warm air from her kitchen wafted past my nose. Fried food. Hash browns.

Potatoes!

Bitch! Yes, I said it! Fucking liar! That's why she'd been so uncomfortable when I'd asked her. She knew she had some. She knew and she lied!

And as I write this, I don't know who I'm more angry at. Her or me. I could have confronted her about it. Knocked on her window, totally gone apeshit in her face. Or maybe just called her out in that cold, judgy, sarcastic way Mom used to use. "Oh hi, Bobbi, I just wanted to let you know I was trying to save your herb garden just now 'cause, you know, we gotta look out for each other, right? Sharing, pulling together. Community, right? RIGHT?"

Why didn't I do that, do anything? Why do I never—

What the hell is Dan doing? Coming around the side of the house now. This giant, bamboo pole.

Wha

At this point the a *ends with a long, deep squiggle that extends to the bottom of the page.*

From my interview with Senior Ranger Josephine Schell.

Mrs. Holland's probably too young to have seen *Fantasia,* but that's what went through my mind when I saw the animals migrate . . . and freeze. Remember that scene, the plant-eaters smelling the T. rex? That's what I saw, all those skinny, starved deer suddenly raising their heads to smell the air, just like Mrs. Holland described in her journal.

Again, like with the bone fragments, I didn't have the time or mental clarity to dwell on it. I do remember feeling sorry for them. I don't think I'd ever seen so many animals look so hungry before. First the berry harvest, then having to flee. You could understand why so many of them were getting aggressive. I witnessed a couple squirrel fights that seemed to go on forever. Buddy of mine in another team saw two black bears just rippin' the shit out of each other over an elk carcass. I kept praying I wouldn't find a similar situation but with the corpse of a human refugee.

And that almost happened, not with a person, but a deer. I stumbled across this pack of coyotes gnawing on a skeleton that'd already been gnawed by something else. Coyotes are pretty wimpy by nature. They'll almost never confront a large adult human. But this pack did. They stood their ground, growling and snapping at me. I don't think they were looking to hunt me, but they woulda definitely fought for the last strips of meat on those bones. Even when I yelled back, made myself big, threw a couple rocks, and finally fired a shot in the air, it took the rest of my team showing up for those little buggers to finally bugger off. I've never, in my whole career, seen animals be that bold.

Shows you what hunger can do.

JOURNAL ENTRY #7 [CONT.]

I can't stop shaking. Half a day later and my heart still won't slow down. I'm glad I decided to keep writing in this journal. I know you won't see it for a while, and I know it's probably silly to pretend like I'm still writing it to you, but just the act of writing, putting everything down on paper where I can see it, is so helpful in organizing my thoughts.

And I have *so* much to organize from six hours ago when I got interrupted by Dan trying to clean the solar panels. This all goes back to last night, when Mostar and I were discussing the ration plan. As she was talking about the problems of making more rabbit traps, Dan said, "We got a bigger problem."

He hadn't really been listening, focused pensively on his tablet. "We're running out of power." He flipped the iPad around to face us. I recognized it as some kind of energy monitoring page, an icon of our house with the wall battery in yellow and the roof solar panels in orange. "I think the ash's covered them." He tapped the panels, which showed 25 percent. "Yours too." He tilted the screen at Mostar and swiped over to her house. He explained that, normally, these "smart panels" would automatically signal the Cygnus maintenance team for immediate cleaning. But now . . .

"Do we really need electricity?" Mostar didn't look too worried. "Losing the freezer means we'll have to find other ways of preserving what we have, and eat first what we can't. But trust me, when the power's gone you realize what a luxury lightbulbs are."

Dan countered with, "Not for the garden. When the shoots come up, they're going to need a ton of artificial light, and warmth." He explained that our heating system was electric, not gas, that all that homemade methane beneath our floor was only used for cooking and fireplaces. I asked, innocently, if the rain wouldn't just wash the ash off our roof. Dan nodded, digesting what I'd said, which makes me realize now that it's been so long since he's actually done that with anything I've said.

He acknowledged I had a point, "but eventually, the rain's gonna give way to snow." He took a breath, then asked Mostar if she had a broom, and on her nod, perked up. "Great, I can just get up on the roof tomorrow and brush them off."

"You can't!" I surprised myself with how quickly that came out. "We . . ." I tried to find a "safe" answer. "We don't have a ladder."

"We can make one." Dan was still positive, even enthusiastic. His eyes suddenly sparked with an idea. "The bamboo! I can cut some stalks, tie or tape them together and—"

"You'd get in trouble!" Okay, so maybe that wasn't a lie. I did, do, always worry about getting in trouble, but it was still a "safe" answer and not the one I was really hiding. "The bamboo belongs to the whole community, and if we cut them down, won't that . . ." I looked to Mostar for backup, and got nothing. Thanks, Mostar.

But off her silence, I said, "Maybe we can eat the bamboo!" It was a brilliant redirect, I thought, and honestly, a pretty good plan. "The shoots, we eat them all the time in ramen!" I actually don't. I love ramen but I've always ordered it without the bamboo shoots. I'm sorry but they smell how I think horse manure would taste. Still, I tried to enlist Mostar again. "The neighbors might not mind us harvesting the shoots! And if we get enough, we might not even need the garden!"

I don't think she meant to shoot me down. "Is this type of bamboo edible?"

Damn you, Mostar.

"I'll just make a ladder." Dan. The rise in his voice, the light in his eyes. "I can saw a few . . . do we have a saw?"

"But you'll burn so many calories . . . ," I tried.

Dan didn't hear me. "Maybe using the bread knife as a saw . . ."

"What if you fall!" There it was. The real reason I pushed back so hard. "There's no doctor! And we can't get you to a hospital! If you hit your head, break a leg . . ."

"What, you're saying I'm not up to it?" Dan's face, surprise verging on hurt. Dan's not, how do I say this, the "athletic" type. And it'd never mattered, to either one of us, until now.

"She's right." Finally. Mostar nodded at me with glum recognition. "Injury turns you from a giver to a taker. Taking up our resources, our time to care for you. That's why most weapons of war are designed to injure instead of kill. Wounded are more of a drain than the dead."

Um, okay, I could have done without the obscure military trivia, but her argument produced the exact reaction I hoped for, and feared. Dan's face fell, his shoulders sagged. I swallowed as he sighed and looked down at the table. I remember thinking this would undo everything, his whole new positive, productive attitude. Popped like a bubble. Back to depression. Back to the damn couch.

But then, suddenly he reinflated, tapping furiously at the iPad. "Maybe I can work on the efficiency settings for the houses. And maybe"—his eyes widened—"no, no maybe . . . we all donate a percentage of our electricity to the Common House to help charge the delivery vehicles. Why can't we share power with each other? Your house to ours?"

The last sentence was directed at Mostar, who shrugged. Dan smiled at himself. I could have cried with relief. "That'll buy us some time to think of something." Still smiling at the screen, he reached out to grab my hand. "We'll think of something!"

And then he was on his feet, clearing all our dishes and rushing them over to the sink. "Black hole sun . . . ," singing above the rush of water, "won't you come, and wash away the rain . . ." He was scrubbing away, head bouncing to his own rhythm.

Mostar smiling at his back, then at my unconsciously shocked expression, leaned in and whispered, "How?" I knew exactly what she was talking about.

"I don't . . . ," I stammered. "I mean . . . when his business . . ."

"This isn't business," Mostar whispered, "this is life or death. This is when the real you comes out." She took my hand. "This is when, as the saying goes, adversity introduces us to ourselves."*

* "Adversity introduces us to ourselves" was originally attributed to Albert Einstein, but spoken in this particular version by President George W. Bush on September 14, 2001, at the National Day of Prayer and Remembrance Service at the National Cathedral in Washington, D.C.

Then she sat back, nodding proudly at my husband. "Nice to meet you, Danny Holland."

"Wha'?" he asked over his shoulder, to which Mostar replied, "Nothing."

"Cool." Dan grinned back at us, dramatically drying a cup. "Don't worry, I'll think of something."

And by this morning, when I was writing that last entry, I saw what "something" was.

Using our bread knife, Dan cut down the longest stalk of bamboo he could find, trimmed away the branches, then attached it to Mostar's broom with some of our packing tape. And it works. The first storm of ash that settled on the car told me that he'd reached the highest panels on our roof. If only he'd remembered to cover his nose and mouth! Dan went down coughing. So did I, when I got out of the car to help him. We coughed, sneezed, then laughed. It was a wonderful moment. Nice to meet you, Dan.

Then we heard someone scream.

Back behind the houses. Dan and I looked at each other, then ran into the alley between our home and the Perkins-Forsters'.

Palomino was still in the yard, alone at her apple tree. Effie and Carmen, grabbing each other's hands, watched her from the back stoop. Nobody moved, nobody spoke.

A mountain lion! Long, skinny, with muddy paws and ash-covered fur. It stood right at the edge of the yard, eyes locked on Palomino.

What are you supposed to do! Make yourself bigger? Yell? Throw something? Run? What do you do when any mistake could be fatal?

Dan whispered, "Don't move," so close I could feel his warm breath on my ear. Palomino must have heard him because she turned in our direction. I could see Effie mouth something and hunch her shoulders toward her daughter. Carmen blocked her with one arm while lifting the other hand toward Palomino in a pained "stay still" gesture. But the girl wasn't looking at her moms. Her eyes were on me. That expression. Fear. Pleading. I took a step toward her, then froze as the cat gave this low growl.

Palomino backed up half a step.

Effie shouted, "Stay still!" and the puma's crouch deepened. The flesh of its mouth curled back, revealing these long, yellow fangs. The growl rose to a sharp hiss.

Palomino turned and ran.

A high-pitched "Stay!" from Carmen.

Everything happened so fast! I saw Palomino stoop under raised arms, Effie and Carmen running toward her, the cougar rising up, and then this pole, this long, thin, green stick streaking past my face to smack right into the animal's ribs.

The mountain lion fell sideways, skidding clumsily on the ground. It jerked and twisted, clawing at the stick with rapid swipes. I'm not sure if it actually succeeded or if the motion of its running dislodged the point, but in a flurry of sharp, phlegmy snarls, it dashed into the trees, leaving a trail of blood.

"Are you okay?" I turned to see Mostar stepping out from between the houses, her attention on Palomino, who was practically smothered by her mothers.

I looked down at the spear, or javelin, whatever you call Mostar's weapon. Because that's what she'd made, a weapon. A bamboo stalk, a half inch or so wide and about as tall as her. Taller when you include the tip, a bloody paring knife, stuck on with equally bloody packing tape.

Mostar said, "Thank you, Katie," as I handed the pole to her. I don't remember picking it up. In fact, I don't even remember how I got there. I just remember wiping bloody hands on my jeans as she turned to Dan. "This is what I needed it for."

I guess Dan had cut the shaft for her when he was making his roof-cleaning thingy. Dan managed a shaky "uh-huh" as Mostar pursed her lips at the knife's bent blade. "Would have never worked on a deer," she huffed. "Too flimsy. And I need to figure out a way to barb the blade for it to stick." She shook the dripping weapon back at me. "See how easily it came out? If someone has a file, maybe I can . . ."

"What are you doing!" That was Yvette, behind us, with Tony in tow. They must have been standing in between the houses, along with everyone else. The whole neighborhood was suddenly there, crowding the alleys. Shocked faces. Pale.

Not Yvette though. Her cheeks were red. She looked angry; no, I take that back. Indignant. A parent or vice principal when a child has made "bad choices."

"What are you doing!"

Mostar ignored her, kneeling next to Palomino. "You okay?" Her free hand reached out to stroke the girl's cheek. "I'm sorry if I scared you."

I looked over at Yvette, who was glaring at Tony, who wasn't saying anything. I noticed he was licking his lips a lot, sucking them in and taking short, loud breaths through his nose.

I saw Yvette's eyes widen slightly, that silent "Well?" look couples give each other. Without facing her, he responded with another lip chew. Yvette whipped her head back and called for Mostar, who remained focused on the Perkins-Forster family.

"Mostar!" Demanding this time. Commanding. I could see she was gripping Tony's arm, giving it slight, signaling yanks.

"Uh, yeah," Tony said without making eye contact. "You know . . . I think . . . maybe if we all just . . ."

Mostar interrupted by turning away from them back to Palomino. "I don't know about you, Little Doll . . . but I was so scared, I may have just wet myself." That was the first time I saw Palomino smile, which became a tearful giggle, which set off both her mothers. All three of them, crying and laughing, and then Effie let out this loud snotty-snort that made everyone smile.

Except Yvette. I could see her jaw muscles throb. She let go of Tony's arm, threw it aside, and strode over to Mostar. "That was incredibly selfish and irresponsible what you just did!"

Mostar gave a slight "oh, here we go" sigh, then grunted as she stood up to face her. "It was?"

Yvette seemed taken aback by this answer, as if she expected Mostar to cave. "It was!" she repeated, and I noticed, as she spoke, that her accent had definitely changed. A strong hint of, what, Australia? New Zealand? "That animal wasn't going to hurt her!"

"It wasn't?" Mostar responded calmly. "You didn't see it about to pounce?"

Yvette said incredulously, "No, I didn't! I saw a frightened animal that you hurt for no reason!"

"Actually"—my heart skipped a beat when I heard Dan speak—"it really did look like it was gonna jump." His voice was shaking a little, and it got louder as he said, "She . . . like . . . saved her."

Yvette's eyes flicked back to Tony, her head cocked to one side. He was gone. Not physically, and I'm not being poetic—well, maybe a little—but the guy we'd first met, this dynamic, confident alpha with the big neon sign above him that flashed TRUST ME, I KNOW WHAT I'M DOING? Gone.

I remember reading somewhere that perception of height is distorted by positions of authority. Doctors, cops, anyone we designate as powerful sometimes appear taller than they actually are. I'm not sure if I 100 percent believe this, and maybe Tony was just hunching badly, but I can swear, at that moment, he seemed a lot shorter.

Yvette's eyes flashed this microburst of anger at her husband, so subtle but so hot that I felt my stomach gurgle. And when she turned that look on Dan, I nose-burped acid. She spat, "Do you know that? Do you know what mountain lions are like? Do you know that it wasn't just scared by us all and trying to get away, and now it's hurt unnecessarily, and what you did could've provoked it to attack . . . kill Palomino!"

I should have said something. I should have stood up for Dan. I might have, if Mostar hadn't jumped in. That's what I hope. But Mostar just shrugged and sighed with, "Well, it didn't and now it's gone. It's all over."

She was trying to defuse the situation, and it seemed close to working. I noticed people around me start to relax. The Perkins-Forsters got to their feet. Reinhardt raised his hands in a "well, that settles it" gesture. And the Boothes even turned back to their house. But Yvette . . . how big are her veins that I could see them bulging from that distance? A half beat to think, regroup, find a way to reassert her authority.

"No, no! No, it's not over. You could have seriously hurt her with that!" Her arm shot toward the javelin. "You're making this an unsafe space! And"—her hand opened—"I'm going to have to confiscate this."

"No."

The word, the tone. Absolute fact.

Yvette exhaled through her nose, eyes flicking from side to side. Was she looking for support? Judgment?

"Mostar."

"No."

"Just give it to me."

"No."

"Mostar!" One step closer, Yvette's fingers curling around the green wood. Did Mostar wait for that, for her to get a good strong grip?

I remember this in slow motion, the hard yank, pulling Yvette forward and down into Mostar's face.

"NO."

And then something happened. Something that still makes me want to run and hide from the memory. Mostar's lower jaw, jutting out as she lunged. An inch, barely, and so quick. A rapid stab forward of her face into Yvette's.

And that face, eyes wide, jerking back suddenly.

Fear.

I keep coming back to this moment, the notion of strong and weak.

I understand beauty or money. Wit, popularity, sex.

Influence.

But I've never seen a physical fight, or even the threat of one. Not with girls, not even boys. Not in my world.

Primitive. Primal.

Dominance.

I have the power to cause you pain.

Yvette released the spear, retreating from the waist up. Mostar gave another lunge, shoulders back, head forward.

Yvette winced! Head turned, eyes shut, retreating a couple steps as her hands came up to shield her face.

"Go home, Yvette."

And it was done. Mostar relaxed, shoulders sagging, weight resting on her back leg, the semblance of a smile pulling at the corners of her mouth. "Just go home, okay?"

Yvette straightened, cheeks and lips completely white. She backed up another half step, glaring at Mostar as fear gave way to anger. But she didn't say anything this time, didn't even look at us. She gave this little half-hearted faux chuckle, which ended in a clownish grin. She turned quickly, heading for her house, and grabbed Tony by the wrist. Tony. Face lank, eyes down, trying to swallow his bottom lip, as his wife led him away.

The next few seconds were a blur. I think I almost passed out from the tension. I remember Dan's arm around me, shaking, nausea.

The first clear vision I had was the group starting to break up. The Boothes' backs, Palomino being carried inside by Carmen.

Then the voice.

"Um."

It was Reinhardt, of all people, and of all things, muttering to Dan, "I . . . uh . . . couldn't help but . . . um . . . well, if you're already cleaning your own solar panels, I was wondering if . . ."

"Huh? Oh yeah, sure," Dan mumbled, suddenly snapping back to the moment, trying to catch up with a flurry of affirmative hand gestures. "Yeah, totally, soon as I finish and—"

"And what are you going to do for him?" Mostar, cutting him

off, standing beside him, facing Reinhardt, blood dripping down the spear onto her hand. "If you need Dan to do something for you, then you need to do something for him."

Her voice was loud, louder than it needed to be at that distance. Loud enough to make everyone turn back and take notice.

"Well, I . . . naturally, yes, yes." Reinhardt tried to shrug it off like that was a given, then, I could see, got a little worried when he realized what he was agreeing to. "What would you . . ."

"Food." Mostar's head jerked in my direction. "Danny needs to replace all those calories he'll be spending. And that's why Katie will be going with him to catalog everything you have in your kitchen. And so, if you ever need his help again, and you know you will, he'll know exactly what to ask for in return." No room. No questions. All he could do at that point was refuse. Which he didn't.

"By all means."

And as he waddled away, Mostar turned to Dan and said, "Need. That's what makes a village. That's what we are now, and what holds us together is need. I won't help you if you don't help me. *That* is the social contract."

I couldn't really process what she was saying. Still trembling, I felt like crying. All that tension whooshing out like a balloon. I must have grabbed Dan's arm harder than I wanted. My legs buckled. My head swam. All I wanted to do was go home and lie down.

"And you . . ." Mostar snapped me back to attention, eyes front, staring into her utterly befuddling smile.

"I knew you had it in you."

I didn't understand. I opened my mouth to ask.

"When you ran toward Palomino." Mostar beamed. "I'm sorry I almost speared you."

Toward!

I honestly had no idea what she was talking about, and when Dan said, "Yeah, you totally got in between her and the cat." I looked at them both like they were crazy, then down at the ground I was standing on. It was, in fact, right in the puma's path. How did I get there? I literally cannot remember!

"That was pretty badass, you know." That was Dan, surprised and, what, a little aroused?

"You didn't even think about it, did you?" Mostar asked pridefully. "All instinct, eh?"

Before I could come up with a response, the sound of footsteps turned our heads. Palomino came running over, holding what looked like a pillowcase in her hands.

Mostar started to say, "Hello, Little Doll, what have you . . ."

But she ran past us, into our house, then a few seconds later, came right back out, and gave Mostar a big hug. Mostar returned it, kissed the top of her head, and sang, "Thank you, Lutko Moja."*

Then she turned and hugged me! I just stood there like an idiot, frozen for a second, before awkwardly rubbing her back. She didn't seem to mind. She looked up at me with a big smile, gave me another squeeze, then ran back to her house.

After a moment of shared puzzlement, we traced her steps inside, and found the pillowcase resting next to the garage door.

It was full of beans, or rather, it was full of her little beanbag fidgeters that were spilling their beans out from cutoff corners. There're over a hundred in total. I haven't stopped counting since. Red, black, white, speckled brown. I don't know all the types, and I can't imagine that all of them will germinate. Again, do I soak them? Wet paper towel? No idea. I'll probably just stick them straight into the mud. There's enough here to fill the whole garden. How much food will that produce? Enough to feed the whole neighborhood?

Village. Need.

Thank you, Pal.

* Lutko moja: Little doll.

Chapter 8

The unearthly cries swirled through the darkness into our open-walled hut and enveloped us. . . . It was the sound of Satan.

—Birute M. F. Galdikas, *Reflections of Eden: My Years with the Orangutans of Borneo*

JOURNAL ENTRY #8
OCTOBER 7

Screams! They woke us up tonight. I felt the bed bounce as Dan jumped over to the window. I got up groggily and followed him out onto the back balcony. The first thing I noticed was the night's chill, coldest yet. Then more screams, echoing clearly from the woods. Not human. The same hissing growls I'd heard from the mountain lion that afternoon.

Rrraaawww. Rraaaawwww.

But they weren't alone. Another sound, underneath, like the bass in a song. Deeper, fuller. At first, I couldn't make it out, but then it rose to the same howls I'd heard before. That first time when I'd been hiking, the second time when I'd been chased. But it was much louder now, as powerful as the heavy, spoiled smell. Again, familiar. This was real. Not a figment in my head, not a spot in my eye. There was definitely another animal out there with that cat.

Those screams, the sharp hisses. The puma sounded angry or scared. The howls boomed, then rose to high chatters. I'd never heard anything like it. No, that's not entirely true. I'd never heard anything *exactly* like it.

I've heard monkeys before. From nature shows, and at the zoo. Monkeys or apes. But much louder, much more powerful. It was like I could feel the sound waves hitting me, like the windows might rattle if they'd been any closer. The cat's screams suddenly changed, from growling rage to rapid, staccato yowls.

Rawrawraw!

Fighting.

Quick, sharp. Grunts of muscles working and muffled growls trying to escape a full mouth?

Then a roar, rising above the rest. Deep, bellowing, as the puma's voice cracked into this horrible wail.

And then it was all over. Utter silence. I realized that Dan and I had been holding hands tightly, so tight that I could feel the blood rush back into my fingers when he let go. He said, "Wait," and went downstairs. I started to say something after him. He paused at the bedroom door. "I'll be right back." It was so quiet I could hear him locking the front and back doors. I'm not sure why. Not like animals can open a door. Can a bear? Can they use their paws or claws or whatever they have to manipulate a knob? It has to be a bear. At least I know I'm not crazy. What else could fight a mountain lion?

And how did it end? Did one chase the other away? Or are they both out there now, circling our houses?

I've just gone to the bedroom's front windows. Lights are on all over the village. Everyone except the Durants. No one is coming out though. Dan just came in and closed and locked the balcony door, then got back into bed. "Nothing more to do," he said to me, just, I think, to reassure me. I asked if we should go knock on Mostar's door, maybe ask her if she's heard sounds like that before. Dan's against it. What's the point? Wait till morning light to see. Maybe he's just scared. Nothing wrong with that. So am I. Also noticed he locked the bedroom door. No argument there.

And he just turned over like everything's fine. Jealous. He's exhausted from cleaning our roof and Reinhardt's. All I did was catalog the man's kitchen. A lot of frozen diet meals. Maybe I should copy them down here from my other list. Something to do to help me sleep? Boring enough.

No, screw it. Time for half an Ativan. No, Ambien.

JOURNAL ENTRY #9
OCTOBER 8

Bad idea. I still couldn't sleep. I tried. So easy for Dan. Zero to sixty. He just crashed out, snoring away. I was so pissed. At myself this time. It was my idea to get rid of all our DVDs when we moved. All uploaded to the cloud.

Cloud.

What a beautiful image, something pretty and puffy way up in the sky. Heaven. What a lie. I remember one of Dan's former business partners talking about the "data parks," the real cloud. I remember him saying that the Pacific Northwest was packed with data parks because of the cheap hydroelectric power. I wonder if one of those parks was buried under boiling mud. People's personal data: work projects, financial records, priceless photographs they scanned because someone told them it was safer than leaving them in a house that could burn or flood. That was just one of ten thousand thoughts that kept me awake last night.

I should have felt bad for all those people, but right then, all I could do was miss the new *Downton Abbey*. It's supposed to be set in the '40s! They even showed those teaser shots of Lady Mary in a uniform with that bombed out London backdrop. Could Granny Dowager still be alive? What about Robert and Cora? They specifically didn't show the whole cast because they wanted to torture us about who was still alive by then. Bastards!

Even just one classic. Just *Princess Bride*. Of course, I never thought to download it. Losing the cloud was "incontheivable."

No TV, *and* no books! Again, my genius. No more paper novels because they're all on my Kindle, which I hadn't charged to save power. Yay.

So, I took half of an Ambien and got back into bed to wait for it to kick in. And it did, but I didn't know that yet. I sat there in the dark, waiting for delicious sleep to roll over me, and when it didn't, I got back up for the other half. I didn't know how stoned I was. That's why I lit the candle.

All my stuff is in the guest bathroom. Old habit from our last house. Different sleep schedules. I didn't want to disturb Dan . . . when I'd get up for work to support us both. Never thought I deserved the master bath. Again, old habit.

I didn't need the scented candle for light. Or to chase away the stink from a few hours ago. I was so wasted, I probably confused the memory with the real thing. That reek. I thought I could still smell it in the air. I fumbled for the matchbook, lit the candle, slid it to the side, then opened the medicine cabinet for the pills. I didn't realize the flame was resting right under the towel rack.

The flicker, the smoke.

Fire!

A cold, waking snap hit me and I threw the flaming towel into the shower. Water, steam, smoke. A lot of smoke. The alarm. Piercing through my skull. I opened the window, hit the fan, climbed frantically onto the sink to pull the physical disc off the wall. I forgot it was just a sensor wired into the whole house. I pulled and yanked and probably shouted, "C'mon! Goddamn it! C'mon!" before slipping and falling into Dan's arms.

He got out half of a "what the hell did . . ." before seeing the charred towel in the tub. Then his arms were around me, a soft "It's okay" in my neck.

That's all it took. I burst out crying. Melting into him, sobbing, babbling about everything that was happening, everything that *could* happen.

Dan just held me, stroking my back, kissing the top of my head, whispering, "It's okay, it's okay."

He switched everything off, led me back to bed.

And.

All I'm going to say is that it's been a very, very long time.

Nice to be home again.

We slept late. About nine A.M. I probably would have slept a lot later if Dan hadn't shaken the bed when he got up. I opened one eye to see him putting on his pants. When I asked where he was going, I meant it in a lazy, flirty way.

But when he tried to answer, "I . . . I'm gonna . . ." His face. So busted! That's one of the things I've always loved about Dan, even in our worst moments. He can't lie.

"I was thinking, I'm just gonna check out what we heard last night." He noticed that I saw he'd tucked that stabby thing, the Boothes' coconut opener, into his belt.

I said, "Okay," and started grabbing my clothes.

"No, it's okay," he said, and raced to get his shoes on.

I repeated, "It's okay," and did the same.

We got into this little "it's okay" ping-pong, trying to convince each other not to bother. We must have done it, like, three or four times, racing to get dressed.

I won.

"Kate." Dan's voice deepened. His hand raised. "No."

I stood there, kind of stunned. There was this man, back straight, shoulders squared, looking just the tiniest bit taller than I remember. It's nice, yes, nice, to know that he has this protective instinct. Maybe it was always there, or maybe it's just grown out of what we're going through. But there it was, for the first time, trying to keep me safe. I'm proud of him for trying, and I'm even more proud of him for not totally deflating when I smiled, kissed him on the cheek, and said, "C'mon, let's go."

We headed out the back door and up onto the trail. I could see Palomino watching us from her upstairs window. Not creepy, expressionless. But not smiling either. She kept glancing at the woods behind us, like a lookout, I think, and gave us an "all clear, good luck" wave.

And Vincent gave us a thumbs-up when we passed his house. I'm sure he meant to be encouraging, but his nervous face, the way he darted from the window afterward. I took it as, "Better you than me."

"Wait!" We stopped at Mostar shouting from down the trail. She came huffing and puffing after us, carrying her javelin. "Here!" I could see that she'd cleaned and tried to straighten the blade. "I'm making a better one," she said, and stuck it into my hand. Looking at Dan, she said, "Don't stay out there too long."

The stink hit us as soon as we crossed over the ridge onto the downward slope. Strong, pungent. I smelled it on the palm of my hand, coming off a tree I'd just touched. I put my nose to the bark. Rotten eggs. My hand also came away with something else. Plant fiber, probably. It was long and black. Thick like a horse's mane. I'm not sure if it stank, it could have just been my fingertips. Animal hair?

Then we saw the white specks, standing out in a patch of turned-up earth and reddish leaves.

Reddish from blood. It was everywhere. On the bushes, the bark, soaked into the ground, mixing with ash into these solid, rusty pebbles.

The white specks were shattered bones. It was hard to even recognize them at first. Most were just chips. They looked like they were smashed with a hammer. I found a few rocks, nearby, with blood on one side. Not splatters. Deep, thick stains mixed with fur and bits of flesh. And this is weird, but they looked, okay, painted? I know that sounds funny, but the blood on the rocks, on the trees and leaves, there were no droplets. Other than in the ash, all the other stains looked like they'd been smeared with a brush, or a tongue. Like whatever killed the cat went around licking every last spot.

Even the bones. They were clean. The marrow'd been scrubbed out. In fact, there wasn't any meat anywhere. No organs, muscle, brain. I found what had to be the remains of the skull; just a curved, polished fragment next to a collection of broken teeth. That's how I knew it had to be the cat. Those yellow fangs. I found one, intact, still stuck to a piece of upper jaw.

What could have done that?

If my mind wasn't already shaken by what we saw, Mostar's reaction made it worse.

She just listened, without judgment, eyes off to the side, taking in every detail without the slightest reaction. It scared me, scares me, that she didn't immediately respond with, "Oh well, what you saw was . . ." She always has an answer for everything. That's why I didn't like her at first. Bully. Know-it-all. "Go here, do this, believe me when I say . . ." This is the first time I've seen her genuinely perplexed. No, that's not right. The first time was when I'd been chased, when she turned her eyes on the woods.

Does she suspect what I'm trying to dismiss? The smell, the howls, the large "boulder" I'd seen on the road. Now this. I'm sure I'm just trying to come up with an explanation for something that doesn't make any sense. That's me. A place for everything and everything in its place. I'm just grasping on to what I've heard. And I haven't heard much. I'm not into that stuff. I'm the practical one. I've never been interested in things that aren't real. I've never even watched *Game of Thrones*. Dragons and ice zombies? Really? When Yvette was going on about Oma, she was speaking metaphorically! It can't be real or else everyone would know. That's the world we live in, right? Anyone can know anything. We'd know about this.

And yes, I know I saw something. We both did. But knowing you saw something is different from knowing what you saw.

I spotted the first one, the first clear footprint. It was next to the skull fragment, so deep it pressed right through the ash into the soft earth. It couldn't be a wolf or another puma. The shape was all wrong. Maybe a bear? I don't know. I've never seen a bear track, so maybe that's the simple answer. But the print looked almost like a shoeless person right down to the five toes. But it couldn't have been. Dan took off his hiking boot. He wears a size 11. He took off his sock as well, and placed his bare foot right next to the print. The toes matched, the overall shape. But the size. That's impossible. It must have been a trick of the ash, or maybe the way it was planted.

Nothing could have such a big foot.

Chapter 9

There is evidence to indicate the possible existence in Skamania County of a nocturnal primate mammal variously described as an ape-like creature . . . and commonly known as "Sasquatch," "Yeti," "Bigfoot" . . .

—Ordinance No. 69-01, Skamania County, Washington State

From my interview with Senior Ranger Josephine Schell.

Yes, I've heard the legend. And no, it's got nothing to do with my heritage. I'm from the Southwest, not the Northwest.* Not that we don't have our own stories. Everybody does. You've got the Almas in Russia, the Yowie in Australia, the Orang Pendek in Indonesia, and a bunch of Sisimite stories from Latin America. And that's just today. The Judeo-Christian Bible has Esau, the primitive brother of Jacob. And the *Epic of Gilgamesh,* the first written story, has "Enkidu," the wild man. Show me a culture anywhere on this planet, and chances are, they got something.

Including this one, and by this one, I mean mainstream pop culture. Bigfoot's as American as apple pie and guns in schools. That's how I learned about it. Like any good Gen Xer, I was raised by TV. I've checked out my fair share of the modern Bigfoot media.

I've seen a lot of the newer, shaky-cam *Blair Witch*–wannabe flicks. I've flipped through a couple of the faux documentary

* Josephine Schell (maiden name Begay) is a member of the Navajo Nation.

cable shows. I keep meaning to check out the one from the survival guy, not the British fraud, the real deal. The Canadian. He knows his shit, and maybe he's actually on the right track. But all the other stuff I've seen, fiction and "managed reality," I gotta say, just feels like a polished rehash of the '70s–'80s craze I grew up on.

You know! I read your article about the five classic films, and, yeah, they scared the crap outta me too. That one where a yeti attacks a ski resort. I think you're right about them not being able to afford a whole costume,* but the result, the whole *Jaws* POV, terrifying. That scene where it breaks through a window . . . comes down from the mountain, right into town . . . It wasn't supposed to do that! It broke the prime directive of horror films! If you don't go looking for trouble, trouble won't come looking for you!

That's why our generation's scary movies were essentially cautionary tales. That's why I never had any sympathy for the horny teenagers going to the summer camp, or the greedy town mayor keeping the beaches open, or the rule-following spaceship crew that just had to investigate an alien distress signal. I knew I'd never be like them. I'd do my part and stay home. But after watching the snowbeast attacking Aspen, I thought, *What's to stop the real Sasquatch from doing the same?*

Because it did! The other movie you wrote about, with the host from *Mission Impossible,* and exhibits like footprints and photos and an interview with a "psychic detective" and, most important, oh my God, those "dramatic re-creations." When the girl . . . Rita Graham, I remember the name . . . when she's sitting at home that night, watching TV, minding her own business . . . just like me . . . and a shadow appears across the window shade behind her two seconds before this giant, hairy arm smashes through the glass. I might have actually pissed myself on that

* Only after finishing my interviews for this book, did I discover that the film in question, 1977's *Snowbeast,* did, in fact, produce an entire creature costume.

one. It scared me so badly that years later I actually tried looking it up. Turns out the incident did happen, but was seriously dramatized for the show.

What wasn't dramatized was another incident, two of them, really, that were re-created for that other movie, the one that actually ran in theaters! The first account comes from the 1920s where some rogue miners are prospecting near, of all places, Mount St. Helens. One night their cabin is attacked with boulders and fists and the classic animal screams we now associate with the legend. That's why, to this day, the canyon where it happened is nicknamed Ape Canyon. The second story is from Teddy Roosevelt.

She reaches into her desk and thumps the old, dog-eared copy of The Wilderness Hunter *onto her desk.*

Fair warning, the first part's pretty cringy. It opens with Roosevelt talking about how lucky he's been to shoot every kind of large animal in North America.

Douche.

Anyway, it goes on to "recount," not tell firsthand, recount, the story of an Idaho fur trapper named Bauman, whose partner was torn apart by a "goblin."

Is either story true? How the hell do I know? I thought they were at the time, when I kept asking my parents to move my bed away from the window. I'd be like, "These are real accounts! A president wrote about it!"

To their credit, my folks didn't just blow me off. They tried to get me to verify it, to look beyond words and see if there was any physical evidence. I think that's why I got interested in zoology, why, to this day, I get excited when any new species gets scientifically proven. And there're thousands of them. Every year! I've seen a live Goliath spider and the corpse of a giant squid. I've seen all types of specimens recovered from hydrothermal vents that would have been considered science fiction when I was born. And as soon as the Congo gets safe enough for eco-tourism, I'll be the first one in line to see that newly discovered Bili ape. I'm open to any discovery, as long as it's based on hard, physical evidence. Facts are supposed to banish monsters . . .

She sighs.

. . . not invite them in.

JOURNAL ENTRY #9 [CONT.]

The animals are gone. I didn't notice it this morning, but as the day's progressed, I realize I haven't seen a deer or squirrel. Anything. And if there are any birds, they haven't made a peep. Why did they leave? It can't be hunger. There're still a few apples on the Perkins-Forsters' trees. I bet if I check the others, I'll also find some remaining fruit. Was it the fight? Are they scared of the animal that killed the cougar?

Listen to me. "The animal."

I can't even write the word down. I also haven't talked about it since telling Mostar. Neither has Dan. To be fair, he's really busy.

Dan got a new "gig," that's what he calls it. We were having breakfast at Mostar's, the last of the rabbit stew, watered down, when Vincent Boothe came around. He said to Dan, "I, uh, noticed you were cleaning Reinhardt's solar panels yesterday, and was wondering . . ."

"Sure." Dan was already licking his bowl. "I'll be over in a few minutes."

"Great!" Vincent looked relieved but stiffened when he caught Mostar's eye. "And, you know, of course, we'd feed you for your time." Then he looked at me. "And you're more than welcome to come over and, uh, go through our supplies."

I smiled uncomfortably. Mostar gave an approving nod.

Dan couldn't have been happier. As Vincent left, he flashed this goofy, almost childlike grin. "I'm in demand."

Mostar playfully cuffed him on the arm and said, "Look at you, village handyman."

"Handyman!" That should have destroyed him! Would have a

few days ago. How many job offers, how many helpful, hopeful dinners with Frank? "I'm not a salary man." That was Dan's default defense. "I'm a builder, not a maintainer." And, oh, the surly tailspins that I had to nurse him through.

And now, thanks to Mostar's big mouth.

Grip the wheel, brace for impact.

But, once again, my head nearly spun off my shoulders as Dan's grin widened. "Village handyman." He licked his spoon like a lollipop, bounced, *bounced,* up from the table, and said to me, "Time for work." Then hummed his dishes over to the sink.

He hummed all day. Through every job the Boothes gave him. They had a list, FYI. Even before he could get to the solar panels, the air vent in the bedroom was rattling, the shower drain was stopped. Little things here and there. I kept my own list. I'm charging them in rolled oats (we're out of cereal). While Dan bopped his merry way between tasks, I went meticulously through the Boothes' pantry, cataloging everything they had, down to the last drop of Lucini Italia premium olive oil. A lot of calories in olive oil. I don't think I'm overcharging them.

Maybe a little.

I've gotta get past the potato thing. Bobbi tried so hard to be nice. She was so open about everything they had—or had left. (Sorry. Let it go!) She even suggested sharing their house's electricity as well as a little blue teapot that "would make a perfect watering can for the garden."

How does she know about the garden? Does everyone? What else are they saying behind our backs? The shift seemed so sudden to me, the acceptance that we might have to survive the winter. But it must have been building for some time, as they listened to the news, watched the empty sky, saw that Tony and Yvette were still clinging to the status quo while Mostar, at least, was trying to adapt.

Whatever the reason, the Boothes certainly seem to be on board with us now. Bobbi even offered compost from her bin for extra fertilizer, and asked if maybe some of her brown rice or puffed quinoa could be planted. I don't think the quinoa will work. Doesn't "puffed" mean "cooked"? And as far as the rice, I took a handful to experiment with. Just enough for a square foot of earth. We don't have a lot of space left, now that Pal's beans are planted. But if they don't sprout and the rice does, it might be a welcome backup. No matter what, we can always use more compost. And I do give her credit for suggesting that her buckwheat pillow stuffing might be edible.

Vincent laughed at that last idea, but when he saw her hurt expression, he explained that their pillows are stuffed with the husks, not the kernels. He kind of slurred the explanation. They were both a little buzzed, opening a bottle of chardonnay as soon as Dan and I came over. Who knows how many 120 calorie glasses they'd had before we showed up. Vincent definitely had another 240 before getting up the courage to ask about the mountain lion.

When I described the blood and bones, Vincent wrote it all off as scavengers. "All the birds and small animals. Insects. Gotta be insects. So many insects. They must have all come out after the poor cat died. Everything's so hungry out there. Died of its wound. That's what we heard last night, all that screaming. Poor thing must have suffered badly. Hopefully it was gone before the smaller animals started feeding on it."

When I brought up the rocks, Vincent just shrugged it away. "Who can tell in all that mess."

Maybe that's why I didn't mention the footprints. Afraid that they'd disregard it with another tipsy theory. Or maybe I was afraid that they wouldn't, that it'd open the door to questions I couldn't answer.

I still can't. Maybe that's why I went over to the Durants' afterward. I'm still convinced that Yvette thought she was talking about some quaint, indigenous fairy tale. But if I could learn more from that tale. Some details. Where it comes from. What it wants. Doesn't all folklore have some basis in reality? Wasn't there really a great flood sometime way back? Prerecorded climate change? And isn't there a theory about the tides of the Red

Sea being so extreme that it might have looked like the waters parted?

I can't remember where I've heard this, or if I'm just totally making it up. I'm pretty sure one of Dan's college friends talked about how mammoth skulls inspired the Greeks to believe in the Cyclops. The cartilage between the eyes looking like one giant socket. I thought Yvette might have some nugget of useful information like that. If I could just get her talking.

And Tony, I wanted to ask about that day he tried to drive away.

Go for help! Oh my God. The day he tried to go for help! The day I was chased. Did he see something too? That look he had. I assumed it was from seeing the lahar, the realization that we were cut off. Maybe that was part of it. But on the way home, or maybe when he was standing there at the edge of the smashed bridge. Did he see something? Did it chase him too?

Those were the questions spinning through my mind as I nervously stepped up to their door.

I'm not sure what I was afraid of. Yvette slapping my face, yelling at me for betraying her? Both would have hurt the same. I took a deep breath, put on a fake smile, and knocked gently. No answer. I tried again, a little louder. Nothing. I thought I could hear talking. But it sounded far away. I glimpsed a faint, flickering glow coming through the living room window curtain. The TV. A recorded show. That's what I must have been hearing. A shadow passed in front of it, heading in the direction of the door.

I stuttered, "Tony? Yvette? It's Kate." I thought about ringing the doorbell but chickened out as my finger grazed the button. I watched the shadow pass the glow again, heading in the opposite direction. I moved sideways down the front of the house, to the garage. I could hear the steady *zzzzzp-zzzzzp-zzzzzp* of Yvette's elliptical, and the muffled mumbling of voices. She must have been working out, because the *zzzzzp*-ing stopped as the voices grew louder. One voice, really. Hers. His stayed at this low murmur. I couldn't make out her exact words, but the tone, high and clipped. I thought about putting my ear to the thin aluminum of her garage door, maybe even knocking on it. But instead I just waited like an idiot for a minute or so, until the voices faded and the *zzzzzp-zzzzzp-zzzzzp* resumed.

I turned back for home, stopping as Dan came out of the Boothes' house to do his roof cleaning. He saw me, waved, and even blew me a kiss that I returned. For a moment, I considered staying, to help or just to keep him company. Something about him being outside all alone. I didn't like it anymore. I felt, feel, uneasy.

Everything's too still. No wildlife. No sound. But the smell. It's constant now, like it followed us down from the kill site. And the eyes. I didn't feel like I was being watched this morning. Maybe I was just too focused on the dead cat. But I feel them now. Walking home, I kept looking up and around me. Up to the ridge above the houses, scanning the trees. I didn't see anything, but does something see me? That's why I couldn't wait to get inside. That's where I am now, sitting on the couch, keeping an eye on Dan through the living room window. Blissfully scraping those panels, then jumping back from the falling ash like it's a game.

I don't mean to keep glancing up at the woods. I'm trying not to memorize every tree, rock, patch of open space, to see if any of them change between glances. I'm trying really, really hard not to head back over to the Boothes' to see if they have binoculars. With all their hikes, they must have a pair. I'll be going over there for more compost, or staying home to work in the garden, something other than watching Dan out there by himself. I thought about getting in the car to listen to the news. But the car faces the house.

I don't want my back turned.

From Steve Morgan's *The Sasquatch Companion*.

The official history of cryptid hominid encounters has had, shall we say, a checkered relationship with indigenous oral evidence. In the words of J. Richard Greenwell, secretary and founder of the International Society of Cryptozoology, "Native peoples tend to not have a very clear line of demarcation between the metaphysical world and the physical world. We in the West very clearly separate those."* This is obviously a heavily biased and debatable point of view, especially when so many "Western" (i.e., Caucasian) eyewitnesses claim to have seen supernatural, even extraterrestrial, elements associated with Sasquatch. Nevertheless, Greenwell's statement typifies a substantial reliance on a Eurocentric record of encounters, a record that until the mid–twentieth century was woefully lacking.

Given the chaotic, often competitive nature of Europe's American invasion, and the incurious, illiterate nature of so many individual invaders, it is a wonder that any written accounts emerged from this period. While there are, of course, notable exceptions such as Fred Beck's Ape Canyon Siege, Roosevelt's "Goblin" story, and the writings of British explorer David Thompson, who discovered "the track of a large animal" which "was not that of a bear," we simply cannot know how many trappers, traders, and gold-fevered prospectors took their Sasquatch experiences to the grave. For all we know, some modern-day Russian may have a mysterious, malodorous hide nailed to the wall of his dacha that his ancestor brought back from the tsar's American colony.

So why the change? Why did contact with Sasquatch suddenly go from a trickle to a flood? The answer is simple: World War II. Before this cataclysmic event, fewer people (of all ethnicities) lived between Northern California and the Canadian border than lived in New York City. With Pearl Harbor came industry, military installations, infrastructural expansion, and millions upon millions of Americans. Small wonder that, barely thirteen years after V-J Day, in Bluff Creek, California,† a road construction crew discovered what appeared to be strange, giant, humanoid

* Interview from the History Channel's *In Search of History*, 1997.

† Bluff Creek is also known as the site of the 1967 "Patterson film" of Bigfoot.

tracks. This discovery prompted the investigation by a local newspaper, which, in turn, unearthed previous stories from the surrounding area.

By the end of the year, the tracks had made headlines around the country, along with a name for their creator: Bigfoot.

Chapter 10

Eyewitness testimony in the case of Bigfoot . . . ahhh . . . I don't think is very good because you can't test it. It's . . . it's the credibility of the person . . . and these people . . . they want to see something strange . . . they can imagine it.

—Dr. Thomas Dale Stewart, former head curator of the Department of Anthropology for the Smithsonian Institution

From my interview with Senior Ranger Josephine Schell.

Why haven't they been found? That's the ninety-nine-thousand-dollar question. And my two-cent answer is timing. See, the people in a position to prove their existence, who know how to find and analyze physical evidence, they won't go anywhere near it for fear of ruining their reputations. And that fear goes back to the time when Sasquatch first came to light.

If we'd had a rash of sightings way back in, say, the '40s and '50s, when we were still a cohesive nation with shared beliefs, maybe there would have been enough traction to force the scientific community to act. And if they had, if they'd proven these creatures are as real as the gorilla or chimpanzee, icons like Dian Fossey or Jane Goodall might have built their careers studying the great apes of North America.

The problem was that sightings peaked in the late '60s, early '70s, which was, coincidently, the dawn of public mistrust. We're talking Vietnam, Watergate, "do your own thing" counterculture. Now, I'm not saying any of that was bad, especially in a democracy. You need a healthy degree of critical thinking. You need to question authority. But Bigfoot came along just as everyone started questioning everything, including academia. This was a time when university profs were getting hit from both sides; the right with their creationist agenda, and the left who'd suddenly realized the connection between science and war. The upshot was that already cautious PhDs got even more skittish about their grants and tenure.

Which led them to drop Bigfoot right into the "crackpot" files. Where it has stayed till . . . yeah . . . till this day . . . even with what's happened . . . which we'll get to.

There's a big reason Uncle Sam hasn't released a full report on Greenloop. But . . .

Holds out her hands like a traffic cop.

"One thing at a time," as Ms. Mostar said.

Point is, public skepticism dissuades qualified experts from searching for physical evidence, and lack of physical evidence only fuels public skepticism.

Which is why the burden of proof has been mainly left to amateur adventurers who either never find anything or make it worse for themselves like that time with the FBI.* You know about that, right? Came out a couple years ago? Some whack-job group in the '70s pressured the Bureau to test a hair sample they collected and the sample turned out to be a deer. And it's those kinds of public, Al Capone–vault fiascoes that keep credible eyewitnesses from going public. And I've talked to more than my share of eyewitnesses. In this job, you get a lot of folks who are sure they've *encountered* something. Not hoaxers. They don't come to us. They go to the media. That's where the money is, and fame. All that shaky footage that shows up every now and then. The most famous one, the "Patterson-Gimlin film" that

* In June of 2019, under the Freedom of Information Act, the Federal Bureau of Investigation released a twenty-two-page file detailing its laboratory analyses of hair "attached to a tiny piece of skin." The sample, brought to them in 1976 by the Bigfoot Research Center, was determined to be "of the deer family in origin."

gave us the image most people associate with Bigfoot . . . Roger Patterson claimed he was out there getting ready to make a Bigfoot movie and just "happened" to run into the real thing. Really?

No, the folks I talk to, I believe them, or rather, I believe that they believe themselves. But like Mrs. Holland said, "Knowing you saw something is different from knowing what you saw." That's why, even now, when I think about one of those BS documentaries from my childhood, I still believe the guy who passed the lie detector test. He wasn't acting. He really thought he saw it. They all do.

Remember, I'm from the Southwest, where it's, like, UFO central. If I had a nickel for every time somebody said they saw lights in the sky . . . and they do. I'm sure there were lights in the sky, and I'm sure they were sure those lights were coming to give them an anal probe. If you gave them all polygraphs, asked them, under oath, what did you see, or hear . . .

You get a lot of those too. Hearing stuff. Noises in the night. Footsteps or breaking branches, or that grunt. A couple times, I've talked to folks who've sworn they heard or smelled something. I've had several hikers or campers who've consistently reported that refuse and spoiled eggs odor. I might have smelled it myself, that time when we found the dead deer.

A thumb over her shoulder to the map.

Maybe that was it, or maybe it was just us hoofing it for three straight days without a shower. I don't know what I smelled but I know that I smelled something. I trust my nose, ears, eyes. But my brain . . .

I think the human mind isn't comfortable with mysteries. We're always looking for answers to the unexplained. And if an answer can't come from facts, we'll try to cobble one together from old stories. If we've heard about UFOs when we happen to see a light in the sky, or a Scottish lake monster when we happen to see a ripple in the water, or a giant, apelike creature when we see a dark mass moving among the branches . . .

That's why I dismissed everyone who ever reported anything to us. Even the credible ones. And by credible, I mean embarrassed. They didn't want to be there. They didn't want to look crazy. They always asked to speak to me in private, remain anonymous, make sure that they weren't being recorded. They were almost positive that their minds were playing tricks on them. They didn't want to believe it.

She sighs.

I should have believed them. Each time I almost did, because once they started talking, the doubt fell away. I should have followed up every time someone looked me straight in the eye and said with confident clarity . . .

JOURNAL ENTRY #10

OCTOBER 9

I saw it!

I don't know what woke me up tonight. A sound, or the outside porch light flicking on. It wasn't ours, not at first. The Perkins-Forster house, shining up onto the ceiling above my head. I got up, rubbed the sleep out of my eyes, and crept to the back window. I didn't want to wake up Dan. He has a lot to do tomorrow. Village handyman. That's why I didn't risk opening the back balcony doors.

But just looking through the window, I could tell that something wasn't right. Their compost bin had been knocked over, which was weird because they're supposed to be animal proof. They've got these deep stakes that go way down into the ground. And the lids are locked with twin rotating levers. The lid was unlocked now, or wrenched off. I could see it lying near the overturned bin among a carpet of scattered trash.

Then I saw something moving. Just a shadow, I think, on the other side of their house. Rustling bushes along the edge of the tree line. It was gone when I looked up. Probably a raccoon. That was my conscious thought. Raccoons are smart, right? And I've seen them go through trash cans in the heart of Venice Beach. Still, I checked to make sure the balcony was locked, then crept silently downstairs to see about the other doors.

I checked the front first, wondered if I should set the alarm, then realized that I had no idea how. That was when our back porch light went on. I started switching on the inside lights. Actually, I hit the downstairs master switch and squinted hard in the glare.

That must have scared it, the whole bottom floor going from night to day. It was turning to run just as I entered the kitchen. It must have been standing right on the back step.

It was so tall, the top of its head disappeared above the doorway. And broad. I can still picture those massive shoulders, those thick, long arms. Narrow waist, like an upside-down triangle. And no neck, or maybe the neck was bent as it ran away. Same with the head. Slightly conical, and big as a watermelon. I'm also not sure if its hair was black or dark brown. And the long, wide, silvery stripe running down its back. That might have been reflected light.

I wasn't scared. More startled. Like when a car swerves too close. That moment of focus, where you're outside of your body. That was me, watching the thing run through the bushes bordering our yard. I inched up to the door and pressed my face against the glass. That's when I saw, and I'm sure about this, two pinpricks of light through the brush.

It wasn't a reflection from inside. I had my hands cupped around my eyes. And they weren't anything mundane like glistening leaves. I saw those too. These were different, set slightly behind the foliage, at what had to be, maybe, seven or eight feet off the ground. I'm not exaggerating the height. I know all those plants, and where I come up to them.

I stared at the lights for a second or two. They stared back. They blinked. Twice! And then they were gone, darting sideways into darkness as a branch snapped in front. I must have kept leaning against the door for half a minute, fogging up the glass with increasingly deeper breaths.

Then the hand grabbed my shoulder.

Okay, a little melodrama in writing this, and now, I see the humor in what happened next. But, holy crap, when I felt that grip.

Who knew that Dan has such quick reflexes? If he hadn't caught my wrist mid-swing, I might have totally nailed him in the nose.

"Whoa, whoa, whoa!" Dan backed up, dropping my arm, holding up his hands. "What the f—"

I cut his babbling off with my own, trying, failing, to cohesively relate everything I'd seen.

He was looking past me, his repeated "What is it?" answered by my repeated "I don't know." We looked from the brush to the ground, to this line of big footprints that led right back to our doorstep.

As he slid the door open, this wave of cold, stinking air *whoosh*ed in. It was "that" stench, so powerful I almost gagged. Dan grabbed the coconut stabber off the kitchen counter and took a step out onto the porch. I reached for the knife rack, then realized, like an idiot, that Mostar's javelin was resting against the wall in front of me. I probably should have left it there. I nearly stabbed myself in the face as the long wobbly pole caught on the doorway. But I felt like I needed something for protection, especially after what we saw.

Footprints were everywhere. Clear. Sharp. You could see the individual toes, and how they made trails leading from the Perkins-Forster bin, to ours (which was still intact), to the trees, which we were *not* going to investigate!

The smell kept us on the porch, assaulting our noses, nudging us back inside. As Dan twisted the lock, I brought up the burglar alarm. Dan wasn't sure how it worked either. At first, we kept getting these error messages. He finally figured it had something to do with the cracked windows, the ones damaged in the eruption. He's learning how to bypass it now, sitting with his iPad at the kitchen table while I'm waiting for the coffee to brew. It's our new "recycled blend," all the week's grounds pressed together. Mostar's idea. "Gotta make it last." I'm not questioning that anymore. "Watery coffee today's better than none tomorrow."

We should probably just save it. We're jumpy enough as it is. We haven't heard or seen anything for about an hour. Dan thinks we should also set the internal alarms. They're just motion sensors, the same ones the houses use for light and heat. I'm against it. What if I set them off accidentally when I get up to use the hall bathroom? Dan thinks I'm crazy for not sharing the master bath. "So what if you wake me?" He's said that twice. I guess we have bigger problems now.

But do we?

A couple times we considered going over to Mostar's house, but, in addition to not wanting to wake her, we don't want to go back outside.

Too paranoid? "Siri, should we be worried?"

At least we're talking about it openly. And that feels good. Dan doesn't doubt what I saw. He just feels bad he doesn't know more about it. Yeah, he's a total nerd, but a sci-fi nerd, not horror or fantasy, as he's been explaining to me tonight. So many subgenres. All Dungeons & Dragons to me. I will say that I can't believe we've never talked about this before. All these years. This is what it takes? Back and forth, genuine communication. Even if it is just speculating on what's out there.

Where did it come from? How did it get here? And are there more than one? I mean, there has to be, at least in general. We're not talking about magic. This thing's not immortal. There's gotta be more of them to make more of them. But how many? And how have they stayed hidden—no, that's not accurate—hidden enough to remain unproven? How does an animal this big remain off the books for so long?

Dan just learned how to bypass all the cracked windows. Time for bed. I'll put the coffee in the fridge. Gotta make it last.

From Steve Morgan's The Sasquatch Companion.

Some theories surrounding the origin of Sasquatch trace its lineage back to a prehistoric ancestor called *Gigantopithecus*. From teeth and fossilized jawbones recovered in Asia (first discovered by anthropologist G. H. R. von Koenigswald in 1935), it can be hypothesized that this super ape stood as tall as ten feet, weighed up to eleven hundred pounds, and existed as late as 100,000 years ago.

The lack of a complete, or even partial, skeleton has left the posture of this creature to the imagination. Most artistic renderings paint *Gigantopithecus* as a stooped, long-armed, knuckle-walker, while dissenters such as Dr. Grover Krantz postulate erect, bipedal locomotion. In his book *Bigfoot Sasquatch Evidence,* Krantz described his reconstruction of a *Gigantopithecus blacki* skull based on recovered jaw fossils. From this process, he determined that the position of the neck "indicates a fully upright posture."

Not only does Krantz's hypothesis corroborate eyewitness accounts of Sasquatch's humanlike gate, the thesis of *Gigantopithecus*'s terrestrial, rather than arboreal, existence would also explain the physical makeup of Bigfoot's feet. Almost no cast or photograph of a Sasquatch footprint shows the traditional simian gripping digit. The mystery of its absence is solved when we consider that its ancestor *Gigantopithecus,* whose size and weight prevented life in the trees, had little evolutionary need for this feature.

If both hypotheses are correct, that this prehistoric mega-simian was both upright and ground dwelling, it would have stood in good stead to survive the climatic catastrophe that supposedly caused its extinction. According to the fossil record, the last *Gigantopithecus blacki* (the largest of its species) died out roughly 100,000 years ago, when the jungles of South Asia retreated into open grassland. But what if, as Darwin himself lamented, the fossil record is "imperfect"? What if the reason no recent *Gigantopithecus* remains have been discovered in central China is because *Gigantopithecus* simply moved away?

Some might have made it to the mountains of Hubei, where their descendants live today as the Yeren. A second group could have trekked farther west into the Himalayas, becoming what we now refer to as the Yeti. And a third, intrepid offshoot may very well have braved the northern wastes in search of an entirely new world.

For decades, it has been theorized that, like the first humans, *Gigantopithecus* migrated from Asia to America during the last great ice age, across the now-submerged Siberian land bridge of Beringia. This theory has recently run into some controversy, however, as the conventional "inland ice corridor" narrative has been challenged by evidence pointing to an earlier, coastal route. However, corridor or coast, it is logical to assume that these two hominid species reached the new world alongside one another.

This co-migration would explain the many behavioral adaptations that differentiate Sasquatch from other modern great apes. Nocturnal behavior, for example, would have been an excellent way to avoid the sharp eyes, and sharper spearpoints, of daylight hunting *Homo sapiens*. Likewise, their general expertise at stealth in day or night conditions would have been vital in the open, treeless tundra of Beringia. Coupled with swift, energy-efficient legs* and an upright posture to watch for danger, they could have not only survived the Beringian steppe but also the human "blitzkrieg" that annihilated so many other Pleistocene mammals.

The term "blitzkrieg," or "lightning war," comes from the early days of World War II, when the speed and shock of Adolf Hitler's mechanized forces caught an unprepared Europe utterly by surprise. That is why the "blitzkrieg theory" has been used to

* A 2007 study done by David Raichlen of the University of Arizona, Michael Sockol at the University of California, and Herman Pontzer from Washington University in St. Louis "indicate[s] that bipedalism in early, ape-like hominins could indeed have been less costly than quadrupedal knucklewalking."

describe the mass extinctions of large animals that were slaughtered by early humans. Like the Polish cavalry and the French Maginot Line, the wildlife of Europe, Eurasia, and finally the Americas, were caught completely unprepared. Regardless of how much climate is to blame, there is no denying that human hunting contributed to the greatest mass extinction since the death of the dinosaurs. In North America alone, entire species vanished within a thousand years of humanity's arrival.

The ability to elude humans would not have been exclusive to North America's great apes. According to the human paleobiogeography hypothesis, present-day Africa enjoys such a plethora of large animals because their ancestors evolved alongside ours. Taking evolution in steps, adapting to humans before they became fully human, spared Africa the horrors of blitzkrieg. It may also have spared some of the megafauna of southern Asia as well, including a certain giant ape.

We know that proto-humans such as *Homo erectus* began migrating out of Africa somewhere between 1.8 and 2.1 million years ago. They might not have been us, but they were enough like us to sound the alarm for *Gigantopithecus*. By the time fully evolved *Homo sapiens* arrived in Asia, the gentle giants would have had enough warning to avoid us altogether.

Chapter 11

When the event occurred, Bauman was still a young man, and was trapping with a partner among the mountains dividing the forks of the Salmon from the head of Wisdom River. Not having had much luck, he and his partner determined to go up into a particularly wild and lonely pass through which ran a small stream said to contain many beaver. The pass had an evil reputation because the year before a solitary hunter who had wandered into it was there slain, seemingly by a wild beast, the half-eaten remains being afterwards found by some mining prospectors who had passed his camp only the night before.

—President Theodore Roosevelt, *The Wilderness Hunter*

JOURNAL ENTRY #11

OCTOBER 9

We think we have a bear. That was the consensus of the HOA meeting this morning. I went around before breakfast to knock on doors. I tried the Durants again. The same as last time. Vague TV glow from inside, the *zzzzzp-zzzzzp* of the elliptical. No voices this time though, and I am proud of myself for trying the doorbell. And when I got nothing, I even went around to their backyard. The curtains were drawn over their kitchen windows and doors. I rapped on the glass. I called their names. Again, no response. Mostar warned me not to get my hopes up. "They're not leaving Elba." But she didn't explain why and warned me not to waste time wondering.

But how can I not? Are they embarrassed about being dethroned? Hiding in self-imposed exile because their façade has been shattered. I guess that makes sense. The model and the salesman. Smoke and mirrors. I wonder.

Everyone else was receptive though. We all met at the Common House to discuss what happened last night. The Perkins-Forsters saw something too, from their bedroom window. They weren't sure what though, a dark mass at the edge of their porch light. And Bobbi thinks she caught something moving through the trees. Reinhardt didn't see anything. He was fast asleep. So was Mostar. At least we'd been right not to wake her up.

She shocked me at the meeting, what she said about a bear. Earlier, at the door, when we'd knocked to ask her about getting together, I'd told her what I'd seen. I used the word. I made it very clear. And she acknowledged it, at least with her body language. By her nod, her tone, I thought she believed me. So, you can imagine how I felt when I heard her say to the group, "Well, it sounds like we have a bear sniffing around."

Before anyone could respond, she continued by adding that that's all it could be. They're the only animals tall enough to reach the tops of the apple trees. Didn't everyone notice their remaining apples (the ones the deer didn't get) were gone? I had, and I could tell that a few of the others had too. A lot of the fruit trees looked "vandalized." I know there's a better term for it, but so many of the top branches were snapped, the fruit picked clean. Squirrels couldn't have done that kind of damage, and deer, even on their hind legs, couldn't have reached that high. That was Mostar's logic.

She also pointed out that, if anyone was considering raccoons, they might be smart enough to open the compost bins, but certainly aren't strong enough to tear them from their foundations. Everyone seemed satisfied with that. And yes, for just a second, I found myself rethinking everything. I mean, bears are big and hairy. And they have no neck. And when they stand on their hind legs, can't they get pretty tall? It all kind of made sense, and if Mostar was saying it, then maybe Dan and I were just freaking out for no reason. Actually, I was the only one who'd seen anything. I totally expected Dan to agree with Mostar.

But then he spoke up, asking about the tracks. Don't bears have claws or something? I caught a look on Vincent's face, his eyes hitting the floor. Had he already been thinking along those lines?

Reinhardt waved the idea away. "Do any of us really know what bear tracks look like in the wild? And isn't it common for animal prints to change shape over time, grow and morph as the tracks melt then refreeze with passing days. I recall one incident back in Connecticut, when I saw week-old deer prints that looked like elephants had stampeded across my lawn."

That worked on the room, the Boothes and Perkins-Forsters all nodding in agreement. I noticed that Palomino was looking at Mostar, who, again to my surprise, was openly complimenting Reinhardt on his "astute explanation." Palomino looked as puzzled as I felt. I shot Dan a WTF glance and he responded by addressing the crowd.

"Yeah, but we're not talking about snow here. Ash doesn't melt and refreeze. And even if time or wind or whatever could morph them into something else, these tracks are so fresh you can see every . . ."

And suddenly his words trailed off. I didn't understand why at first. I glanced at him. Then I saw that he was looking directly at Mostar. Her eyes were maybe a millimeter wider than normal, and that shake of her head, I don't think anyone else noticed it. All eyes were still on Dan. He just sighed, shrugged, and said, "But . . . yeah . . . now that I'm, like, actually saying it all out loud, you're right, I don't know what bear tracks look like. Sorry, I'm just really tired."

Reinhardt gave a condescending, "Of course, of course," and bowed his head in mock magnanimity.

Mostar immediately followed up with a chuckling, "So we have a fuzzy visitor," and with a gesture out to the tree line, she said, "and we might also have solved the mystery of who killed that wounded mountain lion." At that, Vincent threw up his hands in a silent "eureka" gesture. I heard an affirmative *mmm* from Carmen as well as a grunt from Reinhardt. Mostar, smiling so slightly, continued with, "Which means we've got to be a little more careful, don't you think?"

More approving sounds, more supportive body language. It was crazy, what Dan would call a "Bizarro World" moment. Mostar leading the room.

And then she asked, "So does anyone have bear spray?"

Record scratch.

No one said anything for a tense moment, until Bobbi blurted out "No!" I think her own forcefulness surprised her. But when we all looked over, she continued, "That's so cruel! They're just trying to eat, and you want to mace them?"

Mostar's face didn't change. Serene, diplomatic, I can only imagine the words she was biting down. "I'm just thinking about the cougar," she said calmly, probably with her bones rattling from the strain, "how we don't want anything like that to happen again."

Bobbi argued, "We were surprised. And if we're just more conscientious from now on, watch where we're going, make sure we give the compost bins some space . . ."

Effie looked like she was about to disagree with Bobbi, but as she shifted to speak, Carmen cut in. "Or . . . if we clean out the bins, move the edible waste into the woods, away from the houses, they . . ."

"Then they won't have a reason to come close." Reinhardt completed the thought chain with a very smug expression. No doubt, he was somehow congratulating himself for the plan.

Bobbi looked happily relieved. She grabbed Vincent's hand and turned to Dan. "No one expects you to do that, Danny, we'll all do it ourselves. It's only fair."

Again, no change from Mostar. Okay, maybe just the tiniest tension in her voice? I think I know her well enough by now to see what repressed anger looks like. "Isn't it . . . ," she said slowly, clearly considering each word, "dangerous to feed the bears?"

A pause from the room. Bobbi looked to Vincent for backup. "I think that's only in heavy tourist areas," he said. "More of a long-term, seasonal issue than a one-off situation like ours."

Bobbi added, "And, if you mean 'dangerous' to the bears, I think it's only if they lose their hunting instincts by becoming dependent on humans."

Vincent brought it around with, "Which, again, isn't an issue because our compost can't make more than one meal at best."

"But," again, Mostar treaded lightly, "won't putting that meal out . . . encourage them?"

"For what?" That was Carmen. "Bears aren't aggressive. Not unless you surprise them with their cubs." As if to accentuate the point, she reached past Effie to stroke Palomino's cheek.

Is any of this true? Carmen's explanation for why bears attack, the Boothes' justification for feeding them just this once?

Mostar looked about to burst. I could see the shift, the boiling rise. No more consensus building, no more playing nice. I remember thinking clearly, *Oh shit, here we go.*

But then the craziest thing happened.

Her face. I'd never seen this expression. Drooping, eyes down and to the side, like she was taking a call from someone in her head. This was all new, totally indecipherable. When she refocused on the room, her voice, I'd never heard it so far away.

"All right then, let's get to it."

And her walk afterward. Slow, dragging. Everything about her. Like God had hit the dimmer switch.

She walked right past us, not acknowledging Dan's "Mostar?"

No one seemed to notice her change but us. Why would they? Rushing off with their new, exciting little project. Always looking out for themselves. Our community.

Except Pal. Her worried eyes shifted from me to Mostar as her parents led her away.

"Mostar?" We followed her to her house. I'd called after her this time, and again when she reached the front door. "Mostar, what's the matter?" As she reached for the knob, I put my hand on hers. That seemed to snap her out of it. Eyes again refocused, looking up at me, hand on my cheek.

"I'm sorry, Katie. And you too, Danny." A quick glance around at the dispersing crowd, then hustling us into and through her house to the backyard.

"I'm sorry I didn't warn you first about the 'bear' tactic." We were standing on her back steps now, looking at the tracks across her yard. "I thought it was the best way to reach them. Frame the discussion in something more familiar." She stepped down onto the ash, toward the nearest footprint. The sky had been clear all day and night and these prints were as sharp as when they'd been made. She opened her hands to the first one, looking at us.

"Of course, I believe you, but they wouldn't. Too many mental hurdles. Believing the unbelievable." She shook her head. "Like being warned that the country you've grown up in is about to collapse, that the friends and neighbors you've known your whole life are going to try to kill you . . ." She sighed deeply, hands up to the sky. A flash of anger. "Denial. Comfort zone. Too strong. And who are any of us to judge them?"

I certainly wasn't. I would have given anything to stay in my comfort zone. Even now, when Mostar mentioned the enigmatic trauma of her past. I could have asked about it, just like I could have asked all the other times she'd brought it up. But I didn't. I just stood there, hoping she'd change the subject, then wishing a second later that she hadn't.

"People only see the present through the lenses of their personal pasts." Her lips soured. "Maybe that's my problem too."

She sat down on the steps, focusing on the ash. "Violence. Danger. That's my zone of comfort."

She looked up at us again. "You probably thought I was crazy that first night." Her head jerked toward our house and, I'm guessing, our garden. "But I knew what I was doing. I know how quickly society can burn. I've seen it. I've lived through it. But this . . ."

Eyes back to the footprints. "These may be real." Head up to the trees. "They may be out there."

"They"? Not "it"?

"But how do I know that they're dangerous?" She shook her head. "I don't. They might be friendly. They might just be passing through. And the fight with that big cat. How do I know it wasn't self-defense or that Vincent's not right about scavengers? I don't."

And then I understood what had come over her. And it chilled me.

Doubt.

"Bear spray." She huffed. "That was just the start. You don't know how far I would have taken you all today if the others hadn't stopped me. And maybe they were right to do so." Her eyes, meeting ours. Apologetic? "Do I have any evidence that they're threatening, any proof of anything except"—she blinked, hard—"the lens of my personal past?"

I couldn't take it anymore. I still can't. It's been a couple hours since Mostar told us to go home. We haven't seen her since. Dan's off to work, brushing the Perkins-Forster roof. I'll meet him over there after I've done some gardening. Not much really to do. The seeds are all in, even the rice now, scattered over a square-foot patch with some soil thrown over it. The drip line works great, so there's no need to hand water anything. Not that anything's coming up. Basically, my "gardening" consists of looking over a room full of mud.

I should probably go check on Mostar first. I feel so bad for her, and, yes, scared for the rest of us. We're depending on her, Dan and I, and the whole village, whether they know it or not. We can't have her doubting herself, ending up as lost as the rest of us. We need her to be strong. We need her to be right.

But in this case, with those things out there, what does it mean for all of us if she is?

From my interview with Frank McCray, Jr.

Yeah, I've read *The Sasquatch Companion,* and for the most part, I agree with the official origins story. I think the book makes some good points about being descended from *Gigantopithecus* and the migration from Asia to the Americas. But co-migration? I'm not so sure.

Now, I don't have a shred of evidence to back this up, so if you want to nail me on that, be my guest. But given what happened to Greenloop, what if . . . what if . . . they weren't just co-migrating along with us? What if they were hunting us? Isn't that why we came over? Following the grazing animals across the Beringian land bridge? What if we were stalking the caribou while they were stalking us? It wouldn't discount any of the adaptations, just give them a different purpose. Nocturnal hunting would catch us at our most vulnerable. Camouflage skills are ideal for an ambush. And broad running feet would give them the speed to chase us down.

And when they caught us . . . if the stats are right, then we're talking about three times the strength of a gorilla, which is already six times stronger than us. And that large head, the same conical shape we see on gorillas, that's a sagittal crest, the skull plate that anchors their jaw muscles. Those muscles give a gorilla one of the most powerful bites in the world, thirteen hundred pounds per square inch. Now triple that in a Sasquatch and picture what it would do to our bones.

Maybe they used that bite, and strength, and speed to compete with us for food, or maybe we were the food. You'll have to talk to Josephine Schell about that part. She knows more about carnivorous apes than me.

But for whatever reason, we were the ones, not them, who couldn't wait to flee into this vast new continent. And what if enough time went by for us, this weak little species, to build up our numbers, and our confidence, to eventually challenge the larger primates for dominance of North America? What if that's why they've remained so elusive, because they knew what would happen if they stepped out of the shadows? They saw what we did to the saber-toothed cat, the dire wolf, the giant bulldog bear. They saw what we did to enough of them to realize that they were on the wrong side of evolution.

At least until Rainier.

Josephine Schell thinks I'm going too far. She's all about ecosystems and caloric needs, and maybe she's right. But maybe there was also some latent gene that woke up in those creatures when they stumbled across Greenloop and found themselves facing a herd of cornered, isolated *Homo sapiens*. Maybe some instinct told them it was time to swap evolution for devolution, reach back to who they were to reclaim what was theirs.

Chapter 12

Violence, as unpleasant as it may seem, fulfills a necessary social function in chimpanzees.

—Andrew R. Halloran, *The Song of the Ape: Understanding the Languages of Chimpanzees*

JOURNAL ENTRY #12

OCTOBER 10

So much has happened. Where do I even begin?

That idiocy with the compost. Spreading it up on the ridge? I watched them all day. Vincent and Bobbi, chatting giddily over buckets of slop. The Perkins-Forsters, Effie doing most of the heavy lifting. Carmen with her rubber gloves and white paper flu mask. Germophobe. Palomino sticking close, apprehensively looking around. At least they only took up the top portions, the stuff that still looked like food. The bottom, newly minted dirt, we'll need for the garden. Maybe they were thinking that, or were just too lazy to haul it up. I bet you that was the case with Reinhardt.

I busted him taking his burden to the Common House bin. "Busted" is the word because of the guilty look on his face. I watched him hoof his office trash pail (doesn't he own a bucket?) across the driveway to the Common House. I feel a little mean doing what I did, but the way he looked around suspiciously . . .

I just had to knock on the window. That priceless freeze on his face when he saw me. It was worth it for the follow-up fake smile, and the ridiculous pantomime. I think he was trying to relate that the steep incline of the ridge was bothering his hip or something. Yes, I have seen him walk with some discomfort, but now, as he shuffled back to his house, his irregular step was a full-on limp.

Weenie.

I thought Mostar would get a good laugh over that. I thought she might need some cheering up. But when I got to the house, I noticed that the lights were on in her workshop. I'm sure I could have gone in, asked what she was doing, but after what happened that morning, she didn't seem to want company.

And that was confirmed at dinner. She always cooked for us, either at her place or ours. That night she was MIA. I thought about going over again, and even asked Dan if I should. He responded matter-of-factly, "If she wanted to see us, she would."

Dan and I didn't eat together either. He was too busy trying to get all the windows re-alarmed. He wasted half the day on the glass, trying to seal the breaks with packing tape. It turned out the real problem was the screens. The connections had been loosened during the quake. He cursed not having a soldering gun, or any real tools for that matter.

Can you believe that? No tools, anywhere! I asked around, the Perkins-Forsters, the Boothes. Nobody. I mean, I guess it makes sense when you're supposed to have a handyman on call 24/7. But now. I did talk to Mostar about maybe using her 3-D printer, which Dan thought was a great idea. But Mostar reminded us that her only raw material was a polymer-silicon mix. Glass tools? Dead end. So Dan made do with tape, paper clips, and, of all things, glue with a King Kong–ish ape on the front.

Looking at the ape, watching him work, it kind of dawned on me how vulnerable our house, all houses, really are. They're not built for physical safety. That's what cops are for. I remember Matt, Dan's roommate sophomore year. He was a history major. I remember him talking about how rich Romans could afford to live in comfortable homes because they were protected by army forts down the road. But when the empire fell, those ruined forts got built back up into castles. Slit windows. Few doors. Security was everything. Matt always talked about this French movie where a medieval knight travels forward in time to the modern age, and is horrified at what's happened to his castle. "Who put all these windows in? We're defenseless!" I was thinking that as Dan tried to re-alarm all our windows.

And I wondered, without telling him, what an alarm would actually accomplish. It's just a signal, a call for muscle that can't get to us even if they heard. Maybe the siren itself will do some good. Scare them off, hopefully.

Dan must think so, the way he worked today. I did force him to eat something, a bowl of Bobbi's puffed quinoa. He was so frustrated by then, almost getting in a fistfight with the upstairs window in the guest bathroom. It's really small, and against a flat wall. No way for them to climb up or squeeze through. He wasn't listening by that point, getting obsessive about "finishing the job." When he started cursing it out, I put my food down and made him take a break. After "dinner" and a hot shower, he admitted that I was right. I was also right about him heading off to bed. I promised to wake him if I saw anything.

And for a few hours, I didn't. The sky darkened, the house lights went on, then off as our neighbors turned in. I sat at the desk in my office, going over the village's collective food list. The Boothes and Perkins-Forsters both asked me to make ration books for them. They weren't shy about their ages or levels of physical exertion. Reinhardt was the only holdout. Maybe he's too ashamed to get that personal, or maybe he just figures he's got enough fat reserves to outlast us all. I'm not being mean here, just stating a fact. Technically he could outlast us all, because everyone's pantries are about as shallow as ours. I'm trying not to think about what we might all look like by January, living on crumbs and the last licks of olive oil. I'm depending on the garden more than ever now, and hoping against hope that Bobbi's new seed rice will sprout. Does rice need water to grow? Pictures always have it in flooded paddies. Did I totally mess up by sticking it in the ground? I really don't know what I'm doing.

I also keep telling myself that, no matter what, it's great that everyone's starting to cooperate. Trading food for Dan's handiwork, letting me go through all their stuff. People want to help, they want to work together. You can't deny that kind of progress, and I was starting to feel pretty good about it, sitting there at my desk, when I noticed the first motion light flick on.

The Durants. I saw it a second before a shadow moved in between their house and the Boothes'. Then the shadow took form as the thing slouched up the slope into view.

It looked just like what I'd seen the night before, and it was definitely not a bear!

Broad, powerful shoulders, long, muscular limbs. I saw fingers. Four and a thumb! Don't get me wrong though. It was not human! The size, the fur, the head! From the back, that huge neckless head almost looked like a helmet. And when it swung that head toward me, I got a good, clear look at its face. Hairless, shiny dark skin. A jutting jaw, lipless, under flat, flaring nostrils. A pronounced brow, shading deeply recessed eyes.

I don't think it could see me. I'd switched off the desk lamp the second I saw the Durants' porch light switch on. It wasn't even looking at our house, more of a slow scan, left to right, across the whole neighborhood. Its movement was smooth, casual. Unlike last night, the motion light hadn't scared it away.

I whispered, "Dan." Then, a little louder. "Dan!" My response was a disturbed, hoggish snore. I got up slowly, afraid that it might detect the sudden motion, and walked swiftly but quietly back to the bedroom. Dan was dead asleep when I shook him. "Dan, Dan, wake up. It's here!"

He groaned slightly, started with, "Wh . . . ," then his eyes snapped open and he practically shot out of bed.

We spoke in whispers: "Where?" "The Durants'." "Where!" "Look!"

It was gone by then. I pointed to the empty spot on the slope. "Right there, it was . . ."

"There!" Dan's finger pointed farther up the ridge, amongst the trees. Right where the Boothes had dumped their compost. Something was moving up there. Dark shapes in the dim porch light. More than one. We could see branches moving, a brush of fur. I caught sight of a full body, with lighter fur than the rest, auburn. Then it disappeared.

I suddenly remembered and said, "iPad!" Dan grabbed his tablet off the night table. I didn't think about the light from the screen, how it illuminated both of our faces.

Eyes. At least three beady sets. They'd been darting around, attracted by each new porch light. But when we turned the iPad screen to our faces, all three turned on us. I wanted to duck, but instead told Dan to zoom in. The image was too grainy, especially on video setting. I still can't believe we don't own a real camera! They stared at us for a second, we stared back. Then a bright funnel spread out between our house and Mostar's. Another one behind us!

We turned for the back window. We should have gone on the porch. Too "chickenshit," as Frank would say. We did catch a view of it crossing from Mostar's yard to ours. This one had patches of gray fur. The muzzle. Down the swinging arms. The skin was lighter than the first one I'd seen, and spotted. Age? I still don't know. But I'm pretty sure it, she, was female. I haven't mentioned this before, mainly because I didn't realize I was looking at them, but the other one I'd seen had a large, dangling scrotum, noticeable even across the village. This one though, she didn't have anything between her legs, and I could clearly see small pancaked breasts sagging on her hairless chest.

We only spied her for a second, not enough time to get the iPad up. She ducked under the balcony. Then a scraping, popping noise, and the lid from our compost bin flew across our yard like a Frisbee. We could hear grunts now. Low, quick.

Hm-mhmh-hm.

Rummaging through our bin, probably frustrated because we haven't been here long enough to leave much. We listened for a few more seconds. Dan looked at me questioningly, making a two-fingered walking motion with his hand. Should we head downstairs? Just close enough to get some video? The porch light would catch it perfectly, and the burglar alarm was still on. I was considering it when this sharp, loud growl pulled us back to the front window.

The Common House. There were two of them. Males. They were smaller than the first one I'd seen, a little shorter and narrower across the shoulders. Younger? They were also identical. Twin One and Twin Two. Brothers? Do brothers fight like that?

Because they were fighting! One had a hand on the bin's lid. Two tried to nudge him aside. One snarled and with bright, bared teeth, he bodily shoved Two away. Two snarled back and charged, grabbing the other side of the bin. One gave a gurgling bark noise and slapped or sideways punched Two in the face, knocking him back before turning on him with a loud growl. Canine fangs biting down hard into Two's shoulder. And hanging on despite the three quick punches to the ear.

I could see the blood, bright red in the Common House light. Ironically, the light almost killed our view, catching the ash as their tussling threw up a thick gray cloud. It would have been cartoonish, this flurry of flailing limbs, if it hadn't been so utterly terrifying. I've seen a few fights on Animal Planet and once in our neighborhood a couple of dogs got into it. But in real life, and with this much power. The size, the rage. I don't know if I'm imagining it, but I think the ground was shaking!

One rolled off Two, kicking him in the face, then rose to a crouch. Two mirrored his stance. They circled each other for a few seconds. Teeth bared, arms raised. Their shrieks, high, chattering calls. They lunged at each other, swiping and dodging. One finally caught Two, biting him in the stomach. Two howled, bashing One repeatedly with hammer blows to the back. Thumping, bass drum impacts.

Then this *ROAR*! From the darkness, rolling across the village like a wave. The windows *did* shake this time. I'm sure of it. And from out of the gloom, this hulking mass. As tall as the first male I'd seen. Taller, I'm sure. And female! Wider hips. Breasts. Breast! One had been torn off. I'm not making this up. I checked the iPad footage later. Torn or bitten and scarred over. Her whole body was scarred. Claw marks, four jagged lines down the side of one thigh. Scrapes across both forearms. A bite mark, from a bear, maybe, or another one of them, in her left shoulder, like the kind One had given Two.

One must have regretted that now, when this new woman, the mother? The alpha? Isn't that the right term? When she smashed him on the side of the face with her hand. He went sprawling, from the blow or just fear, rolling to a squat at her feet. Two didn't need the blow to assume that position. He shrunk as she turned to him. She roared again, at both of them, and raised her arms for another strike. They cowered, heads down, with these little, doglike whimpers.

I must have done something. My body or just my head, some movement in the iPad's glow, because suddenly that giant, scarred nightmare head whipped up in my direction. Her eyes locked on mine. And she saw me. I know she did. She reacted. Her lips pulled back into a growl.

And then a burglar alarm.

It was coming from the Boothes' house, and as Dan and I looked over, we saw another one dashing up the slope behind the house. Its legs seemed much longer than the others, reminding me, now that I look back, of the one that chased me that day. Because now I know I was chased. I know it was one of them. This guy? Because it was a guy, I could see. The first one to arrive? A scout? These are all thoughts I'm having now. Not then.

At that moment I was just shocked at how quickly the other ones had fled. Because when Dan and I turned back to the Common House, we saw that the other three were gone. All of them. All the movement up and around the village, even behind us. We checked the back window as well. The older one scrounging in our compost bin. Gone.

We waited. Watched. Listened. We didn't move for a full five minutes, which feels a *lot* longer than it sounds on paper. Silence. Stillness. One by one the outside motion lights timed out. And just as I was mulling over the idea of going outside to check on our compost bin, Dan grabbed my arm and said, "Mostar?"

There she was, all five determined feet of her, trudging across the driveway toward the Common House. She stopped at the black and gray patchwork from the fight, stooping as if to examine something. She looked over at the compost bin, turned back out toward the ridge. Hands on hips. Placid.

Dan muttered, "What the hell . . ."

But I knew. I could see that all the house lights were still on, and a few people—Reinhardt and the Boothes—were staring at her from their upstairs windows. I told Dan, "She's letting us all know it's okay to come out. She's calling a meeting."

We were the first ones to reach her, but not by much. The Boothes, robe and slippers, came jogging out toward us. So did Reinhardt (in a kimono!). Carmen was the only one from her house. Effie and Pal watched from the living room window.

"Did you see them?" I'm not sure who said that first, Bobbi or Carmen, but Dan answered with, "Oh yeah, we saw them!" and before anyone could respond, he added, "Those were definitely not bears!"

Whatever Vincent was going to say, Dan's words shut him up. Carmen too went into reset mode. Mostar kept quiet, maybe waiting to see how that truth would land. She might have regretted it a second later when Reinhardt raised a questioning finger. "I'm sure," he said in this very professorial tone, "that we all *think* we saw something other than an ursine family, but . . . let me remind everyone that given this poor light, the stress we're all under, the human mind's ability to fabricate—"

"Oh, come on!" Dan cut him off angrily. "Dude, you totally saw that! Them!" He looked at all of us, and while Mostar again kept silent, I mumbled, "I saw them, pretty clear. I think I know . . ."

I could have been a little more forceful. Me and confrontation. But at least I tried to stick up for Dan, even if it didn't work on Reinhardt.

"You *think*"—eyes glimmering, hand out; Reinhardt looked so smug—"*think* you saw, and that is, indeed, the issue when confronted with an arcane situation . . ."

"Oh Jesus Christ." Dan took off running for the house. "Wait!" he called over his shoulder. "Just wait!"

Reinhardt didn't. "In the interest of full transparency, I will admit that my limited expertise terminates at anthropology"—he bowed his head slightly toward Carmen—"but haven't there been recorded cases of mass hallucinations?"

Carmen took the bait and recounted something about a town in the Midwest during World War II where people blamed a bad smell on an "anesthetic prowler." And, also about a school in Ireland in 1979 where kids all thought they were getting sick at the same time and ambulances were called and ultimately it turned out to be mass hypochondria.

"Exactly," Reinhardt said with a tip of his imaginary hat to Carmen, and then his eyes went wide with another newly remembered epiphany. "Wasn't there a story recently from India? Residents of a Delhi slum believed reported attacks of a mysterious giant 'ape-man.' But when the authorities declared it a case of mass psychosis, no new attacks were reported."*

I looked at . . . to . . . Mostar. C'mon, we need you! That was my expression. But she responded with a blank look and the slightest out turn of her hands. No, you go. That's what I took from it. I couldn't understand. Still doubtful? I muttered, "Well, uh . . . that's . . . like, smelling something and feeling something, right? But we all saw . . . with our eyes . . ."

* In 2001, reports of a "kala bandar" (Hindi) or "monkey man" began to terrorize residents of East Delhi, India. These reports were later debunked as a case of "mass hysteria."

I'm such a wimp. Thank God, Dan came to the rescue.

"Look!" He was running back with the iPad. "Look at this!"

And we did. There was the fight, clear and steady. He'd even rested the tablet on the windowsill. No argument from anyone. Not even from Reinhardt. Silent, defeated, he seemed to shrink as Carmen, of all people, switched sides. "They're real." It came out shocked, but Vincent's "Bigfoot is real!" was definitely excited. Bobbi even smiled, grabbing his hand, and when Carmen waved for Effie and Pal to join us, I took the whole mood as relief that we weren't all crazy.

Mostar must have interpreted it the same way, nodding at us and speaking for the first time. "There is no denying that these creatures exist." And the chatter started, everyone talking at once, sharing stories they've heard. It felt cathartic, to admit what we all suspected, to make it "okay" by group agreement. I admit I was kind of taken up in the moment, re-watching the video with Effie and Pal. "Look at them"—that was Carmen—"look how big they are!"

"Do you remember?" That was Effie to her wife. "That time before we were married, when we were camping by Rimrock Lake and we smelled—"

"Now that they're real," Mostar cut her off, "what are we going to do about them?"

The chatter hushed. Everyone looked at her quizzically, including Dan and me.

Carmen asked, "What do you mean?"

And Mostar, kind of theatrically, reached into her robe for what looked like a sharpened stick. It was about a foot long, bamboo, and angled to a point at both ends. "We're going to need a lot of these." And she tapped the stick, the spike, against the bamboo growing behind her. "Hundreds maybe, but if we work together, and place them in a deep circle around the village . . ."

"Why?" Vincent asked, knowing, I suspect, but needing to hear it out loud.

"A defensive perimeter," Mostar answered, waving the spike

like a baton. "If they try to cross and one of them steps on one of these . . ."

"You want to hurt them?" Bobbi looked like she'd been slapped.

"Just deter them," Mostar responded calmly.

"That's what the burglar alarm did!" answered Bobbi.

"This time," Mostar volleyed back. "But now they know it's just harmless noise. And why do you think your alarm went off in the first place?" And to the group, she said, "They were trying to get in!"

Vincent, stepping up next to Bobbi, said, "Maybe they were just curious."

Bobbi grabbed her husband, rallying to his point. "And you want to hurt them!"

"So they don't try to hurt us," Mostar answered with supreme confidence, all her previous doubt gone. "You heard what they did to that big cat." A glance in our direction, then, "You all saw what they just did to each other." As if to accentuate the point, she stooped to pick up a section of beaded ash. Holding it up to us, mashing it between thumb and forefinger, we could all see the red paste. "They've just shown us how violent they can be."

Bobbi countered. "Not against us." And this time Carmen came in with, "Why do you have to assume that they're evil?"

Mostar took a breath before speaking. "Carmen, they're not good or evil. They're just hungry." A nod to the darkness. "The berries are all gone, and the fruit from our trees, and your compost, which probably kept them here instead of following the other animals . . . assuming they haven't already eaten those animals."

Vincent shrugged defiantly. "So, then there's nothing left."

Mostar looked us over. "There isn't?"

Nobody spoke. I felt Dan's grip tighten.

Mostar was clearly hoping the group would come to this conclusion on its own. And maybe they would have if Reinhardt hadn't spoiled it. "In point of fact"—he stepped into the circle—

"we may be in a more advantageous situation than if these visitors were, in fact, ursine." He must have been waiting for the opening, crafting his lecture while the rest of us debated. "After all, bears are omnivorous while . . . and I confess my knowledge reservoir of primatology is even shallower than psychoanalysis . . ."

And he gave a chortle of faux humility. Has anyone ever deserved more to be punched in the face?

"But I seem to recall that most hominids are herbivorous in nature." Mostar made a sound and he bowled over her with his pontificating. "Great apes! Gorillas and orangutans subsist only on fruits and vegetable matter. In fact"—I could actually see when the cartoon lightbulb appeared above his head—"if I'm not mistaken, one anthropoid species, the bonobos of southern central Africa, are matriarchal pacifists by nature."

I couldn't believe what came out of his mouth next. He actually looked over at the Perkins-Forsters and said, "And correct me if I'm wrong, but don't said bonobos even practice a form of inter-female sexual diplomacy?"

Was it the shock that kept Effie and Carmen silent? Or were they, like the Boothes, and Reinhardt himself, just so damn determined to hold on to anything to keep the fear away? Ego-defense mechanism. Reinhardt continued his classroom speech with, "In fact, since we know nothing of these hominids' social order, or their method of interaction, accidentally injuring one of them might precipitate the very regrettable incident we seek to avoid."

From my interview with Frank McCray, Jr.

Are you serious? Why would any of them have a gun? Just consider your question. Why does anyone have a gun? Barring this unique circumstance . . .

He nods to the weapons around us.

. . . there're only two legitimate reasons. Once you take out the toys and treason, the man-boys who want to play real life Call of Duty and the domestic terrorists watching for "black helicopters," you're only left with hunting and home defense.

Reasonable, practical, and completely incompatible with life in Greenloop.

When it comes to hunting . . . well . . . I can't judge who I used to be. Like my former neighbors up there, I somehow thought I was superior to deer shooters because I chose fish over meat, and chose Apple Pay over bullets.

And as far as protecting my house . . . our houses, from a break-in . . . who's gonna do that? And how? Greenloop is completely off the beaten track, the ultimate cu-de-sac, with a gated private road, and alarms to both private security and county cops.

So, unless you're pulling off a *Mission Impossible* airlift, or you're some hermit meth head who can't believe his luck, Greenloop was probably the safest place in America. That was one of Tony's selling points. That's why none of the houses have surveillance cameras. Or dogs. Did you notice that? No dogs? The HOA guidelines forbid them. I remember thinking how strange that was when I first moved in. I mean, wouldn't it make sense for those people to be the ultimate dog lovers? Problem is, they might scare away the wildlife, which, again, is another reason we all moved up there.

It all goes back to the core philosophy of Greenloop: People are the problem. Nature is your friend.

Chapter 13

At midnight, Bauman was awakened by some noise, and sat up in his blankets. As he did so his nostrils were struck by a strong, wild-beast odor, and he caught the loom of a great body in the darkness at the mouth of the lean-to. Grasping his rifle, he fired at the vague, threatening shadow, but must have missed, for immediately afterwards he heard the smashing of the underwood as the thing, whatever it was, rushed off into the impenetrable blackness of the forest and the night.

—President Theodore Roosevelt, *The Wilderness Hunter*

From my interview with Senior Ranger Josephine Schell.

Dr. Reinhardt was right. He didn't know jack about primates. All apes practice some kind of faunivory, which is a fancy way of saying they eat other animals. Apes have all the biological hardware to be predators. Canine teeth for gripping and ripping flesh. Forward-facing eyes for locking on a moving target. And a brain designed to outthink food trying to get away. I heard a theory once that if aliens ever do come calling, they may very well be hostile, because the same brains that mastered spaceflight learned to think by hunting.

Different primates have different preferences, of course, with gorillas and orangutans tilting sharply toward the fruit and veggie side. That's why they have such big bellies. Their guts are packed with plant matter, which takes a long time to break down.

That's not how eyewitnesses describe Sasquatch. What they do describe, consistently, is an omnivorous diet.

Fish seems to be their main source of protein. One story has them stealing drying fish from a cabin, another where they were digging for clams. And the guy in that movie who took the lie detector test. He says it grabbed his fishing net. With all the rivers we have here, all the salmon and trout, they probably had more than enough fuel for those gigantic bodies of theirs. Until Rainier's eruption drove them from their traditional fishing spots. Throw in the bad berry harvest and you've got a biological imperative to adapt.

She refers back to the map, specifically the spots where dead deer were found.

You know that old saying, "If you can't be with the one you love, love the one you're with?" In the animal world, it's called "prey switching," where a predator ends up developing a preference for a certain food source simply because it's more abundant than their traditional prey.

I think that's what happened with the deer we found and it must have just happened or else we would have been finding these bone fragments for centuries. Rainier must have been their ecological tipping point, which has to make you wonder what was ours.

You know that's how we got started, right? We were the first apes to start cracking bones. Way back in Africa, when the first skittish little scavengers climbed out of the trees. Using rocks to get at the marrow, realizing what a caloric jackpot meat was. A lot less energy to convert animal into animal than vegetable into animal. And the brain boost we got from that bonanza. Tools, language, cooperation. You can see the incentive for all the advances that make us human. More meat. Bigger brains. Bigger brains. More meat. I wonder what it looked like, when we first tasted fresh blood. What did we think? What did we feel? That moment when everything changed. From scavenger to predator. Hunted to hunter.

JOURNAL ENTRY #12 [CONT.]

The knocking interrupted Reinhardt.

It was clear and consistent, so much so that I think a few of us thought it might be mechanical. A loose pipe or maybe, just for a second, an approaching vehicle. But as we all quieted down to listen, I could definitely make out the undertone of animal grunts.

Carmen stated the obvious. "Do you hear that? It's them."

thock-thock-thock

I couldn't see anything. Nobody could. They must have been farther away. Among the trees or on the other side of the ridge.

Effie asked, "What do you think it means?"

No one answered at first. Not even Reinhardt.

The more we listened, the more we could make out a single source. A branch against a trunk? I'm not sure if the grunts were meant for us. Something about them; soft, low, chaotic, like they didn't want their voices to drown out the knocks. That's, at least, what I think now. I didn't have a clue at the time.

I glanced at Dan, who was equally perplexed, and then at Mostar, who seemed to be waiting for something. For the knocking to end, or change? I didn't ask.

"That's communication!" Vincent surprised me. I would have expected it from Reinhardt. I looked over at him, the gasbag prof, who was, amazingly, yielding the floor.

Vincent stepped out of the circle, head craned toward the trees. "They're trying to talk to us!"

"They're friendly," said Reinhardt, who, I think, was trying to get a jump on the next possible conclusion. "They must be! Communication implies intelligence, which implies an innate desire for peace."

Is that true?

The Boothes seemed to believe it, or wanted to, along with

Carmen and Effie. But Palomino, she kept her eyes locked on Mostar's dubious face.

"Maybe we should . . . ," she started to say, but Vincent cut her off with, "Hello! Hello there! Friends! We're friends!"

Bobbi let go of his hand and lightly slapped him on the shoulder. "They don't speak English!" she scolded playfully, to which Reinhardt yelled out, "Bonsoir, mes amis!" The Boothes and the Perkins-Forsters laughed. Vincent, grinning from ear to ear, snatched Mostar's bamboo spike.

"Everyone, shhh," he whispered, smacking it against the wall of the Common House. Three hits, then paused.

The knocking stopped. We all froze. The grunts grew louder. Vincent beamed. The knocking resumed, faster this time, louder.

THOCKTHOCKTHOCKTHOCK

"Okay, yes, yes!" Vincent whispered to us and banged back faster with his pole. I heard him whisper "Friends, friends, friends" as he hammered the Common House wall. After a dozen rapid strikes, he stopped. They responded in kind.

Vincent waited for a crazy tense three count, then gave it another few whacks. Nothing came back. I could see the sweat beading up on his forehead, his glasses beginning to fog. Bobbi saw it too because she took them off, wiped them gently on her sleeve, and wrapped her arms around her husband.

We waited, we listened. Silence.

How long before someone spoke? Time really does crawl in those moments. But it couldn't have been that long before Vincent looked back at us with earnest surprise. "We did it."

Did he permit the group to accept this outcome or did they permit him? Once he said it, the sighs that broke out, the sudden choked sob from Bobbi. "We did it!" A hissing whisper, squeezing her husband's waist, shutting eyes that sparkled at the edges. "You, you did it!"

Carmen hugged her daughter with one arm and reached out to touch her wife with the other. And Reinhardt, nodding as if he approved, gave Vincent a hand-rolling salute.

From my interview with Senior Ranger Josephine Schell.

Wood knocking seems to be pretty common in eyewitness encounters and no one knows for sure what it means. Likewise, no one knows how a wood-knocking response will be received. Language is tricky, even among our species.

She holds up her rounded thumb and index finger.

In this country it's "a-okay," in Brazil it's "you're an asshole." And when you include the extra layer of inter-species contact . . .

She raises her head slightly, showing a discolored scar under her chin.

Six years old, over at my cousin's one time, I didn't know their old beagle would take my staring contest as a challenge. And for all we know, wood knocking denotes a challenge, which Vincent Boothe unwittingly accepted.

JOURNAL ENTRY #12 [CONT.]

The mood shifted; it was suddenly like a cocktail party. Everyone hugging and chatting, and a few people, Bobbi and Effie, wiping droplets from the corners of their eyes. Reinhardt was the first to leave. Beaming proudly for some reason, he placed a hand on Vincent's shoulder and said, "Tomorrow, I believe we should begin collaboration on a paper detailing this historic anthropological discovery."

Vincent, who was a little overwhelmed by his own achievement, just nodded. "Yes, yes, by all means, tomorrow . . . thank you!" And with a dramatic bow, Reinhardt stumped off.

"We should all have dinner tomorrow night!" That was Bobbi, correcting herself with, "Tonight!" It was after midnight by then. "Here in the Common House, all together. We need a healing moment."

Carmen echoed, "We do, that's brilliant! Like when we first welcomed them!" And, smiling at me, she gave Bobbi a big hug.

"Tonight"—Bobbi waved back at us—"see you tonight."

Carmen called, "Thank you, Vincent," as he, arm around Bobbi, headed home.

I watched them a little ways, her head on his shoulder, hand rubbing his back, before Carmen's next conversation caught my ear. She was talking to Dan about coming over tomorrow to "muck out" one of their two biodigester tanks. I knew Dan, "new Dan," would totally be into it. A gross demanding job that only he, the village handyman, could do. He practically did the Superman stance, hands on hips, with, "Don't worry, I got this." And as I turned, Carmen made sure to invite me over to pick out their payment. At that moment Effie, who clearly had something to say, touched Carmen's arm. "Oh, and we were thinking," that was Carmen, "if it's all right, could Palomino volunteer to help in the garden?"

I said, "Sure," then added that there really wasn't much to do at this point since nothing had come up. Effie spoke for herself this time. "Maybe you could dig for worms. I've heard they aerate the soil and their castings make great fertilizer."

As I gave a positive shrug, Carmen added, "Palomino would love to do that. In fact, it was her idea."

I think, if it had been any other time, she might have matched the enthusiasm of her moms. But at that moment, all that little girl could do was dart her head around like a nervous squirrel. From the trees, to the spaces between the homes, to Mostar, where her eyes lingered just long enough for contact. And that contact, Mostar's face. The exact same expression she wore at the end of our first emergency meeting. "So, this is what I'm working with."

She didn't say that out loud. Instead, as we walked home, her only comments were, "I hope Vincent's right. I hope they all are." Now it was her turn to scan the ridgeline. "You two should get some sleep. You'll need it. And I'll need you later tomorrow after you're done in the garden and," to Dan, "shoveling shit." I should note that she was gesturing to us with the bamboo spike. "And if you need me, I'll be . . ."

We didn't need to ask. In her workshop sawing more bamboo. And that eventually, we'd have to join her, and that, probably, if no one else came on board, that perimeter of stakes would only encircle our two houses. Nothing had to be said, with her or between us.

Dan and I didn't talk about what had just happened, or if we believed in what Vincent had done. We didn't talk about anything on our way home except Dan's new and dangerous job. And I really was convinced it was dangerous. I mean, crawling around in other people's feces? Who knows what kind of germs would be crawling around with him? Isn't human sewage dangerous? Doesn't it have to be treated? Heavily? What if he got an infected scratch? What if he just inhaled something?

I can't believe I did that, bombarding Dan with worries. But just like with the solar panels, I didn't care about looking like a nag or about his feelings, or about anything except keeping my partner safe. And he took it, all the way back to the house. No argument, no obvious ego wounds. Nothing but acknowledgment and, I believe, genuine acceptance of my argument.

Until, about two steps from our front door, he suddenly turned on me and stuck out his hand for silence. My heart jumped. I thought I'd gone too far. I was swirling between surprise, fear, and, yes, sudden anger at being shushed. Then I realized that his eyes weren't on me. He was looking out toward the night, listening.

I shut my mouth, opened my ears.

thmp

That's what he must have heard. Soft and dull. Nothing like the sharp hard knocking from before.

thmp

There it was again. A little louder. Closer?

Now I was looking out too. Up to the trees, over the rooftops.

I saw it from the corner of my eye. Small and fast. Coming down in a puff of gray dust near Reinhardt's house. I took Dan's hand, led him out to where I saw the impact. Although I didn't know it was an impact until I spied the other one right in front of us. It had landed about halfway between Mostar's and the Common House, lying in a "crater," which is the only way to describe it.

You know those pictures from the moon, the ringed holes? That's what we were looking at, except this hole had a grapefruit-sized lump half-buried in the middle. We knelt to examine it as another *thmp* sounded on the other side of the driveway. Dan dug in the dust and held up a jagged, roundish rock.

Two more *thmps* sounded, one far, one so close we both jumped, then a crisper *thnk* as a third rock hit and rolled off the Common House roof.

Then a loud *KSHHH* as someone's window shattered.

And suddenly the sprinkle became a torrent.

A *thmpthnkthnkthmpthmpthmpthnk* of rocks all around us, crashing down amid the rising howls from the darkness.

"INSIDE!" My voice over Dan's shoulder, turning him, pushing him, running through the hail.

I don't know how we managed to make it home without being hit. Were they aiming for us? Could they see us? They must. One or two at least. Purposeful shots.

I remember the whistle. I couldn't have imagined that. The cliché I've always heard of a bullet speeding past someone's ear. This version wasn't so much a high whistle as a deep *whoffff*. Right past me, bouncing off the front doorframe just before we jumped inside.

Chapter 14

Most accounts tell of giant boulders being hurled against the cabin, and say some even fell through the roof . . .

—Fred Beck, *I Fought the Apemen of Mt. St. Helens*

JOURNAL ENTRY #12 [CONT.]

A rock struck the door as I slammed it. I can still feel my hand vibrating. Dan pulled me upstairs. I shouted, "Lights! Get the lights!" I meant from the master switches at the top of the stairs, not the central control from his iPad. But that's what he tried to do, halfway up the stairs. He stopped to fumble with his tablet. "No . . . not . . . ," but he'd already dropped it. The glass face cracked as it hit the naked wooden step.

"Go!" I yelled as the house shuddered, kneeing him in the butt as he swiped up the iPad. "Go! GO!"

We ran into the bedroom just as the balcony doors took a direct hit. I yelped at the loud hollow *BOP* and turned to protect my face from the glass. But the doors stayed together. Like our iPad, and maybe our car's windshield, the plate just bulged in a spiderweb of sparkling cracks. I had maybe a moment of shock, gratitude, then I yelled, "Drapes!"

We split up, yanking the cloth covers together, then turned to do the same with the front windows.

I can't believe I did that. Hesitating for just a few seconds. But the view of our entire village, rocks sailing in from all directions, bouncing off roofs, kicking up ash geysers.

If I hadn't stopped to look.

If Dan hadn't noticed.

"Lookou—" His voice, his weight. The force of his shoulder in my chest. We hit the floor just as the window above us shattered. I felt little cold flakes pepper my neck and ear as the baseball-sized rock bounced across our bed.

Panting on the floor, Dan picked glass from my hair. "Don't move." The warmth of his breath, the pressure of his fingertips. "Here . . . ow . . . here . . . here's one." Maybe a minute, maybe longer, before it felt safe to move. Squat-walking to the bathroom, the only glass-free space. As I flicked off the light, Dan found the master switch on his iPad. I noticed some of the screen's finger smudges were red. "I'm fine." He showed me a tiny bubble on the end of his forefinger. "It's not from the screen." That had been the *ow* when he'd checked me for shards. Now it was my turn, crouching in the shower with the curtains drawn, using the flashlight from my iPhone, looking for any sparkling hints.

thmpthnkscrkthmp

That was our soundtrack, a symphony of impact sounds that, after a couple of minutes, we could pick out like instruments in an orchestra.

Thmp. The ash.

Thnk. A roof.

Thomp. Our roof.

Ksssh. A window.

And one big, crazy *kssssh . . . weeeeueeeeeueeeeeueeeee*. A car, its alarm wailing like a wounded animal.

Then footsteps. In the house! I looked at Dan, who reached for his stabber that wasn't there. He'd left the coconut opener downstairs on the kitchen table, just like I'd left the javelin in the bedroom.

Time to get it? I wondered for a second before rapid strides clattered up the stairs.

Then a frantic banging on the bedroom door.

"Kids?" Muffled shouting. Mostar!

"Kids! Are you in there?"

We practically flew to the bedroom door; it was so dark we nearly felt her arms before actually seeing her. Shaking, all of us, on our knees, crouching in a group hug.

A second, a sob, then Mostar breaking to grab a face with each hand.

"Danny, downstairs!" twisting his head to the living room. "Get a . . . two . . . two seat cushions from the couch! Go!" No argument. Dan bolted.

"Katie!" Still clutching my jaw. "Come with me! Come, come, come!"

I ran across the upstairs walkway, past Dan's office with its newly broken window and basketball-sized boulder in the middle of the floor. Into my office where Mostar, crazily, started opening the windows! I couldn't understand. I was halfway under my desk. But when that little oblong, mango-shaped rock came spinning in through the open window, the words "what the fuck are you doing" were almost out of my mouth. Those words stopped short as the "mango" bounced harmlessly against the back wall, then rolled to a stop at my feet.

No window. No glass!

"Katie!" Mostar motioned to my side. I jumped up, opened the window, then pressed myself up against the wall as a rock whooshed through open space. This one, ironically, almost hit Dan, who'd just come puffing in with the cushions.

Mostar yelled, "Here!" She grabbed one of the cushions and jammed it against her half of the open window as Dan copied the action on my end.

thmp

His cushion recoiled slightly as a rock bounced harmlessly off the other side.

Simple. Genius. Mostar.

She was already sliding my desktop monitor behind her cushion when I slid over next to Dan.

"Behind me!" Taking the soft barrier from him, I jerked my

head to the two smaller steel shelves against the far wall. Dan got it, rushed over, and tipped their contents on the floor.

As he lifted the first into place, I felt another rock punch my cushion. The impact nearly knocked me down. "Are you . . ." Dan's hand on my back.

"Fine!" Nudging him away. Shifting my weight, widening my stance, I barely felt the next two hits.

Across the room, Dan grunted, "Look out," and plopped the second shelf on the desk. Then restocking; files, printer paper, printer—the Ikea desk groaned under their weight. But they held! An audible *thmp,* a quick sliver of light between cushion and windowsill. But it held! I did the same, hands free, stepping back. A soft *thmp* and rattle of something hard and loose on my shelf.

Barely audible above the rest of the bombardment. That's what Mostar called it, resting on the floor, back to the wall. "They never warn you," she breathed, "they always come in before the sirens." I heard her sniff, hard, then cough. "Never get caught in the open, always away from the doors. The old streets are best, narrow. They shield you from shrapnel." More cryptic Mostar-isms.

She yawned, breathed some indecipherable foreign phrase, and then dropped right off to sleep. Seriously! Snoring! Louder than Dan's! He's at it too, now, by the way. Both of them, like characters in a Disney movie.

At least Dan waited for the "shelling" to stop. It petered out about an hour ago. Maybe ten minutes in total? God, what a ten minutes! Mostar's still sleeping upright against the wall. Dan's curled up at the foot of the closed office door. I was worried that we'd suffocate in here, but he insisted we keep it shut. "The alarm's out." Those were his last words before dropping off. "I'll fix it tomorrow . . . fix it . . . I'll fix it."

I guess I shouldn't worry. The barrier's not airtight. I can feel little drafts of cold air drifting down around my desk. That's where I am now, next to it, wedged into the corner, writing all this down.

My fingers are cramping. I need to pee. I want to sleep but I also don't. I'm afraid of tomorrow.

Why did the rocks stop? Why did they start? What does it mean?

I can't hear anything outside.

I really need to pee.

From my interview with Senior Ranger Josephine Schell.

Like wood knocking, rock throwing is deeply embedded in the lore. Again, there's a lot of conjecture. It might very well be a peaceful . . . well . . . nonlethal means of intimidation. That might explain the howls as well. One theory is that they use it to drive another troop or individual away. That would make sense, given that chimps sometimes throw rocks at each other, or at people, like at that Swedish zoo.* Santino probably wasn't looking to kill anybody, just make them leave.

JOURNAL ENTRY #12 [CONT.]

So much to do this morning, so much to do today. I have to get this down quickly while it's still fresh. The pain in my neck woke me up. Sleeping on the floor, on my side, arm for a pillow. I've had neck aches before but *oh my God*. Shoulder, ribs, face! And so cold! Last night it was kind of nice. The room was so hot and stuffy. But now, the chill outside, it must have dropped twenty degrees. I can see my breath. *This* is what Frank must have been talking about, that plunge in temperature right before winter.

* In 2009, "Santino," an adult male chimpanzee, shocked visitors at Sweden's Furuvik Zoo by pelting them with prepositioned rocks.

While the rest of me was freezing, my bladder was absolutely burning. Not only did it cause me discomfort, but when I opened my eyes, I almost peed out of fear. Dan and Mostar were gone, and the door was wide open!

I called out for both of them, and got nothing back. I stood up, shivered, sneezed repeatedly, then poked my head out of the office. The house looked empty, the front door was open. The curtains covering the living room window were raised. I checked my phone, a little past eight, but the darkness . . . Lead gray, obscuring everything. I couldn't see lights from the other houses, or the other houses. It was like they'd had been teleported to another world.

I ducked into the hall bathroom quickly, then came out and called again for Dan. No answer. I could hear voices, distant but clear. I hobbled downstairs, rubbing the blood into my needle-stung right leg, and half limped over to the front door.

Fog!

Dark and thick. And cold! I could feel it through my skin, seeping into my bones. The village was barely visible, but I could just make out the small group by the Common House.

Dan was there, talking to the Boothes, along with Carmen and Reinhardt. Vincent was all decked out in his hiking gear, boots, poles, CamelBak. The pack itself was bulging, crammed with stuff it wasn't meant to hold. So was the laptop bag on his hip, round and overstuffed. And Bobbi's pink yoga mat on the other hip, tied around his shoulder with an improvised rope of shoelaces. And around the mat was a blanket, one of those ultra-soft airport types you buy at Hudson News. It was wrapped with more tied-together laces that typified his entire ensemble.

"I don't need to worry about getting lost." Vincent kept gesturing down the road. "Just follow the driveway to the bridge . . ."

Dan countered with, "But then what? If there's no bridge . . ."

"I'll just follow the lahar." Vincent swallowed. "It must have cooled by now. Or hardened, whatever the proper term . . ."

Dan persisted. "But does that make it safe to cross?"

Bobbi cut in. "He doesn't need to cross. Like he said, he'll just be walking alongside it, following it down where the stream used to be."

"To where?" Dan saw me enter the group, slid an arm around my waist, then swooped his free hand to the sky. "You can't see anything!"

"It'll burn off." Vincent didn't make eye contact, just nodded quickly to the ground. "It does." Then, to his wife, "Last fall, remember, by midday . . ." She nodded back, clutching his arm, trying to smile.

"I'll be fine." I'm not sure if Vincent meant this for her or Dan or himself. "Take it slow, careful . . ." He looked up. "I don't need to make it all the way, just enough to get cell reception." He patted his jacket, the high-end trekker kind with solar panels woven into the lining. He repeated, "I'll be careful."

"But you'll be all alone."

A pause at that. A warning.

Dan filled me in later about the argument I'd already missed. How he and Mostar had gotten up early, decided to let me sleep, and gone out to check on everyone else. That was when they'd found Vincent getting ready to leave, and how he'd already made up his mind.

The philosophy, the justification. Somehow Vincent and Bobbi had convinced themselves that the rocks were meant to scare us away. Our land was the goal, the shelter of our houses, possibly, as well as the food inside. They still weren't ready to cross that mental line, to admit what those creatures really want. And when Reinhardt showed up . . .

Reinhardt.

He'd been listening, that's what Dan thinks, through one of his broken windows, and came over to see what was happening. When he enthusiastically threw his support behind Vincent, Dan said Mostar gave up after that. No one, not even Carmen, who showed up at the same time, was willing to accept the truth. That's why Dan had switched tactics, focusing on the perils of the hike. But, as I personally witnessed, this logic wouldn't work either.

Someone just *had* to go for help. There simply wasn't any other choice.

Why? Why are we always looking for someone else to save us instead of trying to save ourselves?

"Here it is!" We all turned to see Mostar shuffling back to the group. Dan told me when he'd pivoted to the terrain argument, she'd rushed back to her house for "something." And that something turned out to be a bamboo spear. A proper one this time. Not the slapdash javelin from before. An eight-inch chef's knife jutted from the hollow center of a thick, strong shaft, held there by what I thought was brown string but later learned was rubber-coated electrical wire. It looked powerful, deadly, and a little bit comical when held next to Vincent's diminutive frame. (I also learned, later, that she'd been making it for Dan.)

"Here"—she held out the weapon to Vincent—"this is what I was talking about."

"Thank you." Vincent kept his hands at his sides. "But . . . I think . . . it's a little . . ." His eyes followed the six-foot-plus shaft.

"I can cut it down." Mostar started to turn away. "Give me thirty seconds."

"I'm okay," Vincent insisted, and held up the twin telescopic poles dangling from his wrists. "They're better for balance anyway, I have more experience with them, and . . ." He ran his hand over his glistening upper lip. "I don't . . ."

A glance at Reinhardt, who, surprisingly, had been silent all this time. "I . . . don't want to make things worse."

"Then don't go!" Mostar jammed the butt of her spear into the ground.

He shrugged. "I have to." Then, softer to his wife, "I have to."

And that was that. A whole conversation in agreed code. Hints, warnings, even a weapon without mentioning aloud what it was for. Mostar just sighed, withdrew the spear, and gave him a big hug. So did the rest of us. I could feel the nervous heat coming through his clothes, the sweat of his neck on my cheek. Reinhardt gave him this confident pat on the arm, like one of those old black-and-white war movies where somebody's sending the hero off to glory. I always hated those movies. Whenever someone said "Good luck" or "Godspeed," I only heard "Better you than me." Bobbi kissed him deeply and, for a second, I thought she was going to cry.

We followed him as far as the Common House and then stopped to let Bobbi walk him to the bottom of the driveway. Standing there waiting, our backs turned to give them some privacy, Mostar looked at her shoes and said, "They never listen. No matter what you say, sooner or later someone always tries to run the blockade." And she muttered something in her native language, something I couldn't catch. I half expected her to cross herself. Isn't that what they also did in war movies, the old stout foreign women?

This one didn't. She just clapped her hands twice with, "Okay, let's get to work, a lot of broken glass to clean up." As Reinhardt took Dan aside, mumbling something about his bad knees, I looked back to see that Bobbi was now alone.

I could see her head was bowed slightly, as she hugged herself, shoulders heaving.

"C'mon, Katie." Mostar took me by the arm and escorted me down the hill toward her. "Let's get her home."

Vincent was gone by then, disappeared into the fog.

From my interview with Senior Ranger Josephine Schell.

Not all chimps throw rocks for dominance. In West Africa, primatologists recently observed them hurling stones against trees. No one knows why. There's a theory that it's some kind of "sacred ritual" for some yet undiscovered goal. Personally, I couldn't care less why they do it, just that they do. It shows me rocks have multiple functions, and we can't be sure about what all those functions are. If some chimps use stones in their monkey-hunting tactics and those tactics are being used by some of their larger, North American cousins, then both the Mount St. Helens attack and the bombardment of Greenloop weren't meant to drive the humans away, but to drive them out into the open.

Chapter 15

When meat is available, it is treated as a valuable resource; bonobos have been observed to beg the meat holder for a share.

—From *World Atlas of Great Apes and Their Conservation*, edited by Julian Caldecott and Lera Miles

JOURNAL ENTRY #13
OCTOBER 12

There's no more lying. To each other, to ourselves. No more denying what they are and what they want.

I haven't written for two days and so much has happened. I'm trying to keep everything in order in my head. It's like I've lived a year.

After Vincent left, we spent the rest of the day trying to repair our houses. I wondered to Mostar if we, the three of us, shouldn't just focus on making more sharpened stakes. If they were hostile, and clearly the rocks had proven that, shouldn't security be our most important priority?

She said, "You're right," but followed up with, "broken glass is a security issue. If we don't clean it up, if someone gets cut and needs stitches . . ." She also pointed out the need for sealing up the spaces left by broken windows. "We can't have anyone catching a chill. We'll need them strong and healthy when they come around." And before I could ask, she answered, "They will, Katie. Trust me. They're on the line . . . no . . . fence. That's the American term. They're all on the fence right now, waffling because of Vincent's heroic gesture. But they'll need us soon enough. And we'll need them."

There it was again.

Need.

I didn't ask what would make them come around. I figured I'd know soon enough.

As far as our house is concerned, the master bedroom had to be abandoned. The rock that hit our balcony door pushed the safety glass right out of its frame. Even if we put the mattress and box spring up against the opening there's no practical way to seal up all the drafts. Better to move them into my office. Move all our toiletries to the guest bathroom down the hall, keep the master bedroom door shut all the time.

The same goes for Dan's office, which he actually sees as a plus. "More energy efficient." That's his rationale. "Two rooms we don't have to heat." He's programmed the system to shut their air ducts. Amazing you can do that. Smart house. He showed me how many amps we're saving. "Which can all go toward the garden."

I pretended to share his optimism, his enthusiasm. I didn't tell him how it feels like a retreat. One more step back. First, they took the forest. Then they took the night. Then a couple rooms in our own house. How many more steps back do we have?

The house told us one of the solar panels was offline. Not cracked, their flexible makeup is shatter-proof. It was just a loose wire connection that could be fixed from the balcony. Still, the idea of Dan out there with his back to the woods. Just one well-aimed rock. I stayed with him the whole time, facing the trees, looking for any movement. Nothing happened. No rocks, no sounds. At least the fog might have given us some cover. That was what I hoped even though it was starting to burn off. Vincent was right. I wondered where he was by now, how far he'd gotten. It was hard to focus on what I was doing. Tired. Achy. But so much to do!

The village took a lot of hits. Back windows smashed. A few

balcony doors fractured. Same with the kitchen doors. Safety glass. Fissured but intact. Reinhardt's took a hit, but unlike our balcony, it was still in the frame. Even the door itself worked, although Dan thought it might be dangerous to use it. He came up with the idea of closing the drapes and setting the kitchen table against it. Reinhardt got lucky. There's no way to seal off the kitchen. That potential heat loss makes me grateful that the living room window-wall is also paneled with safety glass. Ours now looks like an asymmetric checkerboard, panes intact, others "fogged" with cracks.

None of the other houses were hit on their inward-facing windows. Did that have to do with being seen? The Perkins-Forsters all hid right behind their front door. Bobbi sheltered in the downstairs bathroom. Who knows what the Durants did. Mostar warned us not to waste any time trying to check on them. She'd sheltered in her workshop before running over to check on us. We, I, was the only one standing right in front of an upstairs window. They must have seen me, targeted me.

That moment during the compost fight, when the large female, Alpha, locked eyes on me . . .

Stop it. Stick to recording what happened.

While Dan helped Reinhardt, Mostar and I went over to see what we could do for the Perkins-Forsters. That car alarm we'd heard last night? That was their Nissan Leaf. Right on the roof, right up and over the house. How much strength does it take to hurl a stone the size of a medicine ball?

At least their master balcony doors were intact, which prompted them to turn the whole bed up against it. They'll all be sleeping in that room from now on. Palomino's room was a disaster. Multiple rocks. Window glass mixed with mirror shards. I tried not to think about the stone chunk in the middle of her pillow.

No cleanup there, just abandoned. Another retreat.

Effie must have seen the way Pal was looking at me, the way she held my hand when we came in. "Do you want to stay here for a bit, help Pal move some of her stuff into our room?" I was going to agree, especially when I saw her eyes brighten. But Mostar killed that idea with, "We haven't stopped by Bobbi's yet."

"Bobbi's." I just realized that now. Not "the Boothes'."

Effie gave a resigned, "Oh, of course." And as I turned to leave, Pal refused to let go. "Would you like to come along?" I asked her, then up to Effie, "Is that okay?"

"By all means," that was Carmen stepping in, "we can take care of this." There was something in her face, all of their faces, including Bobbi's when we came over.

She was in her kitchen, Band-Aids covering her right thumb and forefinger. A rock had gone through the window above her sink. She'd cut herself trying to fish a few fragments out of the drain. "Can't have them clogging the garbage disposal."

I noticed the room smelled like chardonnay and some of the pieces on the floor were olive green. Did the rock knock a bottle over, or had she done it herself in a frustrated fit? She looked listless, bleary-eyed. The room's smell masked if she'd been drinking. I started to regret bringing Palomino along, but seeing her seemed to energize Bobbi. "Oh hi, Pal!" And she jumped up to open the freezer.

"I've been saving these." She came out with an ice cube tray of toothpicks poked through cellophane. "The last of the lavender berry lemonade pops." Palomino took one with a smile. "Please," she said, proudly holding out the tray for us. "All from our garden." Summer, that's what it tastes like. I savored every lick. Mostar, on the other hand, crunched through hers with one bite, thanked her quickly for the "extra sugar ration," then asked for a broom and dustpan.

As Mostar swept the kitchen floor, I asked if I could get to work on anything upstairs. Bobbi said it didn't matter. "I'll be sleeping on the couch until Vincent gets back."

"Are you sure?" Mostar called from the kitchen. "Maybe you'd like to stay with me?"

"That's very kind." Bobbi smiled and glanced through the living room window. "But I'd hate for him to come home to an empty house."

I didn't like the idea either, but not for the same reason as Mostar. She was all about security. I was about emotion. The look on Bobbi's face, the same as Pal and her parents. I got it now. A longing.

Need.

"Bobbi, are you still up for having that community dinner in the Common House tonight?"

Three people looked at me like I was crazy. Nothing to do but press on.

"Just . . . you know . . . to remind ourselves, each other that . . . well . . . we got us." I couldn't believe I'd actually said that phrase. We got us.

When I was little, Dad bought us the DVDs of the old *Muppet Show*. And in one of the episodes, when that guy, Dom DeLuise, I think, is trying to comfort Miss Piggy about something, he says, "You're here, I'm here. Us is here," and when she repeats "Us is here?" he doubles down with a song: "We Got Us."* That was our song, our family anthem, and though I'd tried to forget it since the divorce, it was now playing at full volume in my head.

"We . . . ," I blathered nervously, ". . . we've been pooling resources, right? Food, skills . . . but there's another resource . . . ," directly to Mostar, ". . . and I know we blew it off in the beginning because we had to handle the practical stuff . . . and we still do . . . But we can't forget . . . we need . . ."

"Comfort." Mostar came forward with a look I recognized as contrition. "You're right, Katie, we need that as much as sharpened sticks." She reached up to wrap her arms around myself and Bobbi. Pal completed our little huddle, grabbing my hand while clinging to the waist of a trembling, sniffling Mrs. Boothe. "To-

* *The Muppet Show,* Episode 211, "With our very special guest star, Mr. Dom DeLuise."

getherness, belonging . . ." Mostar repeated, with a hint of whimsical fascination, "We got us."

Of all the ironies. Wouldn't Yvette, the old Yvette, have just died for a moment like this? And we tried! The first thing after breaking our circle was to march, all four of us, right next door to invite them. Naturally we got no response. The doorbell rang without answer. The methodical, eternal *zzzzzp*s of the elliptical never ceased. I even coaxed Bobbi (who I figured had the least emotional baggage with them) to shout through the door about community and healing and everything they'd preached at the first emergency meeting.

Oh well.

At least the rest of the village agreed, and it couldn't have felt more comforting. Food, wine, and friends . . . and more wine. Everyone brought a bottle, all of us talking about how "every calorie counts." Even Pal had a few sips from her little glass, prompting an approving "How French" from Reinhardt.

The food, portion-wise, was nowhere near what we'd eaten our first night. Anyone in normal circumstances would have looked at our puny dishes as appetizers. It was so gratifying that everyone wasn't just obeying the rationing guidelines, but doing it enthusiastically. To quote Carmen, "El hambre es la mejor salsa." Hunger is the best sauce!

Hunger aside, her egg frittata was delicious. Brilliant idea mixing in ground-up veggie bacon. So much better than ours, which was essentially just scrambled eggs with salt and pepper.

And hunger had nothing to do with enjoying Mostar's dish. It was legitimately scrumptious. She calls them "siege fries"—deep-fried sticks of compressed dough. I noticed that Bobbi didn't eat much of her share; either she didn't like them or, maybe, it was Mostar's comment about "the best substitute for potatoes." Does she still feel bad? That feels like a hundred years ago. Anyway, she gave the bulk of her fries to Pal. "You'll probably like these more than what I brought."

She didn't have to bring anything. We'd agreed on that at her house. But she'd whipped up another noodle soup. It was thicker, darker, and rougher than her soba. She explained that she'd tried to make naengmyeon but apologized for using too much arrowroot starch. I don't think anyone cared. I didn't. For the first time since the eruption, I felt the bliss of a full stomach!

And it was also an entertaining dish, because when I looked over at Pal and exclaimed, "Oh look, worm soup!" the whole conversation shifted to eating bugs. Effie asked if we'd had any chance to dig for garden worms, which jump-started Carmen on a *Washington Post* story about the insect element of the real "paleo diet."

Dan brought up the time he'd tried a dish of fried crickets at this restaurant in Santa Monica. (I'd been there and politely declined to partake.)

Effie asked if anyone had heard about cricket flour, and Bobbi joked, or not, that she'd consider cheating on her veganism for a dish of grubs. "Some curry powder, or soy sauce . . ."

"Or Vegeta," I added, to Mostar's approving nod.

That really got Dan going. "We should totally try it! Wash them good, cook them, all that protein! There's gotta be, like, tons of grubs under all those rotted logs out there." He glanced out at the dark window, then at the suddenly cooling faces. One step too far, mentioning the woods. I felt bad for Dan. He blew it and he knew it. Under the table, I supportively pressed my knee against his.

He tried to recover though, adding, "Obviously not now, tomorrow, when it's light and . . ."

And it was Reinhardt, of all people, who rescued the mood of the group.

"While we're all clearly eager to become orthodox insectivores"—he patted Dan's back—"might I suggest making do with . . ."

Like a magician, he made a dramatic gesture of approaching the small Common House freezer, waving his hands in the air, then opening the door to reveal six pints of, I'm not kidding, ice cream!

We all stared. I think Dan even said, "Whoa . . ."

I just stuttered. "Waitwhat . . . where?" I'd gone through every inch of his kitchen!

"My apologies." Reinhardt raised his hands in mock surrender. "I hope you'll forgive the prevarication of concealing this cache in my inner sanctum."

"A freezer in your bedroom?" Mostar chuckled with a shake of the head.

"Decadent, I admit," Reinhardt began, scooping the containers out in one arm, "and empty now, I assure you." He placed them all in a ceremonious line down the center of the table. Halo Top ice cream!

Oh, the cravings I've been having!

For a second, we just ogled it, like treasure hunters opening the pirate's chest. I don't think anyone has run out of frozen desserts by this point. I mean, it's only been a week and a half since the eruption. But the psychology of rationing, I get it now. I understand what Mostar was trying to tell me about our country, and why we were all so grateful for Reinhardt's gesture. For just this moment, we could go back to normal, to have as much as we wanted, to feel American again.

I'm not sure if anyone thought about it that deeply, but when Carmen said, "What, no cookie dough!" we all broke into laughter. It felt so good to laugh.

Reinhardt, doling out bowls and spoons, invited us all to dig in. Dan scooped out a gluttonous chunk of sea salt caramel, then, bypassing the bowl, shoved the whole thing in his mouth, and moaned what I think is the word "sploosh" (a reference to his favorite show, *Archer*). Nobody seemed to mind. Bobbi even joked, "You must really like the protein." I don't know if she meant Halo's extra grams of protein or . . . something else, go Bobbi.

Pal, with eyes now half the size of her face, glanced at her parents for permission, then practically leapt onto the pancake and waffle. My favorite. I wasn't greedy though, a few scoops at the bottom were more than enough.

Oh my God! You forget. Even though I'd been having a sweet ration since this began, a spoonful of agave or honey, or some of Mostar's real brown sugar. It's not the same. The surprise! That cold mix of cream, ice, and sweetener cocktail: sugar, stevia, and what, heaven?

"Not having any?" I looked over to see Dan offering the mint chip pint to Reinhardt. Sitting back in his chair, hands on his belly, he shook his head. "I've had enough." And for a second, he looked genuinely chagrined. "I've been hoarding these for too long, intending to engulf them alone."

"And in one sitting," added Carmen, which made us all laugh again. Reinhardt too. Pink cheeked, he took the jibe in stride with a theatrical bow.

Still laughing, he gripped his wineglass and, to my utter surprise, pointed it toward me. "Our hostess!"

"We got us!" added Mostar, which prompted a chorus of "We got us!"

I felt my eyes sting, my throat tighten, as everyone burst out into spontaneous applause.

And only when the applause died, in that first moment of silence as we drank, did we hear the cries outside.

Chapter 16

Chimpanzees nearly always eat meat slowly, usually chewing leaves with each new mouthful as though to savor the taste for as long as possible. . . . Often, too, I saw them actually licking the branches of the tree where the kill had touched them or where drops of blood presumably had fallen.

—Jane Goodall, *In the Shadow of Man*

JOURNAL ENTRY #13 [CONT.]

No one spoke, all of us probably wondering if we'd really heard it. But then, a moment later, crying. Human.

As a group, we dropped everything and rushed out into the night. It was clear, close to the village, maybe halfway up the ridge, in a densely wooded clump above the Boothes' house.

A lone voice. Piercing. Agony. Like when you're little, the sound you first hear from a friend who's fallen hard. That long rush of diaphragm torment after the initial shocked inhale.

"Vincent?" Bobbi's voice, wobbly, questioning.

Then she hollered, right next to me. "Vincent!"

Effie covered Palomino's ears, leading her back inside as Vincent's next long shriek broke into echoing sobs.

Bobbi looked at me. Why me? "He's hurt," then, to Dan, "We have to go get him!"

Dan stepped toward the sound. Just one step, because Mostar reached out to grab his arm. She missed, but held him firmly by a clump of shirt.

"No."

Her expression was blank, practical.

"Don't."

More distant sobs, quick, soft, then suddenly launching into another long scream.

"He's hurt!" Bobbi looked incredulously at Mostar, then to Dan. "He needs help!"

I saw Dan wiggle his arm slightly, pulling at Mostar's grip. Testing?

She wouldn't budge. "That's what they want."

It took me a second to realize what she meant. I suddenly wanted to throw up everything I'd just eaten.

Dan got it. I saw his shoulders sag.

Carmen and Reinhardt too, not the shoulders, but the understanding. A moment of surprise, then a mental shift, Carmen facing back out to the ridge with Reinhardt studying his shoes.

But Bobbi, "They!" She threw her hands up. "What 'they'? You can't hear them!"

"Can't you smell them?" asked Mostar.

Even with the wind at our backs, the stench was overpowering.

"They're keeping quiet on purpose." Mostar kept her attention on the ridge. "They want to draw us out, pull us apart." The way her eyes squinted, flicking from side to side. "Sniper trick."

"Wha . . . ," Bobbi started to say, then, as if she'd just picked the winning lottery ticket, her whole face broke into this wide smile. "You're crazy!" Shaking her head with this little half-chuckling gasp. "Crazy! Sonofabitch post-trauma . . ."

And then she spun back to the darkness. "Vincent! We're coming, baby! We're coming!" And over at Dan with a head-jerking *c'mon*!

And when he didn't move.

"What's the matter with you!" Her eyes focused on him, then out to the wider group.

Dan, just standing there, believing Mostar but wanting to help

Bobbi so badly. The way his eyebrows narrowed, lip quivering. I would have said something, I know I would have, but then I noticed his face. The light thrown on his skin, just the barest shade brighter. And behind him, Carmen shouted, "There!"

She was pointing past us to the space between the Boothe and Durant houses. None of us had noticed it until then. We didn't realize that the lower half of that space had been partially blocked by something. And that something was now running up the slope behind the houses. The one with long legs. Scout. Watching us all this time? Frustrated when we wouldn't take the bait?

I watched him vanish into the brambles, just below a gap in the trees. And in that gap, at the top of the ridge, lit by the glow of the houses . . .

I can't be sure if it was Alpha. You can't tell at that distance. And I'm not sure of what I think it was waving at us. Had to be a branch. And it must have been cracked in the middle. Why else would it have dangled like that? And there's no way, no way I could have seen what my brain keeps telling me were fingers.

"We can't." Reinhardt, speaking to the back of my head, then, as I turned to the group. "Mostar's right. We can't go out there." And to Bobbi, "I'm sorry."

"Sorry?" In the pale motion-light glare, I watched her lips go white.

"Bobbi"—Reinhardt gave a resigned shrug—"please just look at the situation with—"

Another scream and Bobbi pointed to the darkness. "Listen!" Eyes wet, bouncing slightly like a child. At the next scream she grabbed her hair with both hands. "OhmyGod ohmyGod . . ."

Dan tried another quick lunge away from Mostar, his free arm reaching behind his back for the stabber he'd hidden under his shirt.

She must have seen the bulge. Or just suspected? "Dan!" Her voice raised in warning, her other arm grabbed his.

Bobbi looked at both of them, hands out, rasping, "Please."

Carmen edged toward her. I followed. I don't know what we thought we would do. Comfort? Restrain?

Carmen barely touched her shoulder before she threw it off in a wild, frantic swipe. "Please! Please!" To all of us. "*Please!*"

"Bobbi," said Reinhardt, soft and soothing, "you have to understand that there's nothing we can—"

"YOU!" She growled, turning on him. "You're doing this!"

Then the howling began, Vincent's pain drowned in a bellowing chorus.

Like a starting gun, that's how I think of it now, because the sound seemed to launch Bobbi at Reinhardt.

She caught him mid-turn. I could see where her nails scratched his ear. He reached up to grab the wound just as Carmen and I reached out to hold her back. "You told him it was okay! You let him go!" Thrashing like a hooked fish. "You're letting him die!"

My mind flashed back to Vincent's departure. Did he confer with Reinhardt before leaving? Ask his advice? Is that why Reinhardt had been so generous with the ice cream? Guilt?

"Bobbi, just think . . ." Reinhardt, hands out, palms open, lip quivering, steam rising from his glistening forehead. "Think . . ."

"You!" Bobbi screeched, kicking up, out, barely missing his face. "YOU!"

"What do you want!" I jumped at the bass, the sheer volume of Reinhardt's voice. "What do you want from us?" He smashed his hands against his face, frantically rubbing, like he was trying to wipe off reality.

"They'll KILL US, Bobbi!" His hands out, clawing the air in front of her, punctuating each word. "THEY—WILL—KILL—US—AAALLLL!"

Instinctively, I pulled Bobbi back. I thought he was going to hit her, the way he came at her like that. But he wasn't coming at her. His face. Shock. His knees hit the ground, hands out, mouth open.

Carmen yelled, "Grab him!" Reinhardt keeled forward just as Mostar and Dan caught him under the arms.

I let go of Bobbi, jumped over to help Mostar. God, he was so heavy, hot, damp. "We can't"—wheezing—"can't . . ."

Mostar kept calling his name. "Alex! Alex, look at me! Can you hear me?"

Slack-jawed, glass-eyed, drool dripping from his bottom lip.

"Are you taking something?" Mostar grabbed his jaw, turning his face into hers. "Medication? Do you have pills at your house? Alex, listen to me! Alex!"

thmp

The first stone landed right next to us, throwing a cloud of dust in our faces.

thmp-thmp-thmp

"Get inside!" Mostar grunted, struggling to lift Reinhardt. "In the Common House!"

As we pulled him through the door, Effie and Pal slammed it behind us.

Mostar barked, "Lights!"

The room went dark as we guided Reinhardt to the couch. He *oof*ed into the cushions, hands on chest, rasping.

Mostar ran to the sink, shouting, "Everyone down! Away from the windows!"

China clinking. Rocks hitting the roof. Bobbi's soft sobs. Reinhardt's defiant *mmm!* as he pushed at the water Mostar'd gotten. All of it in half-light. All to the soundtrack of distant wails.

Mostar gave the water one more try. Reinhardt shoved so violently it spilled on me. Then he leaned to the side, gagging. Mostar crawled for the trash bin. Reinhardt retched, gagged, spat on the floor. Mostar got the can under him just in time. I turned away as the room filled with vomit stink.

Reinhardt groaned, spat again, croaked something like, "Can't . . . can't."

"Hold his head!" Mostar took my hand and cupped his slippery forehead with it. As he dry-heaved again, she went back to the sink to moisten a dishcloth.

He was mumbling by that point. Words and groans strung together.

I felt so sorry for him, so helpless. He was suffering right there and there was nothing I could do. That helplessness. Vincent. Bobbi. Feeling so powerless, victimized. I'm not sure when my sympathy turned.

Maybe when the pleading started, high, meek. "Want . . . want to go home." That phrase, again and again. "Want to go home," punctuated with tiny, infantile whimpers. Once he said someone's name. "Hannah," I think, right before, "Home. I want. I want."

Die.

I tried not to think it, feel it.

Die! Just die!

Biting my lip, glaring at him in the darkness.

Please just shut up and fucking die!

That was six hours ago, five hours since the rocks finally stopped. Mostar made us wait an hour. Sitting there in silence, ensuring it was safe to move. Reinhardt was asleep by then. Or catatonic. We can't be sure. It took four of us to get him safely home. He's on his living room sofa now. His breathing is steady. Carmen is watching him.

We still don't know if he actually had a heart attack. Effie thinks it might be something called "stress cardiomyopathy." A panic attack that mirrors cardiac arrest. Effie's not sure though. She reminded us that she and Carmen are psychologists, not psychiatrists. But even if they had gone to medical school, would that solve anything? Without the right drugs and equipment?

Siri, how do you treat a heart attack in your own home?

We agreed to at least watch him in shifts. If he doesn't wake up, we'll have to think about how to take care of him. Needs like feeding and, yes, going to the bathroom. We'll all have to pitch in.

And everyone has. Mostar's our leader now. And everyone who can is working to build her defensive perimeter.

Effie and Pal are home cutting bamboo stalks into stakes. Mostar and Dan are outside collecting more. I can see them clearly, just across the driveway, crouching in the outside lights, rhythmically moving to the flash of their bread knives. Mostar doesn't want anyone outside alone, not while it's still dark. "Just in case they get bold enough to try."

Try what?

She thinks we'll be safe in daylight, especially within the confines of the village. That should give us enough time to finish the perimeter. A couple days maybe. One more night. She doesn't think they'll "work up the nerve" for a home invasion. That's what she told me once we got Reinhardt home. "And besides," why did she have to add this part, "their bellies are full for now."

Vincent.

Bobbi. She cried herself to sleep just now, curled up with her head in my lap. I can see why she said it. "We'll . . . find him . . . dawn . . . we'll look for him . . . find him . . . we will . . ." Denial. Hope. Xanax.

It's obvious why she wants to search for him, but why did I agree to help?

I guess that's obvious too.

I need to do something, to make up for what I thought about Reinhardt. That's not me. Won't be. A quick nap now, set my phone alarm for sunup. At least it's still good for something. So am I. Who thinks thoughts like that?

Who am I?

From my interview with Senior Ranger Josephine Schell.

Have you ever seen chimps hunt monkeys? They form a tight team. Every member has a job. You have the "flushers," climbing the trees, shaking the branches, screaming bloody murder to scare the smaller primates into running for their lives. Terror is a powerful weapon. Terror clouds thought. The flushers are counting on that. Intelligence surrendering to self-preservation. If they can get just one to break away from the group. That's key. There's strength in numbers, even for prey.

Children are the most vulnerable, the easiest to isolate. But even a full-grown adult can be rattled enough to slip up. Fear-soaked brain switched off, running, climbing, jumping, hopefully, right into the arms of the other chimps lying in wait. If the monkey's lucky, it'll die quickly, a twist of the neck or having its head swung into a tree. If not . . . I've seen a red colobus trying to pull itself away, shrieking for its life while the chimp holds it down with one hand and rips its guts out with the other.

The only term I can think of is "bloodlust," because that's what it sounds like when chimps tear a monkey apart. It's not like any other kill you'd ever see, not like when a leopard brings down a gazelle or even sharks rip into a seal. Those are cold, mechanical. Apes go crazy. Hopping and dancing. Don't tell me they don't enjoy it.

And don't tell me that the hunt only exists for pure sustenance. They pass out that meat according to rank. The leader standing over the corpse as the others wait, literally, with their hands out. They treat it like currency. The same social order which allows that kind of disciplined, coordinated attack is maintained by the attack's bloody spoils.

Chapter 17

At first Bauman could see nobody; nor did he receive an answer to his call. Stepping forward, he again shouted, and as he did so his eye fell on the body of his friend, stretched beside the trunk of a great fallen spruce. Rushing towards it the horrified trapper found the body was still warm, but that the neck was broken, while there were four great fang marks in the throat.

The footprints of the unknown beast-creature, printed deep in the soft soil, told the whole story.

The unfortunate man, having finished his packing, had sat down on the spruce log with his face to the fire, and his back to the dense woods to wait for his companion. While thus waiting, his monstrous assailant, which must have been lurking nearby in the woods, waiting for a chance to catch one of the adventurers unprepared, came silently up from behind, walking with long, noiseless steps, and seemingly still on two legs. Evidently unheard, it reached the man, and broke his neck [by wrenching his head back with its forepaws] while it buried its teeth in his throat. It had not eaten the body, but apparently had romped and gamboled round it in uncouth, ferocious glee, occasionally rolling over and over it; and had then fled back into the soundless depths of the woods.

—President Theodore Roosevelt, *The Wilderness Hunter*

JOURNAL ENTRY #14

OCTOBER 13

It was irresponsible what I did. Selfish. And stupid.

I knew it was wrong, otherwise I would have told someone. Bobbi was asleep. Reinhardt too probably, with Effie watching him. I'd seen her take over for Carmen, who'd gone back to cutting more stakes with Pal. I figured Dan and Mostar were doing the same thing. No one saw me slip out of the Boothes' house, and I managed to get a quarter of the way up the trail before hearing, "Wait!"

Dan was coming up behind me, spear in one hand, javelin in the other. He was using them like hiking poles, pushing himself at twice my speed. His red face, that clench-jawed determination. I turned to face him, ready for the fight:

"No, Dan! No, you can't stop me! I'm going to find Vincent and there's nothing you can do about it! And there never was. You're done holding me back, and I'm done babying you. No, no, keep your mouth shut! Here's what's going to happen, I'm going out to find Vincent while you turn your ass around and make yourself useful until I get back."

Wouldn't that have made a great speech? It was already in my head, probably stored, in one form or another, for years. But it never got a chance to be said, because just as I raised my hand to stop him, Dan gave that open hand the javelin and trudged right on by. I gawked at his back for a moment before he twisted to offer his free hand. And that's how we traveled. Hand in hand, mutually supportive. Hiking up the trail the way I'd dreamed about since Day One.

Figures.

We didn't hear anything, didn't see any movement. I couldn't help but hope that maybe they really were nocturnal. Blissfully asleep. Full.

We made it halfway up before intersecting with the footprints. The tracks from last night, Scout, drawing a straight line from the houses to the top of the ridge. That was where the other one, Alpha, maybe, had been standing. She'd left a mess of prints there. And blood. Beaded in the ash, spattered on the trees. More red flecks led us down the opposite slope. It was slow going. There's no trail there. Not a natural one. She'd torn through the foliage, leaving a path of bloody, broken branches.

Those breaks, jabbing our sides with each misstep. The ground was soft there, spongy. No visibility. And no sound, except for my own heartbeat. The path curved around a large pine, which we now realized had been concealing a small clearing.

Bones. Fragments. They were everywhere. Mixing with ash and mud. Too many for just one animal. With bits of fur and severed hooves. The deer we'd seen? And maybe some more we hadn't? I recognized the few bloody stones, the type used for butchering. But these new piles? Each was about a foot high and twice as wide. Each stone looked pristine, and roughly as large as the kind they'd thrown at us. Stockpiles for the next bombardment? If they're smart enough to plan ahead like this, then what else are they capable of?

As we walked slowly among the stones and bones, I began to pick out distinct "islands," leaves, moss, whole ferns torn up by the roots, all pressed into the earth and all of it mixed with the long, coarse fibers I now recognized as hairs. Sleeping mats? The stench, worse than ever. Different. Dan tugged my hand, drawing my attention to several small, brown mounds at the edge of the trees. Feces? What do you call this place? A nest? A lair?

Dan lowered his hand to something just below the nearest mound, a long, thin object that shone in the overcast light. We didn't need to get any closer. It was one of Vincent's hiking poles.

That was when the trees in front of us moved.

He was big, maybe the first one I'd seen. That night at the kitchen door. He was broad, muscular, but missing Alpha's scars.

His eyes flicked between the two of us. His growl, low, languishing.

Dan was the first to retreat, rising slowly, gently pulling me back.

The large male lowered his head, growled again, and took a cautious step toward us as the woods around him suddenly came alive. They'd been right there the whole time! All of them!

I close my eyes now, trying to picture each one. And maybe it's silly to assign names, but that's where my mind naturally goes.

The two smaller, younger brothers from the compost bin fight, Twins One and Two, flanking their, what, father? The first male. Alpha's mate? What's that term for Philip in *The Crown*? "Prince consort"? And there was thin, tall Scout to his right, with the older male, "Gray," between him and the old female, "Granny Dowager," at the end.

On the left, she was young, an adolescent, I think. She'd been the one I'd seen running through the brush. The one with lighter, reddish fur. It seemed to flow around her, soft, shining. "Princess." And on her left, another female, older, bigger, still with patches of soft red fur, but a distended belly that she cradled in one arm. Pregnant? "Juno."

And the young male to her left, at first, I thought he wasn't even a male. They hadn't dropped yet, barely hanging from the fur between his legs. Everything about him was young; his frenetic hopping, his high chattering, his constant, rapid glances over his shoulder. Waiting? Calling for the three shapes looming up behind Consort.

Two females, one old, one young, both holding fur balls in their arms. Babies. Two mothers, hunched, hesitant, following behind *her*.

Alpha.

The whole troop seemed to part when she approached, even Consort, who stared at the ground when she passed him. No growls from her. No chatter. Silently approaching to match our slow retreat up the slope, out of the clearing, back toward the top of the ridge.

Monkeys. That's the image I can't get out of my head, the little monkeys at the zoo, with their wide, darting eyes. That was us, trying to look everywhere at once. Forward to the advancing troop, down to the stone piles at our feet, side to side at the gradually enveloping ring, and back to the open, narrowing escape.

They were trying to surround us, cut us off. That must have been what prompted Dan to speed up. I felt his grip constrict my wrist, the pulling as I locked eyes on Alpha. Her lips curled back, jaw fell.

The roar, I felt the warmth, the stink. It sent the troop into a frenzy. Jumping, dancing, throwing their arms up amidst those piercing shrieks. I didn't think about what I was doing, just raised my arm as she reached one face-sized hand toward us. I don't know if the javelin's blade cut her deeply, or if it just bent around her closing fingers. The grip, that vicious hard tug. I can still feel the rug-burn friction on my skin as she ripped it out of my hand, then tossed it, spinning, above our heads.

That was when Dan turned, brandishing his spear. Jabbing the air, poking harmlessly. She didn't care. She avoided the thrusts with quick bobs of that neckless head. She even tried to grab it, swooping her arms, forcing Dan back. That new sound, short barks. Was she laughing?

I looked behind us, saw the ring close, then back to Alpha, who finally got ahold of Dan's spear. I see it now in slow motion: one hand on the spear, the other, a fist, raised high. Mouth open as the huge face leaned in.

Glowing eyes.

Two flickering beads.

Not a hallucination. They were burning. Reflecting.

"BACK!"

She released the spear, recoiling sharply, just as the flames passed between myself and Dan.

"GET BACK!"

Mostar, barreling in between us, brandishing a fireball-tipped pole.

"Goniteseupichkumaterinu!"* Her language. And theirs. Foreign words mixed with guttural, animal noises. She snarled, she barked, she spat a high, hissing roar as the troop retreated amid jerky, frightened yelps.

Frightened.

* Gonite se u pičku materinu!: Get back into your mother's cunt!

Even Alpha, reticent. Arms down, shoulders up. Head bobbing for an opening amid soft clucking calls.

Mostar clucked back, a sound like, "Mrsh! Mrsh!"*

Then, "Pichko jedna!"† as she lunged forward, backing off Alpha, swinging her torch that I now saw as a burning towel wrapped in electrical wire. I could also see that it was starting to burn out, flames giving way to smoke.

"J'ebemlitikrv!"‡ Mostar barked as she hurled the torch up and to the retreating Alpha. Then, to us, "Run!"

The ring had opened, the slope was clear. Dan and I ran, stumbling up the muddy ground.

"Mostar!" Dan called. I looked. She was right behind us, waving, "RUUUUN!"

And here they came, loping side to side. Still cautious? Wondering if we had more fire? Alpha, standing her ground, stooping to pick something up. I turned to watch where I was going, just as the first rock smashed into the tree next to me.

The maze. Obstructing a clear getaway, but also a clear shot. The crack of rocks hitting branches, bonking against path-blocking trunks. A slurping *thlp* of a stone cantaloupe buried in the mud right in front of me.

"Zig!" Mostar, behind us, shouting what I first thought was a foreign word.

"Zig-zag!" she shouted, then *oof* from a hit. A glancing blow, I found out later, like the one that hit Dan. I saw that one, a low angle grazing his shoulder, but with enough force to spin. Dan pivoted, tripped. I caught his fall, forcing him up, pulling him the last few feet.

We could see the top of the ridge. Up and over, just a few more steps. The moment I could see the village, the downward slope. Relief. I remember that rush. Then the impact. The blow

* Mrš! Mrš!: "Git! Git!" in American folk language or the traditional "March! March!"

† Pičko jedna!: You cunt!

‡ Jebem li ti krv: I fuck your blood.

between my shoulder blades. Winded. Falling forward. Dan's turn to catch me now, and Mostar pushing us both. "Don't stop! Don't stop!"

Racing down the slope, trying not to slip, trying not to notice, to recognize, the object that had hit me. It was still rolling down the incline in front of us. Black and brown, black and brown. Hair and face. Vincent Boothe's head.

Down to the closest house, the Perkins-Forsters'. Kitchen door open, arms beckoning. Carmen and Pal. "C'mon! C'mon!"

In and through, crouching on the kitchen floor behind the counter. Dizzy, lungs burning. Small arms gripping my sides, a warm face pressed up against my stomach. Opening my eyes down onto the top of Pal's head, then over to Dan, gripping his spear, waiting.

They didn't come. Not even close. They didn't even bombard the house. Just wailed at us from the distance.

"Fire." Mostar huffing with closed eyes. "They're . . . still . . . afraid of it."

"Can we make bonfires?" Carmen asked, glancing over the counter at the door. "Surround the village?"

"Nothing . . . to burn." Mostar, pulling herself up, holding on to the counter for support. "Too wet . . . the trees . . ." Another deep breath, fighting for control. "Maybe . . . we have some more time, finish the stakes, before they get over the shock. And we can make torches too if we need them. More weapons."

My head was clearing by then, the adrenaline draining.

I shifted slightly, signaling Pal to step back. Grabbing my hand, we got up together. Her eyes, looking up into mine. "I'm okay"—stroking her hair—"it's okay." Then over to Mostar, who was still fixed on the door.

I reached out to touch her shoulder. A gentle rub. "Thank you."

And when she turned.

A hard slap, loud, knocking me sideways.

"What were you thinking!"

Grabbing my cheek, facing her glare. "Were you thinking?" Before I could answer. "Either one of you?" And another hard slap, this one up to Dan's chin. "Children!"

Dan, white, shaking, "W . . . we . . ."

Silenced him with a finger. "You! Help finish the stakes." The finger swung toward Carmen and Pal. "Stay with them. Stay together!"

I flinched as she faced me, turning to protect my swelling cheek. "And you, you come with me. Now!"

I followed Mostar to the kitchen door, pausing while she checked the quiet ridge. It was empty now. They'd pulled back to the other side. Mostar moved her head slowly from the edge of the Perkins-Forsters' yard to the Boothes'. It took me a second to realize what she was looking for. Vincent's head was lying at the bottom of the slope, within the moat-like depression around one of the apple trees. He was staring right at us. Eyes and mouth wide open. Frozen in time? His last expression? Fear? Regret? Was he thinking about Bobbi or his childhood? Was he cursing himself for making such a horrible decision, the way I cursed myself for mine? That face. Will I ever forget? With enough time and therapy? Hypnosis or a drug I've never heard of? Is there something to help me "unsee"?

But Mostar, she didn't seem to mind at all. Picking it up, like a basketball a kid had accidentally thrown over her fence. She crouched on her knees to grab it, tucked it under her arm, then gave me a quick glance just to make sure I was still in tow.

We ambled straight into the kitchen. Nonchalant. Inhuman. She reached under the sink, took out a white plastic garbage bag, dropped the head inside, then, after washing her hands—washing her hands!—she opened the freezer and rolled it inside. "Don't tell Bobbi." Covering his head with ice. "She knows he's gone. She doesn't need to know about this."

"Here." She held up an ice pack from the freezer door, pressing it to my cheek, waiting for me to take it. When I did, she raised her eyes to within inches of mine. "Are you here?" Her voice was softer now, her face.

I didn't intend to sob, it just escaped quickly like a cough.

Her eyes hardened. "I need you here. Are you here?" I straightened, nodded.

"You need to focus on what I'm about to teach you"—her hand, still on my face—"because what you did today was selfish and irresponsible. And stupid, because you went out there without a proper weapon."

Chapter 18

A'oodhu bi kalimaat Allaah al-taammaati min sharri maa khalaq.

I seek refuge in the perfect words of Allah from the evil of that which He has created.

—Sahih Muslim, Hadith 2708

JOURNAL ENTRY #14 [CONT.]

Mostar released my cheek, took my hand, and led me into her workshop. Her armory. That's what it looked like now. Bamboo staffs against the wall, kitchen knives out on the workbench. Failed experiments, prototypes, were cast in the far corner. I could see unevenly sawed or split shafts, bent and chipped knives. Snapped shoelaces, different rolls of tape, and an unspooled tangle of shiny red Christmas ribbon.

"Stand here." Mostar directed me to the middle of the room. "Back straight." She stared me up and down for a second, then reached for one of the bamboo poles. "Stay still." She placed the stalk against my back. "Almost perfect." Then set the stalk on the bench. "Watch, listen. Remember each step exactly."

That's why I've written the next section down as a kind of instruction manual. I don't trust I'll remember anything after I pass out tonight. I'm also stuck on something Mostar said while we worked. Something about "teaching the rest of the village." I didn't ask what she meant. I didn't get the chance. She just jumped right into the lesson and here it is.

• • •

How to make a spear from scratch:

Choosing the right bamboo staff is critical. It can't be tapered. That'll ruin the balance. And it's got to fit your height. Too long is too unwieldly. Too short and you risk falling on the blade. It doesn't have to be exact, more important that the top section perfectly encases the knife's handle. The staff's got to have the right girth, thick enough to be strong but not so wide that you can't get a firm grip. (Wow, that sounds dirty. Sorry, I'm really loopy right now.)

When harvesting the stalk, you saw just below the bottom connector, or whatever those rings are called. It takes a while, especially with a skinny bread knife. And there's a special method. If you go down one side, like with regular wood, and miss just a tiny bit of connecting fiber, that fiber will tear a strip down the whole length. As Mostar warns, "That will decrease integrity and increase splinters." The trick is to first saw in a complete circle, severing that tough top layer, before going for the deep cut.

Next, you saw off all the branches (which can be made into stakes) and file down the sharp nubs with an emery board. Oh, for just one square of sandpaper!

I didn't actually do these first two parts. That's why she'd measured me. A pre-cut stalk would save time. That was the only part of the lesson she did herself. The rest was hands-on for me.

Like the shaft, choosing the knife takes careful consideration. You can't just use the longest blade. Those tend to be too thin. The best option is the shorter, eight-inch "chef" type, which also needs to be the right design.

One solid piece, the steel going all the way down through the handle. Otherwise, you can't attach it to the shaft. And attaching is the trickiest part. If the knife's grip is held in place by pins, you're in business. Pins mean holes in the steel. And those holes are the best way to tie them on, but I'll explain that part in a minute.

Hopefully the grip itself is made of resin. That way you can smash it out with a rock. (I know . . . not one hammer in the whole village!) Be safe while smashing, those fragments can hit you in the eye. While wearing Mostar's onion goggles, I felt little chips peppering my face.

Once the grip and the pins are removed, the next step is fitting. Slide the handle into the hollow top of the shaft. If it doesn't fit (good strong bamboo might not have enough internal room), you've got to saw out a little groove with the bread knife. Once your naked blade fits snugly, take it right back out for measuring.

That's where the handle holes come in. Place those holes against the outside of the shaft, mark them with a pen (Sharpie, if you got one), then do it again on the other side. See where I'm going with this? You bore those holes out with a paring knife. Take your time. Don't rush. Mostar showed me where she chipped off the edge of a couple of paring knives, ruining them forever. Checking for light shows if they all line up. I got it right the first time, and Mostar seemed impressed. Apparently, that's the easiest way to screw up, not matching the holes, and the more you drill, the more you weaken the bamboo.

Next, you sew the knife in, and that's what the wire's for. Mostar used a five-foot section of electrical cord from a floor lamp. After cutting the cord free (a regular scissors will do), pull the two sections apart (if it's that kind). Set the extra section aside for another spear, and start threading the wire through the top hole. Sounds simple enough, but my first few tries only produced frustration. The tip kept getting stuck because I'd impatiently skipped a step. Shaving down the wire's end rubber to a point turns it into a needle, which makes a world of difference!

Once the wire exits the second top hole, pull it through nearly to the end and tie the last inch or so into a secure knot. Then wrap the cord tightly round and round the bamboo until you get to the two bottom holes. Then thread it through, tie it off, and you're done!

A real spear!

Mostar took the weapon from me, held it in her hands, checking the balance, squinted with one eye at the knotted wire, then handed it back. "Well done, Katie." It was the first time she smiled all day.

I felt so proud. For a minute, I just handled my creation—vertical, horizontal. I even gave a short thrusting motion with both hands and accidentally banged the back end into the garage door.

"Sorry." I felt my cheeks redden at the dent.

Mostar waved it away with, "Forget it." Then, "I knew you'd be a natural at this. You have a logical, methodical mind. Much more than me." She gestured to the aborted prototypes. "This is how it works. Try, fail, learn, then pass on eventual success for improvement."

That sparked my own idea for an improvement. "What about melting the rubber? Won't it hold the blade even more securely?"

"It might"—Mostar gave me that nod an encouraging teacher gives a well-meaning but totally wrong first-grader—"but it would ruin the wire, which we might need to make more spears."

She gestured to a collection of shorter, thinner shafts. "That's what worries me about the javelins. Losing a good knife every time we throw one. Although I guess they'll just slide right out if I don't figure out a way to make barbs."

Another idea stirred, but this one was far more nebulous. I looked at the 3-D printer but couldn't manage a cohesive thought. Instead, I ended up yawning, which gave me a sympathy yawn from Mostar.

"You need to sleep"—she glanced up at the wall clock—"when you take over watching Reinhardt. I don't think he's woken up yet. You'll rest then. And eat."

Eat.

I suddenly felt sick to my stomach. I'd been so wrapped up in making the spear, so engrossed in the step-by-step process. But with some of my focus freed . . .

I must have glanced over to the door, the kitchen, Vincent's head in the freezer.

"We'll bury him later." Mostar, the mind reader. "When we're safe, when we have time."

I felt my head swim, lurching for the table.

"Take a breath." Mostar took my spear, guiding me to the workbench's little stool. "Try to relax."

I did, closing my eyes tightly. I felt the dam bursting in my brain.

To be someone else's food.

You're a person. You think, you feel. And then it's all gone, and what used to be you is now a mushy mess in something else's stomach.

Carnage, blood, smiling yellow fangs. Gnawing flesh. Licking bones.

"Look at me." The hand on my chin, forcing me to open my eyes.

"I know." Mostar's sad smile, the sigh. "It's a blessing and a curse, the human mind. We're the only creatures on Earth that can imagine our own death. But"—she held up my spear—"we can also imagine ways to prevent it."

That was when the doorbell rang.

Palomino stood in the entry, holding a rolled-up yoga mat. "What are you doing here, Little Doll?" Mostar grabbed her and pulled her inside. "You know you're not supposed to be outside all alone. Do your parents know where you are?"

She shook her head, then pointed, with the mat, to something outside.

Then I got it. The mat was to keep her knees clear of dirt. "Hey, Pal, I'm sorry I don't have time to garden with you right now. I've got to get over to Mr. Reinhardt to . . ."

Wrong. Pal shook her head at me, then shifted back to Mostar with a second gesture to . . . what?

I looked but couldn't see anything. Not a specific house, not the volcano, and (thank *God*!) no dark forms staring down from the trees.

She was facing southeast, and, to my knowledge, there was nothing in that direction. Again, Mostar seemed perplexed. "I'm sorry, I don't . . ."

Then, "Oh," followed by a quick glance back at her wall clock. "Ohhhhh!" This big, broad smile broke her mouth wide open and I'm pretty sure the corners of her eyes began to sparkle.

"Oh, Lutko Moja, it's been a *long* time." Mostar pinched the bridge of her nose, used it to shake her head, then looked up with a shrugging, "C'mon, let's see if I remember."

Ignoring my confusion, Mostar put an arm around the girl, and asked me, "Would you mind running upstairs to fetch a clean towel from the hall closet?"

It was my first time upstairs. I didn't intend to snoop.

But her house is laid out pretty much like ours. The hall closet is right next to the master bedroom. I didn't go in. The door was open. And the picture was so big, facing the bed, which you couldn't miss from my position in the hall.

Mostar looked a lot younger, maybe twenties or thirties. She wasn't thin, but her hourglass figure stood out in her belted coat. Her hair glistened, raven black under a knit wool cap. The man with his arm around her, he looked about the same age. Goatee. Glasses. The kind of Euro intellectual you always see in movies, the kind of guy I thought I'd marry when I was in high school. They both had their arms around the kids standing in front of them.

Boy and girl. The boy looked about twelve, the girl maybe ten. Big grins, genuine on the boy, silly mugging on the girl.

They were standing on the rocky bank of a frozen river. A bridge rose up behind them. Narrow, no cars. An old stone arch connecting two sides of an equally old stone town. I didn't recognize the bridge at first, but then it hit me that I was looking at the real version of her glass sculpture!

I couldn't tell where. Maybe Russia. I've only seen pictures of Red Square. I'm also pretty sure it wasn't Northwest Europe either. The buildings and the clothes seemed too drab, if that's the right word. Eastern Europe? Poland? Czech Republic—or, if I remember high school history, back then it would have been Czechoslovakia? What's the southeast called? The part before you get to Turkey. Sounds like Baltics. Balkans.

Yugoslavia, another country I'd read about in school. A war in the '90s? I would have been about those kids' age. I didn't exactly follow current events back then. The '90s were O.J. and Britney.

Even at Penn, I only took intro to poli-sci and all I remember is the term "ethnic cleansing." And Professor Tongun, from Sudan, "Like a tree in the forest, America doesn't hear foreign suffering."

Shelling. Snipers. Siege fries. Mostar.

"Katie!" from downstairs. "We're waiting."

I grabbed the biggest bath towel she had, ran downstairs, and found them in the kitchen. Mostar looked up at me, smirking. She has to know that I saw the picture. All she said was, "Perfect timing."

They must have just finished washing their hands, and, I think, their feet as well. I could see moisture glistening between their toes. I thought Mostar was going to use the towel to dry them off but when she took it from me, the two of them headed into the living room.

"You can watch," she said over her shoulder, "I don't think He'll mind. Or She. What do I know?" She gave a slight shrug, chuckled, then spread the towel on the floor next to Pal's yoga mat. They were at an angle from the living room window, facing in the direction Pal had motioned to earlier.

They both stood ramrod straight, placed their hands up a little past their shoulders, palms out, as Mostar chanted, "Allahuackbar."

I won't try to describe in detail what I witnessed. I know I'd just mess it up. I want to be respectful, although I'm sure neither

Mostar nor Pal would mind. The beauty of their prayer, the fluid, ballet motions. Raised arms, turned heads. Knees bending and rising to Mostar's sung phrases. And then the name, through a cracking voice:

"Vincent Earnest Boothe."

Chapter 19

It is from the farming class that the bravest men and the sturdiest soldiers come. . . .

—Marcus Porcius Cato

JOURNAL ENTRY #14 [CONT.]

Leaving Mostar's house, I turned left instead of right. I wasn't supposed to be at Reinhardt's for another few minutes and I wanted to spend that time in the garden. Not that there'd be much to do. I figured I'd turn on the drip line, maybe shower and change while it ran.

I opened the front door, then the garage door, and gasped.

SPROUTS!

A tiny little arch was poking up near my feet, right at the spot where I'd planted the first large white bean!

"Pal!" I called, then sticking my head out the front door, shouted, "Palomino! The garden is sprouting!"

I bent down to examine the little, upside-down *u*. It was whitish, about half an inch high, and as I peered closer, I could see that tip of the bean below one end.

The spot next to this arch looked like it was bulging a little, so, using Bobbi's teapot, I dripped a few drops on it. Sure enough, as the dirt fell away, the first hint of an arch as well. I tried it again with the next one, and the one after that. So many *u*'s struggling to free themselves from the soil.

And they weren't the only ones!

The entire garden! Every inch!

"OhmyGod!" That was Carmen, who'd just come in with Pal. "Did you plant all those?"

"Just these," I said, referring to the marked beans. Ironically, nothing was coming up where I'd planted the Chinese peas and sweet potatoes. Or maybe they just weren't coming up *yet*! And it really didn't matter because their seed beds were surrounded by mysterious little shoots. They were everywhere, those shoots, scattered randomly across the entire garden.

"What are they all?" asked Carmen as Pal examined them on hands and knees.

"No idea," I said. "I don't even know where they're coming from."

"Maybe the earth we brought in?" That was Mostar, who'd just joined us.

"Maybe," I said with a little disappointment. If they were all just wild weeds . . .

"Compost?" That was Dan. This was turning into a real party. "The compost we mixed in, the older stuff at the bottom of the bins that turned into soil . . . could there still be old seeds from . . ."

"Cucumber slices," mused Mostar, who squatted next to Pal. Together they were examining a little wild sprout with round green leaves. "And tomatoes?" She pointed to a three-inch thread with two tiny narrow leaves. "This one, I think. How many times do we cut off the bruised parts?"

"I do that all the time!" said Carmen, with more energy and excitement than I'd ever seen. "The extra slices of something, or cutting out pits. And salsa!" This was directed down to Pal. "When we have taco night! All the leftover salsa we make! Right in the bin!"

Our own tomatoes! Even now I can't stop thinking how good they might taste.

Mostar looked at Pal, who was gently brushing her fingertips across the wobbling tomato stalk. "You know, we still have a lot of older soil-type compost. That has to have more seeds."

"And rice." I pointed to the little square foot where I'd sprinkled Bobbi's brown rice. It was now a solid patch of grass.

"Rice!" Mostar beamed at me. I explained where I'd gotten it and how much more I thought Bobbi had left. Mostar's lips rounded into a tight O. "We can live on that, rice and beans." She looked at Carmen. "Do you have any more of those beanbags lying around?"

"We might." Carmen looked at Pal. "And maybe some extra loose beans we didn't use. Maybe in the arts and crafts chest?"

Pal nodded enthusiastically.

"Then that would be worth it . . ." Mostar nodded back. "Worth the calories to build more gardens."

"More gardens!" Dan almost hit the ceiling. "Totally! Another garage! Maybe two, drip lines, compost"—he glanced at Palomino—"more worms and shit!"

"And shit?" Mostar asked with cocked eyebrow. Dan laughed, his cheeks reddened.

"Yes, really—the biodigester tanks!" And to me, with outstretched palms, "C'mon, I won't get cut, or sick. I promise!"

Before I could answer, Carmen asked me, "Can we do it?"

I wasn't sure if she was asking for my permission or expertise. Not that I had either to give. But Dan, Carmen, Palomino, the way they were all looking at me. And Mostar, hanging back, crossed arms. Judging my call?

My mind had already been racing through calculations, judging if the math added up. One cup of brown rice was around two hundred calories. One cup of beans, depending on type, might be the same or more. And fattening too! Most beans had fat in them, about a gram per cup. But how many cups of beans and rice could we hope for?

"We can," I started to say, but held out my hands quickly, "but after . . . after we finish the perimeter. First things first, right?

Safety, then food. Soon as we get the stakes up, soon as we know they work, we'll focus on more gardens."

"Yeah!" Dan pumped his fist as Carmen hugged her daughter.

Behind them, Mostar smiled and nodded.

I felt ten feet tall.

Then she jerked her head to the door and tapped her wrist like an old-style wristwatch.

Reinhardt! My shift!

I ran over to Reinhardt's house and saw through the window that Effie was reading in the chair next to his couch. She saw me, smiled, and got up to join me in the foyer. I could see Reinhardt was sleeping and she said that he'd been out for most of the morning.

I tried to apologize for being late and described what had happened in the garden. She brightened, but not for the reason you'd think. "Thank you," she said, "thank you for all you're doing with Palomino. She needs the purpose now, routine." She looked across the circle to her house, where her wife and daughter were waving from the window. "And now"—her eyes scanned the ridge—"she needs to focus on something positive. We all do." More waves from her family, and a final "thank you," before heading home.

So many thoughts were racing through my head. How many gardens can we build? And what about this one? What now? How much warmth do those little plants need? Dan had been right about cleaning off the roof. We'd need every kilowatt to keep the garage at summer temperatures. And what about summer light? Happy lamps? Everyone has one. Enough? At least the walls are white. Reflective. Aluminum foil? That hydroponics store in Venice. A plant in a reflective box? And fertilizer. Can we really use our own poo? Safe for Dan? Worth it? Smelling up the house?

So many questions, sitting here writing all this down. Foggy brain. Should nap. Reinhardt's still out. But his library. So many books. Gotta be something useful.

JOURNAL ENTRY #14 [CONT.]

Nope. There wasn't. Not one practical text, and believe me, I looked! Lots of philosophers though. Descartes, Voltaire, Sartre, and shelves of historians like Gibbon, Keegan, and Tacitus. Beautiful novels too, leather-bound first editions with gold printed names like Proust, Zola, and Molière.

And, of course, there're *his* books. *Halfway to Marx, Walking with Xu Xing,* and the famous *Rousseau's Children,* in at least a dozen languages: French, Italian, Greek, Chinese. (Or Japanese, I can't tell. Can't be Korean because I didn't see those little circles.) I noticed a lot of Rousseau's works were intermixed with various volumes of his book, as if they were buddies who got published at the same time.

At one point I thought I'd hit pay dirt when, going through the larger coffee table books, I came across the title *Vanishing Cultures of Southern Africa*. I thought I might, at least, get some helpful tips from the pictures. I didn't. It turned out just to be "white man's porn"; a lot of voluptuous, topless, or totally naked women dancing and jiggling in various indigenous ceremonies. Okay, so maybe these are culturally accurate photos, and maybe I'm projecting too much from memories of my "Colonialism and Male Sexuality" class at Penn, but Reinhardt's the exact age to have collected *National Geographic* the way later generations "read" *Playboy* for the "articles." And besides, the picture on the spine above the title should have been a giveaway. It showed a beaded G-string between a woman's legs.

There was one section though, which I almost missed. It was of a young woman during a coming-of-age ceremony carrying what looked like a hybrid sword/spear. I say "hybrid" because the shaft was shorter than I'd ever seen (barely three feet), while the blade was longer (about a foot and a half). The caption underneath described the weapon as an "Iklwa," which made me skip to the index for a closer look.

It's a Zulu weapon, invented by a guy named Shaka, which

"revolutionized Bantu warfare." Unlike earlier throwing spears, which could be knocked away by the other side's shield, the Iklwa was meant for "close combat." The wielder would get right up into the face of his enemy, knock the shield away with his own, then stab the short spear's long blade under the man's armpit. That's where the name comes from. The sucking sound of pulling it out of the dead man's heart and lungs. "Iklwa."

Gross, yes, and horrifying to think of whole armies fighting this way. But I couldn't help being fascinated by the book's comparison to Roman legionnaires who fought in a similar way. Different places, different ages, completely different cultures, and yet they came up with similar weapons and tactics. Is there something about how we're wired, something universally human? That was my last fuzzy thought before I finally nodded off.

The comfortable chair, Reinhardt's rhythmic breathing.

I didn't know what happened until my head suddenly jerked up to a dark sky with Reinhardt coming out of the entryway bathroom. Must have been the flushing that woke me. After half a couple disoriented seconds, I realized that Reinhardt was supporting himself against the wall. I jumped up to help him but he waved me away with, "I'm okay, I'm okay."

He clearly wasn't. Even as I struggled to get him back onto the couch, I could see how pale his lips were. I asked if he was hungry and he nodded weakly. I remember thinking that must be a good thing. Don't really sick people lose their appetites?

There wasn't much, at least when it came to frozen diet meals. But I did find plenty of "secret goodies," little packets of gummies and candies squirreled away. He must have hidden them all upstairs, like the ice cream, when I came over to catalog his food. Now they were everywhere, stuffed into drawers and cabinets all over the kitchen. It actually gave me a little bit of sympathy to see all those caches. I'd hid more than a few Twix bites from Mom.

Shame.

I didn't feel too sorry for him though, not when I asked if

there was anything he could and couldn't eat in his condition. I got a feeble, "Anything is fine, I guess."

You guess? Aren't you supposed to know if you have a heart condition? Lord knows his library isn't much help.

Hey, Flaubert, what can't a heart attack victim eat?

I settled on his second to last packet of insta-waffle. The kind you eat from a cup. Just add water, stir, and nuke. I tried not to keep reflexively checking the windows, or note that there were no kitchen knives to be seen. The man has probably never cooked anything in his life, or has had people do it for him.

Amazing how your perception of a space can change so quickly. If I'd been invited into Reinhardt's kitchen two weeks ago, I might have just thought about the décor (or lack thereof). Then, when I came in with Dan a few days ago, all I could think about was what there was to eat. Now all I could think about was what I could use to defend myself. Same room, different priorities.

The microwave chirped and I stuck a spoon in the expanded, muffin-looking thing. Reinhardt was sitting up now and swallowing with obvious delight. "No sugar?" I told him it looked like it already had plenty but his "aw, c'mon" shrug sent me back to the kitchen. "Some salt too . . ." I heard him call from the living room (with what sounded like a full mouth) and then, after probably realizing his tone, he added, "Please?"

I grabbed the salt shaker off the counter, the box of white sugar from the pantry, and returned to discover that he'd practically finished.

The world-famous scholar looked up at me like a ten-year-old boy. "Couldn't wait."

Something rattled. I jumped and spun. My eyes flicked to the source of the noise. It was the kitchen door, the cracked glass rattling in its fixture.

Reinhardt said, "It's been doing that. The wind."

I apologized, told him that Dan would be happy to look at it, and felt my body relax. That was when the yawn came out, big and loud, and I covered my mouth with embarrassment. As my eyes opened, I saw Reinhardt looking at me with an expression I hadn't recognized before, a kind, almost fatherly smile.

He said, "I'm the one who's sorry. I shouldn't have kept you here to watch me. You've got to get home and to bed."

I told him that I was fine, to which he responded, "Balderdash," and asked how many hours I'd slept in the last two days. I confessed to a couple of catnaps.

"Aha!" A tiny twinkle, a wag of the finger, and a dramatic, two-hand sweep toward the door.

"Do you want me to set the alarm?" Then, remembering all the window damage, said, "At least the internal sensors? Maybe just the kitchen?"

"What if I need a midnight snack?" He patted his stomach lightly. "You think I know how to disarm that infernal apparatus?"

"But you can't make it to the kitchen," I protested, "if you get dizzy, fall, and hit your head or something . . ."

"Go, go. I think it was a . . ." He hesitated before saying, "Nerves . . . I used to get . . . when I was young . . . these spells . . . I could have been more forthright last night." He scowled at the floor. "It's a cruel joke, those formative years, when your brain learns the rules of the universe. Your childhood is spent being nurtured, protected, loved unconditionally while your adulthood is spent searching in vain for substitutes. Mate, government, God . . ."

He suddenly looked up at me, embarrassed, angry. "Sorry." He waved his hand like those words had been a bad smell. "Intellectual coward."

I felt so bad for him, all that puffed up veneer stripped away. Embarrassed old man, admitting his weakness.

All I could say was, "It's all right, I mean, who doesn't want to be taken care of when things get scary?"

He repeated that phrase, "taken care of," and blinked hard with a long, wet sniff.

I suddenly found myself asking, "Do you want to stay at our place, you know, just in case it isn't a panic attack? If you need something in the middle of the night?"

He paused at that, genuinely surprised, then said with a smiling swat, "Will ya get outta here already?"

"Just let me clean up first," I said, and carried his cup and spoon to the kitchen. It didn't take long, spoon in the dishwasher, disposable cup in the trash. But when I came back, he'd already managed a trip to the bookshelf. Three small, thick, red hardbacks were sitting on his lap. I'd noticed them before but couldn't read the Latin titles. "Childhood friends," he said, "Cato, Varro, Columella, their writings on agriculture."

And of my questioning look, he answered, "I overheard you telling Effie about the sprouts. I wasn't really asleep." He opened the first book, grabbed his glasses off the table, and said, "Maybe I can find something useful in here." Then with a derisive snort, added, "Maybe I can be useful for once."

And with a really bitter chuckle, he muttered, "Work sets you free."

Where have I heard that before?

I told him not to stay up too late. He said, "I won't, I won't," and shooed me away with a smile and a big yawn.

That was about an hour ago. I'm home now in my kitchen, writing all this down before getting back to work. Dan's on the floor, sitting cross-legged amidst a pile of bamboo. Two piles, actually, a smaller one of finished stakes and a much larger, rougher pile resting across his lap. He's out, by the way, back against the fridge, snoring, half buried in his bamboo blanket.

I thought about waking him to go upstairs, but I know he'll just want to get back to work. I think I'll crash on the couch for a couple hours, set my phone for midnight. Then I'll get up, maybe wake Dan as well, and the two of us can saw spikes till morning. Mostar thinks we'll have enough by tomorrow night to completely ring the neighborhood.

And after that?

I keep getting up to check on the garden, to see how all my little sprouts are doing. They're so beautiful, so vulnerable. I gotta figure out the best way to raise them.

Raise?

Whatever, so tired.

Tomorrow, or rather the day after tomorrow, after I get a really good night's sleep, after the perimeter is done. By that time Reinhardt might have found some tips in his books. I hope he's okay. As I started to leave, back turned, my hand on the knob, he said, "Good night, Hannah."

Chapter 20

Grant that we may lie down in Peace, Eternal God, and awaken us to life.
Shelter us with Your tent of peace and guide us with Your good counsel.
Shield us from hatred, plague and destruction.
Keep us from war, famine and anguish.
Help us to deny our inclination to evil.
God of peace, may we always feel protected because You are our Guardian and Helper.
Give us refuge in the shadow of your wings.
Guard our going forth and our coming in and bless us with life and peace.
Blessed are You, Eternal God, whose shelter of peace is spread over us, over all Your people, Israel and over Jerusalem.

—The Hebrew Hashkiveinu, a blessing of protection

From Golda's Daughter: My Life in the IDF by Lieutenant Colonel Hannah Reinhardt Roth (ret.)

Intellect. That was the only way to reach them. Emotion? Passion? Never. That was debasement, the language of animals. I tried to remain calm and to keep the conversation along the lines of an academic debate.

I discussed Egypt's expulsion of Soviet advisors as punishment for Moscow's armament moratorium. I delineated the specifics of said armaments, from MiG-23 fighter bombers to the Frog intermediate range ballistic missiles. With Sheehan's *New York Times* story as ammunition, I demonstrated how these offensive weapons were no different than the columns of T-55 main battle tanks Nasser had unsheathed against Israel in '67.

Father, again, insisted that Sadat was not Nasser, which I maintained justified my point. Sadat, in order to prove that he was not a clone of his predecessor, had to prove to his people, the Arab League, and the world at large that he could accomplish what Nasser couldn't—driving the yehud into the sea. Wasn't this strategy, painting victory over defeat, the motive behind so many past wars? In fact, hadn't Nasser tried to erase Israel in order to erase his debacle in Yemen?

I couldn't help but be proud of my campaign. Supporting facts. Inarguable logic. I could almost hear the phantom applause of Clausewitz, Mahan, and Jomini. Only Schlieffen withheld his praise, clucking at my critical mistake of avoiding a two-front war.

"Hostilities are impossible." Alex always knew when to strike, just when Father needed him the most. "The United Nations will see to that."

I responded with a question. "What 'United' Nations do you mean? The declining British? The anti-Semitic French? The Communist bloc that takes its orders from the Kremlin or the so-called non-aligned state hostages of Arab oil?"

I could see another thought readying to charge. I broke it with a preemptive, "The same United Nations that stood by and did nothing after fourteen Syrian probing attacks, and who pulled their peacekeepers out of the Sinai to make way for the Egyptians?"

Alex spluttered, "But America . . ."

I'd won. I knew it. America? I buried him in counterpoints. Vietnam. Watergate. The inward distractions of cultural civil strife. Alex huffed, retreating before my onslaught. If I'd only been magnanimous in victory and refrained from that conclusive nail. "America can't help us."

Just two letters. One word.

"Us?" The resurgent flames blazed in Father's eyes. "Us? Hannah, aren't we Americans?"

"American Jews," I countered, regrouping before those smug, tranquil faces. "Haven't we learned anything from our past?"

"Mmmhh," mused Father, pretending to ponder my point. "Learning is indeed the key, learning to understand ourselves." His hand sailed theatrically over the bookshelf behind us. "Biology, psychology . . ."

"Political economy," Alex added, winning an approving smile from our patriarch.

"Without unearthing the roots of our desire for conflict," Father lectured, "we are no better than pre-Pasteur physicians who acknowledged the existence of microbes yet failed to connect their existence to disease."

Poetic, dramatic, and directly lifted from the pages of his last book. His eyes had even shifted from mine to the sacred arc of his latest shelved tome. *Jung's Hiroshima: Examining the Psychosis of War.*

"There's nothing nobler than working for a peaceful future," I said, trying to appeal to his vanity, "but there won't be a future if we don't secure the present." I opened the window, and like a released djinni, the sounds and smells of the Upper East Side gushed in. "And that present has an entire region's armies mobilizing to wipe us off the map."

Alex gave a slight, amused chuckle. "So, you're saying we should burn our books and just club our way forward like troglodytes?"

"I'm saying," I shot back, "that it's suicidal to waste time deconstructing the Versailles Treaty the morning AFTER Kristallnacht!"

Father, still sitting, smiled that insufferable, victorious curl. "Ah," he said, waving his infuriating finger to the sky, "and now we come to the final keep in your crumbling fortress. Should we have fought?"

It was an old argument, as worn and comfortable as the old leather throne he occupied. Should we have fought? The first time I'd been six, asking about the black and white faces on our mantel. Who were they? Where is Strasbourg? Why did they die? Why didn't they leave with you? And with the final question, "Why didn't they fight back?" came the inevitable dismissal.

"Because it would not have made a difference."

Those same pictures stared down at us now, those smiling, innocent death masks.

"An eye for an eye," my father continued, "only leaves the world blind."

I parried his Gandhi quote with another saying from the Raj: "If the Indians all pissed at once, the British would be washed out to sea."

"Are you dismissing nonviolence," said Alex, shaking his head, "are you really going to deny the progress made in this country by Dr. King?"

"Are you going to deny that King's leverage was based on the fear of Malcolm X?" Sensing an opening, I tried to break the siege. "An open hand works when the alternative is a fist."

Quoting Einstein, Alex said, "You cannot simultaneously prevent and prepare for war."

"Said the man fleeing Dachau's oven."

"Such a zealot," my father moaned, the words dripping with disappointment. "You claim to defend our traditional homeland yet the method of your defense is exactly what lost that land to begin with."

I could feel my cheeks flushing, hear my voice rising. "I'm not saying war is good! And I'm not saying that going around the world attacking people is right. It's not! It's a last resort, always! If there's any other way to solve problems, *any* way to avoid bloodshed . . . but when they're coming for you, when you know they're coming, when they won't listen and it's too late to even run, you have to defend yourself. You have to fight!"

I'd done the one thing I'd sworn against. I had allowed my heart to take command. "Oh, Hannah." Alex chuckled victoriously through his nose, his hands stretched out sympathetically. "Hannah, Hannah." Only my brother could make me hate the sound of my name. *Hannah, you're such a child. Hannah, don't be so hysterical. Hannah, if you'd just let me help you be more like me maybe Papa would love you as much as he loves me.*

"You intellectual coward!" I hissed. "Both of you! Sheltering behind books and quotes and other people's protection! But what are you going to do when reality's jackboot comes crashing through your door?"

My fist shook at Father, then to the ghosts on the mantel; all those lives now reduced to piles of shoes, eyeglasses, gold fillings, and ashes.

"What did you do for them?" I shouted at my frozen audience. "When the letters stopped coming, when your whole class enlisted. Where were you?"

I leaned over my father, fixing my gaze on the passive, cool, utterly unresponsive brain. Because that was all he'd become now; no heart, no soul, nothing but dispassionate gray matter. "You stayed. You hid. *You* didn't make a difference." I didn't realize I was crying until I saw a tear stain his shirt. "You didn't even try." Through blurring vision, I sputtered to Alex, "And you won't either, when they come for you, you won't resist." Over my shoulder I said, "You'll just lie there and die."

Passing the kitchen, I heard Mother putting away the dishes. I couldn't condemn her for not coming to my defense. She never had. She never knew she could. Amid the china clatter and the dull thud of cabinet doors, I could hear her muttering to herself. Soft and steady with the repetitive musicality of prayer. As the door closed behind me, I caught the last lines of the Hashkiveinu.

JOURNAL ENTRY #15

OCTOBER 15

I've just read back over all my previous entries. I don't recognize who wrote them. A life lived by a stranger. Somebody I can barely remember.

If only time travel was as easy as turning a page. Flip back to a couple days ago, warn that person I used to be.

That morning, October 13, the alarm woke me at seven, hours later than I'd planned. Dan told me he'd reset my phone after waking up around midnight. He thought sleep was more important than helping him with stakes. I saw that he still had a few more to finish but he just smiled and said, "Why don't you check the garden."

He already had, saw what had happened, knew how happy it would make me.

It felt like Christmas morning. More pale arches rising from the soil. Yesterday's strongest seedlings had managed to raise their entire bean up into the air. I could see the beginnings of tiny green leaves growing from the split. More little shoots, volunteers from the compost. Rice grass taller by at least half an inch. All in one night!

"You'll need to support them," that was Dan calling from the kitchen, "I mean, when they get taller. Isn't that what you do for plants, you tie them to things, like tomato cages? Or baskets? What are they called?" He was behind me now, hand on the doorframe, smiling down at me. "We still got, like, a whole ton of little thin bamboo branches. Once we get time, you know, down the line, I can help you turn them into those cage-things or whatever."

His arms around me, his kiss goodbye. Off to work, coconut stabber on his hip, spear in one hand and bread knife in the other. The Common House was almost denuded of bamboo. A dozen or so stalks to go. It wouldn't take long, and when he stepped out onto the driveway, we couldn't see or hear anything from the ridge. Still, I couldn't help but utter "Be careful," and got a grunting, caveman spear to chest in reply. I returned his salute with one of my own, a raised middle finger and the silently mouthed, "Love you."

I stayed in the open doorway, shivering in the freezing air, watching him pass Effie and Palomino on their way to Reinhardt's. It was Effie's turn to take over from me, and despite her friendly wave, I suddenly worried that she thought I'd abandoned him. Of course, she didn't, and of course I didn't need to run over and explain how he'd kicked me out. But I did anyway, and ended up being grateful for the chat. She had good news. Finally, some positive stories from the Boothes' car radio.

She told me they'd got that crazy shooter on the I-90. The road was open now, supplies in, evacuees out. The Canadians, just like in Katrina, were also on their way. The president had finally swallowed his pride (that's what Carmen thought) and allowed foreign relief efforts in through the north. And because Seattle was "secured" (I guess that means no more riots), the authorities could focus on the towns damaged by Rainier.

Effie said, "That means they'll be finding us soon." She rubbed her daughter's back vigorously. "When they start spreading out again, looking for survivors, they have to come across us!" I'd never seen her so animated. "Maybe we should put out a HELP sign. You know? Like they always do after storms? On roofs and stuff? I can't believe we never thought about that until now! Maybe we could use a sheet"—she gestured to the grassy "helipad" in front of the Common House—"or just write it in all these"—a nod to the thrown rocks at our feet.

"Good idea," I responded, but tempered it with, "once we make sure to finish—"

"Oh yeah!" She cut me off. "The 'perimeter,' of course! Definitely."

I could see reality begin to cloud her zeal, reminding her of what still faced us. "Maybe tomorrow," she tried.

I answered, "Maybe," and, looking down at Pal, asked, "but for now, you still up for working in the garden?"

Her head bobbed enthusiastically as her mother headed for Reinhardt's.

"It's so beautiful," I said, leading her inside. "When we finally get some time, we can start putting aluminum foil up on the wall." More happy nods as she stopped to check each little plant.

"And we should start thinking about supporting them," I continued. "Dan had a good idea about how to use extra bamboo for . . ."

A muffled scream.

Distant, from Reinhardt's.

We rushed back outside just in time to see Effie stumbling from his front door. I told Pal to go home, to find Carmen, and ran to catch Effie before she collapsed.

Eyes wide, voice and body shaking. Even before I got to her, I thought, *Another heart attack. The first one was real and he's just had another one last night!* Effie didn't talk, she couldn't. Hyperventilating, trying to get the words out, she just waved frantically inside. Darting past her, into the living room, I'd already imagined what he must look like, lying on the couch, cold and blue. "Please don't let his eyes be open."

I saw the blood trails first. Two of them, narrow and wide, running parallel to each other from the hole in the back door to the empty, red-soaked couch. I felt Dan's arm around my shoulders. I couldn't look away. I couldn't stop reading the story in front of me, imagining what must have happened while I slept peacefully at home.

They'd been so silent, pushing the cracked kitchen glass, testing it, waiting for a sound that would send them running. Patient, thoughtful. They must have edged the crinkling pane just enough from its frame to reach one long arm inside. Fumbling with the lock, solving the simple puzzle of the small metal switch. Sliding the frame open, pulling back the drapes, edging the table away. To accomplish all that with the dexterity and focus to not wake him up. Only one had come in, I could tell by the bloody footprints. A small one, maybe? Princess, or the younger, barely pubescent male? Would this have been his coming of age trial? A test of stealth, intelligence, and the strength to tear Reinhardt's head off?

Because that's what it did. Twisting, pulling. The darkest, deepest stain was at the base of his pillow. And he hadn't struggled. Nothing was disturbed. Even his books, lying neatly stacked on the coffee table next to his glasses. He'd probably read them for a little while, realized he was too sleepy to concentrate. Set them aside, switched off the lamp, pulled the afghan up to his neck. He probably hadn't heard it come in until it was standing over him. Did he wake up? A brush of fur against his face, the feeling of rough skin over his mouth? God, I hope he didn't. Please, God, let him have slept through it all.

And yet, why does the alternative keep running through my mind? The story of him waking to this black hovering hulk. Pinprick eyes, warm breath, the clench of fingers around his throat. Why do I keep imagining that he chose not to fight back? As those fingers crushed his windpipe while another hand held him down. No kicking, no scratching. No attempt to save his own life. Why do I imagine that his few seconds of waking consciousness were frozen in terrified acceptance?

It has to be the bloody footprints. The space between those two enormous feet. So close together. I've seen them run, the stride would have only left a pair of prints between the couch and kitchen. These were too close, too numerous, and mixed with far too much blood. The parallel trails, thicker one left by the body, thinner by the head. Reinhardt's head, splattering across the walls and floor, as if the killer, holding it by the mouth, had let it swing back and forth. Unhurried. Unafraid.

And why not? Why fear us when we can be invaded so easily, when we won't even try to fight back?

Chapter 21

Many people are horrified when they hear that a chimpanzee might eat a human baby, but after all, so far as the chimpanzee is concerned, men are only another kind of primate. . . .

—Jane Goodall, *In the Shadow of Man*

From my interview with Senior Ranger Josephine Schell.

Boulder, Colorado, 1991. The town looked like a paradise. Lush and green and totally unspoiled by humans. Only it wasn't unspoiled because it wasn't supposed to be there in the first place. The area around Boulder is naturally semi-arid. It was the townsfolk who pumped in all that water for their lawns and fruit trees. And when the fruit trees came, so did the deer. Locals loved it. "Hey, Honey, there's a deer in our yard!"

And with the herbivores came the inevitable carnivores. Mountain lions were pretty scarce back then. Early Europeans had driven them to the brink of extinction. Those that were left went deep into the Rockies, far enough to avoid any possible contact with humans. But when they followed the deer out of the mountains, they found that this new breed of human wasn't anything like their "shoot on sight" ancestors. These humans shot with cameras. "Oh wow, kids, look! A real puma!"

Some wiser individuals tried to speak up. "You're not in a zoo. These are predators. They're dangerous. They need to be tagged and relocated before somebody gets hurt."

No one listened. They couldn't believe how lucky they were

to see big cats "out in the wild." Who needs a zoo when you've got the woods right behind your house? And then the dogs started disappearing. The little ones at first, the tiny toys who couldn't defend themselves. That's why no one listened when folks with badges tried, again, to convince them of the danger. "Oh c'mon, what do you expect if someone's bichon-poodle mix gets off leash?" I think one of the casualties was a cockapoo literally named "Fifi." Never mind that the attack didn't happen in the woods but right in front of Fifi's house. Naysayers still thought she was "low-hanging fruit," that no way a cougar's gonna go for a full-sized, fighting canine.

Until they did. A Doberman barely escaped with its life. A black Lab and German shepherd didn't. "What do you call a dog on a leash? A meal on a string." That was one of the jokes going around, like that cartoon in a local paper. It showed a dog's owner handing her pup a letter from a cat saying, "Welcome to the food chain."

She shakes her head.

The food chain. Nobody remembers where our link is supposed to be. The warnings were right there. The trail of escalation leading right to people's front doors.

They did start to react, I'll give them that. One lion was killed after it attacked a game ranch, and there was a town meeting on what to do. But like so many other problems, it was too little too late. The cats were there, they were multiplying, and after testing our boundaries, they were getting bolder every day.

Once killing dogs became common, it was only a matter of time before they worked their way up the chain to us. A jogger was chased, treed, and only survived because she'd learned to fight back in her "model-mugging" course. A hospital employee was chased in the parking lot. Several people couldn't leave their houses. The list goes on.

And then Scott Lancaster went for a run and never came back. Scott was eighteen years old, healthy, strong, doing a cardio workout on his free period up the trail behind his high school.

Two days later, they found what was left of him, chest torn open, organs eaten, face chewed off. Those remains were found in the stomach of a cougar. The investigation proved that the cat wasn't rabid, or starving. You know what that attack also proved, along with all the other fatal attacks we've had since then?*

They're not afraid of us anymore.

JOURNAL ENTRY #15 [CONT.]

"It wasn't your fault." Mostar, standing behind us. Reading my mind again, the inevitable punishment she knew I'd inflict on myself. I didn't have to go home. I could have pushed back. Together with the lights on, with me calling for help. I might have saved him. If I'd only stayed!

"Not your fault," she repeated. Then, "It's mine."

A flash of something I couldn't recognize. A nervous swallow, an unwillingness to meet my eyes.

Guilt?

"I didn't think they'd be this bold this soon." Her voice was low, just loud enough for me to hear. "I thought with the fire . . . their first kill to satiate . . . I thought we'd at least have one more day. . . ."

She shook her head, dry-spat another foreign phrase that sounded like, "Majmoonehjedan!"†

Then it passed. Back straight, eyes clear, looking us over like a general in a war movie.

"We don't have time anymore, not enough for a full perimeter. We have to make a smaller one, right now, around the Common House. Carmen . . ." The poor woman practically dropped her

* At the time of this writing, ten humans have been killed in North America by cougars since the death of Scott Lancaster.

† Majmune jedan: You ape.

hand sanitizer. "Go get Bobbi out of bed. Do whatever you have to do but get her up and dressed. Go."

Carmen dashed out as Mostar pivoted to Effie and Pal. "Go home and grab some blankets, the heaviest you've got. One armload, one trip, and get them over to the Common House."

Without question or pause, they left.

Turning back to me, she said, "Go through Reinhardt's kitchen. Grab what's frozen, canned, dried. One bag."

I nodded as she grabbed Dan's sleeve. "C'mon." And they were gone.

There wasn't any emotion in her voice. There wasn't time.

I raced back into Reinhardt's kitchen, my shoe sticking on the floor's red trail. I grabbed a plastic garbage bag off the roll, shoved in the remaining frozen meals, then ran for the Common House.

Their stink was stronger, and it wasn't my imagination. Neither was the figure on the ridge. A tall black outline between two trees. Just standing there, watching me. My eyes flicked down to avoid a rock from two nights ago, then back up to a now-empty slope. The howls began a second later, a solo swelling to a chorus. I felt naked. My new spear. Back at home. I hadn't thought I'd need it. No time now.

I kept my head down, trotting the last few steps to the Common House. I threw the meals in the freezer and ran back outside to see Mostar and Dan exit her house. Both had armloads of stakes. Both dropped them when Mostar pointed up to something just behind my field of vision. Dan reached for his spear leaning against Mostar's entryway as she called for Effie and Pal. "The Durants!" Voice like a megaphone, frantic waves to follow her.

We all met her at their house; myself, Effie and Pal, and Carmen with a very dazed, pajama-and-robe-clad Bobbi in tow.

I'm not sure what Mostar was thinking by then. Rallying us all to their door. All of us together? Societal pressure? Or maybe just the physical force we'd need to drag the two of them out.

"Yvette! Tony!" No doorbell or even knocks. Mostar hammered at the elaborate wood with side fists and open palms. "Open up! Open the goddamn door! Now!" The urgency, the violence of her assault.

Bobbi, now fully awake, pulled back a step. Carmen and Effie both hugged their daughter. I grabbed Dan's arm. A new thought closing my throat: What if Reinhardt hadn't been the first house?

I was about to take Dan with me around back, my brain filling with what might be waiting, when the front door slowly swung open. This relief wave broke though as soon as I saw the ghoul who answered.

Red, wet, unfocused eyes glimmered out from sunken, dark cavities. Thin, unshaven cheeks hung above chapped, cracked, scab-rimmed lips. Shoeless feet, a stained white T-shirt, sagging, worn sweatpants held up by a shaking hand with dirty nails. The reek slammed me a moment later, wafting out from the doorway in an invisible, humid cloud. Body odor. Bad breath. The slightest hint of feces.

"Tony?" I could see Mostar's slump, thought I heard her sigh. Am I projecting? Filling a gap? I feel like she wasn't surprised. The rest of us though, that collective flinch.

"Tony." A little louder this time, her words matched by the slow, air chop of her hand. "Where's Yvette?"

"Oh . . ." His mouth hung open at a crooked angle, exposing a row of stained teeth. "Yeeaaah." A slight narrowing of the eyes, like someone who accidentally walked into the wrong room.

"Yvette." Mostar tried looking past him, around him, then back for a third, "Yvette!"

Licking of the lips, and another "Yeah . . ." as he turned his back.

"No, Tony . . . ," Mostar started to say, then followed him in. A slight jumble from the rest of us. Dan's spear catching on the doorframe. A quick "Sorry" to the nearly struck Effie as he left the weapon outside.

I was already ahead of him by then, almost gagging from what

I smelled inside. Sweat, feet, and concentrated, stale urine wafting from the downstairs bathroom. And what we saw . . .

Had it been anyone else, in any other circumstance, I would have just considered the homeowners to be slobs.

Towels on the floor. A few clothes. Wineglasses amid the bookshelves and empty bottles. The pillow and comforter on the couch, stained brown with the darker residue of body oils. No worse than a college dorm room, or a few of my fellow twenty-somethings in their first apartments. But this home, these people.

And it wasn't just the mess that got to me, or the smashed iPhone lying under an iPhone-sized dent in the wall. It was the magazines. Covering the glass coffee table, over and under and wedged in between crust-bottomed coffee mugs. *Wired, Forbes, Eco-Structure*. All of them wrinkled and bubbled with water damage. All of them with Tony's face on the cover. THE DAWN OF ECO-CAPITALISM, THE GREEN REVOLUTIONARY, FIGHTING THE GOOD FIGHT.

"Tony!" Mostar took his arm, turning him toward her. "Where is Yvette?" Gentle, firm. "We need to talk to both of you."

"Sure, yeah, Yvette . . ." His eyes—is that what you call a thousand-yard stare?—gazing into space, brow furrowed, tongue circling his lips. "Yvette."

His pause gave us all a moment to hear it.

zzzzzp zzzzzp zzzzzp

Mostar shook her head, maybe angry with herself for not realizing it sooner. (That's how I felt, at least, forgetting to check the garage.) I might have knocked on the door if Mostar hadn't pushed past me and thrown it open.

Bright light flooded in, with an invisible, acrid mist.

Yvette, or what she'd become, practically fell off her elliptical.

"WhatWHAT?" Her voice was high, scratchy. Bounding into the living room, dripping, wild. That's how I'll always think of her eyes. Wild. Frantically darting to everyone and everything. Her face, her frame. We were looking at a skeleton. Under the soaking sports bra and yoga pants. Skin wrapped so tightly over sinewy bone. Had she been eating at all? What can you do to your body, your mind, in so short a time?

It hadn't even been two weeks. That quick for someone to fall apart? That easy?

I guess it depends on who you are to begin with, how tightly you're already holding on.

Adversity introduces us to ourselves.

Nice to meet you, Mr. and Mrs. Durant.

"Whatwhatwhatdoyouwant!" I could still hear gibberish squawking from the noise-canceling headphones around her neck. Not music, some kind of talking. Inspirational? Guided imagery? Her own voice?

Mostar barely uttered, "Yvette," but was cut off with a frantic "Whatyouwant!"

Recognition, adaptation, Mostar shifted from the command stance with Tony to a conciliatory, de-escalating, "Yvette, Love, we have to get you out of here." Soft, easy, as with a child or a jumper. "You know about the animals out there?" A slow, non-startling gesture to the unrepaired broken windows. "You know they're surrounding us, right? That they're getting more aggressive? Did you hear the—"

Yvette cut her off with a chattering, "WhatnoIdon'tknowanythingaboutanyanimals." Skin steaming in the cold air, head quivering with each syllable.

"Don'tknowwhatyou'retalkingabout." Her breath, five feet away. I could smell the starvation.

Mostar, caring, concerned. "You must have heard the screaming. Vincent? You heard him, right?"

At that, Carmen put a comforting arm around Bobbi.

Mostar continued with, "And now, last night, Alex . . ."

"Idon'tknowanything!" Yvette chattered. Her accent, upper class English, gone. This new one, old one, a thick Australian twang. "Youneedtogo!" Head bobbing maniacally at the door. "Go . . . gogogogo!"

"We all need to go," Mostar said slowly. "We need to take

what we need to live on, and all move into the Common House, where we can protect each other."

I was already thinking, planning ahead, as to how we'd take care of them. The shower, first, hot water and a scrub. We could hold her down, if we had to. At least Tony might go quietly. Two more mouths to feed. And clothes, I'd wash theirs by hand. I wouldn't mind. Clean, safe. They'd come around. They'd have to. All of us together, cramped, sharing everything. No choice.

"You need to hurry," Mostar continued, enunciating each word slowly. "Don't take anything, just come with—"

"Nonono!" Yvette backed up a step, jutting out her lower jaw. A cornered animal, that was all I could think of, a monkey in a cage. "Youneedtogetout! Allofyououtc'monnownow!"

Tony had sat back down by then, melting into his sleep stain on the couch. He didn't seem to acknowledge what was happening around him. Didn't look or move.

"Yvette, please!" Mostar, losing patience, almost pleading, holding out her hands with a desperation that tightened my abs. "We don't have time for this! They're not afraid of us anymor—"

She never finished.

At that moment her head happened to face the huge living room window behind us.

I turned just in time to see the dark shape standing right in front of the curtained window, right before that window collapsed.

Chapter 22

If this had been a bluff charge, they would have been screaming to intimidate us. These guys were quiet. And they were huge. They were coming in for the kill.

—Primatologist SHELLY WILLIAMS, BBC News, on the "Mystery Ape" of DR Congo

JOURNAL ENTRY #15 [CONT.]

The scramble.

Shouts and running bodies. An elbow in my chest, hair in my face, a shin tripping mine. I started running before I'd fully turned. I stumbled, fell, tried to get up, and slipped again on a copy of *Eco-Structure* magazine.

My face hit the carpet just as the head-sized fist whooshed into the wall above. I heard the crack, felt the vibration, then looked up to see Dan's face through the blue cloud of denim insulation. His hands shot out, cupping me under the arms.

Pal! That was my first conscious thought. Where was Palomino? My head spun around the room. All I could catch was Tony, sprinting over the couch, practically flying through the door to their garage gym. Yvette, a step and a half behind him, calling his name, reaching for him as the hooting colossus reached for her.

The flash of a moving figure outside (Mostar?) disappearing from sight.

A stampeding sound above my head. Small feet on the second floor. Human feet?

"Pal!" I shouted to the ceiling as Dan pulled me to my feet. A loud "C'mon!" in my ear, and a hard tug on my arm.

Together, we rushed toward the kitchen door. Around the table and chairs, just a few more steps. I was already reaching to slide it back. A shape loomed in front of us, a recoiling fist.

"Back!" Dan pulled me away as the veined safety glass wrapped, literally wrapped, itself around the attacker. Blinded for a second, thrashing in the crunching coat.

"Here!" A shout over our shoulders, Mostar beckoning us from outside the hole in the living room window.

She'd waited for us. She could have gotten away and she waited. Mostar.

We dashed across the living room, past the creature trying to batter its way into the exercise room. A grunt of recognition. A look of terror from Mostar. It must have turned toward us, followed us as we jumped through the window's car-sized opening.

Mostar shouted "Run!" and gestured with Dan's spear. Then a thrust, an inch or two past my face. I spun just in time to see the huge bloody hand, still gripping the blade.

The wail, that painful, sustained bawl. It rang in my ears as Mostar pulled me forward and kicked me, actually kicked me, in the direction of my house. "Go! GO!"

I sprinted across the driveway, dodging moon-cratered rocks. I thought they were right behind me. Mostar and Dan. I even held the door for them. But they'd broken left instead of right, around the other side of the Common House. Mostar's idea? Multiple targets? Or was the ultimate goal her house? Her workshop? Her weapons? Watching them reach the door, I felt this sudden rush of panic, like a little kid whose family got on the other subway car.

I called, "Dan!" and he actually stopped for a moment. A look, a recognition, and the first formation of a word. Then a hard shove of Mostar's shoulder drove him through the entrance. A roar behind us. I jumped inside.

I should have gone upstairs. I should have at least grabbed my spear. It was right there! Leaning behind the front door! Stupid! So many mistakes. If I'd armed myself, barricaded the office, or holed up in the bedroom where I might have escaped out the back balcony. Choices, chances.

Anything except what I did. Staying downstairs, crawling to the window, spying the horror across the way.

I'd looked just in time to see the Durants' garage door begin to slide up. A foot of space, maybe a little less, just enough for Tony to slither out. Skittering for his Tesla, his right hand closed around what had to be his key fob. He jumped behind the wheel just as Yvette crab-walked out behind him. I watched her run to the passenger side, try the handle-less door. She slapped, then punched the window with her bony hands.

I couldn't see Tony at first; the car was parked facing their house. But when the backup lights came on, when the tires skidded in four clouds of ash, when Yvette leaped back to prevent being run over.

His face. A photoshopped mask of mundanity. He wasn't running for his life. He hadn't just abandoned his wife. An everyday three-point turn on his way to the store. Even when Yvette jumped in front, pounding the hood.

"Cunt!" Her screech, clear and sharp through my double paned windows. "Youfuckingcuntyoufuckingshiteatingcunt!"

He honked. Actually honked! Behind flapping windshield wipers, he looked, what, perturbed? Delayed by road construction or a pedestrian too slow to cross? Frowning slightly at the hysterical Yvette, whose back showed four long, bloody stripes. "FuckyoufuckyoufuckfuckfuckFUCKYOUUUUU!"

And what did I look like? Probably the same? If Tony was stuck in traffic, I was watching a movie. I didn't move, didn't speak, didn't try to warn them as the brown, shaggy ogre leapt from the hole in the window, rupturing the windshield as it landed on the roof like a wrecking ball.

Alpha. Arms raised. Hooting.

I couldn't look away as she gripped Yvette, flailing and screaming, by that long stringy rope of hair. She kicked, she shouted, she swiped up and back at the forearm-sized fingers. The yank ended everything. One hard jerk snapping her head back against her spine. Flicking a switch. Yvette dropped.

Then another yank, a full circle up and around. Her body slammed into the car's windshield, caving in the opaque barrier. I caught a quick peek of Tony's rump disappearing into the backseat. Was he trying to climb out? I didn't see either of the back doors open. He might have just been cowering in the footwell. Cornered, helpless.

Still gripping the dangling, almost fluid Yvette, Alpha reached her other arm through the holed windshield and pulled Tony out by his right leg. I saw the left leg catch on the seat, twisting at an impossible angle. I know I didn't hear any screams. The way his arms flailed, grasping at the smooth metal as he was dragged backward across the hood. He reminded me of an insect, a captured butterfly trying to flap away.

Tony was still moving when she tossed him to the ground, bouncing him on his stomach, bringing her big foot down between his shoulder blades. Why did he have to be facing me? Why did I have to see that frothy red bubble from his mouth? Another stomp, the crack of ribs. A thicker, darker spurt followed by the spasm of lungs trying to find breath.

She was standing on him now, both feet alternately pulverizing his neck and back. I saw his head burst. Not break. Burst. Fluid in the brain case? Was that the red pressure pop from the nose and eyes?

She held him aloft, this limp, dripping bag of skin and soaked clothes. And Yvette, the hanging puppet in her other hand, still recognizable, still staring with open eyes and a wide, crooked mouth. Alpha howled, a long, triumphant wail that seemed to vibrate the glass in front of me.

A rallying cry. The rest came running. The Twins from around the back of the house. Scout, galloping across the circle with old Gray trying to keep up. From down the slope, Juno and the two new mothers. The small young male squeezing through the front doorway as Dowager climbed through the hole in the living room window. And behind her, tall and broad, Consort with his dripping bloody hand. He must have been the one Mostar stabbed with Dan's spear. Licking the wound, bloody tongue.

Hopping, whooping, beating their chests as they surrounded their leader. And all with eyes averted. None would look at her as they got close enough to hold out open hands. Begging. Submission.

Alpha dropped Tony's amorphous pulp at her feet. The crowd surged forward. She barked. They withdrew. With her now free hand, she reached for Yvette's exposed stomach. Sharp nails tore through the flat, muscled belly, spilling a red torrent down her white skin. A slow, almost gentle pull, and a fistful of bloody hose flopped out.

The circle closed, the shrieks rose. Alpha's hand lowered as the small male, the Goldenboy, grabbed the first taste, then spun its back to the group, a length of intestine still connected to Yvette's corpse.

The troop went wild, some running in small tight circles, some rolling spasmodically in the ash. What do they call it when sharks do this? A feeding frenzy? Alpha looked down for another grab into Yvette's torso. That was when she saw me.

Spy. Voyeur. Why did I stay? Why did I have to look? Just like that first night, the compost bin fight, when she'd locked eyes on me. A challenge? That huge head stopping halfway up with another fistful of gut. The glint from those two black marbles.

The roar! Yvette's body tossed aside as the mountain charged.

I jumped back from the curtains, running, stumbling, scraping my knees up the stairs. Again, I forgot the spear. Again, I chose the wrong hideout. The guest bathroom was right at the top of the stairs. The door was open, and so was the back window. Why did I think I could slip through it? Slamming the door, locking it, jumping onto the closed toilet seat, trying to inch my shoulders through.

Too narrow.

I pushed again, trying to relax my body, forcing my flesh to give. The scraping, the burning. I tried again, faster. Again. Straining. Skin scraping off on the metal sill. The definition of insanity, repeating motions with the baseless hope of a different response. I kept trying to jam myself through, a Kate-shaped peg in a rectangular hole. Back and forth, twisting my arms, bashing the back of my head on the sill. I don't know how many times until my neck seized up. And when it did. That knot at the base of my skull, like a hand grenade behind my eyes. Pain rippling down my neck, across the right side of my face. Ear, jaw. Spine.

Crippling. Freezing.

I sank back on the toilet, unable to move my head, neck, right arm. I tried to rise, make it to the door. I reached for the knob.

It vibrated in my hand as the whole house shook.

I felt the living room window smash, heard the curtains pulled from their fixtures. I didn't move. Didn't breathe. Adrenaline must have deadened the shock waves surging from my neck. I remember that cold line of sweat running from my armpit to my hip.

She couldn't have seen me. That was what I hoped. The curtains had to have blocked her view of my escape. There was no way she could know which way I'd gone.

Another roar, rattling the mirror in front of me. I heard a hard bang from the coffee table. A soft thump from the couch. Three quick, shaking booms told me fists were bashing in the downstairs bathroom door, and the lingering crack said that door was caving in.

A frustrated huff, then silence. She paused to listen, which gave me pause to think. I don't know where this idea came from.

But as I heard the first creak of a foot on the staircase, I grabbed for the phone in my pocket. Still charged, still able to communicate. I tapped the music app, hit the room choice, heard it blasting from the kitchen.

A grunt, a shuffle, then the clang of pots and crash of plates.

Thank you, "Black Hole Sun."

I took a careful, painful breath, trying to think, to plan my escape. Out the door? Through another window? Could I make it to Mostar's house? Flashes of Alpha's speed, her reach. At that moment the floor jumped, killing the music. I checked my phone to see that the connection was gone. Something delicate she'd severed. I could hear more destruction below, the overturned roll of the kitchen table as she stomped back out into the living room. Then the hard, shaking bang of another door caving in.

The garden. My sprouts!

Low grunts. Long, slow. Sharp cracks and muffled thuds.

A second source. High and distant out the window. Next door. *Pop-papop-pop!*

Alpha must have heard it too. She paused. Both of us listened to the noises, followed by grunts, growls, and suddenly a wail.

The same sound Consort had made when Mostar'd speared his hand.

Pain.

He was hurt!

A crashing sound, furniture turning over. A childlike whine lowering to an angry yelp.

An answer from my house, Alpha's bellow from my garden.

The *BOOM,* this deep bass from somewhere at Mostar's. Not furniture, not wood, not alive. I couldn't begin to imagine what had made that kettledrum din.

The screams. Human—Mostar and Dan.

Dan! I tried the phone again. More music to cover my escape. No response. Zero signal. A flash of anger and I almost threw it against the mirror. And in the mirror, I saw the smoke alarm. Memories collided into an idea just as I heard the roar.

She must have heard me. The faintest creak of my feet?

Thundering footsteps.

I grabbed the towel, wrapping it around my arm.

Louder, closer.

Match in my free hand, box wedged between towel fist and sink.

The staircase shuddered.

First strike, breaking with a curse.

The force of a truck, crashing against the door.

The second try, a flare, holding the flicker under cloth.

Second blow, wood splintering.

Light. Please. Light!

Door bursting open, thick fingers grabbing my shirt.

LIGHT! Orange licks through billowing smoke. My toweled fist burning!

Alpha pulled me toward her. Chipped teeth, stinking, moist breath.

One punch.

Into her mouth!

A muffled bawl. Biting down as I yanked my hand from the towel.

Flying cinders, stinging eyes. The smell of singed hair and burnt meat.

Coughing.

Snarling.

Staggering back, pulling me with her.

Hitting my head on the doorframe.

Falling forward.

Spinning.

Somersaulting.

Stairs.

Fur in my eyes, mouth.

Smooth skin over hard bone.

My nose cracking, white spots on black.

Chapter 23

From the early days of Gombe research, Goodall noted that the chimpanzees periodically had hunting "crazes," during which many colobus or baboons would be caught.

—Craig B. Stanford, *Chimpanzee and Red Colobus: The Ecology of Predator and Prey*

From my interview with Senior Ranger Josephine Schell.

Do you know that more people are hurt by bison in North America than by sharks all over the world? Do you know why? Because they try to ride them. Tourists from New York or Tokyo, whatever urban bubble, literally try to jump on the buffaloes' backs. Feed them, hug them, take selfies with them. They think they're at a petting zoo, or in a Disney movie. They've never learned the real rules, so they think they can just make up their own. This is called anthropomorphizing. This is why families let their little kids play around coyotes, why the Venice Beach "Grizzly Man" tried to live among Alaskan bears, why a whole town in Colorado couldn't imagine that mountain lions would ever be a threat to human beings. All these overeducated, isolated city dwellers who idealize the natural world.

And they don't stop with animals. My people too. All that "noble savage" shit. From Rousseau to that alcoholic, woman-beating, racist anti-Semite. Ever see the movie he made in the Yucatan? The simple, sweet natives living "in harmony with nature" until, oh no, here come the evil, pyramid-building, crop-growing, corrupted Mayans! Thank God the Spanish show up as divine punishment. Movie shoulda been called *Them Injuns Had It Comin'*. I've heard versions of that philosophy all my life.

Nature is pure. Nature is real. Connecting with nature brings out the best in you. That's what I hear from the poor dumb dip-shits who come up here every year in their new REI outfits, never having felt dirt under their feet, just aching to lose themselves in the Garden of Eden. And then a few days later we find them crawling through the muck, half-starved, dehydrated, nursing some gangrenous wound.

They all want to live "in harmony with nature" before some of them realize, too late, that nature is anything but harmonious.

JOURNAL ENTRY #15 [CONT.]

The touch on my hand woke me. I sprung back, legs up, ready to kick. I opened my eyes and saw Palomino hopping backward as well.

"Oh God, sorry!" I think I said, and got up to pull her to me. She shook in my arms, or maybe that was me. My neck was aching, my back. As I bent my head to rest it on Pal's, I felt my skin burn from under the right ear to the base of my shoulder. I discovered, later, that I'd scraped the top layer completely off.

I also discovered, later, how Pal and her moms had survived. Effie said that when the Durants' window wall had caved, when the first monster stormed in, Carmen grabbed Pal with one hand, Bobbi with the other, and ran up to the master bedroom. Effie'd been right behind them. She'd been the one to slam, lock, and throw a chair under the knob while Carmen forced Bobbi and Pal under the bed.

Then Carmen started grabbing all the dirty clothes she could, and there'd been a lot to grab. Apparently, upstairs was even gnarlier than the living room. Stained, dirty, skid-marked. That's right. Effie even gagged at the memory of Tony's shit-streaked underwear, which her germophobe wife snatched up without hesitation and jammed all around the sides of the bed. Carmen thinks these creatures depend on smell as much as sight and sound. She thought clogging the space between the bed and the floor with a noxious moat would mask their own scent.

And it must have worked. By the time their pursuer, Dowager, I think, beat down the door, they were all hidden under the Durants' bed, behind a berm of filth. I can't imagine what it must have been like for Carmen, lying there in that dark stuffy stink. Maybe that's why she hit Bobbi, although Effie insists it was necessary.

That happened right before Dowager barreled in, as the door began to buckle. They'd just gotten under the bed, Carmen stuffing this damp moldy towel over the last open space. Bobbi started to lose it. Heavy breaths, faster, louder. Effie said that Carmen whispered angrily for her to be quiet. That Bobbi kept saying, "I can't, I can't!"

Effie said the third "can't" was when Carmen hit her, not an open-mouth slap, but a full-fisted punch right in her eye. I don't know how she managed it with them all lying on their stomachs. I don't know how she found Bobbi's eye in the darkness. But she connected, and Bobbi was stunned into silence. But that wasn't good enough for Carmen. She grabbed Bobbi by the neck, put her lips right next to her ear, and whispered, "Shut up or I'll fucking kill you."

On "you" the door fell in. Effie said she could feel the footsteps vibrating through the floorboards as Dowager stomped past them into the bathroom. The old female must have just poked her head in, reached out to pull the shower curtain down, then come back out to tear the doors off Yvette's walk-in closet. For a few seconds they heard clothes being ripped down, drawers pulled open. (Why? Just curious or thinking they made a small entrance to another room?)

Then Dowager growled angrily, frustrated, probably, and turned for the bed. She couldn't have been looking for anything, the way Effie described the sheets, pillows, and eventually mattress tossed around the room. If Dowager had just made it to the box spring, if Alpha's outside whoops hadn't pulled her from her tantrum.

They owe them, the Durants. That's how Effie looks at it now. The grimy concealment, the distraction of their murders. When Effie described it, she couldn't help but repeat, "We owe them our lives."

I know I'm getting ahead of myself. Sorry. Back to the moment when Palomino woke me up. I was so dazed, bouncing between thoughts and feelings.

Alpha! That was my first thought, hugging Pal closer as I looked nervously for some dark hairy shape hiding behind a corner. I noticed the scorch marks on the wall at the bottom of the stairs, followed the trail of cinders out to the hole in the window. Through the waving curtains, I saw what had to be the black, charred lump of the towel resting in the ash.

"Pal, what ha . . . ," I started to ask, but she broke away from my grasp, keeping my hand in hers, and tried to lead me toward the door.

"What . . . where?" I asked, but she was insistent, a silent pleading in her eyes. I took a few steps, felt my ankles pop, then caught sight of the caved-in garage door.

The garden.

She'd destroyed it.

Alpha had torn the irrigation hose right out from the sink, which was still gushing into the dirt. The dirt, all our carefully sculpted rows were gone, replaced by the thrashed lumps and holes of a kindergarten sandbox. Our seedlings. I saw a few lying among the debris, torn up by the roots, or probably just lifted along with all the other backhoe-sized handfuls.

She'd tried to eat a few, I guessed by the small, slimy green nodules. The tomatoes, the cucumbers, all of Pal's precious little beans. Chewed up and spat out like miniature horse droppings. Not her droppings though. She'd left that behind as well.

A large, slick pile sat right in the middle of the room. An involuntary function? Just an animal doing its business? Or was there a conscious message?

"Fuck you, Little Prey. Here's what I can do to your nest."

I'm just glad I couldn't smell it. My broken nose was too swollen. Pal could though, with nostrils buried in her sweater. She kept pulling my hand, leading me away.

At first, I resisted. "Don't you see this? All our work! Everything we tried to do!"

She wasn't listening, wasn't even looking. Her face was fixed on the entrance hall, the open front door, something beyond it that I absolutely needed to see. When she looked back toward me, I could see the tears begin.

"Okay, okay." I gave up the fight, let her lead me out into the falling ash.

At least I thought it was ash. But when the first flake landed just under my right eye, I blinked hard at the icy surprise.

Snow.

Must have been early. I didn't think we'd have snow for a few more weeks. It wasn't heavy. It evaporated before hitting the ground, before it could cover the large footprints leading away from my house. Or the blood trails leading to Mostar's.

Red footprints amid spatters, a track leading from her kitchen door around the front. Pal let go of my hand then, running on to Mostar's house, disappearing through—through?—the garage wall. I thought there was something wrong with my eyes, or maybe Mostar had opened her garage. I couldn't see from that angle, or even as I stopped at her open front door.

More blood in the entrance hall, tracking back to the kitchen among a sparkling carpet of broken glass. So much glass. So many colors. Mostar's artwork. All those intricate pieces. I could recognize little bits; a pink petal, the blue head of a bird, and the cleanly broken leaf of the fire piece I'd been so taken with earlier. All gone. That'd been the popping sound I'd heard during the attack. One by one they'd been hurled against the floor. Not by the creature, not like my garden. I suspected then, and I confirmed it later, that Mostar and Dan had smashed them in a last-ditch defense.

That had been the howl of pain I'd heard from my bathroom hiding place. The blood trail. And the hollow boom. I finally saw the source of that sound after a few more steps. The garage's sliding aluminum wall had been bashed in. That's how Pal had seemed to walk through the wall. She was waiting for me inside, along with everyone else. Effie held her. Carmen held Effie. Bobbi leaned against the back wall, hand cupped against her puffy, darkening cheek. Their collective, red-rimmed eyes told me where to look.

The body was lying facedown. Flat, smooth, tremendous feet glittering with so many embedded shards they looked like a treasure trove of rubies. The blood trickling from those wounds mixed with the large red circle that spread from the breathless torso, from the knife-topped bamboo that sprouted from its silver back. Consort. I could see my reflection in his blood, following another trail that led to the far corner of the room.

Dan, sitting against the wall, cradling Mostar's limp form. For a second, just a second, I thought she might be sleeping. The rise of her body under Dan's heaving chest. I should have known right away that no human neck can twist so far to one side. But the closed lips, the gently shut eyes. She looked peaceful, alive.

Dan told me later what had happened, how she'd pulled him inside the house and ordered him to start smashing her art. She'd disappeared into the workshop as he'd grabbed all her sculptures off the shelves. One after the other he'd hurled them against the floor. He wasn't sure how many he'd destroyed, half a dozen maybe, when the kitchen sliding door had toppled down. Mostar must have heard it too. She shouted from the garage, "Keep smashing!" And he did.

He told me that the beast had half stepped, half leaped at him, and come down hard on a floor of broken pieces. The whole village must have heard the roar. Dan watched the giant stumble backward, tread on more shards, then disappear back outside. He told me he felt like cheering, even crying, but Mostar had shouted, "Don't stop! Expand the minefield!"

Her word, "minefield." Always with the war metaphors.

He'd thrown everything to the ground. "Hard as you can," she'd said, "everywhere!" He'd covered the kitchen, the living room, the entryway, every direction leading up to the garage.

Mostar was still inside, working on another spear. This one had been for her. You could tell by the short shaft that was now rising from the dead ape's back. She'd just been tying off the wire when the garage door imploded right in front of her.

"She didn't call for me." That's what Dan said. No cries for help as she'd turned and braced the butt of her spear against the wall. She must have known she was too little and weak to cause any damage, but if she could use the animal's strength and size, if it was angry enough to charge without thinking . . .

That's what she must have counted on as Consort came at her, impaling himself on the blade. But it worked too well. All that weight and speed. Dan doesn't know if it was the inertia of the attack, or if the monster actually intended, despite the pain, to pull itself down the spear's shaft to Mostar. Dan didn't see any of this happening.

She was dead before he reached her. All he could do was drag her body away from the dying killer. And it didn't die right away. It lay there for several minutes, facedown, coughing up blood, jerking every so often as the spear swayed like a flagpole in the wind.

Dan, holding Mostar in the corner, watched as Alpha came stumbling out of our house, clutching her charred, smoking mouth. He'd heard her pained cries, and that's why, he believes, the rest of them didn't finish us off. Their leader was hurt, unable to command. She probably wasn't thinking about anything but getting away, finding a safe place to lick her wounds. They probably followed without question. Obedience trumping bloodlust.

Dan couldn't stop apologizing later, about how he didn't think to come looking for me, about how he just huddled there, sobbing quietly, holding Mostar's cooling corpse. I didn't judge him. I still don't. He couldn't even talk when I first saw him. The grief, the loss. I envy him. I didn't feel anything at that moment, bending over him, reaching out to touch his tearstained cheek.

I remember his face darkening with the shadows of everyone crowding around us. I remember turning to face them. The silence. No one knowing what to say.

Then:

"We have to kill them."

That was me. And it wasn't.

I hadn't planned on saying those words, or the ones that followed. Someone else was talking, a part of me I'd never met.

"Kill until they're too afraid to hunt us, or until none of them are left."

All eyes were on me. No pause. No debate. One by one they silently nodded.

I looked down at Dan, then over to Mostar's face. "We have to drive them off or wipe them out."

I felt Pal's arms slip around my waist, her head nodding into my stomach.

"We have to kill them."

Chapter 24

According to Darwin's Origin of Species, *it is not the most intellectual of the species that survives; it is not the strongest that survives; but the species that survives is the one that is best able to adapt and adjust to the changing environment in which it finds itself.*

—Leon C. Megginson, professor of management and marketing at Louisiana State University, 1963

From the NPR program Fresh Air with Terry Gross (2008).

Gross: . . . And so you've taken on the name of your city as a form of public remembrance.

Mostar: Well, I know to some it sounds like . . . what did Jerry Seinfeld call "Sting"? "A prance-about-stage name"? [*Chuckles.*] But the inspiration came from Elie Wiesel, when he said, "For the dead and the living, we must bear witness." That is what my life, this new life I've been given, is about. That is why I became an artist.

Gross: To remind the world of the tragedy of Mostar?

Mostar: Yes, but not in a tragic way. I'm glad you used that word "tragedy," because it exemplifies what I believe is the critical danger of negative remembrance. Most humans are not masochistic by nature. The human heart can only absorb so much pain.

Gross: And you feel that discussing tragic events in their barest form runs the risk of repelling people?

MOSTAR: Not always, but far too often. We can't just mourn the deaths, we also have to celebrate the lives. We need Anne Frank's diary, but we also need her smile on the cover. That is why I decided to become an artist, when I had that inspiring moment.

GROSS: Can you talk for a little bit about that moment?

MOSTAR: It wasn't long after the siege.

GROSS: The second siege.

MOSTAR: Yes, when the Serbs had gone and the Croats turned on us. This was in May, when we weren't sure the cease-fire would hold. There was a house I passed every day on my way to the hospital. It was just a charred wreck. I'd never really looked at it before. I must have passed it hundreds of times. But that one day, that moment when the clouds cleared and the sun caught a special verdant glint . . . I stopped. I turned around. I couldn't believe it. A sparkling waterfall of ice.

GROSS: But it wasn't ice . . .

MOSTAR: No, it was glass. Wine bottles that had melted down their wrought iron rack.

GROSS: Oh . . .

MOSTAR: It was truly exquisite, the way these hard rivulets had dribbled through their black cage. The frozen fluidity, the way it captured the rays. I couldn't believe that something so beautiful could come from fire.

JOURNAL ENTRY #16

OCTOBER 17

They're probably full. Why else haven't they attacked? The Durants and Reinhardt. A lot of meat. They know we're not going anywhere. They think we're just here for the taking. Or maybe it's Alpha. Recovering from her wound. Is she spooked? The deterrence Mostar was hoping for? Wouldn't that be nice. I don't want to believe it has anything to do with the body rotting under the tarp in Mostar's workshop. Dan doesn't think any of them saw it on their way out. Hopefully, they think Consort's just run off. Maybe they're looking for him. I hope that's the case. I can't afford to think about them mourning.

Not yet.

I also can't delude myself into imagining that they've moved on. We're all still choking on their smell. It's heavy in the air, thick despite the crisp, frosty chill. For whatever reason, they've given us about forty-eight hours' peace, and we've used every last second to prepare.

"Hacking the houses," that's what Dan calls it. Manipulating the internal alarms, biogas tanks, stoves. That "hacking" part's hard for Dan. Not the technical, the emotional. It drove him crazy, hunched over his iPad while the rest of us worked with our hands. Physical work. Male pride.

Three times he tried to take a "study break" to help us out. Once he even ran outside to help Effie and Pal carry a big box of stuff. I yelled at him. I didn't mean to. I just saw him through the hole in Mostar's garage door and shouted at him to get back to work.

He apologized to me later. He understands. We can't afford bruised egos any more than we can afford wasted time. "Specialization. Division of labor."

One of Mostar's many lessons.

That box I yelled at him about, it was filled with supplies. It's Effie and Palomino's job to stock the Common House. Blankets, medicine, what's left of the food. Everything we need to survive there. I'm glad Effie didn't argue about the personal effects. Not that I'd expect her to argue about anything. But she did have a point. What about all the photos? The mementos? We can't just leave them. No, but we can't waste time on them either. Once everything's in place, we'll pack up our treasures.

Effie seemed to get the logic of that argument. So did Carmen, who's in charge of placing stakes. She and Bobbi have been cutting and sharpening new spikes, as well as "modifying" the ones already made. And by "modifying," I mean dipping them in our own poo.

Again, Carmen's idea, in the hopes that it'll give them an infection. I have my doubts. Who knows how tough their resistance is. But if it works just a little bit, if even one of their wounded wanders off to sicken or die days later . . . That's why I haven't publicly "poo-pooed" Carmen's idea (sorry, lame joke), and privately, I'm blown away that she's been able to turn her phobia into a survival skill.

I don't know how she stands the smell though. I haven't seen her reach for the hand sanitizer once. She even personally scooped out the bucket of slop from the biogas digester, even after Bobbi offered to do it. Bobbi hasn't mentioned anything about Carmen clocking her, even though her cheek looks like half a hard-boiled egg. I noticed neither of them talk much about anything.

They've been going nonstop, laying stakes in between the houses, on the front lawns, in a semicircle ring around the Common House. "Semi" because the driveway leading up from the road can't be staked. Same for the actual loop around the house. The asphalt is too hard, the ash too shallow. That's where the glass comes in.

I took the idea from Mostar's "minefield." We've swept up all those shards and combined them with every single glass object in the village. I heard Carmen and Bobbi smashing them for hours. Glasses, bottles, picture frames. Shattering them all in the second story bathtub above my head, then carting the buckets downstairs to spread out along the entire circle. Maybe not as effective as bamboo, but maybe just enough to give them pause. That's what I'm hoping for. That's what I've been working on.

I'm the village "weaponsmith." That's what Dan calls me. I've been in Mostar's workshop for two days, trying not to nap, trying to ignore Consort's body next to me, and Mostar's one floor above. We placed her on her bed. We'll bury her later. I know she'd understand. I can picture her yelling at me to get to work. "Stop messing around, Katie!" She probably would have chastised us for carrying her all the way upstairs. "Just toss me on the couch or stuff me in the freezer next to Vincent's head!"

Knowing Mostar, she'd probably have told us to pump her body full of poison and lay it out for those creatures to eat. I've actually thought about it a couple times. I haven't said anything to anyone though. Morbidity aside, I don't think the idea's practical. I can't afford to waste time trying to find something that might be toxic (of course nobody here has rat poison!) and I wouldn't even know how to get it into her.

The fact that I've even thought about it, that I haven't cried once since she died . . . I do think about her though, every waking second. I picture her over my shoulder, barking orders and correcting each mistake. I think she'd be proud of how I'm using her 3-D printer. I hope she'd approve of my creation.

Spearheads. Well, to be specific, javelin points. I'm surprised she didn't think of it herself. That first weapon she threw at the mountain lion, how she lamented not being able to barb the blade. Well, these have barbs, these new, six-inch-long, half-inch wide, razor-sharp glass blades. And they're beautiful, if I do say so myself, and so easy to attach. Gift-wrapping ribbon through the pre-printed holes. I've got a whole spool of it from Effie. Pink and shiny, it's just the right width to fit through the ports. I've tested the strength, trying to pull it apart. It'll work once, and that's fine for disposable weapons.

Not like the real spears. They're taking a lot of time. In between each javelin, when there's nothing to do but wait for the printer to finish, I've been making spears for each member of the tribe.

Did I just write "tribe"?

Punchy.

There are a lot of personal spears to be made. And while we're mainly following Mostar's design, I've made one slight modification. A crossbar, or guard, or whatever you want to call it. Five inches long, slightly thinner than a dime. I've inserted one horizontally through bored holes just above the second to last connector. A little glue seems to hold them in place, enough, hopefully, to stop the spear from going too deep. I don't want any of us to risk what happened to Mostar. Who knows if it'll work. At least the spears themselves have been proven, and fortunately we've got enough raw materials. The bamboo and electrical wire were easy but scrounging for high quality, compatibly constructed chef knives took some effort. Dan and I had one, Mostar had two.

The Durants' knives were great. A couple of solid, eight-inch blades that I've crafted into formidable killers. The Boothes, ironically, have the most useless knife set. Maybe it's not ironic, the whole foodie thing. From a culinary point of view, their high-end Japanese cutters are magnificent. But for our needs: no pins, no holes, just thin, steel cores that look like they're glued.

"I'm sorry," that was Bobbi, frowning as I lifted the first naked blade from its smashed wooden grip. "Maybe these will help." I saw that she'd brought two more items with her. The first was kind of a U-shaped cleaver; the blade extended down and parallel to the handle. A riveted handle!

"Soba kiri." That's the official term. Bobbi reminded me of the soba soup she served us that night in another lifetime. This was the tool she'd used to make homemade noodles.

My first thought was "hatchet," and what an amazing bamboo-chopping, time-saving implement this *could* have been if I'd only known about it sooner. But I hadn't, and if it could chop through plants, it could sure chop through meat. It wasn't hard to picture how I could turn this hatchet into a full-blown axe. I could already see it fixed to a short, sturdy bamboo shaft.

And if that project got my creative juices flowing, Bobbi's next gift practically took my breath away. Not only was the blade thicker and at least two inches longer than any other knife we had, but the finish! I didn't know steel could be a work of art.

Bobbi calls it a "Damascus blade" after the medieval Arab swordsmiths who invented it. The metal looked like water, and I'm not being lyrical. The wavy lines across the surface looked exactly like moonlight shimmering on the ocean.

Holding it to the light, I said dramatically, "I have never seen its equal."

"*The Princess Bride.*" Bobbi smiled at the reference and said, "You're actually pretty close to the truth. It's not a Zwilling clone. Bob Kramer custom made it for Vincent. They knew each other for ages, and when Bob found out that Vincent had cancer, and we were trying a vegan diet . . ." She paused, sniffed slightly, and ran her fingertip over the handle. "It worked, you know. Veganism, or at least, it didn't hurt. Vincent used to love a good porterhouse, but with the full remission . . ."

Her eyes suddenly glazed. Her cheeks flushed. I was going to give her a hug when she turned and said, "I'm sorry. I've got to get back to work," and trotted outside to help Carmen.

I tried to push her feelings, and mine, away and focus on what I was doing. I was about to begin measuring the blade for a standard spear shaft when my mind came back to the soba kiri. I'd initially envisioned a three-, maybe four-foot shaft for the new axe, and that image made me realize I hadn't constructed any indoor weapons! Spears were too long. Javelins too weak. Yes, we could use regular paring knives, and Dan had his coveted coconut killer, but they were so small and you had to get so close.

We needed something in between. Not the axe (although I'd still make it) because the swinging motion needs a lot of room. The idea of a cut-down mini-spear sent me jogging over to Reinhardt's house, to the book that was still lying right where it had fallen.

Vanishing Cultures of Southern Africa.

And there was the picture, the short Zulu Iklwa.

It didn't go quietly. The grip, I mean. Like a lot of the high-quality knives, the grips couldn't just be smashed away with rocks. I had to chip, chisel, and whittle a lot of material away with paring knives. I even ruined a perfectly good six-inch blade, literally broke pieces of steel off trying to chop through the aluminum pins. I feel bad about destroying that cook's knife, but it was worth it for a new axe, and a really lethal-looking Iklwa.

I wonder if Shaka would accept it? I know Dan will. I'm going to give it to him tomorrow. Along with the new shield. It's a nutty idea, I admit, but after seeing the pictures in the book, and mulling over how these creatures fight, I wondered if it might not be worth the time to make one. And it really didn't take that much time. Half an hour to lift one of the steel mesh shelves off its support poles, tie up a handle of electrical wire, and wrap the front in aluminum foil. That last part is the whole reason I made the shield. I don't expect it to stop one of their punches. The impact would probably break my arm, but if Dan has to get close with the Iklwa, maybe the reflected light could distract them long enough to get a shot in. I've been going over Dan's iPad footage, how their eyes locked on each new source of light, and how most of their attacks were overhead blows. It might work.

And the steel grating might also provide some protection from thrown rocks. I've actually never thought about that until writing it down just now. I'm also thinking about finding a use for the shelves' steel support poles. They must be as strong as bamboo, and hollow, but how could I ever drill holes for the knives? If I only had more time to experiment.

But I don't. From Mostar's workshop I can see everyone asleep in the Common House. I can see everyone sleeping, curled up in comforters and sleeping bags. Bobbi on the couch. Effie, Carmen, and Pal on cushions. Dan on an air mattress we found in the Durants' house. Probably my imagination but I think I can hear them snoring.

That's not all I can hear.

That's why I can't make any more shields, or Iklwas, or anything else anymore. For the last few minutes, the woods have been coming alive. Branches breaking, the occasional grunt. I hope my work didn't attract them, the high-pitched metallic banging. Maybe it's just time. They're fully digested, well rested.

There it is, the first howl.

They're back.

No motion lights yet. The sounds seem far away. Maybe they're psyching themselves up. Harder to hunt on a full stomach?

Deep hooting cries now. Alpha. Rallying them to finish us off.

I wish we had more time. If just to practice with the javelins. No chance now. I probably shouldn't have wasted all this time writing. But just in case something happens to me, I wanted there to be a record. I want someone, anyone who reads this, to know what happened.

The hoots are getting louder now.

Time to wake everyone and apologize for not getting their keepsakes. I'm good at apologizing. Specialization.

I thought I'd be more afraid. Maybe I am and just don't feel it. Maybe I'm just too tired to care.

Fear and anxiety. I've lived with the latter all my life. Now it's gone. The threat is here. I feel strangely calm, alert, focused.

I'm ready.

Another howl. Closer.

Here we go.

Chapter 25

Red colobus are most aggressive and most successful at counter-attacking in habitats where they can mount an effective defense without being scattered.

—Craig B. Stanford, *Chimpanzee and Red Colobus*

JOURNAL ENTRY #17

OCTOBER 17

My man is dead.

It was hard to wake Dan up. He was sleeping so soundly. I had to shake him a couple times. He looked up at me, started to ask something, then got his answer from the distant grunts.

We roused the others. No need to explain the plan. Everyone knew their jobs. Palomino hid under blankets behind the couch while the rest of us headed to the workshop for our "bait." So heavy, slowing us down. I worried about the sound of the flapping tarp, the smell catching their noses before we were ready. If they'd jumped us at that moment, unarmed, hands full, in that narrow stake-and-glass-free path.

Once the "bait" was placed, we started the knocking. Short, wide bamboo rods, hollowed out for maximum sound.

thock-thock-thock

Slow and synchronized, striking them together like kindergarten woodblocks.

thock-thock-thock-thock-thock-thock . . .

We drummed for a full minute, standing in a line outside the

Common House door. I glanced back inside at the wall clock, held up my hand for silence.

They didn't answer.

We waited. I held my breath, straining to hear some kind of reply. I started to think, hope, that maybe they weren't coming. Maybe my theory about the full belly was right. They were done with us, watching from a respectful distance before slinking away for good.

I really did hope that was true. And yet, there was this tiny part of me, no point in denying it now, just the barest thread of disappointment.

"Do you . . . ," Carmen started to say.

thk

We almost missed the first one. My hand went back up.

thkthk

Soft and muffled, the other side of the ridge.

thkthkthkthkthk

I looked at the group and we answered as one.

Thckthckthck!

Faster. Louder. I could feel my palms moisten, my ears warm, and suddenly I really needed to pee.

More knocks followed by the howl. Long, powerful. Familiar.

I knew that voice.

I answered it with mine.

I'm sure I sounded ridiculous. Trying to match those lungs was like a flute taking on a tuba. But I did try. Laying my knock-sticks down, stepping forward and raising my head to the ridge, I let go the deepest, harshest boom my diaphragm could muster.

A pause, maybe bewilderment on their part?

But then she answered, followed by the chorus of her troop.

These hoots were much closer now, direct instead of echoed.

They'd come over the rise. They had to be watching us.

I looked back at the group and said, "Now!"

Dan hit a button on his iPad, manually igniting the house's

outside lights. There was no way they could miss us now, or the "bait" as we whipped the tarp off Consort's corpse.

The sounds, I thought I'd heard them all before. The call to challenge, the rallying hoot, the roar to charge, the chatter of food. But this, this cacophony of wails. Shock? Did they not know Consort was dead? Grief? Suddenly seeing him like this, no time to process his passing or conceive of how he died? Or was it hope? Belief that he might actually still be alive and that we were somehow holding him prisoner? "Please don't hurt him! Please let him go!"

Whatever emotions drove their soprano screeching, it rose to a fever pitch when we began our mutilation.

I stepped up onto Consort's lifeless chest, raised my spear, and with another challenging howl, I jammed the blade into the dead ape's gut.

Everyone else followed, mimicking my howls as they drove their spear points into the fur-covered flesh. As with everything, we'd meticulously planned this act. Ten seconds, no more. We raised our spears, waited. But they didn't come. Still cautious? Still clearheaded enough to plan? That was what I was afraid of when I stepped over Consort's face, dropped my spear, and then my pants. I couldn't make my bowels work on command, but my bladder was another story. I hoped the house lights made me visible to all, and that the message behind my action was clear.

"Fuck you, Ex-Predators. Here's what I can do to your family."

The bellows washed over us.

They were coming.

They were mad.

The first motion light snapped on somewhere in our backyard, followed by a large slouching shape darkening the space between our house and Mostar's.

The shape grew, the roar echoed.

Then the step, the high yip, and those points jerked upward as the brute recoiled in pain. It had worked; the challenge, the taunts, the sight of their loved one's body being desecrated. They were enough like us to fly into a mindless rage, and miss the spikes right under their feet.

Another leviathan loped in between Mostar's and the Perkins-Forsters' house. Another sharp cry, and the darkened mass retreated out of sight. Other motion lights, more quick blobs skirting between our homes.

We waited, watched.

No more blind charges.

They'd learned.

It only took a few seconds before we heard the faint crinkle of our kitchen door collapsing. They were trying a different tactic, going through our homes instead of around. *Please don't let them smell it*. That was the prayer in my head. *Or let them still be too angry to care!*

Dan's iPad chirped, the home security app flashing. One, hopefully more, was now passing directly through our kitchen. The angle of Dan's tablet gave his face a demonic expression. Rising smile, narrowing eyebrows. Even now I don't know how he'd done it. Hacking the stove to pump all that homemade methane into our house. Bypassing all the safeguards to ensure a remote ignition. Dan's eyes flicked to me for permission, finger poised above the screen.

I mouthed, "Yes."

Dan answered, "As you wish."

Face warmed, eyes squinted, my ears popped as blue flames blew out our windows. The creature must have run (if it did run) out the back. It might have just been stunned in the blast. There wasn't time to see what happened.

More chirps. More home invasions. Mostar's, Reinhardt's, the Perkins-Forsters'. How could they have been unfazed by the first explosion? Were they that brave or simply that eager to reach us? Dan didn't wait for my permission this time. Three quick taps. *Boom-boom-boom!* Heat and pressure rolled over us, along with the sight of our first confirmed kill.

This one had made it to Reinhardt's living room. Goldenboy. The force of the explosion blasted him right out onto the front lawn. He landed on his hands and feet, dazed, shaking. Wisps of whitish smoke rose from patches of smoldering fur. He tried to rise, slipped, and face-planted right into a patch of bamboo.

We heard a hacking, wet wheeze as he pushed himself up to show us his punctured front. Some stakes were still embedded, some had left gaping holes. Stomach, chest, the higher ones puffed small red clouds. He tried to stand, slipped backward, hit Reinhardt's door, and slid back down under a slick of blood.

Then the whole house jumped. Reinhardt's home seemed to rise off its foundation as more fireballs erupted from every window. Dan shouted, "Battery!" and we ran for the safety of the Common House.

Dan had rigged up the houses' energy cells to explode, hacking their fire suppression systems and packing their bases with oil-soaked towels. He'd tried to warn me that it might not work, or work too well. "We don't know how big the explosion could be!"

"Bigger the better" was how I'd responded, mentally salivating about how many it could kill.

But as we all crouched under the table listening to, feeling, our houses detonate one by one, I will confess to thinking, *Oh shit, what have I done!* I'm sure Mostar wouldn't have given it a thought, probably compared it to an artillery bombardment from her past. "Oh no," she would have scoffed, "this is nothing." And then rattled off the names of some army cannons that made these explosions look like firecrackers. I could have used those comparisons now, because the rain of debris made it seem like World War III. Bangs and thuds and, at one point, a *crack* as the roof's central beam absorbed a piece of something we used to live in.

We couldn't see anything outside; blowing ash fogged the windows. One of them cracked suddenly from a small strike. I threw my body over Pal, ready for another hit to send flying glass our way.

A final *BOOM* above our heads, the last solid objects hitting earth.

A few tense, quiet seconds. Then—

"Listen!" That was Dan, holding my hand and cupping one ear toward the door.

A sound, rising above the crackling, creaking collapse.

A new call. High, lamenting bawls mixing with pain-filled yelps.

Fear.

Alpha? That's all I could think as my ears strained to pick her out. *Is she calling them all back?*

I listened for another cryptic cry, but instead got an earful of cheers.

"Yeah!" That was Dan, squatting at the open door, staring out at the fires, pumping his fist in the air. "Yesyesyes!"

Bobbi picked up the cheer, whooping right into my ear with Effie and Carmen behind her.

I shouted, "Quiet!" and rushed for the door. Dan, reaching for my hand, mumbled something like, "Wait."

I couldn't. I had to be sure.

The dust was still settling along with some light debris. I coughed at the smoke, tried to see through stinging eyes. Greenloop was gone. Nothing but a ring of bonfires.

There!

Two of them running over the rise behind the burning wreckage of our home. Backs orange in the flames. One lighter than the other, Princess, her pristine fur ruined. And Scout, far out ahead. Just those two? I grasped my spear, whipping my head right and left. No more movement, no bodies.

Then a yelping cry behind me. From the driveway, still in darkness.

I was afraid of that, planned for that, and reached into my pocket for the two car fobs. We'd parked our Prius and the Boothes' BMW on opposite edges of the road entrance, making sure to angle their noses down the hill. When I hit both buttons, their headlights turned night into day. A startled Gray shielded his eyes, along with Twins One and Two. They must have also been surprised by the broken glass, the only barrier we could lay across the ash-covered asphalt. But between the glass and now the light, we'd spoiled any chance for a surprise attack.

I shouted, "Javelins," but Dan was already next to me, shoving one of the long thin missiles in my hand. I held it next to my face, arm cocked, legs bent for balance. The glass point glinted in the light.

Something beautiful from fire.

I threw. I missed. My shot landed just short of Gray. The old male kicked it aside, trampled, forgotten.

But the second.

Carmen, like an Olympic athlete, threw hers from a running stance! She was still balancing on one leg when I turned to see the reflected orange sparks vanish into the target's chest. She must have hit right between the ribs, sliding almost to the hilt.

Twin One roared, skidding to a halt in a storm of ash. He grabbed the shaft angrily, threw it aside, then skipped sideways and backward, clawing the tiny wound.

It worked!

The barbs had held the blade in place, allowing it to snap clean off. Yipping, dancing, Twin One pinched and fingered the bloody hole. Finally, in an explosive fit of rage, he pounded furiously on his chest. That must have driven the point through the lung.

The sound. Megaphone hacks of wet, crackling bubbles from his nose and mouth. I could have watched it forever, then . . .

"Throw!"

Dan's mouth in my ear, his hand pointing to my left. Twin Two, barely a dozen feet away. Arms out, mouth open, eyes narrowed.

Two javelins. Mine and Dan's. His was knocked away in midflight. Mine hit low, planting deep in the upper thigh. Two jerked to a stop, like hitting an invisible wall. As it reached to break off my wiggling shaft, Dan launched another right into its shoulder. Two jerked back sharply, roared, reached up to tear it out.

I actually heard this one, the whistle of a third javelin that whipped between Dan and me. Carmen again. Straight on to burrow in the smooth, muscled gut. Grasping, pulling, the whole barbed point came out. A long yowl, a flash of pink, tubular intestine.

One hand swatted the air in front of him, the other cupped his wounded stomach.

Enough? Self-preservation instinct or an intelligent calculation of odds?

"Not worth it!" That's what Two seemed to yelp as he backstepped a few paces down the driveway, then turned and ran. *Ran!* He didn't even stop to help his brother, who was lying on his side, panting, bleeding, trying to crawl away. Two didn't look back as One wailed after him. The mouse from the cat, the antelope from the lion. Distance, safety, life.

"Effie!"

My eyes flicked to Carmen, thrusting spear in hand, sprinting over to her kneeling wife. I watched Gray catch Effie's javelin mid-flight, stop to bite it in half like a piece of dry spaghetti, then bound the last few steps toward her.

Speed, weight, momentum. What does it take to knock a hurtling asteroid aside? Carmen, Dan, and I running with outstretched spears. We hit at exactly the same time. Dan's blade buried itself into the sinew of Gray's left forearm while Carmen's pierced its bulging calf. And mine, falling forward, steadied by the grip on my shaft. It skewered him under the lowest rib, stopped only by the spear's crossbar! Gray yowled, spun, swiped at my head. Six inches, maybe. Three? Close enough to whip the air across my face. The crossbar'd kept me, literally, at arm's length!

If I'd only been smart enough to let go and duck. Gray pivoted from the hips this time, using my own weapon to catapult me back into the ash. My head hit something. Hard. A bright star burst in the center of my vision. I rolled over twice, saw what I'd struck.

A thrown rock from the first night's bombardment. Rough, oval, heavy, I grabbed it with both hands, struggling to my feet. I don't know who'd acted first, Dan or Carmen, but as I turned to face them, I could see both had Effie's spear now, and were driving it up into the goliath's chest. The angle was perfect, just under its rib cage, right into the heart.

Thick, sticky spray. Down the pole, into our faces as Gray toppled backward.

And that was when we made our mistake.

Leave him there. Recover our weapons. Scan for other attackers. That was the right choice, the one we'd planned for. Gray had to be dying, and dying or not, he couldn't hurt us anymore. I remember Carmen bracing her feet against the heaving ribs, and the spurting streams that followed her retracting blade. I remember her jamming that blade right back in, her red-stained teeth grinning wide. I remember Dan retrieving his spear, striking Gray in the chest, the stomach, the groin. I remember the old ape's splotchy, sun-damaged face, upside down as I kneeled above it, eyes clear, mouth opening, driving the rock down.

Bouncing off the skin-covered bone. Again. Teeth breaking, lips torn. Again. Muzzle cracking. Again. Skull giving. Again. Broken bone slicing up through damp fur. Again. The first hint of brains. Again. Again. Again. Eyes popping, skull collapsing, brains spilling out into the ash, onto my jeans, a mass of hairs and liquid and steaming, shiny meat. I remember everything.

I remember laughing.

No words, words are for thinking animals, for human beings. Laughing and grunts and tight little moans of joy.

Then the scream.

Up and alert. Me again.

All of us scrambling. Remembering where we were, who we were.

One mistake. That's all it took.

There were others out there, braving the dying flames, watching for the shadow of stakes and flicker of broken glass. We'd stopped thinking just as they'd started. Moving through darkness, silent, creeping up to the Common House behind our backs.

The scream was Bobbi. It had her by the hair. Dragging her in a puffing furrow, spindly legs kicking, delicate, pale hands grasping backward at air. Screaming, sobbing, pleading.

I don't know if what happened next was an act of self-defense, the old lady, Dowager, using Bobbi to ward off Dan's charge. All I saw was Mrs. Boothe, still writhing, swung back and up into the air. Like Yvette, spun in a complete circle. I pray that her neck broke quickly. The Common House roof thudded as her body broke on its edge. She had to have been dead by then, by the time my eyes followed her down, and caught on the image of Dan's spear rammed up into the killer's chest.

That was when we all heard the second scream.

Pal!

Juno had slipped completely past us, right into the Common House without a sound, right over to the pile of blankets hiding her.

"Palomino!" Carmen ran after the withdrawing titan. Like Bobbi, this one had Pal by the hair. Unlike Dowager, Juno wasn't looking for a fight. She was limping, bleeding from her right foot. A stake? Probably why she'd gone after Pal. Easy pickings, limited risk. Withdraw, escape, feed somewhere quiet and safe. That was what must have been going through the pregnant sow's mind.

Carmen and I were running toward them, with Effie—the only one still armed—leading the charge. She threw her heavy, clunky spear in a high arc. Over Effie's shoulder, I saw it *thunk* into the small of Juno's back. A shallow hit, maybe glancing off the pelvis. Enough to get her attention though, force her to turn and swipe at Carmen with her free arm.

The open hand caught Carmen on the side of the head, grabbing it, lifting. I saw her feet rise off the ground. I heard the crack as Juno crushed her skull.

Juno hurled Carmen's body at us, forcing us to stop and duck. With a growling hoot, she held up Palomino, dangling her like a taunt, or a warning.

"Don't come any closer. I'll hurt your baby. Get back. I'll kill her!"

Intelligence, reasoning. I *know* that's what it meant, and I think it might have worked except—

"Mamma!"

That was the only word I've ever heard Pal speak, and before I could react, I witnessed that word's power.

Effie shot forward, springing past her daughter and into her captor's grasp.

Hands out, clawing the sides of that watermelon head, thumbs jamming into Juno's tiny eyes.

The snarl. Effie's snarl. I didn't know human beings could sound like that. Rising to a sandpaper screech as the back of her head disappeared under the monster's chin.

Juno staggered back, dropped Pal, and raised her arms above her head. Those arms came down like hammers, smashing Effie's shoulders.

She dropped to Juno's feet. Eyes open. Broken doll.

Effie.

Mamma.

Her mouth was full of fur, skin, and blood. She'd literally torn Juno's throat out with her teeth. The giant fell back, hands groping for the holes that had been her eyes and windpipe. I rushed over to Pal, who was already crawling toward me. Struggling to rise, she reached up as I fell to my knees beside her. I think I said something like, "C'mon . . ." and turned us both to the Common House. The door was right there, only a few dozen steps away. But there was something wrong. The shape. It'd changed. The rectangular door now seemed triangular, like it was framed in some kind of arch. And that arch seemed blurry, the edge of light and dark in soft focus.

Fur. Legs.

I followed them up to the scratched stomach, over the scars and torn breast, past the singed, raw, oozing mouth into those two glinting points staring down.

Was she as surprised by Effie's actions? Or just savoring the sure kill?

Still on our knees, I tried to move Pal behind me. "Get ready to run."

Alpha roared.

"GO!" I shoved Pal sideways, crawling in the other direction. I knew the blow would land. I just wanted a few more steps. A few more seconds to give Pal time and space. I didn't expect the padded vise grip on my ankle.

The hard yank dragged me back, face plowing in the ash, breathing it in.

Coughing, choking. And suddenly I was upside down. I hoped it would be quick like Bobbi. My eyes cleared in time to see a grotesque smile. The result of my fire punch. Cooked, peeling lips pulled back over mottled teeth.

Her growl vibrated my own teeth, filling my nose.

Her mouth opened as I shut my eyes.

Then the squeal. Surprise, piercing, numbing my eardrums as I fell.

On my hands, rolling to the side, looking up at Dan poised for another swing.

The soba-kiri axe in his hands, painted red, matching the gash in Alpha's right hip. She wobbled, spinning awkwardly to face him.

"Getouttahere!"

I rose and ran, bolting for the Common House.

I didn't see what happened next. Pal explained it all to me later.

She'd run in the other direction, toward the darkness, under the gutted remains of the Durants' car. Hiding on her stomach, she could see everything that happened to Dan.

He raised the axe for another, higher strike, probably going for an eye. But the blade glanced off the socket's protruding bone. It must have hurt though. That must have been the roar I heard. Pal saw Alpha slap one bloody hand over her split brow while grabbing and throwing the axe away. Dan tried to retreat, backing up and ducking as she swung.

Speed, that's what he must have been banking on, his small size allowing him to dodge the bludgeoning storm. She was fast too, but she was hurt, and she was angry. He kept just out of her grasp, missing half a dozen punches. He could have run, maybe. He could have hopped over and around enough stakes to maybe get her impaled on a few. A chance to let her bleed, to get fed up, to give up. He had a chance.

Dammit Dan.

The coconut knife, still in his belt, then in his hand. Sidestepping another blow, he sprang forward with a quick stabbing thrust. He had to have been going for the heart, just under the rib cage, just like before.

So close.

Alpha charged at just the same moment, spoiling the spike's angle, pushing it up toward the sternum, where it lodged between hide and bone. Alpha roared, reeled back, taking Dan with her. She raised her fist just as he freed himself.

The blow came down on his shoulder, spinning him sideways, knocking him on his stomach. She stepped on his back. Pal heard the crack. So did I.

I'm not sure what I said at that moment, running out to see her raising a foot to stomp on his head. Something profound, or just profane? I must have made some kind of sound to get her to twist in my direction, for her eyes to catch the reflected light of my shield.

That light on her face, the expression. Annoyed at my distraction, or just glad to finish me off? I remember her fists raising high above her head, aiming for the shield, exposing the soft dark dent of her armpit.

I drove the Damascus blade through skin and muscle, heart and lungs.

The world spun. Alpha jerked herself away, throwing me aside, losing my shield but still gripping the Zulu spear. The sound it made sliding from the wound:

IKLWA

I landed flat on my back, ears ringing, eyes and mouth filled with her blood. I managed to crawl backward to the edge of the Common House, sitting up against the wall. I watched through tunneling vision as Alpha took a long, thundering step toward me.

She tried to roar, but all that came out was pink foam. She tried to move, but her knees buckled. She knelt, raised an arm, reaching. She fell on hands and knees, eyes never losing mine. A final stretch, fingers brushing my shoe. She collapsed without a sound.

I crawled past her and over to Dan. I stroked his face, called his name. Pal's hand touched my shoulder.

My man is dead.

Epilogue

I found a way, I found a way to survive with them. Am I a great person? I don't know. I don't know. We're all great people. Everyone has something in them that's wonderful. I'm just different and I love these bears enough to do it right. I'm edgy enough and I'm tough enough. But mostly I love these bears enough to survive and do it right.

—From the video diary of TIMOTHY TREADWELL, self-proclaimed "Grizzly Man," recorded right before he was eaten by a bear

From my interview with Senior Ranger Josephine Schell.

A knock at the door interrupts my interview. Two rangers enter, hesitate respectfully, then on her nod remove several of the heavy boxes from the room. The time is eleven forty-five A.M. *The government's lease officially expires at noon. Schell rises from her desk, stretches slightly, winces, and rubs her lower back.*

We got there the following week. Shoulda been the following day. But that's how long it took for the heat signature picked up by an NOAA* POES† bird to make its way through the bureaucratic labyrinth at Lewis-McChord to the closest team, which happened to be us. . . . If those houses hadn't burned, we probably never would have found them until spring, until some family

* NOAA: The National Oceanic and Atmospheric Administration.

† POES: Polar Operational Environmental Satellite.

member finally got a phone call through or maybe, honestly, some bill collector logged enough complaints.

Mrs. Holland was gone by the time we got there, her and the little girl, but everything we've found backs up everything in the journal she left.

We found what had to be the garden, which just looked like a patch of raised, charred dirt by then. I can't help wondering if it might have worked, if they'd been able to plant more in the other garages. . . . I know a little bit about gardening. Mom always kept a vegetable patch behind our house. I honestly don't think they could have lived on it indefinitely, but under the right conditions and with a little luck, it might have eked out enough to make it till spring. Hypotheticals aside though, who can't sympathize with all that work down the drain?

War does that, I guess, and this place looked like a war zone. All that blackened rubble, debris strewn everywhere. We found the glass "minefield" and the bamboo spikes. Had to be really careful with those, one of our guys almost lost a foot. Reminded me of the story my uncles used to tell about Vietnam. Punji pits, complete with human feces. Amazing how different people at different times can come up with the same ideas.

We found eight stone-covered graves on the Common House helipad—four big, four small. We didn't exhume them. We left that to the follow-up forensic team. The long graves, I'm told, contained the remains of her husband, along with Roberta Boothe, Carmen Perkins, and Euphemia Forster. The small ones . . .

She grimaces.

Those were . . . collections. The smashed bones and tissue shreds of Mr. and Mrs. Durant, the head of Vincent Boothe, and the black, burned skeleton that DNA evidence later identified as Ms. Mostar.

When I think about the time it took for her, the two of them, to dig that miniature cemetery, scraping out the frozen earth, collecting the bodies, covering them with rocks . . . and still having time for the "other" corpses . . .

We found a lot of meat in the Common House freezer. Newly cut steaks—well butchered, I might add—along with pots of stew. And in the cabinets, these endless Ziploc bags of jerky. They must have had the dehydrator going night and day. Some of the guys in my group, they . . . yeah, me too . . . we kinda kick ourselves for not sneaking just one of those little dried strips. I mean, c'mon, who doesn't want to know what Sasquatch tastes like?

But it's all gone now. Confiscated, along with the piles of broken, scraped bones we found behind the Common House and the heavy, stinking skins we found nailed to the walls. Investigators also took every last shard from the other bone pile. The one up behind the ridge, the "lair" according to her journal. They even scooped up the frozen pile of poop from the garden. All under lock and key now, along with the cellphones, laptops, and tablets we found stacked neatly next to Mrs. Holland's journal. If I'd only thought to charge up Dan Holland's iPad before turning it in. The compost battle video's gotta be on there. Woulda been my chance to actually see what they look like. Well, I guess, we all will eventually.

Schell reaches for one of the two remaining boxes. I grab the other one. Together, we carry them out to the parking lot, loading them into the back of a battered U.S. National Park Service pickup truck. On the way out, I ask my final question.

Fuck if I know. At least they're not writing it off. I think if they were going for a straight-up cover-up, it'd all be explained away by the fires. Community gets stranded, starts fiddling with their newfangled biogas systems to keep warm. Accidental explosion, yada yada yada. But they haven't done that. The investigation is still very open. Ask anyone directly connected with it and they'll tell you they're gettin' to it, as soon as they dig, literally dig, through all the other investigations going on right now.

And there's no lying there. That backlog is real. We're still finding bodies in the woods, who died of exposure after abandoning their cars. And the bodies still buried in those cars? Lahars dry into concrete! Even with ground-penetrating radar, they're having a bitch of a time.

Between those entombed corpses, our frozen finds, and all the other remains they're still pulling from under the smashed towns . . . how long did it take for loved ones to identify body bags from Katrina? How long do you think it'll take to empty that mega-morgue we've got in what used to be Tacoma?

So officially, it's just a matter of red tape. But unofficially . . . look, we were "encouraged" not to talk about this, and if I thought my job was on the line, I'm not sure I would, but you didn't have any problem getting through to me, and you don't see anyone right now trying to get in between us. They're not gonna bury this, stick the evidence in a crate and warehouse it like the end of *Raiders of the Lost Ark*. I think the truth'll come out for no other reason than they want it to.

Think about it. Tourist dollars! Zoo fees! You know what the Chinese make on their pandas? You know how long Loch Ness had been dining out on a few faked photos? Please. We'll be able to rebuild the Rainier damage and then some when the whole world flocks here for the chance to glimpse a living legend.

They want to go public, the only question is when. Rainier showed us what can happen when people lose faith in the system. We need to restore that faith, rebuild it along with the roads and bridges and other structures that make up a civilization. And that's why it probably won't help with public confidence if the government announces it just discovered Bigfoot.

That's why they have to wait a little bit, till the lights come back on, the water starts running, and all the dead are finally laid to rest. Maybe they have a PR plan for that day. Maybe your book is part of it. No, really. Maybe that's why they're letting me talk to you.

It's not the craziest idea. The book comes out, puts a toe in the water. If no one gives a shit, they've got more time to get their story straight. But if it stirs the pot, they can back you up with their findings, blame their own bureaucracy for the delay. Whatever. I guess we'll know soon enough.

From my interview with Frank McCray, Jr.

McCray has finished cleaning his BioLite stove. He places it in his backpack, checks his watch, then ushers me outside. The wind has gotten colder since our conversation, despite the rising sun. McCray reaches into his parka for a small, bright orange handheld radio and keys the mic three times. Turning toward the mountains, I watch one of the bushes move, a human figure walking down the game trail toward us.

What happened? What's the next chapter of this story?

There are a lot of scenarios and they depend on who you ask.

Scenario One is that the surviving creatures regrouped for a counterattack. That's what the scuzzbags at [website name withheld] believe. They think Kate and Palomino tried to hole up for the winter in the Common House until one day, or night, they were ambushed and taken away. I'll admit it's possible. She did write about several of them escaping. Scout and Princess, running up the slope after the explosions. One of the twins with all those javelin hits, although I'm betting he later bled to death. And the other two females, the new mamas. She didn't write about them during the fight.

Yes, it's possible they reorganized, then came roaring back out for a rematch. Possible, but not probable. Kate wouldn't have let that happen. Not the Kate I've read about. Even when they buried the bodies, she would have been armed and alert. Those graves were dug right next to the Common House, which meant that any of those approaching fuckers would have to cross a lot of open space to strike. Kate probably had plenty of javelins waiting within arm's reach, and her new spear.

That's what I think she did with the Iklwa blade. Nobody ever found it. Schell was kind enough to make some discreet inquiries for me. Through all the wreckage, all the stockpiled supplies and homemade weapons in the Common House, they never found a knife with a Damascus blade.

That's the key piece of evidence to back up her leaving. That and the soba-kiri axe. They never found that one either, and it would have been essential for a long trek. I can't be sure about any other items. Backpacks, sleeping bags, cooking gear. I don't know what else they had. She didn't leave a list. She also didn't leave a note, which is why some people suspect she was taken. I don't buy it though; I think she wasn't sure where she was going.

That's Scenario Two, and it's backed up by the fact that they didn't have a map of the area. She wrote, more than once, that they didn't know which was the best way out. It's possible that they tried a series of day-hikes to get the lay of the land, and that she didn't leave a note because when they stepped out the door that morning, it wasn't supposed to be for the last time. They could have gotten lost or hurt, or stuck in the first storm of winter.

Remember how brutal that was? I mean, c'mon, God, give us a break! A contact at the USGS told me that those kind of one-two punches can happen, like the typhoon after Pinatubo. If she got caught out in that polar vortex, with the blizzard and bitter cold . . . Their bodies might still be up there now, half-buried in snow and ice, thawing and rotting as scavengers pick at any exposed pieces. That's the ending of Scenario Two, and it's a lot less attractive than Scenario Three.

In this one they make it! Found some cave somewhere in the mountains, kept a fire going, lived on melted snow and Sasquatch jerky. Then, when the weather cleared enough to get moving, they started off again and are right now about to walk out of the wilderness next to some busy road. They might have done that already. The two of them, in some hospital, too weak and traumatized to speak. Someday soon she'll open her eyes, whisper her name to the nearest orderly. I love Scenario Three.

But my gut tells me it's Scenario Four.

"We have to kill them all." That's what she wrote. That's what she's doing.

I'm not talking about revenge. This is deeper, more primitive. What if those poor dumb brutes flicked a switch in Kate that's waiting in all our DNA?

What if she didn't stop at driving those creatures away? What if she went after them?

She knew their tracks, their scent. Kate had winter gear, and I'm betting little Palomino did too. I'm also betting that the jerky we found was made for that purpose. It's light, easy to transport, and if you add up all the meat the rangers found versus what those animals probably weighed, I bet the deficit would be enough to get them to their first kill.

And that kill would mean more food. That soba-kiri axe was perfect for chopping up bodies, roasting a nice juicy leg on a spit. I wish I didn't think of her that way, sitting in the dark with Palomino, the two of them warming their hands by a roaring fire, stomachs growling at some steaming limb.

It's also hard not to feel sorry for the surviving troop. Wounded, scared, cringing at any sound that might be the smaller hungry primates coming for them. Kate's not the only one in our family with a vivid imagination.

I've pictured her stalking them, maybe using Palomino as the flusher. The little girl'd yell, beat the brush, make enough racket to scatter them in terror as Kate waits patiently for some straggler to blunder into her spear. I can even picture one of them. Princess, the youngest and most vulnerable, chattering in torment as Kate jams the Damascus blade between her ribs. I can also picture my sister "playing" with her kill, torturing her. Not for fun, that'd be a waste. She'd try for a Vincent Boothe tactic, hoping to draw out a lone rescuer. And maybe it'd work. Scout, running to help, turning in surprise to see his Achilles heel severed by Pal's swinging axe.

And the others, the two young moms, holding each other,

hearing the screams die, then smelling smoke and cooking meat. I hope their brains aren't too advanced to imagine fate, to know their babies won't live long enough to reach adulthood. I also hope they're not intelligent enough to feel remorse. "What have we awoken!" If there's anything worse than visualizing your own death, it's knowing that you caused it.

Maybe I'm totally grasping at straws here. Maybe they did just get caught in a storm. For all I know, their bodies are on a Tacoma slab. I check every week, and so far, no remains match.

But if by some miracle they kept stalking those things, killing them one by one . . . living off them long enough to . . . find the others? We haven't talked about this till now. There can't just be one troop out there. That wouldn't be enough to sustain the species. What if Kate and Pal let those young mothers live just long enough to lead them to another troop? Hard to believe, I know, but so is everything about this story.

At this point the figure from the game trails has come down to meet us. It is Gary Nelson, McCray's formerly estranged husband. The two men share a long embrace. Gary shows McCray the map in his gloved right hand, and the red grease pencil marks he's made. McCray utters a resigned sigh and unslings his rifle.

Hard to accept why she left the journal behind. She never said it, but I know. One journey ends, another begins. Hard to reconcile the memories of my soft, sensitive baby sister with the predator that might be out there now. Mother of a tribe of two. The killer apes.

The wind howls in the distance. At least I think it's the wind.

You hear that?

Acknowledgments

First and foremost, a giant, Sasquatch-sized thank-you to Thomas Tull, who generously gave me back the novel rights for a movie I once sold to him.

To my editing team, Julian Pavia and Sarah Peed, for their relentless diligence and objectivity.

To Carolyn Driedger (USGS), Leslie C. Gordon (USGS, Ret.), and Professor Barry Voight of Penn State for their technical help with the Rainier eruption.

To my friends Kevin and Jo for introducing me to the town that inspired Greenloop, and to Jo's brother John for his technological guidance in turning that inspiration into reality.

To Rachel and Adam Teller for their advice on glassblowing.

To Diana Harlin and Jonny Small for their culinary and pop-culture references.

To Nate Pugh for his knowledge of home construction, Cousin Robert Wu for kitchen knives, and Arigon Starr for her navigation through the world of Sasquatch in Native American cultures.

To Rosemary Clarkson at the Darwin Correspondence Project for setting me straight on the real author of that Darwin quote.

To Major John Spencer (US Army, Ret.) for his military language.

Professor Lionel Beehner (United States Military Academy at West Point) and Major Michael Jackson (US Army) for introducing me to my Bosnian experts.

And to those experts, Jasmin Mujanovic and Leila Disdarevic, who expertly brought Mostar to life.

To my agent, Jonny Geller, who filled some very big shoes.

To my childhood friend Richard Cade, for his unforgettable, second-grade declaration that "Bigfoot is indestructible!"

And, always, to my brilliant, supportive, and superhumanly patient wife, Michelle.

ABOUT THE AUTHOR

Max Brooks is a senior nonresident fellow at the Modern War Institute at West Point and the Atlantic Council's Brent Scowcroft Center for Strategy and Security. His bestselling books include *Minecraft: The Island, The Zombie Survival Guide,* and *World War Z,* which was adapted into a 2013 movie starring Brad Pitt. His graphic novels include the #1 *New York Times* bestseller *The Harlem Hellfighters.*

maxbrooks.com
Facebook.com/AuthorMaxBrooks
Twitter: @MaxBrooksAuthor

ABOUT THE TYPE

This book was set in Bembo, a typeface based on an old-style Roman face that was used for Cardinal Pietro Bembo's tract *De Aetna* in 1495. Bembo was cut by Francesco Griffo (1450–1518) in the early sixteenth century for Italian Renaissance printer and publisher Aldus Manutius (1449–1515). The Lanston Monotype Company of Philadelphia brought the well-proportioned letterforms of Bembo to the United States in the 1930s.